HOW
TO PLAY

DEAD

Also by Jacqueline Ward
Perfect Ten

HOW
TO PLAY
DEAD

JACQUELINE WARD

CORVUS

Published in Great Britain in 2019 by Corvus,
an imprint of Atlantic Books Ltd.

10 9 8 7 6 5 4 3 2 1

A CIP catalogue record for this book is available from the British Library.

Trade Paperback ISBN: 978 1 78649 380 4
Paperback ISBN: 978 1 78649 379 8
E-book ISBN: 978 1 78649 381 1

Printed in Great Britain

Corvus
An imprint of Atlantic Books Ltd
Ormond House
26–27 Boswell Street
London
WC1N 3JZ

www.corvus-books.co.uk

To Kathie

Chapter One

Day 29

I'm standing backstage on a Tuesday night looking out at the audience when Danny texts me. When I say backstage, I mean behind a set of dusty burgundy curtains, half drawn back to reveal a rickety podium laden with plastic, star-shaped trophies. And when I say audience, I mean a half-full meeting hall in a run-down cul-de-sac just outside Manchester.

It is what it is. I know that. I also know that every woman here, especially me and Janice, is holding her breath, waiting to see what happens. This is one of the most important nights of our lives. I read the text and my heart warms.

> Day 29. I'm there. Here. Flight wasn't too bad. Can you believe it? One day down, 29 to go and we'll have enough to buy our own home and be back in the black. It isn't going to be easy but it will be worth it. I love you x Always x Good luck tonight, babe

I'm giddy with delight, even though I don't share Danny's desire to be the master of his kingdom. His settled kingdom. I'm a serial mover. I've lived in fifteen places since I left home twenty years ago, seven of them since I married Danny. Three of them since I had children. It's not that I don't want to settle down. It's just that I can't. But I do want to be out of debt. He's right. It's going to be difficult with him away, but he is right. And I love him.

I love my job, too. It's harsh, but I love the success stories, and I hope tonight will be one of them. I stare out into the hall: it's filling up. Women looking for their names, which I so carefully Sellotaped to the backs of the tiny wooden school chairs earlier today. The local press snapping away at every fourth chair. Empty. Carefully labelled. I'd briefed them with the standard 'One in Four' message, but I knew it was all in the visual. On my rise to the top of refuge work I've learned that words often fall on deaf ears because people don't want to hear bad things. They switch off. But if you show them, it sinks in.

That's why I insisted on holding tonight's proceedings in the hall right here at SafeMe; in a domestic violence refuge with the women affected as guests. Each one of those empty chairs, one in four, represents a woman who has not survived; each one will help us get funding for those who came afterwards. Like a silent legacy. I know for a fact that it is exactly what the women who should be sitting there would want.

It's a strange dynamic. Although it's heartbreaking, I know it has worked and I am happy. I'm happy Danny is away too, even though I will miss him desperately. He is doing this for us, finally dragging us out of the one-pay-packet-away-from-poverty life we have become used to.

I see Sheila James hurry to the front, seeking out her seat. She's all peroxide-blonde, false lashes and fake tan massaged deep into her ageing skin. She looks a little shaken and, as she sees me and waves, I see that her wrist is freshly plastered. I panic. Making sure she is OK means more than some award, but I can't get off the stage. I rush around the barrier and bump into the PR woman I hired to run the event. She's wearing a headset and Bluetooth earpiece and carrying a clipboard. It's all completely out of place in the small hall and much more at home at the O2 arena. She holds my arms and moves closer, wide-eyed with adrenalin and hissing frantically. 'Two minutes to go. Look, I know you must be nervous. God knows, anyone would be in these circumstances.' She looks around as if we were just about to take the stage at a stadium gig. She shakes me. 'You need to get a grip.'

Get a grip. I look around. PR woman extraordinaire. Sheila James, obviously hurt again. A room full of women who are relying on me. Yes. I smile. She doesn't know me. She doesn't know how many times I've had to get a grip, to fight my way through. I have elbowed myself into the place I am now, at the top of my profession. *Get a grip.* I got a grip, all right. Tough and strong-nerved at work, I shed that steely exterior like a second skin when I am home with Danny and the kids.

She's counting down silently now, complete with arm movements. A loud fanfare sounds and the mayor appears on the stage along with one of our trustees, Marjory Bates.

I know it's going well. I know when the audience clap at Marjory's speech. I know when the members of the borough council who hold our future in their spreadsheets start to pay attention. I know when the funders, who turned up right at the last minute and were directed to their junior-school seats at the back, stop looking annoyed and start to look surprised. I know when the pictures of all the women who have passed through our doors are flashed on the walls one by one; those who survived stay there while the others fade. I know by the complete silence in the room and the realisation on the faces of the funders that I have made the right impression. My message has got through. This time.

Then it's time for the awards. Mine is second to last. Marjory turns and smiles at me as I feel the confidence I have cultivated push its way to the front. The fanfare that heralds each award is overkill now and, from my elevated position, I can see people fidgeting. I wish Danny was here. But I know that if he doesn't do this work in Dubai, just for a month, things will only get worse.

'And the award for Superwoman of the Year for services to SafeMe goes to Ria Taylor.'

I stride on to the stage and smile and take the lightweight star with my name on it. Sheila is clapping and smiling and the photographer beckons. I pose and smile and blink into the flash. I feel for the envelope in my pocket, folded over. I always have a plan. They usually work, but sometimes my plan is not enough. My nerves are truly jangling when I think about the bailiff's letter and the debt collectors. This is not the time. I know I could get another job, better paid, but I love this place and if I left, what would happen to these women? No. I know Danny is right. His thirty days away will get us out of the shit. And more.

Marjory is heading my way with Trevor Jones, the funding coordinator, so I fix a smile again and hold out my hand.

'Trevor, how lovely to see you again.'

This is a huge lie, which I dress up in its own elaborate outfit of a fuck-you tone. Trevor takes the bait and my hand, which he grips harder and longer than he needs to.

'And you, Ria. And nice to see you looking so … colourful.' We all pause to take in my trademark Day-Glo orange jumpsuit and the matching scarf wound around my dyed-red hair. Trevor smiles benevolently. 'Of course, it does the customers good to see you looking so cheerful amongst all this …'

We look around. We know what SafeMe is. It's the brink of change for some women, and for others the last stop. We are at the front line of services, the only small pocket of funding left and only for those people whose situations are absolutely critical. These are women with nothing left, nowhere else to go, often injured or scared to fucking death by violent partners. Life or death, for some of them, which is what I had tried to convey this evening. I fill in for him.

'Crisis? And they're people, not customers.' There is always a crisis here. But it doesn't look like crisis. Not tonight. We're putting on a show for the people in charge of the purse strings. They never see what it's like in the cold light of day when we're all leaning on a door in front of a terrified woman whose ex-partner is trying to get to her. I look at the empty chairs and his eyes follow my gaze. He looks back at us, unsmiling now.

'Look, we'll be considering the funding in a month and this definitely helps. Definitely. You know, if it were just my decision ...'

I feel the rage creep up. I will defend this place to the end of the earth.

'Well, let's hope that everyone else feels the same, Trevor. Or there won't just be more empty chairs. There'll be no chairs at all.'

I stare at him, my infamous 'Ria stare', which has warded off hundreds of angry men over the past twelve years, allowing their frightened partners space to breathe and recover and decide what to do next. Trevor Jones nods and shifts uncomfortably until Marjory guides him away. I want to check my phone, check if Danny, now thousands of miles away, has sent any more lovely messages. But Sheila is heading my way. I sit down on the low stage and she sinks down beside me.

'Went well, didn't it, lovey?'

Her voice is gravelly and thick. I see her bright red lips twitching, her hand on her ciggie packet. She's dying for a smoke but she doesn't want to miss anything.

'Yeah. Really well. So ...'

It did go well, and I feel a surge of pride. I glance at her arm.

'Oh, don't bloody start. I fell. On the stairs.'

Her dead, glassy eyes tell me that she did not fall on the stairs. That this is yet another of the well-practised lies that she has rehearsed over the years. I have been Sheila's advocate for ten weeks now, since she left her husband Frank. She's lives in an independent apartment but spends all her time at SafeMe because she is scared shitless. Frank is a has-been local bent politician, ex-mayor and councillor, but he definitely still has connections. Shelia regales me with tales of how they are coming to get her. In reality, it's Frank she is scared of. Just Frank, because Sheila could take on the rest of the world with no problems. Sheila, five foot nothing in her bare feet, is a human dynamo at sixty-three years of age.

But the rest of the world hasn't controlled her every move for decades, and Frank has. She is completely conditioned, and my job is to change her thinking so she can be safe, away from this man who claims to love her. The day I met Sheila, she was wearing a neck brace and her arm was in a sling. Before I said a word, she had qualified her appearance.

'Looks worse than it is. A bit of whiplash.'

But I knew she had been found abandoned in a car park in the middle of the night, crying and afraid. The two men who found her told the police she had been pushed out of a moving car, which turned out to be Frank's limo. Of course she refused to press charges. She also refused to go home. Frank came to our office, palms turned upwards like some used-car salesman to claim his property. He reasoned with us then threatened us with legal action but we all knew what he really meant was that Sheila would pay for this.

I look at her now, her shoulders hunched and her eyes ever on the door.

'Did you go back to your house, Sheila?'

She nods. 'I needed to get something.'

I put my hand on her shoulder. 'I'll get Janice to give you a lift home. Will you be OK on your own or do you want to stay at SafeMe? You can, you know.'

We officially have twenty-four emergency places in the ex food warehouse that is partitioned into tiny rooms, each with a bed, a toilet and a sink. Some rooms have cots and smaller beds for children. They resemble prison cells but represent the biggest freedom most of these women have had in a while. Pull-out sofa-beds in our spare rooms and lounges extend the places to thirty-six at busy times.

Janice, my co-manager and best mate, and I have transformed the main area into a veritable wonderland. It is a grotto, complete with charity shop chandeliers, fairy lights and donated rugs. Chesterfields we have done up with patches where they are worn out. The, mostly, women who have been driven out of their own homes love it. The men who drove them out and turn up here to try to reclaim them, not so much. Sheila smiles without looking at me.

'It's all right, lovey. This is nothing.'

I know it isn't nothing. But to Sheila, she got off lightly. I hug her and beckon Janice over. She knows me so well and reads me immediately.

'Shit. Has he gone?' I rest my head on her shoulder and she

envelopes me into her. I hear her sigh. She knows me and Danny are a strong team. 'Won't be long, though. Thirty days? It'll fly. And you've still got me.'

I can't help but smile, even with Danny in Dubai and the prospect of the bailiffs banging on my door.

'Give her a lift, yeah, Jan? Make sure that the building is secure as well.' I touch Sheila's shoulder. 'You've got your physio tomorrow, so I'll be round the day after.'

They leave, and the evening is wrapping up. I get my phone out and text Danny.

It went well, love. Don't wear yourself out. I love you too.
Always x

I know he wants to be here to support me and he'll be waiting to hear how tonight went. He is so patient. All the moving around, dragging Danny and the kids to new flats in new locations, all the jokes about being a serial mover. But I just couldn't settle.

Like lots of people, my difficult teenage years made me afraid to have a relationship for ages. Skipping from each one-night stand to the next, numbing myself with alcohol, cake, new clothes – anything. Only relenting when Danny held me tightly enough to let a little bit of the love he had for me seep in. Later, when we married, the horrible feelings faded. But some days I would wake up on edge and be unsettled for the rest of the day until Danny asked me what the matter was and offered to go to the chippy for tea. I need to settle, I know I do.

I hurry the rest of the way home and let myself into our ground-floor flat. Terri, my babysitter, stands up to leave.

'Danny's going to be away a lot for a bit so ...'

She smiles. 'I need the money, Ria. Any time. They're good as gold, anyway.'

Simon and Jennifer. *Good as gold.* They are gold to me, only more precious. I cannot ever imagine being without them, or them without me. Terri gone, I flick on the kettle and sit in our tiny kitchen at the Formica table. These flats have paper-thin walls and I can hear next door's telly booming out and someone laughing in the flat above. It's strangely comforting because I know I'm not alone.

Tea ready, I open the envelopes that are stacked on the table. The glue is dirty, yellowed and thick with fluff. I pull out the contents, one by one, crumpled now, and unfold them. I feel a little flutter in my heart, a sudden stab of brilliant hope that this is finally going to go away. It isn't as if we are frivolous; we have only bought what everyone else has. Our rent is high even for this tiny flat and the bills are steep. Things have accumulated over time. One loan in top of another, then topped up for Christmas. Then Danny was made redundant. Again.

It feels like failure, but I know it isn't. It's just that I am rubbish at managing money. And school uniforms come before loan payments. I guess I've seen the absolute pits of life at SafeMe and this seems so trivial. Until the default letters began to arrive.

I text Danny again.

All good here love. Goodnight xxxx

And it is good. Danny is getting us out of this fucking mess and the evening went well. What more could I ask for?

Chapter Two

Day 28

I slept on and off. I'm in the kitchen at five-thirty drinking strong tea. I miss Danny. He's completely and happily unqualified and works as a shop fitter. The money is rubbish but every so often he has the opportunity to work long, hard hours on a project for megabucks. Last week he came home and told me that there was a huge shopping complex in Dubai that needed to be ready quickly. He had thirty days' work.

The only catch was that it was thirty days away. Thirty days separated. We've barely been apart for more than one night since we met. I protested. He wasn't getting any younger and it would wear him out. Thirty consecutive days. It was too much.

But Danny wants his own home. A home for us. Neither of us earns brilliant money. I have a good job but it's a charity salary and low for what I do. Danny works when he can. It works for us personally, but it means that if we are going to have our own house, we need a huge deposit. He has saved and saved and now he has his target. Thirty days and he will have enough to put down on a modest house in a decent area and clear all our debts. It's what Danny wants out of life and if it wasn't for my constant fears about money, it's what I want too.

Despite my protests, I knew he was going to do it. He sat at the kitchen table under the fake Tiffany downlight that makes the dark flat look homely. He got out his ancient Casio calculator and worked out how much he would earn, then deducted the air fare and accommodation. I could not imagine thirty days without Danny and when he announced that it would be possible, my heart sunk.

'It'll be fine, love. Fine.'

I knew it would. On the surface. But underneath I know that this unit is what keeps me together, makes me able to deal with my job. I have to be OK for Danny and the kids. I have to be alert at work.

I don't start work until ten because I take the kids to school every day and Danny picks them up, so I go back to bed. I wake up in our bed with Jennifer's face next to mine. Her red curls are damp with sleepy sweat and her cheek is squashed against my shoulder. Danny's side hasn't been slept in and I touch the cold sheets. Jennifer stirs and I envelope her warmth and hug her close. My heart leaps with happiness.

I don't want Danny to get an inkling of how much I miss him, and he can read me like a book – even my voice can give away my feelings. I know what he will do. When we first met we did the usual three dates, then straight to sex, staying awake all night afterwards talking. I made out that I'd done this before – that I was used to the flow of relationships but I wasn't. Danny was so easy and free, so friendly and cool. He hung a string of fairy lights around the bed in the flat where I was renting a room and told me that he would be with me for ever. The inevitable getting-to-know-you questions came up. Tea or coffee? Sugar? Where did you grow up? How many sexual partners? Serious relationships?

He'd pressed me. With a wide Danny smile and a twinkle in his eye.

'How many, then?'

'Serious or ...?'

'Serious. Just so I know what I'm up against.'

It had been easy, really. Danny was beautiful. Quietly sexy and very, very interesting. And he believed every word I said.

'Just a few.'

He smiled.

'So were you engaged or ...?'

'No. Not really. On and off. Came to nothing.' His eyebrows were raised. He wanted more. 'I went on a few dates but I can only sleep with someone I am in love with.'

It was clever of me and I knew it. I'd been saving it until an awkward moment like this, where the surface of my life was about to be punctured with questions. Something grand to distract him. Something to make me stand out from all the other ex-teenagers moaning about their upbringing. He had melted into me and we were a couple.

But one thing I do know about Danny is that he won't take any shit. He told me right from the start that he expected complete fidelity, complete truth, and that anything else was a deal-breaker. Here, with me and his children, he is the gentlest, most patient man. But I have seen his temper flare, rushing out to protect and insulate our little part of the world, our relationship. I know that if he found out how much I was pining for him, he would be back on the first flight.

Simon appears with his games console. He sits on the end of the bed and clicks away at it, his body moving with the game. My two babies, here with me. I close my eyes and listen to Jennifer's breathing. Simon clicks away until Jennifer wakes and pushes her hair out of her eyes. She pats my face gently to wake me and Simon's clicking stops.

'Mummy.' It feels good. I know in that moment I will do anything to protect this. That this is the right thing.

I hurry into the kitchen and start breakfast. This is the metronome of the day and Jennifer is jumping up and down on the sofa.

'Are we going to see Grandma after school?'

'No, love. It's only Wednesday. Saturday is Grandma's day. Grandma Vi's today, love.'

I pop some bread into the toaster and she continues. We both know where this is leading. Finally, we get there.

'Why have we only got one granddad, Mummy? Why do we only have Daddy's daddy? Janet has two granddads. Where's our other granddad?'

I sigh. It's a good question but one that it will never be easy to answer. When I had been seeing Danny for six months, he took me to meet his mother. Violet, a wonderful West Indian woman, welcomed me into her family with open arms. She asked me questions about my life and told me all about Danny's exploits as a child, complete with photographs. His father was an older version of Danny, easy-going and vitally happy. The opposite of my father.

When I left home I visited my parents about once a month. They live in a village at the other side of Manchester, high on a hill that sits at the foot of the Pennines. My childhood was spent traipsing across the heathered moors and running up and down the steep inclines with my best friend. I fancied myself as a Cathy and I was desperate for my Heathcliff. I never wanted to be indoors with my parents. Their semi-detached bungalow has been their home since they married, and my father's armchair in the window was a permanent fixture.

So when I took Danny to meet them he was the first thing we saw. His reaction took me completely by surprise, but on reflection I don't know why, after how he had treated me. I had never seen him answer the door, not even once, always leaving it to my mother. But he was out of the chair, newspapers floating through the air, and at the door before we even got down the drive. He fixed his stare on Danny, stony-faced and hostile. We should have left then, I knew it instinctively, but Mum intervened. 'Ria! Come in. Come in.'

I walked in with only a brief glance down the road to Dougie Peter's house. Danny followed me inside my mother and father's beige home. Mum made tea and Dad just sat staring at Danny, seething. Finally, Mum beckoned me into the kitchen.

'He seems nice, Ria. But are you sure …?'

I totally missed the point.

'He's got a job and we're moving in together.'

I folded my arms and stood firm. She pulled her lips thin and looked down.

'But children …'

'I'm on the pill.'

She turned away and fussed with some Madeira cake. I could hear the silence in the lounge and then Dad got up and went upstairs. Danny was very still. It's the only time I have seen him visibly hurt. He took my hand.

'Come on. Let's go.'

Mum stood in the lounge with a tray of cake, her hands shaking. We moved towards the front hallway and she followed us. Dad was standing at the top of the stairs.

'If you leave with him now, don't bother coming back. Not you and not any kiddies. Bloody hell, Ria. I thought I'd brought you up better than … that.'

I looked at Mum but her face was set in a look I had seen so many times before when he had proclaimed that we would not go abroad on holiday. Or that we would not eat that foreign shit when she cooked pasta. She looked from me to Danny and back again but she didn't do anything. Not for a full minute. Then she put the cake down on the table and ushered us out. As I stood bewildered on the front doorstep, she smiled stiffly.

'You can still phone.'

She said it hopefully, and I still did. But if she wants to see Jennifer and Simon she must meet me in town. We've met almost every Saturday since I had them. I meet her outside Boots and she takes them to McDonald's while I wander around the shops or sit alone in a coffee shop thinking about how I can make things right with her. She always manages to make it sound like she's doing me a favour.

'Come with Grandma while Mummy does some shopping.'

The way she says 'Mummy' holds a mild sarcasm, as if she doesn't really believe I'm their mother. That I could have produced these beautiful creatures with Danny. In many ways it suits me as it means I never have to think about my childhood. But it also means that my children have never met their grandfather.

I still need her at times like this. I think about phoning her but it's early and I know that she will be making his breakfast and might not answer. My father has never made a cooked meal in his entire life; she has to do everything for him. I once asked her why – why she let him treat her like this. But she told me to keep quiet. That nothing ever came of making accusations you can't prove. *To keep my mouth shut,* which is the very opposite of what I tell the women I work with every day. I knew deep down she was thinking of my father. Of the trouble it would cause. Interrupting his going to work and coming home. Eat. Sleep. Repeat. She was telling me to do what she did: keep quiet and suck it up.

I take the kids to school and go into work. The whole day is spent dealing with enquiries from the awards evening. The reporter who took the photographs phones and asks me for a quote. I answer him almost mechanically.

'Two women per week are killed by their partners. I am making it my life's work to stop this happening, whatever it takes.'

He pauses and I hear him clicking away.

'So what made you want to work in this area?'

I snort. Journalism 101.

'I grew up around controlling people. I just wanted to save others from it.'

Vague enough for most people, but hopefully my father will read it and know it's about him. The reporter is satisfied. He tells me it will be in tonight's teatime edition and ends the call. It's like throwing a grenade into a room with my mum and dad, but if change is going to happen, it might as well be now.

Janice organises the rooms back to normal and talks to our guests. Danny's sister Donelle has collected the kids from school so I go along to Danny's mum's to pick them up. I realise as I sit down at the table to dinner with her and Danny's family how much they mean to me. Danny's mum squeezes my arm.

'All right there, Ria?'

I smile at her. She means it. It's not a platitude.

'I'm fine, Vi. Fine.'

She nods. 'Work, is it? You're a bloody saint, you know. Working there. Them women need you. Bloody saint.'

I snort as I sip my tea. 'I'm no saint, Vi. Your Danny's the one who props me up. You did a good job there.'

Jennifer joins in. 'Daddy's amaaaazing!'

Donelle holds up the local paper, which has an old picture of me and the headline 'Ria Taylor – Local Superwoman'.

'But Mummy's Superwoman, isn't she? Or so I hear.'

We all laugh and I'm tearing up again, thinking how this could have been me and my mum and dad. It's not like me. Janice calls me Teflon: tough as nails and nothing sticks. But Danny's barely been gone two days and I'm blubbing.

I don't want anything to spoil this. It may sound selfish, but this family, this round-the-table situation, is what I want to preserve. It suddenly strikes me that the past two days and all the worrying over money has made me count my blessings.

At half seven we say our goodbyes. I finally sit down at home around half eight and ring Danny's mobile. He answers in one.

'Ri. Hi. Look I'm sorry I didn't ring but. I just ...'

It's so good to hear his voice.

'It's OK. I just wanted to check in. It's been a hard day.'

He laughs, deep and true.

'Aren't they fucking all! Look, I'll be back in the real world sometime tomorrow. That flight then a full day labouring's wiped me out. And I can't wait until we have that deposit in our hands. Get looking. It's gonna happen.'

I smile to myself. I want to tell him I love him, and explain how much, tell him how happy he makes me. Because I do. So much. But the unspoken cost of a foreign phone call hangs between us, eating into Danny's house deposit dreams and the debt-busting trip.

'Yeah. Speak tomorrow, love, take care. Love you.'

He ends the call and I immediately open my laptop. It's better to look to the future. That's what we agreed. I'd look for houses while he was away. We could still get a mortgage if we sorted the debts out now. He is right. I flick on to Rightmove and lose myself in what could be my future home.

Chapter Three

Day 27

When I woke up this morning Danny's jumper was in bed beside me. I must have reached for it during the night.

I get up and make tea. It's my ritual, holding the hot cup in my hands and having half an hour to collect myself before Jennifer and Simon burst forth. Our home is tiny but comfortable, most things recycled from either our previous homes or house clearances via work: the houses of women who are gone, their partners in prison or far away.

Yes, I grow attached to them. It's hard not to because they become my friends. I spend hours and hours helping them, sometimes sitting in silent witness to their oppression, other times an endless sounding board. Whatever they decide I will honour, even if it is returning, because it is their choice. But when the end of their world comes, it is devastating. SafeMe is a family, and it is like losing a sister. I always keep a memento of them, and they are here, dotted around my home: a thimble, a ceramic cat, a moulded plastic bangle. Nothing matches in my home, but everything matches people's lives.

I think it's rebellion rather than general untidiness. Even as a child I cluttered my room with bits of toys I had collected from the street and from friends' houses. In my mind, I was creating a toy hospital where I could put them back together and gift them, reconfigured, to my friends. In my mother's mind it was a fucking mess. The bungalow was spotless and washed over with magnolia paint every six months to 'freshen' it. None of that for me.

I sort through the various hats and gloves and boots. I take Simon and Jennifer to school and wave to them long after they've gone in. I walk to work through the backstreets of Manchester, social housing turning to quirky bedsits and old mills turned to posh flats. Once there, I pull out the work diary. Someone has complained about us. They mistook us for a bail hostel. I open a word document and think about how to explain that the women here are not criminals but not victims either.

My thoughts are interrupted by Janice bursting into the room. She thrusts a package into my hand along with a bunch of envelopes with a thick elastic band around them. I see my chance. I produce a bundle of final demands out of my pocket.

'Got a minute?'

She turns around and sinks into a chair. She reads the letters, some of them in bright red ink. Her face reddens a deep beetroot in temper.

'Fucking hell. Is this why Danny's fucked off to Dubai?'

'Yeah. That and a deposit for a house.'

She whistles into the air.

'Bloody hell. Must be some job.' She shuffles the letters. 'Will there be time? I mean, some of these are quite … old.'

I grin at her. We're used to last chances.

'Yeah. I'm going to ring round today. Give them a payment date.'

'So is this why you've been a bit pissed off. Not the usual strength of Little Miss Sunshine?'

I nod and grin still.

'Yeah. That and Danny being away.'

She looks at me.

'Happens to the best of us. Wasn't so long ago our Eamon owed Very five grand. And he's an accountant.' We both laugh. She's right and I know it. She kisses the top of my head. 'Got to run, Ri. But cheer up, Charlie. You did the right thing telling me even if it's only so I know why you've got a face like a fiddle. We'll chat later. I need to tell you about Tony's girlfriend.'

Normally I would be all ears. Janice is my female soul mate and the source of hilarity, but I'm already sorting through the post. I relax. Bills and benefits letter for the residents. I open the package and pull out the box inside. It's a cheap mobile phone. I look at the label and it's clearly addressed to me. Probably for one of the women. I turn it on and the screen bursts into life. There is an icon on the front that says 'media file', and underneath 'play me'.

I press 'play' and it's me. It's me walking away from SafeMe, down the road. It is filmed from a distance, probably from inside a car. I turn up the volume and I can hear rustling, the noise of traffic and breathing. I watch the footage until it ends, then flick to the numbers. There is a single number in the address book. The freeze-framed picture of me on the screen is half astride and there is something mildly comical, almost clown-like about it. I'm wearing black dungarees over a bright yellow T-shirt.

I snort. *Fucking idiots.* I've had this kind of thing before, although not this blatantly – more catcalling and threats on the street outside SafeMe from disgruntled ex-partners who truly believe it is my fault their wife has taken their children and left them.

This is a new turn. They don't usually go to any expense. Except time, but they tend to have plenty of that, having followed their desperate partner halfway around the country. But they usually like to save their money for elaborate deliveries of bouquets and chocolates. As if that will put it right with these women who have been beaten so badly they have left everything. I watch the clip again then I throw the phone into my bag.

I get home to an empty flat minutes before Donelle drops off the kids. I watch the footage of me again, trying to glean any clues as to who could have sent it. There are so many to choose from, so many men who have sworn to take revenge on me for giving their wives and children a better life away from them.

It doesn't scare me. Janice and I have each other's backs, logging anything of concern and high-fiving the rest away. I know it is well within the range of many of these men to harm me; I also know that they prefer to harm someone much more defenceless, isolated, vulnerable. I have people. I feel safe.

Even so, I try to listen to the breathing, to discern if it's a man or a woman. I'm fuming, but competing worries pile on top and I stow it away in the mental box marked 'Disturbing Things', that fuzzy place that stops me losing the plot. I check my own mobile, the familiarity comforting. Danny has not replied to my last text despite my checking every thirty seconds. A new worry has piled on the usual ones because I knocked on Sheila's door earlier and she didn't answer. Her nearest neighbour, Stella, leaned out of her window.

'Went out early, she did. All dolled up.'

I ring Sheila's mobile but she doesn't answer. I text the warden of the individual living complex she lives in – it's part of SafeMe but just around the corner – and ask her to let me know when Sheila gets back, and I ring the hospital just in case. She isn't there. A million Sheila-related scenarios cancel out everything else as I pop some fish fingers under the grill and saw at the fresh bread I brought home.

Donelle arrives with the kids and the panic shuffles to the back as love hurries to the front.

'Fish finger butties!' I proclaim this loudly and Donelle laughs.

'No wonder they call you Superwoman. Is there enough for me?'

I smile at her. I love Donelle. She is a wonderful person, full of vitality and the definition of sass.

'Of course, Sis. Help yourself.'

The kids are ravenous but I just pick at my crusty bread and dip my finger in the tomato sauce. Donelle pauses mid munch.

'You OK? You don't seem yourself.'

I smile. I am OK. Some fuckwit with a camera phone isn't going to faze me.

'I'm good. Just tired.'

She finishes chewing then nods.

'Danny? Look, I know it's hard without him but it kind of gives me a chance to see the kids more. If that's OK?'

She stares in anticipation. Her job doesn't let her be here as much as she would like, and Danny's recent unemployment meant he was picking the kids up most days. I put my hand over hers.

'Course. It will be great to have you here more.'

Jennifer is sitting on Donelle's knee and Simon is beside her as she reads Roald Dahl's *BFG* for the thousandth time. The cheap phone pings and, despite wanting to ignore it, I simply can't.

I get up and go into the back garden we share with the other flats. It's a cool evening and I look up at the stars. I instinctively try to predict what this message will say, veering to the positive as ever – the eternal optimist.

I press the 'open' button, read the words.

I'M WATCHING YOU

I chill but then remember that this is a stupid game being played by someone on the losing end of a long battle. I smile to myself. I know I shouldn't answer. But that small 'fuck you' part of me, the part that doesn't give a shit about debt or threats and what got me into trouble in the first place, can't help itself.

I press 'reply' and touch the phone keys quickly, laughing as I press 'send'.

NO SHIT SHERLOCK

Chapter Four

Day 26

It's Friday. I wake up after a deep sleep and it takes a moment to register why Danny isn't there.

I check my phone straight away and there's a text from Sheila's warden. I ignore the cheap phone. I push the video and message to the bottom of my consciousness to sit with all other things I don't want to think about. I'm good at that.

Sheila's back. Seems OK.

I know this merely means that she is walking unaided and doesn't appear to be injured. I get ready for work, drop the kids off and by five past ten I'm sitting on the wall outside Sheila's building. Danny texts me.

Day 26 Morning, beautiful. Sorry I didn't message you yesterday, I'll call you later. Have a glorious Friday. I love you x always x

I touch the screen. I bring up his name and run my finger over it. I text him back.

Miss you. Love you, love you, love you xxx

Sheila appears in the doorway of her flat.

'Coming in or just thinking about it?'

I hug her tightly.

'Where were you yesterday? You should have phoned me. I came over and I was worried.'

She ignores me and plods through to the lounge. I look around at the neat flat. Some ornaments have appeared on the mantelpiece since I was last here last and some small cardboard boxes, sealed with brown tape.

'So you've been back to your house, then?'

She twists the rings that adorn almost every finger, diamonds and emeralds mostly, and touches the gold chains at her throat. I notice that the knuckles on her unplastered hand are freshly scraped.

'I just wanted a few things. Some of my stuff.'

'Was Frank there?'

She stiffens. Months have passed since she moved into this flat and she has never once admitted that Frank is to blame for her injuries. She hides the plaster cast under her Damart cardigan.

'He lives there, doesn't he? Yes. We had a chat.'

'Oh. So what did he have to say?'

She shrugs and makes a face. 'Misses me. Wants me to come home. The usual.'

She gets up and fetches one of the boxes. She rips away the tape and puts it in a small tiger-print litter bin. Sheila is a big fan of animal print. I've never seen her without at least one item of fake fur on. She reaches inside the box and brings out some framed photographs and then a box of loose ones. I see that the top photograph is a wedding picture: Sheila and Frank, all happy and smiling on their wedding day. She's wearing a smart suit and a corsage and he has a dark three-piece and a rose buttonhole.

They look fabulous, but this shatters my hopes that she is finally making the transition away from him. I had expected her visit to the house she shared with Frank would be to fetch clothes and shoes, her bits and pieces. But all she seems to have brought are pictures. Of them both. I watch her as she sorts the photographs. She passes one to me.

'That's me and 'im at the boxing. When I was eighteen.'

I smile. She's opening up to me at last.

'That's lovely, Sheila. You made a lovely couple back then.'

She laughs – a deep, throaty laugh that reflects a lifetime of smoky bars and unfiltered cigarettes. Her blonde hair is a testament to this: permanently nicotine-stained at the front, as are the nails on her right hand.

'We weren't a couple, love. He paid me. Picked me from a line, he did. I was an escort. You know, like that film. *Pretty Woman*. I'm fucking Julia Roberts.'

She starts to laugh loudly until tears run down her face. I laugh with her, but I'm looking at the picture, and some more she flings at me. She was very beautiful. When she manages to stop laughing, she gulps down her tea and carries on.

'I went everywhere with him. He was up for election then, local council, and he wanted someone on his arm. Then, after a bit, he proposed. I didn't really know how that worked, and where I would get my wages from, but it turned out I didn't get any money. He bought everything. Everything I wanted.'

I nodded. 'So were you happy with that? Is that what you wanted?'

She laughs again. 'Wanted? Ha! There is no wanted at this end of the world.' Suddenly she becomes very serious. 'End of the world. That's what this is for me, you know. I loved Frank. I still do. I've heard you going on about how you can't love someone who hits you, so praps I'm bloody obsessed. And praps he don't love me either. But all I know is that this is the end of the word for me.' She wipes away a tear. 'In my day you stayed, rain or shine.'

I look at the photographs in my hands. This is my chance to talk to her.

'So has he always treated you like this, Sheila? Has he always …?'

'Yes. You see, I could do what he said, mainly. I could put up with him not coming home and the other women, but every now and again I'd blow up and then he'd batter me. Never my face, though.'

I glance at the pictures. They cover a long period and there is no sign of the deep scar she has on her cheekbone. She previously told me this had come from a car crash in Spain.

'So when did it get worse?'

She lights up a cigarette and takes a long drag. She offers me one and even though I don't smoke now I'm tempted, until she starts to cough deeply.

'When he stood down. He never really worked, not a nine-to-five. All above board, Frankie, local councillor, lots of connections, most of them dodgy. Bribes and that. But plenty of money. Then other, younger blokes came on his patch and paid him to take a back seat. He was at home more, so I was more annoying to him. All charity this and benefit concert that, he is, but underneath it all he's bent as anything.'

I shake my head. 'It was never your fault, Sheila. You know that, don't you?'

She snorts, blowing smoke from her nostrils. 'I was all right until I opened me mouth. That's what he used to say. "You're all right till you open yer mouth." I did everything for him. Bloody everything.' I think about my mother, pushing my father's suit jacket on to his arms as he stood motionless in front of her. 'I used to get these little flashes of what it could be like if I, say, went out with me mates. Or got a job. I'd mention it and then he'd start. And then there was the jealousy.'

She turns her huge diamond engagement ring another circuit.

'So you see, he kept me in that house, unless he was going out and then I had to go with him.' She passes me a more recent picture of them in a night club with several generations of Manchester businessmen and their dead-eyed wives. 'See. Two weeks after I'd had a hysterectomy. Going out in that state was easier than the bleeding consequences. Frankie was my world. Still is. Happen not by choice, but he still is. Fish out of water, I am.'

She lights another cigarette and gulps her tea. My face is wet with tears. I had wondered if Sheila had known what had happened to her or if ignorance was bliss. But she's smart. She knew all along and every time she tried to break free Frankie boy held her down. Yet here she is now.

'You're safe here, Sheila. He can't get you here.'

She nods. 'I know, lovey. And you're doing a wonderful job.'

She leans forwards and pats my knee and the cable cardigan rides up and exposes fresh bruising on her arm. She sees me see it.

'Take someone with you next time. The police—'

She roars with laughter. 'Bloody hell. That's a good un. The police. Oh yes. That'll scare the shit out of Frankie.' Then she's serious again. 'Don't you think I went down that route, lovey? Dialling 999 till the 9s on the house phone were worn out. Then broken fingers so I couldn't. They just told me to leave, but every time I tried he just made it so I couldn't.' She lights yet another ciggie. 'Anyway, half of 'em were in his pocket. And to them I was just another prozzie who got lucky.'

She's done with that and she changes the subject to her Asda online shop until she tells me she is tired and she'll see me on Monday.

'Don't forget. If you're going round there, take someone with you. One of us.'

She repeats it. Rolls it round in her mouth like it's delicious. '*One of us*. Yeah. Happen I will.'

I leave and walk slowly down the road. Sheila's flat is in central Manchester, just around the corner from SafeMe. My phone rings and it's Janice.

'Funding bid forms are in. We've got a week to complete and evidence them. This is it, Ria.'

Between the end of Sheila's world and Danny being away I'm already frazzled. My mind and body tell me they need a long soak in a bubble bath. But deep down in my soul I know that if I shirk this admin or trust someone else, someone less experienced or less qualified, we're fucked. They weren't going to fund us at all. Even sending us the forms to fill in depended on the impression we made at the awards night.

'I'll be right there. Just on my way back from Sheila's. She's OK.'

Janice is silent for a long second. She knows everything about SafeMe and what goes on here. She has insight. She also has a Ph.D. in Sociological Methodology and could earn a zillion times what we do here. But she does it for the same reason I do. Moments like this.

She also knows me inside out. From the moment I met her I knew Janice and I would be close. We had shared experiences and we both knew how dangerous this job could be. On our first day working together we were leaning against a door trying to keep out the pissed-up ex-partner of one of the women while she hid under a table. We had stared each other out for strength and no words were needed – we just knew. We knew each other, and we knew the situation. We didn't know what had made us like that, given us that amount of strength. We didn't know what had driven us to have a higher threshold for danger, and stress, but we silently acknowledged it.

When I arrive at work, there is a huge bouquet waiting for me – ten beautiful red roses with clouds of fluffy gypsophila between. They are hand-tied with a pink ribbon. The smell is fresh and I quickly pull away the cellophane wrapped around them and put them in small vases all around the largest conference room where I am working today.

I text Danny:

Thank you – they're lovely xxxx

All feels well with the world again. Janice appears and stares at the flowers.

'Bloody hell. Danny's pushing the boat out.'

I flick my hair. 'It's because I'm worth it.'

She laughs loudly. 'You are, Ri. You are.' But there's something else. I can tell. She continues. 'Look. It's about Sheila. Is she definitely OK?'

'Yeah. Fine. I just saw her. She's been home but ...'

Janice nods. 'I thought so. Something's going on here.'

I try to reassure her. 'She was fine. A bit shaken, but she's bound to be. She readjusting, isn't she?'

Janice blinks at me. 'Right. That's good to hear. Because Frank James has booked himself into the perpetrator counselling sessions on Monday.'

We both know what this means. It's just another step in the pursuit of power. Half the perpetrators are at the sessions because they know it's a step closer to access to their prey. That there is a chance they will see them, be able to affect them. Frank is no different. Except he already has power. Frank James expects to get exactly what he wants.

Friday afternoons are a chance for me and Janice to look back over the week and plan the week to come. We usually sit with our feet up on the chesterfields, talking to our guests and finding out what we can do better. We phone around supermarkets to get them to donate sanitary towels and deodorant, we check that our donation tins are still in place.

Today is no different. It's usually a chance to wind down, and what seems like a distant memory of pre-debt relaxation washes over me. Janice is telling me about some shoes she bought and had to take back and Sally Lewis, recently arrived mum of four, is listening intently, as if she has been starved of conversation. I sink back into the patina of the sofa and laugh with them. The afternoon washes over me and I've almost forgotten about the messages, the video, and the constant and ever-increasing list of stalker candidates who could have sent them.

I glance at my phone and there's a text from Danny. I open it quickly and it's a question mark followed by three 'laugh till I cry' emojis and 'what for'. I look around the room at the vibrant flowers, all in separate vases, then I run through to Reception. Amy, our temp receptionist, is filing her nails.

'Amy, was there a card with those flowers? Who brought them?'

She shrugs. 'They were outside when I opened up. Must've been a courier.'

They're not from Danny. I hurry round the back of the building and ransack the bin to find the wrapping paper that the flowers arrived in. It's under a layer of teabags and milk containers, but I manage to tug out the soggy cellophane. It's a standard florist's wrapping. I search and search but there is nothing to say who sent them.

It doesn't make sense. My mind tags the flowers on to the phone footage and the message. I text Danny back and tell him it was just a joke, I meant the texts he had been sending but didn't explain properly. But somewhere inside me something shifts. The smell of roses sickens me and, deep down, I know that this is not right.

Chapter Five

Day 25

Saturday morning dawns as I sit in the kitchen alone. I'm making coffee and I feel my hips begin to sway involuntarily to a samba-based tune on Radio 6. It reminds me of Danny, and I feel his arms around me, his body moving with mine. I career back to reality when Jennifer rolls into my ankles, buckling me. I look down at her and she's giggling and I feel my mouth curve into a smile.

'What on earth are you doing?'

She laughs, still leaning against me on the kitchen floor.

'I'm rolling.'

She collapses into hysterical giggles and I can't help but laugh too. Somewhere inside I wonder where I lost that, the ability to laugh until I cried.

'Come on. I'm dropping you off with Grandma!'

She pulls herself up and, still giggling, puts on her hat and coat. Simon appears, already wearing a parka and a backpack. We set off, them excited and me reluctant as usual.

My relationship with my mum has never been good, but there was a steep decline when I was fifteen. By the time I was a teenager I had banned the 'freshening' process from my bedroom and covered the walls in pop posters. Mum relaxed a little, sensing this as normality.

How wrong she was. Nothing was normal about that time. I spot her in the distance, looking in the window of the coffee shop opposite Boots. I wonder if she's looking for someone or looking at herself, constantly checking herself like she used to in the mirror at home. I suddenly feel self-conscious, like my fifteen-year-old self. Faced with her appearing every morning fully dressed and made up, a faint smell of hair lacquer around her, I was constantly inadequate.

She sees me and stiffens. No smile for me, but a bent-over kiss for Jennifer and a hand on the shoulder for Simon. I stand awkwardly, toes turned in. The unspoken instruction as she stares at my shoes make me push my feet together and I feel resentment swelling.

'OK. I'll be back here at four.'

She nods. 'Fine. We'll be here.'

That's it. I walk away, glancing behind to see her whole demeanour changed now I'm gone and she is alone with Simon and Jennifer. An internal clock sets itself for the tide of missing them, flowing at me in waves until it is time to pick them up.

I head for the coffee shop, but my phone rings. It's Janice.

'Hi. We've got a situation.'

She sounds out of breath and I know she wouldn't call me on a Saturday if it wasn't urgent.

'Let me guess. Velcro?'

She makes a noise, which, if she wasn't so stressed, would be a laugh.

'Yeah.'

'I'm on my way.'

I hurry to the taxi rank and jump in a cab. It's not far and by the time I get there the police are there too. I pull my ID out of my bag and walk past the first police car and into SafeMe. Janice gives me a 'thank God you're here' look and I gravitate towards the most frightened person in the room.

Sally Lewis is cowering against a wall, drawn up inside herself to make her body small. Her legs tremble and she is ready to defend a blow, her right forearm shielding her face.

Her husband, Jimmy, who we refer to as Velcro because he sticks like glue and will not leave, is dancing around Malc Edwards, our security guard. So far Malc is fending him off. Jimmy is like one of those guys you see in a Manchester night club. Wiry and lithe, arms outstretched trying to break up a fight that he probably started. Handy, as Danny would say. But my priority is Sally. I stretch out my arm.

'Come on, love.'

She stares at my hand, alien to her.

'He doesn't mean it. He's just upset.'

I nod. 'Come on. It's OK. Let's get you somewhere safe.'

Janice catches my eyes and I see, just above the leather sofa and behind an orange stained-glass panel, four little heads: Sally's children. They are in another room but can still hear everything. Sally follows my gaze then looks back at Jimmy.

'Yeah, go on then, you fucking bitch. Go on then. Take my kiddies away from me.'

He's still dancing around Malc. The policemen are outside – I can hear their radios – this is something they see every day. Domestic. Rows. They won't intervene until I say or Jimmy looks like he's going to hit someone. While he's just shouting they stand back. He reaches into his pocket and we all take a sharp breath in, but he produces a phone.

'I'm filming this. Filming you fuckers. For court. Once this gets to court they'll see how I get treated by her. You lot. Them fucking pigs. It's her who should be arrested. She stole my kids.'

He waves the phone around, its red recording light flashing, until it rests on me.

'Big boss lady. Oooh. I must be important for you to come out on a weekend.'

I fold my arms. 'They're important, Jimmy: the children and your wife.'

He continues to film. 'Yeah. Because that's what always happens, innit? Eh? Women can run off with the kids and what can the bloke do about it? Eh? Fucking nothing.'

He moves closer to me, right up to me, and I hold my ground. I hear Sally murmur, like this has happened before, his MO. I see the police out of the corner of my eye move into the hall. The phone is almost touching my nose.

A child starts to cry in the other room. A young child. A wail that provides a background distraction and everyone looks around. Everyone except Jimmy. I watch him not even flinch when his son begins to cry. Sally hugs herself and starts to move but he steps in front of her. They are nose to nose now, him teeth gritted and face red. Her terrified. The police move in but it's too late.

A trickle of liquid runs on to the wooden floor. Jimmy watches as it makes a ravine between the boards, his expression turning to a smile.

'You dirty fucking bitch. You've pissed yourself.' He turns to us. 'She needs locking away. She's not fit to look after them kids. Look, you all seen her piss herself in public. If that were me I'd be ...'

An officer goes to take his arm but he jerks away, suddenly serious.

'I never touched her, mate. I never touched anyone. Just here for my kids, me.'

There's a brief face-off before they escort him off the premises, followed by Malc and Janice. Her shoulders are drooped because she knows there will be reams of paperwork for just this one incident.

Sally still does not move. Then she crouches down on to the floor and pulls her hoodie sleeves over her arms and covers her face. I touch her shoulder and she cowers away.

'Come on. Come in here. I'll sort this out.'

She looks up at me then down at the floor.

'Sorry.'

I shake my head. 'Don't worry about it.'

'I'll clean it up. Just tell me where the stuff is and I'll ...'

I watch as Janice goes through to the room where the children are. Sally's son has stopped crying now and SafeMe is back to the quiet place it was less than an hour ago. I go to the staff shower room and Sally follows me. Once inside she is stripping off her clothes until she is naked. I can see round scars on her stomach, evidence of burns, and longer scars on her thighs. It could be self-harm, but I doubt it. She will tell me in time. She hurries into the shower and stands under the warm water with her back to me, not pulling the curtain. Her shoulders shudder a little.

'None of this is your fault, Sally. None of it.'

There is a slight movement of her head but I can't work out if it's a nod or not without seeing her face. I leave her to have her shower and check the time. I need to be back in town by four. I clear up, then phone Janice.

'Are the police still here?'

She laughs. 'Yep. Didn't arrest him. Just gave him the chat and sent him on his way. He's back in the pub across the road.'

I end the call. That phone. Him recording. Was it a coincidence? I snort to myself. Of course it fucking was. Everyone's got a phone. Jimmy's a psycho but he's a psycho who's only interested in Sally. And would he spend money on flowers? Although he has got a motive. Or he thinks he has.

I check myself. No way am I letting a little fucker like Jimmy worry me. It could all be unconnected: the phone, the message. The flowers could just be an innocent thank-you from someone and the card got lost, but I've built it into something bigger.

Sally is out of the shower. I can hear her padding around.

'Are you decent?'

I try to sound cheery in a desperate situation. She pulls the door and the oversized bath towel that barely covers me exposes her bony shoulders. I hand her a pair of old leggings and a top from the lost property, just until she gets back to her room. She is drained.

'Can I see the kids?'

I stare at her. 'Yes. Of course. Why wouldn't you be able to?'

'Well, after what Jimmy said ...'

I take her hand. It's cold and damp and she flexes her fingers free.

'Look, we're here to help. We'll help you find somewhere. When you're ready. And you can talk to me. You can tell me anything.'

Her eyes flicker up to my face and I know there is something to tell. But we sit there for almost an hour in silence. Sally warms up as the washing machine then the tumble dryer clean her clothes. She finally climbs back into them.

'Can I go now?'

I nod. 'You could have gone anytime. You're not a prisoner, Sally.'

She leaves and closes the door gently behind her. I wait for the rush of gratitude and the tingle of joy that I have Danny and the kids. But all I feel is my fingers gripped tightly around the cheap phone deep in my pocket. Usually, when I see a woman trapped like this, I feel an overwhelming sense of my own freedom, my liberty. I also feel the depth of despair in my heart for women who have not yet escaped. Those in their homes enduring what Sally has.

Tanya

Diary Entry: Saturday

I'm so pleased that I went along to the doctors the other day. That lovely lady doctor was really good; I felt like she understood what was wrong with me. It was really hard to explain it with Al there, especially when she started talking about periods and all that sort of thing. I warmed to her and although Al didn't think writing a diary was a good idea, she thought it would help.

So here goes. It's only an old exercise book, not a proper diary. I probably won't be able to do it every day. After we came out of the surgery Al said again it wasn't a good idea and would just upset me more. In fact, he's gone back to how he was before. He's got this thing that he does, where his face changes just a tiny bit and I know he's annoyed with me. Just a tiny bit, but I know.

Anyway. Where's the best place to start? Probably the other day, when I first started feeling shaky and anxious again. I'd been sitting at my desk in the corner of the office when Jade came over. I could see Mr Simister looking at us through his office window, only his head visible. But like I know with Al when he is annoyed, I know with Mr Simister. His head bobs up and goes to one side. He usually comes out and interrupts, but the phone was ringing and he answered it.

Jade works on the other side of the office with Marcy and Karla. Al says that they are sluts. They wear very trendy clothes and high heels and swear a lot. I guess that's why I have a long-term partner and they don't. They are always talking about different men and how they had fun with them, which Al says means they had sex with them.

It would have been last Wednesday, I think. Jade had leaned over my desk and flicked a paperclip with her false nail. I picked it up and she stared at me.

'Coming out tonight, Tan. After work. Just for one?'

I stared at my desk. She's asked me on and off, and I never go. It was nearly home time, and I could see Al parked outside, staring in.

'No. My husband is waiting for me. We're going out to dinner.'

He's not my husband and we're not going out to dinner. But I had to say something to get rid of her. It didn't. She sat there, looking at me and frowning. Then she pointed a long, French-manicured talon at me.

'Won't he let you? He's always there, every night. Don't you get a night out with the girls?'

I shook my head and carried on typing but Mr Simister was on his way over.

'Get back to work. Come on. This isn't a bloody knitting circle.'

I'm a bit scared of Mr Simister, if I'm honest. Al got me this job about a year after we moved in together. He's one of his friends. I was annoyed at first because I never got a pay packet like all the others. They would go home on Fridays clutching a brown envelope with notes in it. Al told me that Mr Simister was trying out a new system, where he paid employees directly into the bank. As I didn't have a bank account, he'd given him his details. That was all right, wasn't it?

It upset me at first, but when Al started to buy me nice things and let me have a catalogue account, I could see it was the right thing. This way I never had to worry about money, he says.

So when I left work last Tuesday and got into the car I could see his temple throbbing. His hands were gripping the wheel and his knuckles were white. He was staring at Jade and Karla as they laughed and stumbled across the cobbles.

'Thinking of going with them, were you?'

I caught his eye in the mirror. It was the night of my doctor's appointment and I didn't want anything to spoil it.

'No. She asked me. But I said no.'

I always tell him the truth, because somehow he has a way of finding out if I leave anything out. His grip on the steering wheel loosened and he looked at me.

'You can if you want to, you know. Only …'

I smiled at him. I know he only gets like this because he cares about me.

'I know, love. But why would I want to do that?' I patted the hand nearest to me. 'I'm here, they're there. That's all there is to it.'

His temple was still throbbing, but he started the car. In the doctor's surgery she asked me if I wanted to be alone with her. Al did his hand-squeeze thing, the thing we agreed was a sign just between the two of us. So I told her that I wanted him there. For support. Because I really do think I am going crazy.

Chapter Six

Day 24

Despite all the stress, I'm having a lazy Sunday morning, sitting around reading the papers. The kids are playing at my feet and this time last week Danny would have been here.

I'm still annoyed about Jimmy getting into SafeMe yesterday and almost attacking Sally. But thoughts of Danny have damped it down and I make tea and toast. It's an unspoken tradition we've had since the first day, a shared love of thick socks and hot tea and slightly burnt toast. There has never been any need to be 'on show' with him. Dad had always appeared fully dressed in the mornings and stayed that way all day. Mum had very occasionally sat in the lounge in a brilliant white dressing gown with little roses dotted all over it. I was allowed pyjamas on to watch TV just before bed. This is completely different.

Danny usually slumps in the shabby chair opposite mine in his boxer shorts and T-shirt. He's as lean as when I met him and is only just getting tiny lines around his eyes. He wears his hair long and natural and I think about him as I butter the tower block of toast.

I haven't fared as well. Two children have taken their toll on my waistline. I often eat on the hoof, forever promising myself that I will prepare my food in advance and quit the Diet Coke. I did give up smoking, but the result was another stone in weight piled mostly on my legs. But Danny still looks at me just like he did when we met. He was one of the lads, slightly younger than me and rowdy drunk most of the time.

I knew he liked me. He started to go quiet when I appeared and stopped the constant pub-based swearing in front of me. He finally asked me out and our first date was at a posh restaurant in central Manchester. We sat in the lobby for ages, waiting to be seated. We were overlooked for posher, more attractive couples. Me with my badly dyed bright red hair, skinny black jeans and flat pumps. Danny in his brother's too-big suit. We were no competition for the bronzed and Botoxed wannabe wags and their men.

Eventually I took control of the situation. This is what I do. My trademark. My personal statement. Take control of everything, except the one thing you can't. I motioned towards the door and Danny and I escaped. Once outside he laughed loudly and took off the suit jacket. I tied it around my bag handle and we went to a tiny Lebanese eatery in the Northern Quarter. All lamps and candles and, it turned out, love. Yes. I knew there and then that this man was different. He felt like a confidant, someone I could finally be myself with.

I had just started working for SafeMe and I was enthusiastic about the future. Six months later we moved in together, into the back room of a shared house in the city centre. We spent our days working hard, him digging roads. I was training on the job and doing a part-time psychology degree with the Open University. In the evening we sat in dark cinemas holding hands and watching Noir films that we could not tell you the titles of because all we knew was each other.

Danny wanted to settle, he would have bought a tiny out-of-town terrace then and married me. But every time I became nervous. Every time my mum mentioned visiting home on the phone I was straight on Rightmove looking for a new rental. I didn't want to be like them. I would find fault with our current room or flat, and we would soon be packing for our next move. I branded them adventures, but Danny was pissed off with another new set of walls to decorate. Especially when Simon came along, with Jennifer following swiftly fourteen months later.

I had six weeks off work with each of my children. No wonder people think I am Superwoman. But I am not. I worked right up to the first labour pain. Danny, who was still working temporary contracts, looked after them, feeding them my expressed milk. He loved it, but I knew his ultimate goal was a settled family life. I work in a place where I see the best and the worst of human behaviour. I see broken relationships and pain and suffering and, yes, violence. So I know what me and Danny have. We are not lucky because that would imply we have not worked for it. We have built this life, we are still building it, and this is what fuels my strength. But I've never told Danny why I can't settle.

I've seen what lies and deceit can do to relationships and to people, what manipulation and control can do. Everyone has tiny secrets they are entitled to, private thoughts and actions that make us individual. It's the mutual trust and sharing that strikes the balance. I have never told Danny about what my dad did. Or anything that happened when I left home. I know he will never understand why I didn't tell him something so huge, something that damaged both me and other people so much. Danny hates liars. Lies are a deal-breaker for him.

I shudder inside. I'm not usually like this. If anything, I'm over optimistic. I reason with myself that I am tired and missing him. That everyone's teenage years are shit and they aren't constantly offloading on their partner. The fact that my dad is a huge racist has conveniently allowed Danny to think that this is the reason I meet Mum with the kids.

But what if they are right? What if I am not the person Danny thinks he knows? I'm scared that I will lose him and scared that he will think badly of me. Scared that Mum and Dad's assessment of me never amounting to anything will come true. Scared that my colleagues at SafeMe will realise that I am not Superwoman. That I am just an ordinary mortal who can get into debt?

My phone rings and I jump out of my skin, the spell broken. It's Danny. He chats about the job and I am silent. Listening. Thinking about Jimmy and the phone.

'Ri? You all right, babe?'

I panic. 'Yeah. Just this funding thing,' I lie, then hate myself. This is how it all goes wrong. This is how it starts. 'Now the gov have changed it from national to local funding we need to step up. Or we'll close.'

He knows what SafeMe means to me and the women.

'Close? Jesus. What'll happen then?'

'Well, they'll have to rehouse the women and there will be no service.'

He is silent for a moment. Then he asks again, 'So what will happen to … you know …?'

I shake my head. 'Nothing will happen. There will be no help. Well, 999 and an emergency helpline with an answerphone. So nothing.'

There is silence as we take in this possibility. I change the subject.

'Donelle came round. Telling me she's changing routes. Doing Japan for a bit.'

She works for an airline and she's been promoted. She's my main source of cheap vodka and perfume. I hear him cheer a little.

'Good girl. Told her to look after you.'

We laugh and we're almost caught up. Only one burning question remains. He waits awhile.

'Did you see your mum?'

He always asks, even though he knows how my parents feel about him. Predictably, my early protests that they would 'come round' and 'realise' came to nothing. Now any conversation about them is met by Danny's hurt look. It's the one usually reserved for teenagers who taunt him at bus stops or half-arsed white supremacists who insult him from a distance. But he's a good man and he always brings the conversation. He knows that if he doesn't, he's accepting that it's a problem. And we both know the problem is theirs, not ours.

'Yep. Seven minutes, two fat remarks, one hair remark and a 'pull yourself together'. I laugh and he laughs as I relate the brief chat when I picked the kids up from her yesterday. 'She told me Dad's thinking of retiring. More time for him to judge other people, then, I expect.'

Then on to the question of the day.

'What date will you get back?'

He is silent for a moment. 'I don't know. It's day twenty-four today, so in twenty-four days. Look, it'll get easier. I'm here, but my hearts still there, Ria.'

I almost cry. Yes, his heart is still here. With me.

'Yeah. It'll be done in no time. I've been looking at Rightmove. I've been marking them. Ones with a garden and high ceilings. I've sent you the links. I love these two.'

I haven't looked at them, not in detail. I just typed all our requirements into the page and clicked save. But he seems happy with this.

'We'll look when we have the money. When all those debts are paid. Remember, don't open the door to any of them. You know, babe, I can't believe this; we're going to have somewhere that's ours. Get out of here.'

We say our goodbyes and he is gone.

The kids are bickering at the table over some Star Wars Lego and I push the button to switch on our ancient TV. I limit their time – yes, I am one of those annoying parents, but I don't want them exposed to anything that will pollute their minds too early.

'Come on. You can watch TV for a bit.'

They rush over and sit very still on the sofa just in case I change my mind. I stay with them for ten minutes. Eventually they are suitably hypnotised and I creep into my room and sit on the bed. Evidence of Danny is everywhere. I pick up socks and T-shirts and parking receipts, never wishing to have even the slightest overlap between him and what is starting to niggle me. Finally, I get out the cheap phone. I rerun the video, listening for any hint of who took it. It's like a fly buzzing around my head, not actually doing any damage but very annoying. I am none the wiser.

For now, I get the hoover out and move all the detritus of mine and Danny's life into black bin bags. I clean and polish and soon the whole flat is dust-free and relatively tidy. I iron the children's school clothes and stick a chicken in the oven for dinner, cut some roasties and even whisk up some Yorkshire puddings. I text Donelle and invite her and Vi and Danny Snr round for dinner. They are going to church, but Donelle accepts so I chill a bottle of white. Why not? I am strong. I am assertive. I might even be Superwoman after all.

We all have dinner then the kids have baths and go to bed. I don't even check my phone all afternoon. Donelle makes me laugh until I cry with her stories of 'dickheads on planes' – the drunken customers she has to deal with daily. She entertains me with her early Japanese lessons and she drinks more than half the wine, which I am thankful for as I have a big day tomorrow. She looks happy and it doesn't take her long to tell me why.

'So I met him when I was on that two-day break between trips and, well, what can I say? He blew me away!'

I laugh.

'Good God. Everyone blows you away.'

She nods and gulps the wine. 'Usually. Yeah. But he's different. Sort of … I don't know. Charming? So far so good.'

I laugh. 'Bloody hell. So far so good? It's only Sunday!'

I'm glad for her. Donelle has had her fair share of heartache and I know she would love to have what me and Danny have. She leaves at ten and I feel happier than I have all week. I get ready for bed and as I plug the cheap mobile phone into the charger at the side of the newly shiny bedside table it pings. I debate whether I should leave it until morning, but chastise myself for being so blasé. Even so, I pause, not wanting to deflate my mood, but I have to know.

STILL WATCHING

There's a picture of me getting into a taxi outside SafeMe yesterday. The car door is open halfway and I am smiling at the driver. An involuntary shiver runs through me. I try to pitch the angle, twisting the screen to see if it had been taken from the pub. I lean back on my pillow. *Don't let this get to you, Ria.* I've got enough problems at the moment without this.

Tanya

I've had to find a really secret place for this diary. It was easy to fill it in when Al was out last night. Not so much now, though, when he could come upstairs at any time and catch me. I really do think it is helping me. *Write the problem down.* That's what the doctor said. So here goes.

My problem is: me. I keep upsetting Al. He is a very sensitive man. He likes everything just so. The problem is I keep doing things that make him angry. Like that time when we went to the pub on the way home from work. It's about half an hour's drive from Huddersfield where I work to our house and he was in a particularly good mood. He suggested the pub but I didn't really want to.

When we got inside I sat down and Al went to the bar. There were some men playing pool and I sat with my back to them. Al came back with the drinks and I did my usual thing of looking into my half a lager to try to stop myself doing it. Then two young blokes came in and stood at the bar. The fact that I knew they were there proved he was right: I can't help myself.

I saw the pulse in his temple then he scraped his chair backwards.

'Come on.' He dragged me outside by my arm. 'You can't help yourself, can you?'

This is how it has been for as long as I can remember. At first I used to argue and create a fuss and then … well, he lost his temper. Then I began to think he was right. How could he be wrong every time? So

I controlled myself. Completely. I trained myself to look into my drink or at Al so he wouldn't get upset. Afterwards he told me he loves me so much that he can't bear me looking at anyone else.

So that's the problem. I am anxious because I am doing everything I can and he is still angry with me. He is a good man. We've been together a long time and I know all his little ways. I sometimes wonder if I am like this because he was my first boyfriend. If something inside me is lacking. Maybe if I had been a bit more like Jade and her friends before we met I would have been better.

Al is attentive. Over-attentive sometimes. I can't think of a single time he hasn't picked me up from work or not been at my side for the whole of our relationship. We have a beautiful home. He lets me pick everything from catalogues. It's all clean and white, so easy to look after. The back garden is absolutely gorgeous, all enclosed and quite established now. In the summer I go out there and sunbathe, watching the sky and thinking. Watching planes go over and wondering what that would be like.

He is careful, too. Although the house is detached – Al's parents left it to him – he says you can never be too careful, which is why he had the shutters put on. And that's one of the bad things. The shutters. When I annoy him, he goes out and leaves me in the house. It does make sense, I suppose, and he's only trying to keep me safe but, if I am honest, this is when I feel most anxious. All shaky and tearful. But it's for my own good.

So I try not to annoy him. But the other day all that business with Jade and Karla, then at the doctor's when I nodded when she mentioned the diary; it must have all built up. Because when we got outside I was shaking and my teeth were chattering. We got into the car in silence.

When we got home, he stormed inside and went into his study and locked the door. Something had upset him, for sure. He was in there for ages and even when I made some chilli and rice he didn't come out. It's nights like these that I sit on my own, just thinking. It all starts to get on top of me and I start thinking that it's Al. It's him. He shouldn't be doing this. I should be able to go out and have my own money. I shouldn't have to worry about sitting in a pub with him – I wouldn't have another man thrown at me.

When I'm tired my mind plays tricks on me. And when he came out of the study that night those tricks spilled out of my mind and cut the air between us like razor-sharp knives.

'It's her, isn't it? That's why you're like this with me. You still want her.'

His face reddened and his mouth twisted and he lunged for me, but I ducked out of the way.

'You're hysterical.'

The voice wasn't Al's but someone harsh and cold.

'I'm not hysterical!' I screamed.

It only took one slap. I melted into a sobbing heap, sorry for shouting at him and extra sorry for mentioning her. Why did I do it? Why did I do that? Why didn't I keep quiet and let his mood pass, let him be?

So you see, it's definitely me.

Chapter Seven

Day 23

Monday morning finds me raring to go, despite the horrible message. In the middle of the night I made a decision. I'm going to file this away with all the other psychopathic events that surround SafeMe. Someone is trying to play a game with me, but I am not joining in. Danny must have rung just after I fell asleep as he texted me an amused message:

> Bloody hell, babes, those houses are fantastic. Day 23. Nearly one week down and only 3 to go. It all gets easier after this, I love you xxx Always

Easier. Will it? I pull myself up, gather my strength and tell myself that he is right. I miss Danny. Underneath all the problems and worry, I just miss him: the feel of him there, around the flat or at the end of a phone. I read his text again. I run my finger over the words, over Danny's optimism that spans the miles.

When I arrive at work Janice is in the office. I hang my coat on the back of the door, sit at my desk and wiggle my mouse to make my screen spring to life. Janice turns to me.

'You won't believe it.'

It's her opener to tell me something funny. I feel the corners of my mouth curve immediately and think how lucky I am to have her.

'Go on.'

She doesn't say anything, but she swings around in her chair and lifts her legs. She's wearing odd shoes – clearly odd – similar, but definitely not a match. And this is why I love her. Most women, including me, would be mortified, but Janice thinks it is hilarious. She wiggles her feet and I feel the 'don't give a shit' part of me light up. We collapse into laughter, which feels good, and we begin to put the chairs out. It's perpetrator counselling day and on checking the list we see there are fourteen men and no women booked in today.

Each of these men, and each of the women who sometimes attend, has their own reason for coming on one of these days. They have usually physically hurt their partners; sometimes they have psychologically abused their partners, too. Some will argue and protest; some will tell us that they own their wives or that we are fucking lesbians who could never understand because no one has ever wanted us.

They are keeping their wives 'in line'. 'Sorting them out'. 'Putting them straight'. And this is all said in the same tone that the PR woman used to tell me to 'get a grip', only with a little added menace. It is pure power dynamics and it affects every aspect of people's lives, passed down through generations and regardless of class.

So when I see Frank James loitering outside the SafeMe offices, continually trying the locked door because he still hasn't realised what this is, I wonder what he will have to say. How he will spin his violent behaviour towards Sheila. She texted me early this morning to tell me he was coming. I texted her back to reassure her it would be OK. She responded with a standard but heartbreaking, *Please don't tell him I said anything about him.* This is the risk of holding the perpetrator counselling here: that we lose the trust of the women. But it is part of our funding criteria – if we don't do this bit of it, we don't get any of the money.

The attendees of today's session are gathering outside. They are standing individually in a very small area pretending that no one else is there. Many of them are smoking underneath a huge red 'No Smoking' sign, which does not bode well. I see Frank look around and assume the position: hands in pockets, staring into space, no eye contact.

We deal with terrible, terrible situations, but Janice and I are good at our jobs and get through them with humour. We are a veritable double act along the lines of good cop, bad cop, and we take turns. I have the 'Ria stare' and Janice has the deep, silent frown. She pauses before speaking. Nodding, frowning, pausing. It is unnerving to watch, even for me and I'm used to it. But if it serves to diffuse the power dynamic, then I'm game.

She stands in front of me now as we listen at the door.

'Ready?' she asks me in a very serious voice.

'I am. I want to observe Frank James.'

She nods and faux frowns.

'Frankie, Frankie, Frankie.'

I can't help but smile, even though in seconds we will be surrounded by criminals. She flicks the switch that releases the door, and the switch next to it that activates the panic button in the room. We are also targets of violence and it wouldn't be the first time one of us had been attacked by someone's violent ex for just doing our jobs.

The men file in and find places on the chairs in the circle. The new faces look around at the fairy grotto we have made: the low-hanging twinkly branches and the warm colours of the carefully selected framed art posters. If they were expecting a standard, bleak community hall, they will be disappointed. We care about their exes and this is home, just like the huge distressed wood sign that hangs at the front of the room says. *Home.*

I point to empty places and urge the reluctant ones forward, while Janice stands, arms folded, staring and frowning. I look around, risk assessing the situation and making sure the exits are clear, just in case. The first to address the group is our security guard, Malc, who some perpetrators will already have met under very different circumstances when they tried to get into the building to retrieve what they considered their personal property.

'Right, lads, I'll be just outside if anyone needs any help – tough uns these two.'

There is laughter, but everyone knows the score. We begin. We go through the no blaming and shaming policy, we're here to help, and who will be the first to express why they are angry. We are met with silence, and I take the time to assess Frank James.

He is a large man, sturdy, tanned like Sheila. His hair is unnaturally dark for his age and I wonder if he touches it up. Vanity. He's wearing golf clothes – expensive ones – and Adidas trainers, a statement about his football allegiances. He has a Rolex on his left wrist, loose and casual, and he is wearing a wedding ring. Instead of diamond rings like his wife, he has the full sovereigns. His nails are carefully manicured but he has the same nicotine tattoo as Sheila. His eyebrows are trimmed to perfection.

He screams 'ladies' man'. Yet here he is, enduring this to get Sheila back. He's looking at the other attendees, already thinking of alternative reasons he could be here in case anyone recognises him and word gets out.

We time the session and out of the ninety minutes there are only eighteen when someone is actually speaking. The rest of the time is Janice nodding, frowning, pausing. When they finally pluck up the courage to say something in front of their wife-beating peers, we have one 'she's my property' and a short burst of crying and apology, which I suspect is put on to get probation points. We also have one verbal attack on us both as 'rug-munching muffia who deserve everything we get', which we report to the police as soon as the session finishes as a hate crime. This will be added to his already extensive record of abuse.

Some people can't help themselves, and then there are people like Frank. I know that he is sixty-three, which is not old by any means, even in this city of low life expectancy. He moves with the air of a much younger man. As the other men file out, he comes over.

'Ladies. Looking lovely today.'

We stare at him. I am make-up-less, hair scraped up into a wonky bobble. I am dressed in bright yellow dungarees and a purple Sex Pistols T-shirt that has seen better days. I am quite obviously suffering from the stressful week I have just been through. Janice looks like she is at the pinnacle of a hangover and is dressed in black leggings that are too small and almost see-through, and a too-short T-shirt. This gives the effect that she has missed out an item of clothing somewhere. And the odd shoes. We do not look lovely, nor do we mean to. He tries again.

'So. I spoke to the lady on the phone to book in.' He says it like it is a hair appointment. 'What I need to know from you is how many sessions there are on this course.'

I sense Janice stiffen. She moves slightly forwards to engage.

'Until what, Mr James?'

I seriously wanted her to say Don James, because that is exactly what this is. He is lording it over us. He smiles a thin smile.

'Until the end of the course and I can talk to Sheila.'

To be fair, he stands his ground but does not state his purpose. I intervene.

'You can speak to her any time. In fact, didn't you speak to her last week?'

I emphasis the 'speak' so he knows I do not mean speak at all. He looks at the ground. He is a little pissed off now because we are not bending to his masculine wiles.

'Look, ladies, I just want Sheila home. I don't know what she has told you but this is all a big mistake. She's mixed up. She's on the turn.'

He even makes a face that implies that Sheila is a little bit insane. Janice takes it up.

'Is that why you are so angry, Frank? Because Sheila is on the menopause?'

She sing-songs it and he looks very uncomfortable.

'I'm not angry.'

'But you're here, at anger-management classes, where you learn not to be angry. If you're not angry, Frank, why are you here?'

He is confused now as well as angry.

'I ... I just want Sheila home.' At least he spared us the usual protestations of true love. Even though they have beaten the object of their 'love' so badly within the last three months that a crisis intervention was warranted. I step forward and guide him towards the door. Once he is outside, I smile and tilt my head to one side.

'The thing is, Frank, this is about what Sheila wants, isn't it? She left and she is the one who needs to decide if she will return.'

He's still confused. Confused that everyone isn't doing what he says and that Sheila has an opinion and rights. He looks at Malc for male support, but he just shrugs. Finally, he speaks.

'So why am I here, then?'

I shake my head. 'I don't know. You tell me, Frank? Have a think. Eh? See you next week.'

I close the door, lock it and lean on it. Frank is charming. He's the original 'how could Sheila say anything bad about him? He's so lovely'. Completely calm and reasonable in 99.9 per cent of shit situations, after he has encountered them once. Clever enough to not have to deal with them twice himself. He still looks like the Frank that Sheila showed on the old photographs. I remember the scar on her worried face and the solid rings on his fingers and wonder which one made it.

I make my way back to the room; Janice is stacking the chairs.

'Kids all right?'

She bangs the chairs on top of each other. She's a practical person and she would rather mop a floor than do admin, even though she is easily capable. I laugh.

'Yeah. They're not missing him yet. But I am.'

She stops stacking.

'There's somat else, though, isn't there? What's up?'

She's in my face, watching my eyes.

'Nothing really. Just ... Just ...'

She shakes her head and hugs me tight.

'He'll be back in no time, love.' I nod and my eyes fill up, brimming over. This isn't like me at all. A phone vibrates and I jump out of my skin. Janice releases me.

'You need to have a rest. You're on your last fucking nerve and we all know where that leads.'

'I will. I promise.'

At half twelve Sheila appears in the doorway.

'Did he turn up, then?'

I turn around quickly.

'Oh, Sheila love. You know I can't tell you what happened, don't you?'

She nods solemnly. 'Yes. But I just wondered what you thought?'

Her eyes are pleading with me. I know from experience she'll have been on edge all morning. She'll be wondering what kind of impression 'her Frank' made. She'll have worried what he said about her, and whether we'd believed him. Would we still help her? She sits down on one of the tiny chairs that we have no funding to replace.

'I saw him standing outside. With the others. It's not the same, you know. He's not evil. Not to me, anyway.'

She qualifies it quickly. I nod and smile.

'But he's hurt you. Hasn't he?'

She avoids my gaze, looking away as usual, feeling for her ciggies and lighter. Feet set apart.

'He's had a hard life. Got in too deep with that lot when he was young. Very stressful. Surrounded by it, he was.'

She means violence, not stress. I know that he was an important figure in the Manchester community in the 1960s. He is high profile: suspected of being the figure behind multiple crooked building contracts, although nothing was ever proved. I've even seen their house. After I read about Frank's wealth and lifestyle, which seem to be well beyond that of a local councillor, I looked it up on Google Maps. They live in a detached ex farm in a gated complex. It has a sauna and a hot tub. It's not massive, but it is impressive. I know exactly what Frank James was and still probably is. Her phone rings and she jumps to attention.

She thinks it's him, clearly. I'm disappointed, because she told me he didn't have her new number. But it isn't him, it's her hairdresser and she backs out of the room waving to me as she chats colour coverage and sunbed tubes.

Still thinking about Sheila, I open the cheap phone to see if this joker has sent any more messages and I see it. There in my in-box, and now open on my phone, is a picture of a penis. I close the picture quickly and words appear.

JUST A PEEK. UP FOR IT?

He sent me a dick pic. I pack up my bag and leave the office. I go straight home and sit in the dark kitchen. I will fucking ring whoever it is. I will let him know he is not doing this to me. I am just about to dial his number when Donelle turns up with the kids. She's holding a bottle of wine and right now it's exactly what I need.

By the time she's told me her latest man news and we've drunk more than we should, I've made my decision. Tomorrow I will tell someone. A problem shared and all that.

Tanya

Diary Entry: Monday

Al was still very annoyed this morning and I can't work out what I've done. He definitely doesn't know about this diary. I hid it in a gap under the kitchen unit. I made sure that it looked like I was just putting away a pan because I sometimes think he's watching me.

He's been like this since last week. Apart from the incident with Jade and then the doctor's, I've made sure that nothing is wrong. I've been very, very careful to stick to my routine, to speak to him just the right amount so I'm not ignoring him or nagging him. He hasn't spoken to me. Even in the car driving to work and back. He normally compliments me on my cooking or asks where his shirt or socks are. But he's worse than he's ever been, and it's making me shaky.

I know it must be obvious. Like some of the other things that have happened. But I hardly ever see anyone outside work and it's hard for me to get help. I want to be a better person, I really do. I know what's happening is wrong, but I also know that Al wouldn't be so annoyed if it wasn't for me. But I was quite bad today. All I could think about was the silence and the waiting, never knowing what would happen next. Lying in bed and waiting for the door to open.

I expect that's why Mrs Simister came over to my desk at lunchtime. She only comes in one day a week and I used to fantasise about what she did on her days off. Until she brought her son and daughter in. Then I couldn't think about it any more because I was so sad.

She gave me a Turkish Delight bar and stood in front of me so Mr

Simister couldn't see what was going on. I looked up at her, my hand shaking as I took the chocolate. She smiled at me, a kind, closed-lipped smile.

'Are you OK, Tanya?'

I blinked at her. Was I OK? I don't know. I don't even know who I am any more.

'Yes. I'm fine, thank you.'

She looked at my hands. White, thin and shaky. An expensive diamond-and-gold engagement and wedding ring set.

'Look. I know what's going on. With Alan. I know he's …'

It's terrifying when someone says something like that. Because I do know that something isn't right. I do know that he's stricter than other men. I've seen couples in pubs we go to laughing and joking. When we've been stopped at traffic lights at Aldi I've seen women on their own or with kids, shopping. On their own. But he has an answer for everything. And it's this: he cares about me. He loves me. He can't bear to be without me. He's sorry.

I looked down at my desk. The shaking had spread to my whole body and I tried to keep my shoulders still.

'What?'

She reddened.

'He's not treating you well, Tanya. I do the salaries. Your wages get paid straight to him, don't they? Is it because you're on the sick? Have you been diagnosed?'

This is a new one. Diagnosed? Of course, they couldn't have my National Insurance Number. I knew that. But I wondered what Al had told them. I shook my head and for a moment our eyes met. She handed me a card.

'Look, I know it's difficult.' She looked over her shoulder. 'Me and him haven't had it all roses. But if I am right, ring the helpline. You don't have to stay with him.'

She walked away and I ate the Turkish Delight. I am not allowed chocolate – it will make me fat, another source of annoyance – and I bring a packed lunch. No money at work. *You don't have to stay with him.* Don't I? Even if I could get away, which I can't, where would I go? I have no family now my dad is dead and I have no money. I wanted to run after her, shouting, screaming, what did she know? She didn't know what happened at night, did she? She didn't know what happened when Al gets really annoyed.

I looked at the card. Refuge. I placed it inside the Turkish Delight wrapper, went to the toilet and put the wrapper inside my bra. Then I took it out again. I read the words. *Get help.* A number. I went through it in my mind. How I would walk out of work at lunchtime, just walk, until I found someone who looked friendly and ask them if I could use their phone. But then I remembered that it hadn't gone well last time I tried this. Not at all. I'd ended up in casualty, upset and, yes, almost hysterical because no one would let me use their phone. Then Alan had turned up super quick and took me home. I squeezed my eyes together, trying not to think about what happened after that.

When I got home and Al had gone to the loo, I put the card in the gap under the kitchen unit. I placed it carefully on top of the pile of other various helpline cards people have given me over the past twenty years.

Chapter Eight

Day 22

Donelle stayed on the sofa because she was driving and I was glad. I slept properly for the first time in ages and woke thinking today was the day I would take action. We played cards with Jennifer and Simon before she left and as she left I hugged her tight.

'Thanks.'

She smiled widely.

'Family. Our kid's family is my family. And besides, we're friends, aren't we? I mean, if I ever tie the knot you know it'd be you I asked to stand for me. Anyway. Have a bit of a rest. It's only early and these two are fine.'

They were in their bedrooms playing on their tablets. She pulled me into my room and made me a cup of tea, then left. I was so grateful for her in that moment, just someone looking after me, caring. I lay there, fuming over the gall of whoever sent the dick pic. Like teenagers, or something. I know all about Tinder and social networking and Snapchat but I don't use them and I'm not going to let this happen.

I get up and Simon is sitting at the table. He's ten. He is staring at his tablet, watching a Minecraft video on YouTube. Jennifer is eight. She is looking at a row of socks of assorted colours. She's sorted them into an ever-increasing level of decoration, from white plain to loud pink with green pom-poms. Like mother, like daughter. In this case, anyway.

I check the cheap phone. There are no more messages, but somehow it seems worse now. The videos of me were one thing, something someone would do to try – and, in my case, fail – to scare me. But this is different. My skin crawls with the violation of it, the intrusion. I know what to do. I throw my purse and sunglasses into my handbag.

'Come on, kids. Time to go.'

Jennifer pulls on the brightly coloured socks and her own sunglasses. She's humming 'Jenny from the Block' and, once on the street, we break into its verse and do the dance. Simon pretends to be embarrassed and walks slightly ahead. I can see the rhythmic strut almost turning into a dance, the same walk as Danny Jnr and Danny Snr.

We get to school and I hug them closely. I tell them every day that I love them, more than once, and today is no exception, but I feel it a thousand times more. I hug them to me.

'I love you both.'

Jennifer smiles and runs off but Simon hangs around.

'Mum, are you all right?'

I stop in my tracks. 'Yeah. Why?'

He thinks. 'You seem far away.'

My heart breaks. I do seem far away because I am, lost in a world of bills and missing my man. Someone sending me creepy messages. I take his face in my hands.

'It's a special time, Si. Daddy and me, we're thinking about buying a house. That's why Daddy's away a lot.'

He turns slightly and looks at his school, and my idea of moving away – of starting again in a new stalker-free area – smashes into tiny pieces.

'Will I have to leave my friends again?'

I shake my head. 'No, we will stay nearby.' I make a promise I don't even know if I can keep. 'Don't worry about it now, and I won't. Deal?'

We do our special street handshake. I watch as he runs to his friends, not looking back. Stability. That's what Danny wants.

I arrive at work to chants of 'Ria, Ria, diarrhoea; Ria, Ria, diarrhoea; Ria, Ria, diarrhoea' coming from the main room. It is women's individual counselling day. Before I can even think about what to do about my own problems, I need to see Sally. She still looks nervous after the other day. She came to SafeMe from Gloucester. She has four children ranging in age from three to twelve, three boys and a girl. It is the three boys whose noses are pressed against the window, like the other day, watching me. I open the door and they run over, still chanting.

'Ria, Ria, diarrhoea; Ria, Ria, diarrhoea; Ria, Ria, diarrhoea!'

I fold my arms. 'Come on, lads. You know that's not nice.'

All Sally's children are small for their size. She hurries over, herding them.

'All right, boys. Come on, give her a break.' They run off and she hangs about, pale and shaky. 'Still over there, he is.'

Her gaze moves from me towards the direction of the pub across the road where Jimmy has taken up daytime residence, glaring at Malc.

'Right. Look, the police are aware after—'

She interrupts. I see the tears in her eyes. 'It's too cramped sleeping in one room. And school ... I'm sorry. I'm just worried.'

I touch her arm and she freezes. They are sleeping in a family room in the main SafeMe complex; we've moved in extra beds.

It's not ideal.

'We've applied, but there's a waiting list. Same with school places. But it will happen, Sally. It will. Until then they can stay in the school group.'

We both look at the makeshift school room. Janice holds up her hand. She has a tray of milk and biscuits she probably spent all last night baking, and there is complete silence. The children follow her into the far corner and sit in a circle. I turn back to Sally.

'Right, then. Shall we?'

She sulkily follows me into a side room where I flick on a light and then sit in front of her. She is studying her phone and looks up only to check the door every thirty seconds. As I make coffee, she is silent. Finally, I sit opposite her. I speak to her gently. 'Sally?'

She looks at me. Her eyes are shadowed with dark rings and the bright blond streaks in her darker bob are growing out now.

'They sacked me. I knew they would, but ...' She pauses and looks up. 'Probably better. Because now I can get benefits to pay for here and ... wherever next.'

Her expression is haunted. I know she had a job as a medical secretary at a hospital. She loved her job, but Jim didn't.

'You can tell me anything, you know, love. It's private.'

She isn't sure. She's still looking around. Then she clasps her hands in front of her.

'That, the other day. When I ...' She looks up at me. 'He kept me awake. I couldn't work. I couldn't look after my children.' Her voice breaks and her lip trembles. 'He never hit me. He just shouted in my eardrums if I tried to close my eyes. Pinched me.'

She pulls down her track-suit bottoms.

'He burnt me.' I see the circles on her legs, scars on her skin, some of them not yet healed. 'Held ciggies over my eyes and told me that if I shut them, he'd burn 'em open.'

I take her hands.

'You're safe here, Sally. We're going to help you.'

She doesn't cry or smile. She is past that.

'That night. He locked us out. It … it was raining and I called the police. He wouldn't let us in. There was nowhere for us to go in Gloucester so we all had to sleep in a cell, soakin' wet with no other clothes.'

I've read her file. 'Their' home was in Jim's name only. All the bills were in his name. The social worker who referred them told me that it was eerily as if Sally didn't exist in that house. She has refused to press charges against Jim, or even to report him. She is destitute and I know that if this goes on any longer her children will be taken into care. And she has done nothing wrong. Nothing at all.

Sally's immediate problems are getting suitable housing and making sure Jim does not harm her again. The first one will happen eventually, but the second is trickier. He's texting her now. I can see her eyes follow the words and consider them. Then her thumbs moving quick as light across the keyboard of her tiny phone.

'Sally, if we're going to sort this out, I need to talk to you about Jim.'

Her eyes dim further, if it were possible.

'Has he said somat?'

I shake my head. 'No. Look. If you go back there is a risk he'll do the same again.'

Now she is shaking her head. 'He won't stop, you know. See?' She holds the phone up to my face and I read the standard repeated protestations of undying love and his begging apologies. I am cynical, I know, but I have seen it so many times before. 'So even if I do get somewhere, he's just going to follow me. How do I get out of it? How?'

And I do not know. He has threatened her, but when questioned denies it and calls her 'insane' and intimates she is on drugs and is self-harming. The police won't arrest him for sitting in a pub opposite SafeMe and scaring the shit out of her – not until he does something 'wrong'. Their liaison officer is looking at an injunction for harassment. But it takes time and the evidence has to be gathered from scratch. So I do not have the answer. But I do the best I can.

'You will have a panic alarm, so that if he comes near the house, the police will come.'

She tears up. 'It might be too late then, though. Because one day he'll do what he's been sayin' he will.'

I can hear the children in the room behind me singing 'Ring a Ringo' Roses', the patter of feet as they race across the room to tag the wall then reform their circle. A chill runs through me because I know that she is probably right.

She resumes texting. When she puts her phone down on the table to pick up her half-cold coffee, I can see she has been texting Jim. In response to his last three messages professing to 'be a good boy', 'provide for his family' and then demanding to know who her 'new fella' is, she has typed three words over and over again. *Leave me alone*. She sighs.

'At least the flowers have stopped.'

I freeze.

'What?'

She looks up. 'The flowers. Every single time he did it he'd send me flowers afterwards. The house was falling down and we had no food. But he'd send flowers. To apologise, he said. More like so everyone would see.'

I want to ask her what kind of flowers, how were they tied, but I don't. She's stressed enough. At the end of the session she leaves, still reading and texting. Janice pops in and drops the cupboard keys on the table. I know I should be working on the funding bid, but I need some advice.

Geri Lomas is our independent link to the outside world. She is a volunteer, but an experienced solicitor and a trustee of SafeMe. She is passionate and driven and sitting in my office when I get there.

'So what's burning, then?'

I'd sent her an email to request a meeting. She would assume it was for the women, but I am going to discuss my position with regard to whoever is stalking me. Just to be sure where I stand before I take any action.

'Nothing. Well, this is about me.'

She leans forwards. 'Oh. Right. You are OK, though, Ria?'

The pause in my answer says it all and she sighs.

'Oh no, it's not Danny. God, no. It's something else. I just want to run it by you to check how I stand with a complaint.'

She looks puzzled as I begin to spew out the story. By the time I have finished she looks shocked.

'Bloody hell. And he actually had a phone delivered here?'

I nod. 'Yep, and flowers.'

'And now he's sending you pictures of his cock?'

I nod and look at the floor and almost laugh. When she says it, he sounds pathetic. Like someone having a fucking massive mid-life crisis. But that isn't how it's starting to feel to me. I show her the footage and the messages. And the dick pic.

'Whoever it is is a complete dick, Gez. Problem is, it could be anyone.'

She raises her eyebrows. 'Yes, this is classic manipulation. He has all the power. And you don't want Danny to find out?'

'No. I just … well, Danny's funny about stuff like this.'

I dig my hole a little deeper and lie about the most generous, understanding man alive.

'Well, I have to say that reporting this is not going to be easy. For one, you know they won't act without evidence. Evidence in this case being a positive ID. They might go and have a word if he approached you in person, but, for my money, if you can't pinpoint who it is they will just log it at this point. Might be worth doing that. And don't engage. And tell Danny.'

All the things I know. But she hasn't finished. She touches my arm.

'Look, I know this is scary. You've done the right thing telling me. But these are just texts. This is a common thing now, believe it or not, not that it makes it right. Go home. Tell Danny. Ignore the dick pic and messages. Switch that phone off and if he turns up have him arrested. If it carries on and you find out who it is, I'll prep an injunction. Yeah?'

I nod and smile. 'Yeah.'

But I know inside that this is just the beginning. And moments later, when I am standing outside SafeMe, this is confirmed. I am in the process of signing out when the cheap phone pings.

LIKE WHAT YOU SEE? ☺ PLENTY MORE WHERE THAT CAME FROM. ☺

I gag. Smileys. I want to answer, to tell him to fuck off, but I don't. I do what Gez says and ignore it. I push the phone in my pocket. I haven't got further than the pub opposite, where Jim is still sitting staring at Malc, when the phone pings again. My fingers are cold and I struggle to open the message. It's an mp4 and I press 'play'. It's footage of me leaving work minutes ago.

I spin around, scanning cars and windows and even SafeMe, looking for someone I vaguely recognise. I spin, spin, spin, eventually coming to a halt in the middle of the road. Then I see Jim, watching from the window of the pub, smiling. I stare him out. He isn't going to get the better of me. I'm stronger than that.

Tanya

Diary Entry: Tuesday

Nothing out of the ordinary happened at work today. Al is still silent and really annoyed. He did sit at the table tonight to eat dinner instead of taking it into his study, though. He seemed a little bit jollier and, later on, I heard him laughing at the TV in his bedroom.

I feel like I should explain that we have separate bedrooms, seeing that the doctor will read this diary. It's because Al likes to get a good night's sleep and I'm restless. He has a very important job - he's a luxury car dealer. He brokers deals for very rich people, which is how he can drive me to work and back every day. He can keep his own hours.

He stays up watching TV until all hours in his study. I can hear it faintly through the door, sometimes I hear him laughing. The study is below my bedroom and I know every single floorboard creak in this house. I can hear when he opens the door and whether he is going to the kitchen or to the bathroom. I can hear when he is walking across the landing and when he gets to my room. He always stops outside for a moment. I am always listening.

He doesn't like me watching TV. I'm usually sewing in the evenings, or, in the summer, watching the birds outside. I sometimes hear the children from the house nearest to ours playing outside. They have a plastic pool and I hear their dad get the hosepipe and all the laughter. My childhood wasn't like that. Not at all. Maybe that's why I was attracted to Alan. Because he was so much like my dad.

There was a fall-out. Well, not a fall-out. I couldn't see Dad any more because we would get into trouble. When it first happened I didn't even want to. We both thought it would be best to leave it for a while. It was fun back then; we were rebels, two young people setting up home. We would lie in bed every day we could, wrapped up in each other.

But I did start to think about Dad. That's when all the thoughts about her crept in. I hated her. I totally knew that Al must have had girlfriends before me – he knew what he was doing in bed. I loved it then. I loved him. But after a while I started to question myself, then him, about why he had been unfaithful to me. With my best friend. He just laughed and said that it was all in the past.

Then I suggested that we go and see Dad. Explain what had happened. Maybe invite him round for tea? Al became very upset and accused me of going back on our agreement to break free. I tried to explain that I loved my dad but it escalated into a huge row and then he said it.

'It's him or me.'

I told him that it wasn't fair. That Dad would be worried. His face hardened.

'You should have thought of that before you left.'

He made it sound like it was all my fault and I felt even worse.

'I'll go, then. You don't have to come.'

That was the first time. It was quick as a flash. A slap, but hard. I reacted and hit him back, and the next blow he landed made me see stars. He had my hand twisted behind my back and he ran me upstairs, me screaming all the time from the pain. He threw me on the bed, and him on top of me. I was screaming, 'No, Alan. No.' But all he said as he did it was: 'You're not going anywhere.'

About six months later he came home one night smelling of beer and looking very sad. He sat down heavily beside me.

'I've got something I need to tell you.'

I thought it was going to be about her. Or that he was sorry for hitting me and … hurting me. But it wasn't.

'It's your dad. I didn't know how to tell you before. He's dead.'

My heart shattered into a thousand pieces. He told me he had been test driving a car with a client when they stopped in town and he saw Don Jackson, one of Dad's friends, who had told him the sad news.

'I want to see his grave. I want to say goodbye.'

He rubbed his eyes.

'I'm sorry. I should have taken you to see him. I'm sorry.'

I could tell that he meant it. I held his hand.

'I just want to say goodbye.'

He turned to me.

'He wasn't buried. He was cremated.' He stood up. 'Come on. I'll take you to the little chapel at the crematorium.'

I picked some flowers from our garden. We drove up there and, in the moonlight, I said goodbye to my father, my last living relative. Al looked into the will, but it turned out that, after what we had done, he had left it all to Cancer Research. Which answered my questions about what he had died of.

But after that Al and I slept in separate bedrooms because I could not sleep next to him again without crying in my sleep.

Chapter Nine

Day 21

It's starting to get to me. I forgot Donelle was picking the kids up.
I arrived at school and she was already there, leaning against the
railings laughing into her phone. All the extra work has helped
her lose weight around her waist, giving an overall appearance
of youth when you factor in her skinny jeans and a tight T-shirt.

I stepped back as the children raced out and into her arms. I felt
the heat of anger in my chest. This will not get to me. I want to smile
like Donelle, not a care in the world. I hurried home through the
backstreets and arrived before them. I didn't want Donelle to know
I'd forgotten. I washed my face and made drinks and made it look
like I was here on purpose. I quickly knocked up some sandwiches
and poured crisps into a bowl. Some pink wafer biscuits from the
back of the cupboard and a packet of mini chocolate muffins that
Donelle brought round last time she was here.

They burst in and I pulled on a party hat and shouted, 'Surprise!'
Donelle hugged me tight and laughed so loudly that I couldn't
help but join in.

'Celebrating family.'

She laughed loudly. 'Yeah. Family.' She gazes at the kids. 'I just
wish ...'

I sighed. 'You will. You'll make a great mum. This may be the one.'

We laughed and the kids made a start on the food, all of it laid out in front of the TV on a low trestle table with big sunflowers on it. I sat looking at her and her at me. I could tell she wanted to tell me something.

'So. What's up?'

She pursed her lips. 'I don't know.'

I've seen that look before. Man trouble. I wasn't really in the right frame of mind but she looked so sad.

'Tell me.'

She sighed deeply. 'Well. He was Mr Dreamboat. Drinks. Laughs. Meals out. Charming. Seen him every day while I've been working in the office. The minute I say I'm going long haul and I'll be away he goes all funny. Then he started asking if I think women who have kids should work.'

I grimaced.

'Exactly. I thought he was kidding at first. Started saying if we have a future together I need to settle down. I said I was settled and he went into a big huff.' She looked forlorn. 'I didn't know what I'd done. Wouldn't speak to me. Made me feel queasy. Then he was all right after a bit.'

Alarm bells. It sounded like he's training her. But she knows this. She has the instinct and the sense to feel it. I'd be more worried if she didn't notice, or, worse, ignored it.

'It's early days, Don. And you know what they say. No fun – run.' We both laughed. 'Seriously, though, don't allow him to make you feel uneasy. Don't let him put on you, scare you.'

She looked up quickly. 'He's not scaring me. He just had a bit of a strop. I'll see how it goes. Don't worry. If he's not Mr Right, I'm gone.'

Donelle is usually the opposite. It's her it fizzles out for. I worry at her easy defence of this man, but it's hard to say what's going on without all the information. She phoned a taxi and went about ten o'clock.

I woke early, more positive. I'm travelling the main artery into the city to do some training with Janice. I watch all the faces on the bus, wondering who would waste their time sending dick pics. Gez said it's commonplace. I Google it, and apparently it's a thing on the Tube, people sending porno pics via AirDrop.

I called in at work first to see Sheila, but she was in a knitting group. She waved at me like the queen, all serene and airy. Sally was there too, for once not looking at her phone and, as I left, Jim was not sitting in the pub, just watching. The kids were in another room with the playgroup but I could hear the faint sound of the 'Ria, Ria, diarrhoea' chant. I heard Sally shouting at them to shut up as I passed the windows. Maybe it was progress, or maybe just the calm before the storm.

When I arrive at the venue, I see Janice sidling up to the buffet. Janice and me, we are from the same tribe. At SafeMe we work as a team, but outside work we are even closer. These training days are necessary to keep up our qualification, but we agreed early on that no one said they couldn't be fun. It's relaxation time. Time to reconnect and air any grievances we have in the presence of a referee.

We're tough women. Me, Janice, Roz from another refuge, Linda Hall from the courts; all of us hard as nails. We've seen some things but we aren't desensitised, because if we were we would lose empathy and be unable to do our jobs. In some ways this is worse because it is a repeated round of seeing unthinkable things.

I know that one of the reasons I have been able to carry on doing this job is Janice. Her humour is dry, sarcastic and to outsiders it might seem cruel. But it is a coping strategy for both of us. We know full well what faces us every day. It isn't just women suffering, although that is enough. It is the danger of being exposed to the same angry men who had put their partners in the last-chance saloon. It is scary. You don't get used to it.

The world can make a million excuses for them, mostly out of a lack of information. The facts of a case, the exact facts, are rarely disclosed, even if it gets to court. Only hospital records can bear testament to the horrors that happen. And us. Because we listen. We listen to all the details, as many or as few as they need to tell us, as soon or as late as they want to. Some never do, but some tell us everything. Janice and I hold the bad things at a distance for them. Lighten their load until they are strong enough to carry it again.

We don't record it or write down the details. We just listen and those words are held somewhere in the ether, somewhere secret and forbidden to anyone who they might affect or harm. Or use. It is dirty work. But Janice and I roll up our sleeves and birth the truth. We bring the awful stories of how these women have been treated into the world. The previously unspoken and probably unseen violence, because cowards like to do their dirty work in private.

Most importantly, we listen to each other. In all the years we have worked together we have never grown complacent with one another. I have the utmost respect for Janice with all her fucks and buggers, for her frowns and her inappropriate laughter, which I know is nerves playing out. For standing up to bullies and lying on makeshift beds and holding crying women all nights as they sob for the men that have put them in hospital.

I listen to her talk with love about her family and swear about her mother, who is far worse than mine. I listen to her talk about her dog Ruff, who she loves like a child. The endless banter with Malc over football teams – he's City and she's United. I just love that woman and today is a space for that love.

I see her at the end of the training room pushing some tiny doughnuts into a carrier bag.

'Waste not, want not,' she says as I approach. 'It'll just go in the fucking bin. There's a homeless guy out there who hasn't seen a doughnut in months.'

I hug her tightly, like we don't see each other every day at work. I pour myself a coffee from the machine and go and sit next to her.

'All quiet on the western front. I called in on my way. Knitting, they are.'

She nods. 'Yep. So far, so good.' We check our phones in unison. 'So. What's the script then? And don't say nothing because I've seen you. Distracted.'

I suddenly tense. I wasn't expecting this. But I will tell her. Part of it, at least. I get out the phone.

'That package the other day.'

I flick on the screen and show her the videos. She is fuming.

'Jesus. Someone is fucking with you? You?'

I can't help but smile. 'Yeah. And with Danny away I'm ...'

She looks through them again.

'Any ideas?'

I shake my head. 'I don't know. Jim?'

She nods. 'That's what I was thinking. Or Frankie. Or Bill Lyness – over Joan. He had it in for you.'

I take back the phone.

'It could be anyone. But I've told Gez and she'll sort it out if it gets worse.'

She hugs me tightly.

'I'm here whenever you want a chat. Ignore the fucker. Switch the phone off and have a word with Carole.'

I know she is right. I've been keeping Carole, our friendly police contact, in reserve. Janice hugs me and we link arms. I know I have her support, no matter what. We sit through the training, losing ourselves in other people's stories, until it is time to leave. Janice chats about her family and Ruff's exploits on the way back to SafeMe.

It is only then that Janice touches my arm and looks at me.

'I'm worried about you, Ri. That message shit's got to you, and it's not like you. Why don't you and the kids come and stay at mine? Just till Danny gets back?'

I smile as brightly as I can. 'I'm OK. Donelle's stayed a couple of times. It's not cos Dan's away, you know. It' just …'

I pause and it's too late. Sally's arguing with a woman who has just arrived about the cooking rota and she drops a glass that shatters on a table near the children. Janice runs to fetch a dustpan and brush and we're in action again, our own souls on hold until later.

I've been ignoring the cheap phone all day but I know this isn't over at all. As if to confirm it, the phone buzzes. A message appears. It's a picture and I am almost afraid to look. But I do. It's Sheila, going into her flat. I look around and she isn't here. I cast my mind back to earlier on, picturing her waving at me. She was wearing a leopard-print shirt and a black cardy. I bring up the picture again and she is wearing the same. The first thing that runs through my mind is that Frank wouldn't be pleased if he knew someone was following Sheila. Unless it is Frank. The psychopath landscape suddenly widens. I scroll down.

YOU'RE A REAL SAINT, ARENT YOU? FOREVER FRIENDS. KEEP HER SAFE.

I start to delete it, then I don't. I might need this as evidence. I already know I am going to go to the police: Sheila is a client.

Tanya

Diary Entry: Wednesday

Al's working late tonight. He picked me up but then went straight
out. It happens sometimes in his line of business. So I'm home alone.
I thought about making myself some chips and bread, but I'd have
to cook the soup as well so Al would think I'd had that. So I'm not
bothering. I'll cook the soup and write my diary in the kitchen where
it's light – I've been writing it in my en suite so far.

I've been quite upset all day. Probably because I was writing about
my dad yesterday. I'm starting to see why Al didn't want me to write it.
He didn't want me any more upset. Or unstable, as he put it.

Anyway, there was more fun and games with Jade in the office.
She's got a little girl, Juliet, aged about seven. She's single and does
this co-parenting thing with her ex-boyfriend Dave. I could see Dave
drive into the car park, screeching to a halt. I didn't see Juliet at first
because Dave left her in the car. But as he strode towards the door,
red-faced and puffed up, I saw Juliet open the car door and get out.

Dave was calling Jade a whore, and I slipped out of the open door
just as Juliet was making her way across the car park. I took her hand.

'Come on. Let's take you to Mummy.' She looked up at me. 'It's OK.
My name's Tanya. I work with your mummy.'

She stopped and smiled. 'Tanya. Crazy lady.'

I stood beside her as it started to dawn on my why people would
look at me strangely. Why they sometimes stared.

'Crazy lady? Why's that, Juliet?'

I didn't look at her. I was too afraid that I would cry.

'Mummy says you are fucking mad and you don't change your clothes.'

I gripped Juliet's hand and led her back inside, where Dave and Jade were still screaming at each other. When they saw Juliet they stopped. Mr Simister intervened.

'OK, folks. Show's over. Take it outside.'

Juliet turned around and waved at me.

'Bye, crazy lady.'

It registered with Jade and she gave me her 'I'm sorry' face, the same one she gives me when I have to recalculate her monthly sales figures. But I know full well that Juliet had got those words from her. I felt indignant that she actually thought I don't change my clothes. Of course I do. But I could see how she had made the mistake.

Al does not like me to wear certain clothes. He likes me to wear black trousers and a white blouse for work with a black jacket. So I have a rail of them. All the same, so there can be no confusion. When it's cold, I wear a black anorak too. At weekends it's jeans and pretty tops. He doesn't like me wearing skirts because he says he knows men and they will take any opportunity to look up a woman's skirt. *Was that what I wanted?* He asked when, one day, I wore one of the dresses I had brought with me.

He told me I didn't know men, which is true, I don't. I only know Al. He lets me order clothes from the catalogue and has them delivered to work. He makes a big deal of me opening them, just like he does on my birthday and at Christmas when he buys me perfume and expensive moisturiser. Make-up is out as he is convinced that lipstick is for the sole purpose of making the lips look like labia and the vagina. Likewise, mascara is just for making eyes look bigger for flirting. *Was that what I wanted?*

Whether I wanted it or not, I wasn't getting it because I had no money and Al didn't buy it for me. The one thing he is completely extravagant with is jewellery. Right at the start he bought me the engagement and wedding ring set. It would be more convincing, he told me. But since then he has lavished me with a diamond tennis bracelet and a solitaire diamond necklace and earrings. For the past several birthdays and Christmas I have chosen an expensive Pandora charm that has arrived hidden in an expensive bouquet.

We aren't married. We could never be because we would need my birth certificate or some other form of ID. But I use Al's name and he said the wedding rings would make that look real. They are really beautiful. Sometimes, when I am a little bit braver than I am at the moment, I imagine that these will be how I get my train fare to go far away. But then I remember that you need ID to pawn something. I read that in a paper someone left in the ladies' toilets, and hope faded again.

I was more shocked that Juliet said I was fucking mad. Shocked, too, that a seven-year-old said 'fucking'. But I thought about it more and it became clearer and clearer. This was what Al had told Mr and Mrs Simister when I began to work for them all those years ago. I was ill. That I couldn't handle my own money. Keep an eye on me.

The more worrying thing was that they believed it.

Chapter Ten

Day 20

I already know, first thing Thursday morning, when I am standing at the desk in the police station, that I am doing the right thing. What if he goes further? Further than messages? I have held it together so far, I'm used to this kind of shit, but it's getting silly now Sheila is involved. The desk sergeant appears.

'Hi there. May I speak to Carole Barnes, please? Could you tell her it's Ria Taylor?'

He presses buttons on his desk phone and relays the message and, ten minutes later, I'm sitting in an interview room. Carole is everything good about the police, and my main go-to about SafeMe. Except this is about me.

'OK, Ria, how can I help? I haven't got long but—'

I blurt it out. 'It's about me. This guy is causing me … problems.'

She nods as I outline the story to her. I finish and she stares at me.

'I'm just asking for advice, really?'

There is a pause.

'The thing is, as you know, he has to have committed a crime. As you also know only too well, we have to build a case and present it to the CPS. You've told me that you don't know who he is. How did he get your number?'

I swallow hard. 'He sent me a phone. To my office. He's not really threatened me but … in context … And one of the photos is of a client.'

I pass her the phone and she looks through it. She leans back and sighs.

'God, Ria. I can see why you're here. From what you've said, though, and these messages, I don't think you would have a stalking case. And there's no evidence that the flowers and messages are connected. Even with the dick pic. Not these days. We should be able to do something but we can't. Creepy, yes, but probably some psycho with a grudge who's too scared to confront you. Come on. You know all this.'

I nod and look at my hands, clasped together in my lap.

'But the phone?'

'If we did ever find him he'd say it was a present. No law against that either. We could take the phone and get the serial number and track it back to the shop. But even without looking I know it's a pay-as-you go and he'll be sending these messages from something similar. Can you think of anyone it could be?'

'Just to do with the women. Their partners.' Frank. Jim. Bill. It could be fucking anyone. She stares at me.

'That picture of Sheila James? Well, we all know what Frank James is like. I'm not saying it's him but maybe someone connected? Look, Ria, I'll be honest with you. There isn't much chance of us finding him from this phone or some texts or messages. Turn the phone off. If he approaches you, call us out. He'll soon get the message. Just check every now and again. If he keeps texting and emailing or anything else anonymously, keep everything. He'll pop up somewhere eventually and you can go down the injunction route, or we'll get him for harassment if he steps it up. You've done right telling me, and I'll keep a note in case it escalates. I'll log this on Sheila's file as well. But keep away from him.'

I walk out of the police station with a new perspective. She is right. I can either comply or fight. Or I could make sure he stops getting to me. Harden up. And, right there and then, I choose the latter.

I've done the right thing. I've told people. I have marked myself out and put myself on the radar without drawing attention to him and making the situation worse. This is something to do with SafeMe, a crazy ex or a former employee with a grudge. I need to treat it as part of the job. Contain it. But it isn't that easy when it's me.

How the fuck has this happened? I am meant to be helping people. I have gone out of my way to do everything I can to make sure these crises-stricken people get the best chances. It has never been just a job, it has been a vocation.

Nothing is ever completely safe, but I have striven to make the risks here as low as possible. I have fought for funding for panic buttons in every room that activate CCTV and alarms. I have petitioned for a security guard and personally vetted candidates until I found Malc, who is the perfect balance of kind and scary. The last thing we wanted was a bullying aggressor to frighten already terrified women. In many ways this has been my life's work, second to Danny and my beautiful children.

Back in my office I sit alone. Talking to Carole has made this person real, somehow. I have always been there for people. I have been to court and stood in front of women while their armed partners flew at them. I have pulled children out of houses where one of their parents was out of control and the other one was too damaged to save them and understood. I have physically restrained one partner from reaching the other in order to kick and punch them while they cowered in a corner.

The question is now: who will help me? The three people I have confided in so far have not been able to help because no physical violence has happened. So the answer to my question is – right now – no one. It seems like I am in the same situation as everyone else, caught up in a complex web of lies and confusion created by the perpetrator so they can swoop without any pesky interference from the authorities. So no one will help me until the damage is done. Until he makes his next move.

But one thing this fucked-up piece of shit hasn't realised is that I know the process. I know what I am feeling is normal. I know that he doesn't need a reason for what he is doing. He is just a bastard, a sociopath with no regard for someone else's feelings as long as he is suitably entertained. Just like all the rest of the low-lifes I encounter on a daily basis.

The phone pings and the expected dread fills me. I am just thinking that I am used to it, that I am cleverer than him, when I am taken by surprise. This video is freestyled. It is me on the bus this morning. On the way to the police station. I can see it is me only from the close up of the back of my head – my bright red overdyed hair. I quickly flicker back to the almost-empty bus. Who was behind me? As I watch, his fingers move to my hair, the loose bits at the back that hang down. Then there's a snip.

I feel the back of my head. I unwrap my hair from my trademark scarf and feel the short blunt ends right at the back: a chunk of my hair missing. I play the footage again and again, trying to glean a clue, feeling my hacked hair. How did I not feel it? How did I not see him? Who was on the bus when I got on? Who got off? I rerun it over and over in my mind's eye. It can't be someone I know. I would have seen them, recognised them. I turn quickly. This is how it has me now.

No one is here. Even so, there is a sudden movement behind me and I almost jump out of my skin. I turn quickly but it isn't him. A policeman appears in the doorway just as I shut down the screen. 'We've had a report of harassment. Sally Lewis called us about her husband Jim hanging about outside. Banging on the doors with an iron bar, or something.'

I look in the incident log. Jim finally cracked and brought a crowbar. I relax a little. Of course. This has nothing to do with me.

'Yeah. He's been sitting in the pub across the road every day just staring in. There's a file on him.'

I hand him Sally's file and he reads it while I pretend to tidy some papers.

'Right. We'll take him in then. But I doubt we'll be able to charge him.'

I read the incident report again.

'Coming equipped? He had a crowbar.'

He smiles a little. 'Managed to get rid before we got here. But we'll see. Can't promise anything. Not this time.'

I nod. 'It all adds up.'

The policeman gets up and leaves.

It does all add up. I calm a little. It's often the long game. Wait, wait, wait until the perpetrator gets tired of staring and looking mean – or, in my case, of sending messages – and takes action. Then I'm standing there with the police or an injunction.

I sigh. Everything here points to me waiting for him to slip up. To do enough for me to make a complaint that the police will take seriously. But even then, he will probably make my life a misery by trying to make out I am a fantasist. It's standard manipulative behaviour. I know he thinks he is manoeuvring me into a corner, and perhaps he is, for the time being. But eventually he will up the stakes, do something drastic, because for men like him, nothing is ever enough. He will push and push and become crueller until he does something so terrible that he will trip himself up.

It is my knowledge of this that is the advantage, and my ability to wait without cracking up or getting hurt in the process. But I will wait. No matter how bad it gets I have all the time in the world.

Tanya

He didn't come home. He was out all night. I am writing this in the toilet because I heard him come in at about half seven in the morning. I've locked myself in and he will think I am in the shower.

He will think that I didn't know. That I didn't hear him coming in. I can hear everything. Over the years I've become more alert to all the sounds in the house, how close the noise is and which direction it is coming from. I can picture it. He came in the back door – the shutters are almost silent there when they roll up automatically because he oils them every week. Almost silent. There is a tiny click at the top when it rolls itself into the shiny white holder so it is invisible to the outside world.

I know he can raise either all the shutters, like he does every morning, or just one at a time, when he wants to go in and out. He had them installed because he heard that someone's house nearby had been broken into while the occupants were in bed. To keep me safe.

He closed the shutter again. I heard the dull clunk of it hitting the back doorstep. Then he opened the washing machine door and then closed it again. I could hear him as he walked around, first in his shoes, then without them. He placed them on the rack so I would think they had been there all night. He tiptoed up the stairs and now he is in his bedroom.

I'd crept downstairs around five o'clock just to make sure. At first

I was really angry, but what's the point? Downstairs at night is totally black. The shutters block all the light. I couldn't flick on the high-tech lighting system that Al had installed about four years ago because the light is bright white. Stark. I couldn't be sure he wouldn't see a glint of it. Anyway, I'm used to padding about the house in the dark. I made a map of the creaky floorboards and memorised it.

Sometimes, when he has been in my room and I've had a shower, I sit at the kitchen table in the dark. Just so I don't have to be in that room with the smell of sweat and sex and my own terror still ringing from the walls. I put the radio on low and listen to people who are out in the world doing things that sound exciting.

I realised long ago that I am just torturing myself because, like Al says when we have an argument, 'You signed up for it. You knew there was no going back.' But I was so young and I didn't know anything. I thought I did. I thought I was so clever. An older boyfriend. With a car. All the other girls, even her, were at the disco. They were laughing until they cried, a bit like Jade and Karla now, and kissing other boys. Dancing. I miss dancing.

I don't know what I thought would happen. Actually, I do. I thought that I had won. I thought by going with him I had finally got him away from her. But I was wrong. He has never admitted it. But I know that all the times he stays out all night, all the times I am left completely alone here, he is with her.

That's where he would have been last night. I see all the signs. He is stressed, then chipper, then stressed again, then he stays out. A couple of times he hasn't come back for a whole weekend. I smell perfume and I see him preening, his hair cut differently. I used to shout and scream but I soon learned not to. Because those were the worst times.

I'd heard the shower go on this morning and I'd crept down to the kitchen. I opened the washer, listening for the water flow in the pipes. I'd pulled out the shirt and sniffed it. His aftershave and a hint of perfume. I put it back and tiptoed back upstairs. And here I am now, sitting in the shower base writing this. I won't be able to mention it. I will have to act as if nothing is wrong at all. As if I have slept all night and not even known he was gone.

It gets harder every time. I will have to get ready for work, get in the car and be as bright and breezy as possible. I don't know if I can do it. But I know the consequences if I don't.

Chapter Eleven

Day 19

Last night was the very opposite of the day. Donelle had cooked a curry and when I got home I couldn't help but smile when Jennifer proudly presented me with a blue T-shirt with the Superwoman logo on it.

'You can wear it for work, Mummy!'

'I laughed and it felt good.

'Yeah, I'm practically famous.'

She grimaces. 'God, you know what that makes Danny, don't you? That makes him a Bah. Boyfriends and husbands.'

She makes a sheep noise and we collapse into laughter. It's exactly what I need, and when she suggests a bottle of wine and a chat I switch off the cheap phone and put it on the mantelpiece.

In the morning I do the breakfast routine and I kiss the kids outside school. I fret the whole way to work that he knows all about me, about my kids, where their school is. Watching me. But he could have been watching me for ages, I reason with myself, and he is not going to do anything in the open. No. He isn't, I convince myself. I could be scanning every inch of the road, every car, every person for someone watching. Someone I recognise. But fuck that. I have a job to do.

I go straight round to Sheila's flat. It's her day today and she's waiting at the window for me and when she opens the door, she doesn't smile. I hug her and she hugs me back, hard and tight like she doesn't want to let me go.

'OK, Sheila? Everything all right?'

She sits down on the low sofa and shakes her head. The flat smells strongly of cigarettes, much stronger than usual. Her ashtray is full to overflowing and she is wringing her hands.

'Oh, you know, lovey. You know.'

She sits in silence with a packet of Garibaldi biscuits for Marks & Spencer on the arm of her chair. I take my cue.

'Been into town, have you?'

She eyes the new boxes in the corner, stacked on top of the ones she collected last week.

'Yeah. I called in on the way back. From the house. I went to get more stuff. And before you bloody start, he wasn't there.'

I stare at her as she sucks deeply on a Benson & Hedges. She's wearing a huge, jangly charm bracelet – gold, naturally – that I haven't seen before.

'That bracelet's lovely. But you know, you're taking a big risk every time you go back there.'

Her face sets and she looks away from me.

'A charm for every year me and Frank have been together.' She takes a biscuit and crunches it. She turns to face me. 'There are some things in that house I need to have with me. I need to fetch them myself.'

I wonder what could be more important than broken bones, but she's already up, getting the boxes and bringing them over. She opens the top one and I gasp. It's a hat, pink and purple velour in a flapper style, pure 1930s. It is encrusted with red and purple stones. I catch my breath.

'It's beautiful, Sheila.'

'It was my mother's. All I have left of her. Everything else is ... gone.' She passes it to me. 'Put it on, lovey. Try it.'

I pull my hair out of its regulation Day-Glo bobble and pull on the hat. The inside is silk and it feels lovely.

'Suits you, lovey. You could make more of yourself, you know. You're a lovely woman.'

I feel tears well and give her the hat back.

'Thank you, Sheila. I don't always feel lovely. But none of us do, do we?'

She shakes her head sadly, her blonde beehive shuddering. She closes the box and opens another one and just looks into it. I can see knitting needles with something half-finished on them.

'Oh, how lovely. More knitting!'

She looks at me, her eyes watery.

'I wasn't knitting the other day. I was watching.'

'But you can knit. So ...'

She picks up the needles and the white ribbing. Underneath are several strands of ribbon. Sheila had never struck me as a maker. I had imagined that she spent most of her time with Frank, in the house or out at social events. All the pictures of them were in pubs and clubs. I peer into the box. There are more needles and some sea pearls, dressmaker's pins and a beautiful silver thimble. Sheila is holding the knitting very still.

'I can knit. Oh, I can. But this was the last time I knitted – thirty-nine years ago.'

I quickly calculate. She would have been twenty-four. She picks out a photograph.

'Me and Frank at Blackpool on the beach. That's when we found out. When we got back.' The black-and-white photograph shows them on deckchairs, arms and legs intertwined. They are in shorts and T-shirts, but in the background are what appear to be two men in suits. She points to them.

'Tony and Knob. Gone now, both of 'em.'

They look younger than Frank and Sheila.

'Oh. What happened?'

She stares at me, a desolate stare that I have never seen before from her.

'Late for something. Frank thought they were grassing him up. A few things, Then ...'

She shakes her head almost imperceptibly and her eyes tell a story of such deep sorrow that I finally understand the horrors this woman has seen. Who Frank James really is. She reaches down into the box and pulls out a tiny box with a clear cellophane lid containing a tiny gold bracelet.

'This was his. Bobby's. Frank gave it to me when I was three month. He knew it would be a boy. Told me he was calling him after Bobby Charlton. Bloody United mad, he is.'

She takes out the bangle, turning it over and over in her hands. I can see she has done this often.

'What happened, Sheila? What happened to Bobby?'

She cannot meet my eyes.

'It was about seven months and I was in the lounge with my feet up. I'd had some belly ache but the midwife came and said it was nothing. Just pressure. So Frank went out and when he came back, I was rough. Being sick and very weak. We went to bed and I woke up with the bed full of blood. The midwife came back but it was too late. I'd had him. Tiny, he was.'

I take her hand.

'I'm sorry, Sheila. I'm so sorry.'

'Yeah, well, turned out I couldn't have any more. I'd already had seven early miscarriages. Somat wrong with me. That's what Frank told everybody who'd listen. Somat wrong with me. So you see, it was my fault.'

'No, Sheila, love, it wasn't. It must have been terrible for you, but it wasn't your fault. These things never are.'

She is shaking and fumbling for her lighter. I help her and flick the flame up to the tip of her cigarette.

'It were. It were punishment for what I did. With them men.'

I feel my anger rise.

'Did Frank tell you that?'

'No. He didn't have to. I could see it in all their faces. All the other fancy wives. All of them with kiddies. Just me and Frank without. So I deserved it. Like I deserve this. You always say that none of this is my fault but, in Frank's eyes, I'm a failure.'

She rustles in the box and, right at the bottom, is a blue rabbit.

'I used to sleep with this under my pillow. He'd keep throwing it in the bin and I'd get it out again. Bobby's rabbit. Have you got kiddies, love?'

I almost feel guilty telling her.

'Yes. A boy and a girl. At school now.'

She glances at my hand.

'You're married?'

'Yeah. I am.'

She looks hard at me.

'Funny. You don't look the type. Not being funny but you don't keep yourself nice for him, do you?'

I smile. Danny's face if I turned up at home all dressed up complete with jewellery and make-up. But I do make an effort in my own way. We both do. We like nice smells and soft skin.

'He likes me just how I am. He's not one for going out so …'

She tries a smile. 'Well, you're a lucky girl. I hope it all stays fine for you. We had a proper funeral for Bobby, you know. A priest and everything. He's got a headstone up at Hollinwood Cemetery. Big do afterwards. Then back to an empty house. That's what all this is about. He's never forgiven me. He said I had been gaddin' about while he were out at council meetings, but I'd just been in bed. I keep going over it, over and over again, to see if I could have done any different, but I did everything right. Everything.'

She's crying now and so am I.

'It's all right, Sheila. It'll all be all right.'

She pushes my hand away. 'No. It won't. Him in that house on his own. Me here. Bobby up there in the cemetery. When we should all be together. But I feel like I've got Bobby now. That's why I had to go back. To fetch him here.'

I breathe out. For one awful second I thought that she was going to say she was going back to Frank. Instead, she puts everything back in the box and sets it aside. I wait a moment.

'Are you OK? Sheila? Are you going to be all right? You can come back with me if you want. And bring anything you want.'

She shakes her head. 'No. I can't smoke in there. And it's all I've got left.'

I take the tray through to the kitchen. Poor Sheila. I am so glad she is opening up but it is absolutely tragic. The poor woman had been brainwashed. I go and sit back down.

'I know that this isn't what you want to hear right now, but none of this is your fault. No one has any right to punish you for anything, except a court of law. And you've done nothing illegal. You've just been human.'

She nods and wipes her eyes. 'Maybe I will come back with

you for a bit. I can help Janice clean up. Lovely girl. You both are.'
Then she is serious. 'But the reason I'm telling you all this, love, is
to tell you what Frank's like. He'll stop at nothing, you know. You
need to watch out.'

I look at her.

'So do you, love.' I stare at the vase of flowers on the window
sill. 'Those don't mean anything. They don't mean he's stopped.'

She frowns. 'Oh. Them. They're not from Frank. They're from
your friend. That nice man who knows you. Said you'd know what
they were for.'

I want to shake her and demand to know who it was. What did
he look like? But I can check the CCTV. Yes. I can check. She puts
her hand on my arm. I feel her fingers tighten and I feel like crying
into her bouclé cardigan. But we need to go so we walk round to
SafeMe, red-eyed and emotional, and she steadies herself on me
until we get there.

When Sheila is settled I go to my office. I check the CCTV but
this guy knows what he's doing. He keeps his hoodie up, head
turned. It's grainy, anyway. And old system. I don't even know if
it's him. It could be a delivery bloke. It could be fucking anyone.
My insides churn.

He's not going to get to me. I write all the incidents in my diary.
I feel more in control and I settle in my chair and read a text from
Danny.

Hey babe. Baaaaaahhh 🐑 Day 19 on the deposit countdown
And 20 days to go to D-Day. Deposit Day, that is. I love you x
Always.

I imagine his delighted face when he thought of D-Day and smile.

He's obviously spoken to Donelle. Sheila is right, I am very lucky. I sit down at my computer and think about Shelia's lost child. I think about my own children and open my emails. I type an overdue email to the headmistress of Simon and Jennifer's school.

Dear Mrs Hatherton,

Just a note to ask you to not allow anyone except myself, Danny Taylor (father), Donelle Taylor (Aunt) and Vi Taylor (Grandmother) to collect Simon and Jennifer from school. This is without exception.

Thank you

Ria Taylor

I press 'send' and this begins my campaign to protect my family while I do what I have to do to deal with this fucking psychopath. Stay one step ahead.

When I get home Donelle is cooking. She has made tower burgers and chips. They are her speciality and I swear that they are better than any burger chain or restaurant. The kids love them and I manage about half of one as I am full of fear.

'Come on. Eat up. We're going out.'

Every other Friday night me and Danny go out with Janice and her husband. Cheap-as-chips pub with a live band, back at eleven to relieve the babysitter. I would normally be over the moon, happy to shake off the week with a boogie with Danny, but I suddenly feel isolated. He's not here and I don't want to leave the kids.

'I don't know, Don ...'

She laughs. 'Rubbish! Come on. It'll do you good. And I'm at a loose end. Anyway, I already asked Terri to sit with the kids.'

This makes me feel a little better.

'Oh! What's happened to lover boy then?'

She shakes her head and laughs.

'Previous engagement. But that's fine. Don't want to be in each other's pockets, do we?'

But her eyes aren't smiling. I make a mental note to talk to her later when the alcohol has taken effect. I text Janice and tell her we'll meet her at the pub.

Janice is my best mate out of work and in. Even though we work together, we still have a lot of fun. We've laughed ourselves stupid on Friday nights to chase away the horrors that lie underneath the everyday at SafeMe. Tonight will be no different. I drag the straighteners through my split ends and finish with big curls, eyeliner and a lot of mascara. I walk into the kitchen and Donelle approves.

'Wow. You look amazing.' Terri is outside smoking and when she comes in she nods and does a RuPaul.

'Girl, you too good for the local. Don – take the lady into town.'

I laugh and Donelle pulls on her jacket. But I can't help myself. I turn to Terri.

'Keep the doors locked. And don't answer the door.'

She frowns. 'Oh. Why?'

'Just some crime reports in the area. And it's Friday. You know?'

She nods and glances at Donelle and I wonder if I see them exchange concerned looks about a shared worry. About me. Donelle is quiet in the taxi on the way there and by the time we arrive I am on edge. But she isn't someone who will fuck with me so before we go into the bar she pulls me to one side.

'Ri, Ri, Ri, Ri. What's the matter?'

I look into her eyes. My sister-in-law. She, like Danny, has stood at my side for twelve years, while I fight the good fight. She made me family the moment I met her and I pause for long enough for her to know there is something. Her face clouds with concern.

'Oh my God. You're not ill, are you?'

I shake my head. I will have to tell her. Part of it, at least. 'No. It's just … Just this guy. Sending me unsolicited texts.'

Unsolicited texts. I almost laugh at the lengths I will go to not say the word 'stalker'. She fumes.

'Someone from work? One of them? Not happy with just hurting their own woman?'

'You know the score, Don. I've told legals and the police. It'll be dealt with.'

She hugs me tight. 'It better be, because if it isn't …'

I nod. 'It's OK. Really. I'll sort it.'

She nods. 'Look, you've lost weight and you've got a frown line.' She runs her hand over my forehead. 'I'm not surprised with what you have to deal with, but this is different.'

It is fucking different. It is me. And now it's affecting my family. This is how it creeps up.

'I'll deal with it, Don.'

She hugs me and we go in. I grab Janice immediately and go to the bar. She starts to tell me about her brother's break-up and we're back in the moment.

I smile and carry our drinks over, just as the band starts. It's a Blues Brothers tribute band and Donelle pulls me on to the dance floor. We shake a tail feather and laugh and drink until I almost feel myself again. Almost. Because, as I sit down again I glance in the flashing blue light on the phone in my bag and can't help myself.

And there it is: a picture of the back of my head taken seconds before. Whoever it is, they are right here, right behind me.

Tanya

This is why I think I am going mad. He took me to work on Thursday and picked me up as normal. Then he just sat in his study all Thursday night while I sat on the other side of the door, trembling and wondering what the hell was going on. Wondering if I should ask him where he was. I had washed the shirt and pressed it. Hung it back in his wardrobe.

I didn't sleep Thursday night. I lay awake wondering what she looks like now. If she is still pretty. She always was back then. Different to me. I was skinny and blonde and she was curvy. But we jelled. We were best friends, right from the off. She would come round and play dolls with me, and we would play out in the fields behind my dad's house, stroking the horses. She was the sister I never had.

How was I to know that she was a bitch? We were inseparable. I told her everything, but she just sat there, taking it in. Using it to get to Al. By morning I was seething but I had to hold it in. I would talk to him tonight. Friday night, with the weekend ahead to recover if anything bad happened.

But Friday afternoon at work he turned up half an hour early. Instead of waiting in the car he strode into the office, cocky and smiling. I saw Jade look at Karla. He is a good-looking man and their eyes followed him. He had a carrier bag, Monsoon, and I immediately thought of her. He'd bought her something. But my heart beat faster as he popped his head into Mr Simister's office, then came over.

'I've got you something. For tonight.'

I saw Jade look at Karla and they craned their necks to see. I reached into the bag and it was a beautiful velvet dress. The colours graduated from pink to lilac and there was hand-stitched beading across the bodice. It was the most beautiful thing I had ever seen. He stared at the bag.

'Go on. There's more.'

I pulled out a velour box and opened it. A bracelet. It was opal and diamonds, clearly antique. Art deco, if I am not mistaken – I read about it in a *Reader's Digest* when I was at the doctor's surgery once. He clipped it around my arm and I looked up at him.

'It's Jenny and Colin's party tonight. From work. Remember?' I nodded. It was only four-thirty. He pre-empted. 'It's OK. I've made it right. Give you time to get ready.'

All the way home he chatted to me about work, the radio on and his finger tapping on the gear stick. We called at the chip shop for a Chinese take-away on the way home. I had to stay in the locked car but when he brought the bag and put it on my knee, it felt like we'd rewound to the beginning. I started to giggle and so did he.

I showered and dressed and put on the dress with some strappy sandals that he had bought me for a colleague's wedding. I applied a tiny touch of make-up. I know just the right amount, any more and he won't like it at all. But he nodded his approval when I stood in the kitchen in front of him.

'Lovely. You look so beautiful.'

I almost spoiled it by flinching when he moved towards me, but I pushed myself forwards into his surprisingly gentle embrace.

'So we're going to Jenny and Colin's party. It's her fortieth. I thought it would be good for you to meet her. It's at their house. They've got a nice-sized detached over the hill near town.'

I suddenly felt panicky. I hadn't socialised for a long time. What if something happened? What if I annoyed him? I felt like I was going to throw up but he was already calling a cab. I took some deep breaths and calmed myself. Nothing was going to stop this, so I just needed to make sure I didn't do anything wrong.

We got into the cab and I waited for him to click the remote control to close the shutters. But he didn't.

We never went this way. We never went towards town because that would mean going near where we met and everything that happened. But he didn't stop the driver and I moved my eyes as far as they would go without turning my head when we passed the bottom of the road. It still looked the same.

The party was lovely. Tiny cones of food that I could eat. Jenny and her friends were huddled in the huge conservatory, drinking wine and chatting. Al ushered me towards them and they looked at my dress and jewellery and pulled up a wicker chair. The men were in a games room playing pool and drinking beer straight from the bottle. I watched Al for a while. He seemed completely at home. Laughing, drinking, his foot tapping to the music.

Eventually everyone went outside. It was crowded in the garden and I stood with my back against the wall while they did speeches and then there was a band and some fireworks. Then suddenly, I couldn't find Al. I hurried over to Jenny.

'Have you seen Al? Only I've lost him …'

She laughed loudly. 'Oh, he'll be here somewhere. Is he feeling better? Any idea when he'll be coming back to work? He asked us not to mention it to you as you get upset about it, but it must have been a shock?'

I am the master of the poker face. I really had no idea what she was on about, but I looked down at the fake grass.

'It was. And, no, we're not sure.' I hope she will take the hint but she is still staring at me expectantly. 'So how much has he told you?'

She shook her head and took a big gulp of prosecco. I sipped my water.

'Just that he has had treatment and that he'll need another couple of months off, probably. I mean, I'm a social worker. If you two ever need ...'

I nodded.

'Yes. Yes. That's right. You are very kind. So is it affecting business?'

She shrugged. 'Well, it is, but we've managed to get someone temporary in to do the accounts in the meantime.'

I frowned. 'Oh. What about the cars? The supercars?'

She stared at me blankly. 'Do you mean the vans? The transport? Haulage companies don't have supercars, love.'

I'm beginning to get the picture. Slowly. As usual. I laughed lightly.

'Oh, yes, sorry, that's just what he calls the vans. Supercars. His little joke, you know.'

I elbowed her and moved off. More lies. I stood alone in the crowd, just as alone as I would have been in the house. Which is just as well because he reappeared.

'Good girl.'

He whispered it in my ear. It would have probably looked like a kiss to other people. He has no idea. No idea at all.

Chapter Twelve

Day 18

I wake up early as a hungover Donelle accidentally slams the door on her way out. I am on high alert as I remember last night: the small crowd at the back of the pub; people tapping their feet to the band. He was there. In that crowd. Then gone, leaving me shaken and wondering if I had imagined it. But when I look at the photograph on the phone, I know I didn't. I see the back of my head, but I also see Donelle and Janice, laughing. Janice mid-clap.

Jennifer and Simon come into my room and climb in either side of me, their warmth relaxing me until I jump as my phone buzzes. I gently move snoozing Jennifer, red curls splayed across Danny's pillow, to one side. I stand down as I see Danny's name.

> All right babe x Day 18. It's fuckin hot here but it's worth it. I miss you and the kids xx Is everything OK?

I type my reply carefully. I don't know if Donelle has told him anything – I hope she hasn't.

> Just the usual, love. Kids are missing you. Going to meet Mother today. Wish me luck. I love you x always.

I wait nervously. I need contact with my husband. I really need him here, but I know what he would do. His temper. There would be no police if Danny was here. For the first time I wonder if I should tell him. But what would that achieve? He would come rushing home and I don't even know who it is. He texts right back and I finally smile a little.

> Haha. Good luck with that. I'm always here for you, Ri. Give me
> a ring tomorrow, yeah. Eighteen days to go until snuggles. I
> love you x always

Thank God. Donelle hasn't mentioned it. I asked her not to and she knows exactly what Danny would do. I'll deal with it before he gets back. I will. I just hope I can.

Jennifer has realised that it is Saturday before I really want her to. She cuddles up to me.

'You're here so it must be weekends. Are we going to see Grandma? In town?'

I sigh. That's the plan. I could do with staying here and having some down time. If I leave Jennifer and Simon with her for three hours, which is the allotted time she can be in town, it doesn't work – it isn't worth me coming home. So I usually take a book or listen to music while she buys them new clothes. Or takes them for a McDonald's and fills them with sweets so that they are manic until late on Saturday night. But it is what I have to do.

'Yes. We are. But we'll go in early. I want to get you some school shoes.'

Simon looks at me. He is a thoughtful child. Vi tells me that Danny was the same until he hit his teens. He has long dark brown ringlets which I wax every day and he will not let me cut. Long legs, like Danny, but he has my face shape, and my hairline. He is beautiful. Jennifer is mini me. Her hair is straight and auburn and her skin coffee coloured, striking a contrast that makes people stare. She has my blue eyes and Danny's family's long eyelashes and slender build. I know she is going to be stunning when she grown into a woman, just like Aunty Donelle. Simon finally speaks.

'I wish Dad was here. I wish he wasn't away all the time.'

He comes and sits beside me and I pull him towards me. I look at them both.

'Can you keep a secret?' They both nod enthusiastically. 'Well, you know how I am Superwoman, cos it said so in the paper?' More nodding. 'Well, Daddy is Superman. That's why you're not allowed in our room. That's where he gets changed.'

My children have not yet encountered the *Superman* films. So it is easy for me to invent silliness. Their eyes open wide. Simon thinks.

'So can he fly?'

I shake my head. 'Not when he's Daddy. But when he's Superman ...'

They bounce on my bed and clap.

'Superdad!'

I laugh with them and I am secretly happy that I have deflected the usual 'where is your daddy' conversation that crops up every time I mention meeting my mum. Danny Snr is so present in their lives that they are almost oblivious to him as he sits in his leather wing-backed chair snoozing and snoring. He is a lot older than Vi and Danny constantly dreads anything happening to him. I am showered with questions now.

'Has he got a cape? What are his special powers?'

Danny's special power is patience. Especially with my father and mother. He has never forgotten the day we were asked to leave, yet he never mentions it. Danny is used to bullying and insults, and he can handle himself, but I know he has always felt disappointed that someone so close to me could be so unpleasant. I hear him, strumming his guitar to Sinead's 'Black Boys on Mopeds'. He is devastated each time the children ask about Granddad. I see his jaw set and his eyes narrow at my father's small-mindedness. He had been very specific. *Not you and not any kiddies.*

He is also very patient with me and my wanting to move around. He could never know that I am so insecure; I don't even admit it to myself most of the time. But I can feel it now, the dreaded tightness in my chest, the nausea bubbling up inside me. He has been patient with my job, when I have been threatened by angry spouses, by the council, when I have argued with the police. When I have been woken in the middle of the night as someone has arrived or left and there has been a serious incident. Before the kids, we would go together. Now, he just turns over and goes back to sleep as I wait for my taxi. But he never complains. And that is what I am relying on now; that he is patient with me while I sort this out.

As we set off to meet Mum I find myself checking to see if anyone is watching. I know this is getting to me, but it isn't going to spoil my life, or my children's. Jennifer skips along in front of us and Simon walks alongside me telling me about someone at school and how they had been to Spain and could we go to Spain?

I tell him yes, yes we can, and then, in my mind I add on 'when all this is over'. I catch my breath as I realise I have been adding this on to every sentence. It has stopped my life. He doesn't even need to follow me or show up where I am. He has firmly pushed himself right to the front of my consciousness. A faceless figure with a hundred possibilities.

At least I know, and I am waiting for him, ready. So on the surface I am as normal as possible, laughing and joking. Because if he is watching, I don't want him to think I am afraid. I am strong. I am capable. I repeat this in my head all the way to town on the bus until I see my mother standing outside Boots.

I do love her. But she can be so cruel and scathing that I feel dread around this time every Saturday afternoon. My rational mind tells me it is her problem, not mine, that there must be a reason for her impatience with me. Why she can't let me just be who I am without comment. But the little girl inside me still cries out for her approval, and here she is, looking our way and waving.

Jennifer runs across and hugs her and it's only then I start to see that something is different. She is wearing a pair of leather ankle books with three metal buttons up the side, replacing her sensible standard Mary Jane's. These boots have a small heel, which make her look taller. She is wearing grey straight-leg jeans and a grey and mustard tunic under a black denim jacket. As I approach, I see a smudge of eyeliner and mascara. I can't help but smile. She is huffily self-conscious.

'Morning.'

I stare at her, eyebrows raised.

'Hello ... Ria. How are you?'

Yes. It is still the same voice, still the same tight tone, which she reserves especially for me.

'Good. Good. Yeah. So ...'

I look her up and down as she fusses with Simon's coat.

'Ah, Simon, love. How was school this week?'

Her voice is soft and crisp now, like she used to talk to me when I was small. Before I grew into something she wasn't happy with. Simon starts to tell her and I bend down to kiss Jennifer, catching a whiff of Lady Million perfume. My own odour of choice when I can afford it.

'Bye, kids. See you in a bit.'

There is no need to make arrangements with her as we have the same routine every week. I drop them here and collect them by the bus stop, where we go our separate ways, me towards the city and her towards the hills. I turn to walk away but she catches my arm.

'Stay. I mean ... we're going to the games centre. We could have a coffee.'

It isn't a question. For the second I am fifteen again, wondering if this is a trap. Like the countless 'Dad and I want a little chat about school', which would then open up the seething can of worms they had both stored up. Their past regrets bubbling up and fired at me as individually packaged salvos of anger and insult about almost every aspect of me.

I debate whether I should inflict any further pain on myself while I'm under my current stress, but my children are looking up at me, eyes pleading. So I nod.

'That would be nice. Thank you.'

I mimic her, mirror her, something I learned to do to avoid her disapproval. But as she sets off down the high street she is much more playful than I remember, light on her feet. She swings hands with Jennifer and Simon, who considers himself too old to be holding hands now. He walks close to her, chatting easily. I stand down a little, stropping behind them like the teenager I feel.

We reach the games centre and they run off, finding vacant seats at computer monitors. This is all they seem to do, one screen to another, and even though I limit the use of tablets and TV at home, I know they are constantly seeking them. I smile at her foresight; she has done the right thing, spoiling them. I never had grandparents, both sides had died by the time I was born. So the only point of reference I had was my schoolfriends Danielle and Lin's grandparents, who seemed to be constantly doling out ice cream and treats. She finds a table in the coffee bar.

'They're fine in there. I can see if anything happens and they would have to pass me to get out.' She looks at the coffee menu. 'Special request from them. I would have never known it was here.'

I look at her fingers, same nail shape as mine. She is sixty-three, the same age as Sheila but she looks a decade younger. She has never smoked and drinks very little. The tiny lines around her eyes are only just starting, a few on her forehead. Nothing like Sheila's skin. I think about the Beautiful South song 'Prettiest Eyes' and both Sheila's and my mother's lives. Different. So different. She runs a manicured nail, painted the most delicate pink, along the coffee choices.

'Cappuccino. What about you?' She says it brightly, but I am somehow still in teenager mode.

'Flat white. Large. Need the caffeine.'

She goes to order and I check my phone. One text from Janice.

Hope you're OK, mate. I know there's something wrong. Let's have a chat about that fuckwit you told me about xxxxx

I text her back quickly.

Cheers Jan. It'll wait till Monday. After Perps. Don't worry. I've marked it xxxx

In other circumstances I would have been in Costa Coffee with nothing to do for three hours and I would have phoned her straight away. She knows almost everything about my relationship with my mother, but I am aware I didn't tell her I was here. I take a deep breath as Mum arrives back with coffee and cake. Cake. Yes. Actual cake. I think it's a trick at first, to make me eat it so she can scold me, but she takes a slice and bites.

'So. Here we are.' She puts the huge slice of lemon drizzle cake down and smiles. Not directly at me, but it's a start. 'I just wanted to ...' She reaches into her bag and gets out the cutting from the paper from the awards night. It has been laminated and she puts it between us. 'I just wanted to say that I am very proud of you.'

I see myself upside down. The fuzzy letters are unreadable apart from the huge headline. I feel the tears. Here in a kids' games workshop coffee shop, this important thing has happened and I am in public. I panic and scrabble in my bag for a tissue. She continues.

'I had no idea. I thought you were a carer. But I am very proud of you.' She bites into the cake again, chews then sips her coffee.

'Thank you. I've been doing this for about twelve years.'

It comes out spiteful. As if I am spotlighting the years she has relegated me to un-noteworthy. I know when it started. She never had time for me because she was always chasing after Dad. She forced me into what would, later on, become a big problem: me and my best friend Alice.

I can see it in my mother's face. That it is the elephant in the room. The thing between us that will not be mentioned that is always there. Her eyes are on the tablecloth now but I know she will be thinking about it. Reasoning out what happened. About how I was always round at my friend's house. Sleeping over. She liked it like that because at least that way she could placate Dad without me there. I just annoyed him. I was aware of it early on. So I gravitated towards Alice and her perfect life.

We spent all our time together until we discovered boys. Just the thought of what happened makes me hot, and I push it all away. Not that it matters to anyone but me because I became invisible in all the drama. My feelings were inconsequential beside the mountain of problems Alice left in her wake.

That is why I left. This is why I avoid my parents. This is why I keep away. That and Danny. She still lives in that world, near to Dougie Peters, but I escaped long ago. And that's how I would like to keep it.

She doesn't take it up.

'And bringing up the children, too. Who, by the way, are a credit to you.'

I'm really suspicious now. She'd had a part-time job in a local accountant's office because 'looking after Dad' is a full-time job in itself. His man-child demands were ever increasing as I got older until he sat in the window like a huge baby, having food and drinks brought to him. His clothes washed and pressed in the way he instructed. I don't want to as it seems to be going so well, but I have to.

'Me and Danny.'

She puts her cup down gently.

'That's partly what I wanted to say. As well. And that I'm proud of you.' She reddens. 'I liked Danny. It wasn't me, you know.'

I stiffen. 'But you didn't say anything. You just let him do it.'

She shakes her head slightly. 'And I had to fight to see Jennifer and Simon.' She stares at me. 'Give things up.'

It slowly sinks in. There are the good guys and there are the bad guys. And there are the very bad guys. Janice and I made a wall chart, like the ones you get on colours of urine and dehydration. One about happiness and the bastard-level of your partner. A bastardometer. I mentally place Dad now at around 55 per cent on the bastardometer. Controlling but not violent. Ruling with silence. Then I remember when he hit me. How I froze. Like her. Played dead until he was satisfied he had adequately controlled me. More like 85 per cent.

'Give what up?'

'The bit of money I earn at Jones' accounts. He didn't want me giving it to you and ... Danny.' She rolls his name around her mouth as if it were brand new. 'So he made me put it directly into a joint account and gave me an allowance.'

I gasp. 'A fucking allowance? Sorry. But why did you agree?'

She pulls a face and reddens. I want to make her say it. But she doesn't.

'He would have been difficult. He would have stopped me going out shopping, which is where he thinks I am every Saturday.'

I look at her. This is not the person I knew. She is softer, more relaxed. Not, I realise, hidden behind a fake mask of complicity. I smile and she tries to.

'Right. So what about all this? Is he aware of your newfound Madonnaesque vibe?'

She pulls the jacket around her.

'My Great-aunt Edna died. I was looking after her. She made me Power of Attorney years ago and just about six months before she died she wrote me a cheque. I never cashed it, because it would have gone into the joint account and ...' She is talking very fast, and I recognise the fear of being found out. 'I didn't know what to do. Anyway, I read your article and I thought, Why not? So I opened an online account.'

She looks very proud of herself.

'But he must have noticed?'

'Oh yes. He has. But now I've got the money what can he do?' She looks from side to side. 'It was quite a lot. And I checked, it's legal, because I helped out she can pay me the going rate. She left a letter. I can declare it as earnings and pay tax on it. I asked Mr Jones.'

I smile.

'Mum, you don't need to justify it to me. Or to anyone. I'm pleased for you.'

She pulls in her lips.

'Is it too late?'

I shake my head. I think about Shelia and Sally; I look at Jennifer and Simon.

'No. It's never too late.'

Tanya

Diary Entry: Saturday

I don't know why I am doing this because no doctor is ever going to see this diary. It occurred to me when we were in the taxi on the way home. He was drunk and trying to kiss me and the driver watched in the mirror. I am never going to be able to give it to the doctor because he will always be there.

Which, I suppose, begs the question: why don't I just walk out of work and go to the doctor's and tell them? Or the police? I hated myself last night, at that party. When he was probably talking to another woman or tapping his foot while he watched a game of pool. I hated myself for not turning around and walking out. On to the street. Keep walking until I was on the main road. There was bound to be someone around who could help.

But there are many reasons why I can't. The first one is because I would get in trouble. We both would, for what we did. Al has explained very clearly what would happen. I don't really care about that. I know that for all my dressing it up and my excuses this house is a prison, so what would the difference be?

The other main reason is because I know what the consequences would be if he caught me. Which he did last time. No matter what happens, he will always be there somewhere. Waiting for me. That's what he told me. He would find me. This is also the reason for carrying on writing this diary because I know something bad will happen at some point and I want people to know. I don't know if anyone would find it in the gap under the unit, but I need an outlet or I'll go mad.

So I'm going to write something now that I have never told anyone. Never. I block it out, but it's important I write down why I can't just walk away. Then I will know it is real and I'm not a coward.

He bought me a dog. Tina. She was a little girl, wiggly and furry with a funny little face. He gave her to me at Christmas and it didn't take me long to train her. We would walk her at night and it almost felt like we were a normal couple, talking and walking our puppy. Tina loved me. Al built her a little outdoor kennel at the back of the shed for when we were at work. It even had underfloor heating and a little bed. She would run out of the kennel when I opened the back door and launch herself at me.

She slept in the hallway at night, and the times Al crept across the landing she would bark as if she sensed my fear. It didn't stop him. He still came in and I still held my breath, but at least I knew he was coming.

Then one day, a terrible day when I had completely lost the plot after Al had been out all night, I snapped. I waited for him in the kitchen, Tina dancing around me to go out. But I couldn't let her out because the shutters were down. Eventually I heard the shutter click up and there he was. Looking rough, smelling of beer.

'Where've you been?' I screamed it at him. 'Tina wanted to go out. Where were you?'

He stood there for a moment, then he walked up to me.

'Shut up.'

I stepped back.

'No. No. I won't. You can't treat me like this.'

Quick as a flash his hands were in my hair, the strands popping at my scalp. He jerked my head sideways and held me over the sink. He turned on the water and shoved my head under. My hands were on his, scratching and tugging at him and he suddenly let go. I spluttered and gasped for air and turned around.

He was holding Tina by the scruff of the neck right in front of my face. I moaned.

'No. Alan. Please. Don't. I'm sorry. I'm sorry. Please.'

But he turned around and took her. The door slammed and the shutters closed and I heard the car start up. I was screaming and crying and banging on the locked door until I bruised my hand.

Eventually I was exhausted. I lay on the kitchen floor, my scalp raw and my eyes almost closed. I lay there until he came back. He came in and pulled me up. I looked behind him.

'I drowned her.'

He was smiling. I screamed and screamed and I thought I was going to die. He held me against the sink and he pushed his body against me. Pulling down my pyjama bottoms and pushing inside me. I sobbed and sobbed, not even pretending to like it like he had made me do before. Not even checking that he had a condom on; my worst fear is that I would be pregnant because what would he do then? I know what he is capable of. I know. When he had finished, he lolled against me and whispered in my ear.

'I drowned her. And I'll drown you if you ever try to leave me. You signed up for this, remember?'

Chapter Thirteen

Day 17

'So she actually ate a piece of cake?'

I am lying in bed, the Sunday sun pouring through a gap in the curtains, talking to Danny on the phone long distance, and he picks this fact from the whole conversation about my mother. I sip my tea.

'Yeah. It was like she had never had cake before. But I guess there's a lot about her life now that she's never had before.'

He laughs. I can picture him looking puzzled and scratching his head. I miss him so much.

'D'you think she'll leave him?' He pauses for effect. 'You know, using your Superwoman special powers of deduction? What do you think?'

'Nah. But she's making a stand, which is good.'

'Speaking of which. Donelle.' I feel a stab of fear. Has she said something? 'So what's the story, then?'

I pause.

'About what?'

I know that eventually this is going to explode in my face. I need to tell him, but I can't. '

'I spoke to Mum and she said Donelle's a bit moody. Some new guy.'

'Yeah. She met someone. She thinks it's the real deal but ...' I think about Donelle. God. I've been so wrapped up in my own problems that I've missed something. Vi's right. She's fretting. It might be love or it might be worry. Poor Donelle. She's helped me so much, I need to speak to her.

'Right. Well, I'll rip his head off if he hurts her.'

And this is exactly why I can't mention my little problem. If I told him about the texts and especially about the pictures and my hair he would immediately interpret this as a cross between some fucked-up romantic pursuit and terrorism. He would do some serious damage. It's also why I can't talk to him about my past. Danny and Donelle had each other. He was always asking me about my childhood and my friends but I managed to skip over it. It's just too painful. I thought me and Alice would be friends for life. She was like a sister; we were inseparable. Every now and again I think about her and I get a sense of anticipation, like when I was going to meet her. To a sleepover at her house. Or playing out. But I can never tell Danny about her because of what happened. It would just add to his anger about my parents and how they treated me.

'Don't worry, love. I'll speak to her. She's here a lot of the time, I would have noticed if anything was seriously wrong.' I fucking wouldn't, though. Not enough, anyway, it seems. I'm so focused on saving myself. 'Let's look forwards, Dan. We've got a major opportunity to get out of debt and move here. I want this all to go well.'

He tells me he loves me and I tell him. I do love him. I lie there until our beautiful children burst in and jump on me and I am reminded of what is really important. We are off to Vi and Danny Snr's for Sunday dinner. When we arrive I scroll through Rightmove and look at houses I have ticked as possibilities.

'Simon wants to stay at the same school, but there are plenty to choose from,' I explain convincingly to Danny Snr. Even though I cannot really predict what will happen in the next twenty-four hours, let alone the coming years. 'And once we are on the ladder ...'

Danny Snr is impressed. He helps me choose three houses and we email for details. They would stretch us to within pennies of our budget, but we cannot let it stop us. Danny's philosophy is to go the whole hog, take a chance. But my previous avoidance of staying in one place has left nothing to chance and it scares me. I nod and smile because deep down I know this is what I want more than anything. Our own home. Where we can shut the door and close out the world.

I text Danny the details. He replies immediately.

> This is exciting. It's really going to happen, isn't it? They'll have a garden to play in. We can install a glitter ball. Only seventeen days to go.

Yes. All I have to do is hold this situation down for seventeen days and then ... what? At least Danny will be here then and everything will be back to normal. This month has been tough so far and the intervention by some psychotic stalker has not helped. Just seventeen days.

The one good thing that had happened is the surprising show of strength from my mum. As we sit in Vi's front room, the kids playing on the floor and Danny Snr behind them, laughing and joking with them, I have time to sit back and think. Vi will not allow anyone else in her kitchen when she is cooking, despite my protestations. It has always given me a break, just to sit and not do anything – a complete luxury for most working mums.

I hadn't read the news article about me, just glanced at the picture then on to the next client, the next problem. It was never about me, more about the funding message. I hate attention. Hate it. Without even looking I know I will look odd in the photograph, over-dyed and pasty-faced. I've had it thrown at me that my feminist values make me look scruffy and unprofessional. But my appearance is less feminist values and more that I don't have hours in the morning to curl my hair and dress up. I'm already dealing with work way before I get there. Texts, emails, all done on the hoof. My wardrobe of bright colours has no distinction between work, home and going out.

I know I am not someone to aspire to in terms of appearance. I'm slightly overweight and my nails are short and functional. So I had never imagined in a million years that anyone would aspire to be me. Or admire me. Superwoman of the Year, with the tacky star, was thought up by me and Janice. There, in the dingy office we call work-home to get maximum publicity because we have to be everything. Marketing, advertising, services, management, accounts. And still it isn't enough for the council funders, who would love to shut us down just so that they could claim 'savings'.

But the person I least expected to has seen through my hard shell and into my heart and finally seen what I am really about: my mum.

I watch Vi through the crack in the kitchen door, transferring roast potatoes from a tray on top of her stove to the oven. She has always valued me, recognising that Danny loves me instead of resenting me for taking him away from her. She just included me in him. I get up and stand at the door.

'We're going to buy our own house, Vi.' She smiles but her eyes roam to the children and Simon in particular. She knows as well as I do that he's had trouble making friends. But now he is close to two boys in his class.

'Any idea where?'

'Round here; maybe closer to town or nearer Heaton Park. Nearer school.'

For all that she likes me, she has been critical of my constant need to move around, fearful that I will take the children and Danny away, but separating this from our friendship. She laughs now.

'So will this be the last move?'

I laugh too.

'Well, it's the first rung on the ladder. But it will certainly be for a long time. I can't see either of us moving into the next tax bracket just yet.'

Her eyes flicker around her home. They bought their house when the children were little, an old semi in the middle of a middle-class area. This did not go down well locally and they were subject to much abuse. Danny told me they had windows broken and dog shit posted through their letter box. But they stuck it out.

'Kids will love it.'

Which means kids need stability. I know that Simon suffers if things are unbalanced. He does not have my resilience, he has a softer nature that I know, if nurtured, will turn into the love and kindness of his father's character. We stand in shared silence, the way only friends can without feeling uncomfortable. She wipes her hands on a tea towel and herds me to the table. She rips a piece of bread and spreads butter on it thickly.

'Help yourself.' I do, and she pours us a glass of minted water from a decanter. 'Got the idea from a restaurant. I liked it so I bought one. I got one for you too.'

'Thanks, Vi. It's lovely. No Donelle?'

'No. She's working. Too hard. And this guy. She seems … anyway. Her and Danny, lately, and you. Oh yes. And you.' She reaches over and opens a newspaper at the awards page. I shake my head.

'It was staged, Vi. I awarded it to myself!'

'But Daniel is so proud of you. We are so proud of you.'

I nod and smile.

'Well, let's hope the funding people are proud of me or I'll be out of a job.'

She butters another piece of bread. I hear Danny Snr and the kids laughing loudly.

'You're missing the point. This means a lot to us. You're like a daughter to me and Daniel. Let us help you with the deposit for this house.' I sigh. Danny will not let them. He wants it to be all his own work for his own family. 'We've got a bit put by for if Danny and Donelle went to university but they didn't so I was going to save it for grandkids. But you can use it for this. To settle.'

She looks hopeful.

'I can ask, but you know how he feels about it.'

We have a huge Sunday dinner and I almost feel like things are back to normal. But then Vi pulls me into the kitchen. This is her domain; this must be serious. She folds her arms.

'Donelle. I'm concerned. She's not telling me something. Has she told you?'

I smile. 'No, Vi. And I've seen her most days. She's got a new man. Maybe it's love? It can do that. Especially when someone's had a rough ride. Maybe she's just worried about it working out?'

I can't tell her I am concerned because I don't know the details. I don't want to worry her. She shakes her head. 'I don't know. She seems bothered.'

'I'll ask her. Don't worry, Vi. She'll meet someone. This might not be him, but she will. She's a lovely woman.'

We say goodbye to Vi and Danny Snr and Vi reminds me to 'ask him'.

As soon as we get home, my phone rings. I jump out of my skin, but it's a foreign number and I know it's Danny.

'Ria. Go outside, where the kids can't hear.'

He sounds serious and my stomach turns. What could have happened? What does he know? I let Jennifer and Simon in and they hurry to the TV – Sunday is TV day. I go back.

'OK. I'm on the front steps.'

He tuts. 'I just had a call from Mum. What are you supposed to ask me?'

I shake my head. *Shit.* This is Danny's arguing voice.

'You already know. That's why you're so pissed off and I haven't asked you.'

I look around. Our street is a row of rental flats, green with trees and today it's sunny. It's cheerful but rough, and even at a glance I see a discarded painkiller popper pack and a used condom. God only knows what is hiding in the long grass on the spare ground across the road. I saw a needle on the edge of the grass once and donned surgical gloves to pick it up, only to see many more near the beautiful willow trees.

I've watched as people walk through the rough paths that lead to a forested area in the middle of this urban decay. Jennifer and Simon gaze at it, innocent as yet to the dangers it could hold should they go there alone. We need to get away from here before they become teenagers and I can't stop them.

'I'm not taking it. I'm doing this alone or not at all.'

I'm suddenly stung.

'But you're not alone. What about me?'

He is silent.

'You don't even want this, Ria,' he says eventually. 'You're not even bothered. You'd stay there. Which is fine, but I don't want to.'

Tears threaten yet again and I swallow them back.

'I do want it. And you know I'd follow you anywhere.'

He finally softens. 'Yeah, I know. I'm just tired and this job. But not long left now. And this guy … I'm worried, Ria.'

I freeze.

'What guy?'

'Donelle's fella. Pissing me off. And you. I'm worried about you. I always am with your job and those fucking nutters you're constantly fending off. It's worse now I'm not there. You can't blame me.'

He's right. I can't blame him. I think quickly. My stalker is just another one of them, someone who is warped and needs putting straight. But there's only one way to do it: through the law. And I've been down that road. I can't do anything until it escalates. I hear him and make him a promise, one that helps us both.

'Look. This is normal. You're away from your family and you're bound to be worried, love. If it all gets on top and I need you, I will text you. I'll text you a specific word and you'll know to come straight away. Or I'll phone you and say it and you'll know.'

It's a device we use both in practice and to make people feel safer, to make them realise that someone is there for them.

He laughs. 'Live a reverse *Fifty Shades*?'

I giggle. 'Yeah. Our own version. What word? What do you think? Something vague. Not "help" or anything. Something that could be used in a normal sentence.'

The line is silent and he's thinking.

'Superwoman.'

I roll my eyes.

'Hardly normal.'

He laughs.

'Seems to be being bandied about a lot these days. And you are.'

'I'm not. And if I were it would be because you support me. Don't do yourself down, Dan. Don't.'

He is serious again.

'I worry about you being hurt. That hurts me, Ri. That I can't do anything.'

Oh my God. I never covered this angle. Male pride. It hadn't occurred to me. Of course he means everyday danger, which is enough really, but I want to tell him everything. Tell him about this fucking creep. A full 100 per cent on the bastardometer. He's nothing. I've reported him. He is nothing.

'I can handle myself, Dan, don't worry.'

He changes the subject.

'Look, I have to go. I want to come back, Ri; I miss you and the kids. But I want the money. I don't want any more debt collectors knocking at our door. And I can't take it off my mum. If I'd known I was going to meet you and have them two, I would have gone to uni, used that cash then. But I need to contribute. And that money's in the bank for Si and Jen. It doesn't feel right to take it.'

I laugh. 'Yeah, well, we'd all like the benefit of hindsight. Go. I'll be fine. I'll call you if anything happens. With Donelle. With me. Anything. And if you get the Superwoman call get here straight away. OK? But it won't.'

He sighs. 'Bye, love. Bye.'

He's gone. I look up and down the street and then I go inside and bolt all the doors and windows. Just in case.

Tanya

Diary Entry: Sunday

We went out for a walk yesterday. After the party Al was hungover and he suggested going for a stroll on the moors. We drove out past Huddersfield and over to the little cafe that we used to go to when we first met. All the while I was thinking about what Jenny had said and what he must be doing during the day. As if I needed to ask.

It had never ended. It was all falling into place. That's why he was doing this to me. Keeping me in the house, making sure I was too scared to even look at anyone let alone speak. He wanted to keep us separate, like he had before. He wanted me in one place playing the little wife, and her in another as the mistress.

I watched the heathered hillsides roll by then turn to stone houses. We parked outside the cafe and I watched him as he went through his stupid routine of slicking back his hair, like he was still young. But he isn't. He's old now. Older than me. He drinks too much. He's got a paunch. This is how I convince myself that one day everything will be all right.

Right at that moment I hated him. My feelings changed so rapidly from fear to desperation to hatred on a minute-by-minute basis that I was just waiting for the next wave. But it didn't come. And it wasn't just him I hated. It was everyone who sat and watched me day after day and said nothing. I knew I had to do something about it.

Walking away was out of the question – I wasn't stupid enough to do it on the spur of the moment anyway – but somehow I mustered strength from the bottom of my soul and smiled.

'I love this place.' I looked at the cafe wistfully. 'It reminds me of when we met.'

He looked at me from the corner of his eye. It was a cross between boredom and disgust.

'That's why we're here. You really are stupid, aren't you?'

I turned away and looked through the window. It's the anniversary of the day we met. How could I have forgotten? But stupid? Am I? Am I stupid? Let's see. I felt the thrill of risk flood me, cancelling out the fear for a second. I've felt it before and nearly done something. Nearly. But getting caught would mean lasting consequences.

We went inside the cafe, a neat little place where *Last of the Summer Wine* was filmed. It has a shop on the side that sells plants and little ornaments and pictures of the actors. He ordered us a cream tea and we sat down. My heart was thumping but I smiled sweetly when the woman on the next table asked to borrow the salt. I passed it to her and he barely looked up. I waited until he looked calm. Engrossed in a newspaper.

'Al, can I go and look in the shop please?'

He waved me away, throwing a ten-pound note on the table and munching his scone. I got that awful feeling of being nothing, having nothing, and hoping no one would see, and it nearly stopped me.

But I knew what I was doing. I knew this shop well. Where everything was. I browsed for a while, through the themed pencils and coasters. I picked up a few trinkets and looked at them. There were plenty of people about. I made sure he was still looking at his paper, only checking now and again, never suspicious.

The card rack was facing him and I stood in front of it, back turned. Quick as anything, I took a diary page out of my pocket and slipped it inside a greetings-card envelope. I took the envelope and slipped it inside my cardigan, under my arm. I took a birthday card and paid for it. It was his birthday soon. He would inevitably look in the bag, but good. Good.

I sat back down and drank my tea and ate my scone. Al stretched, his arms long with no regard for anyone else's space.

'Right then. Shall we have a walk round?'

He announced it as if he was doing me a favour. I caught his eye and pointed at the Ladies. He sighed an exaggerated sigh and flopped back down.

'Hurry up then.' Like I was a child.

I walked slowly to the toilet, and once inside pulled a pen from my shoe. I almost didn't do it because if he ever found out he would probably kill me. Not probably. Definitely. I addressed the envelope to Oldham Police Station. I didn't have a stamp and the odds were that it wouldn't get there, but at least I had done something.

Once outside, I clutched the letter in my pocket. I slowed down just before the post box in the wall and bent down to tie my trainer. He looked down at me and carried on walking. My heart skipped a beat as I jumped up and popped the letter in the slot. He didn't see. He was almost at the end of the street and I ran to catch him up.

I felt completely exhilarated. I wasn't useless after all. I smiled to myself. Let's see how stupid I am now. Let's see how he likes this. And let's see how she likes it, too.

Chapter Fourteen

Day 16

Monday morning hits me like a brick. I haven't heard anything since Friday night and I almost believe that, as predicted, he'd give up when I resisted. But the pictures on the cheap phone are a lingering warning that he is still in the background of my life.

I drop off the kids, ducking into the headmistress's office just to confirm that she got my email and no one except family can collect them. All sorted, I arrive at work super-early because it's perpetrator counselling again. Janice is setting the chairs out when I arrive. She sees me pass the doorway.

'Hey, you. Come on. Spill.'

She follows me into the office. I pull up the dusty window blind slightly. Some of the men are already outside, carefully avoiding each other. Malc is imposing in his security uniform, arms folded, back against the door, and I turn back to Janice. I know she will never break my confidence, but I am still careful, the truth catching in my gut.

'That guy. He sent me a dick pic and flowers and some texts. He cut my hair. On the bus. Carole said it wasn't enough so I'm waiting to see what he does next.' I take a deep breath. 'And he was in the pub on Friday night. He sent a picture.'

Her face flushes and she reaches for the phone.

'I'm calling Carole.'

I stop her. I place the receiver gently back on the cradle.

'And say what? Some random guy's sending pictures?'

Her hands are trembling.

'Stalker. He's stalking you. Why didn't you mention this the other night? I knew something was wrong.'

I shrug.

'Because you would have called the police. Loads of trouble and we still wouldn't know who it was. And Danny would find out and come home.'

She stares at me.

'Maybe he should.'

'No. We need the money. You know how skint we are. I'm getting letters from debt collectors, Jan. I have to get through the next two weeks. I have to. Besides, what would he do? We've no real idea who this is?'

'A perp? It has to be.'

'Yeah. Maybe. Carole said to go through the correct channels. But he's not approached me. Yet. Yeah, he was on the bus but I didn't see... anyway. They won't do anything until they know who he is.'

'That's assault. Cutting your hair. It's assault. And the phone? Can't they—'

'No. She said he'd have bought it for cash, probably two at once. Pay-as-you-go.'

I pull the phone out of my bag and show her the dick pic, then the picture message from the pub. She stares at the table.

'Fucking hell. Fucking. Hell.'

I smile.

'Quite.'

'But honestly, Ria. You're a fucking angel and this happens.'

'I know. No clues. I've scoured the messages and videos. Carole says ignore it, unless he approaches, which she doesn't think he will. The bus thing. I'd have to prove it was him.'

'Right. Well, he'd better not come here. But you've done the right thing – telling as many people as possible. Which you know, of course, because it's your job. Sorry.'

I laugh. She's right.

'It's OK. It will pass, like everything.' I change the subject. 'Anyway, I need to tell you about Dawn.'

I explain about my mother's new-found independence and she laughs loudly when I tell her about our coffee date. Eventually it is nearly perpetrator time, and we open the blinds a little. No Frank, but Jim is there, smoking a roll-up and having a staring match with Malc. Sally and the children are at the Community Centre seeing the social worker with the other women, and, apart from me, Janice and Malc, the place is empty. We finish our coffee. I get up, but Janice catches my arm.

'Whatever this is, love, don't let it go too far. You know the score. And so do I. And I know the fact you haven't closed it down means there's more to it.'

I move the yellow arrow on the bastardometer, which is actually just a scale of one to one hundred written on a whiteboard with a permanent marker. I push the magnetic arrow past the 100 per cent mark. She meets my eyes and she knows.

'I'm here. Whenever you need me.'

She leaves to open the door for the perpetrator counselling. Malc is at the ready and the men file towards the door until a black limousine pulls up and they all turn to look. It's sleek and shiny, just like its occupant. Frank James. He's not driving, of course, but he gets out smoothly as two burly younger men get out of the front and rear on the other side. They open the spacious boot and remove two large boxes.

Frank, dressed in pale golf slacks and a pink Fred Perry lightweight cotton sweater over a brilliant white shirt, practises his golf strokes. They carry the boxes in and then return for more. I rush through to the main hall to see what they are. Janice already has the first one open.

'Xboxes. Brand new.'

She shakes her head. We should be pleased. It's a donation and the kids will love them. But we know what this is. It's a show of power, an attempt to buy us. The perpetrators file past them, eyebrows raised, and sit down. Eventually, Frank graces us with his presence. He stands at the front of the gathering. His minders wait at the door but he signals them to leave.

'Ladies.' He smiles at us, a thin-lipped smile that would be entirely charming if we didn't know what he had done to Sheila. 'Gents.' He turns to the perpetrators. 'No one knows how hard these girls work. Keeping us on the straight and narrow. Sorting our girls out while we sort ourselves out.' He turns back to us. 'I just want to say thank-you, girls; thank-you.'

He does a bow, hands pressed together. Janice steps forwards.

'Women. We're women. Not girls. Grown women, Frank.'

He doesn't flinch. Or move. But his eyes grow icy cold.

'Same thing, love. Anyway ...'

She moves closer to him.

'Please could you sit down, Frank, so we can start the meeting?'

He stares at her. Then he looks away and around the room.

'I could completely refurb this place. All you have to do is humour Frankie. Come on, girls, Frankie's a teddy bear once he's comfy.'

Some of the men look confused, but those who know Frank James and his reputation as local councillor cum businessmen cum thug look plain scared. I intervene.

'Right, Frank, let's chat this out later on; we need to start now. I'll make sure the kids get these. They'll love them.'

I make a point not to say thank you. He looks satisfied and walks slowly to the back of the room where he sits looking at his phone for the whole session. When we are finished and we have heard the stories, excuses and even some heart-felt regret, Malc guides everyone towards the door and unlocks it. Jim watches him intently and I make a note to make sure all the alarms are on. Frank remains. He stands at the very back of the room, throwing more golf strokes. He is checking his gold cufflinks, a little tic I have noticed he does when he is really fucking annoyed.

'Frank.'

He looks at me as if I have only just arrived and the last two hours have not happened. I see the black limo pull up outside the gated entrance. The two burly guys get out and speak to Malc, and he relaxes and kicks back as they offer him a cigarette. I turn and walk slowly into my office.

Under the desk in every office at every workstation, and also at regular points in the main rooms, are panic alarms. The white switches turn on a recording device in the room, should we need it. A second position transmits the feed to the main room to alert other workers without panicking anyone in the room. The big red buttons activate a deafening alarm that sounds through the building and is connected to the local police station. This is not going well. Frank is quietly aggressive and I guess that this is his style. Cold and calculated, without being overtly obvious. Until the moment he strikes, or he gets someone else to. I activate the white switch to position one with my knee and smile tightly.

'So.'

He sits down facing me, drawing his chair closer.

'Right, love. Is she all right?'

I screen him for any sign of genuine concern: a furrowed brow, caring eyes. But there is none. I nod.

'As well as can be expected under the circumstances. With a broken arm.'

He nods. 'Aye. She told you about Bobby, didn't she?'

I tense. The video is running and this cuts both ways.

'You know I can't tell you about my conversations with Sheila.'

He sighs. 'Aye. Well, I know she would have because she took his things. Is this what this is about? Because I can tell you now, it wasn't my fault, that.'

I shake my head. 'We're not apportioning blame, Frank. We're helping Sheila because she asked us to. She's fine. Settled. No need to worry.'

'He was already dead. Inside her. That's what the doc said. But she said it was my fault. I never bloody touched her. He was already dead. But all she does is go on and on about it.'

I am silent. Everything that Sheila has told me, all the complex issues of this long relationship, all passing through me because neither of them could communicate with each other. Even after all these years. As he fiddles with his British Lion cufflinks, I wonder how it started, how they lost their connection. The early pictures of them that Sheila showed me suggest that they were happy once. He waits for me to say something and when I don't, he continues.

'She's driven me bloody mad. I've given her everything she wanted. Every bloody thing. Except a kid. So praps she's not as bloody innocent as she makes out, eh, lady?'

I meet his gaze.

'I never said she was innocent, Frank. But here's what it looks like to me. You are living in yours and Sheila's house without a broken arm. And she is living in a women's hostel with a broken arm and many, many historic injuries, which she is too scared to tell us about. According to the law, there is never an excuse for violence, no matter what the other person has done. There are other ways to sort out issues. To get help. Or to walk away.'

He stares at me, furious.

'Are you suggesting I hit my wife?'

I shrug. 'I don't know if you did or didn't for sure. Someone has. But if you didn't, why are you here, at the perpetrators' meeting?'

He laughs suddenly and loudly, a fake, over-practised laugh that makes me jump in my seat.

'I'm just playing the game. She's fucking nuts. On the change. I'm only here to get her back.' He leans closer. 'I never touched her. Understand? Never touched her.' He stands up and stretches, far too close to me. 'This place. Up for funding, is it? I might be able to help you.'

I get up and open the door. He walks out, not looking back, and I watch him shake hands with Malc and press some notes into his hand. Frank gets into the car and he is gone. In an instant Malc is in my office placing four fifty-pound notes on the table.

'Just think of it as a donation.' He mimics Frank's thick Manchester accent. I want to laugh but I am so shocked at the terror Frank can impose and the thought of Sheila enduring him day in, day out. I flick off the recorder and sit in silence, contemplating how I can protect Sheila.

I already know I am lucky, but when my phone beeps and it's a text from Danny I slide the yellow arrow to zero.

Hope you are OK, babe. Day 16. Nearly halfway. All good here. I'm there for you every minute of the day. I love you x always x

We have argued just like everyone else, but Danny is a genuinely nice person. And there are a lot of them about; it's just that I work at the other end of the spectrum. It's not that he would never consider doing anything naughty. Years ago he came home with some bottles of home-brewed vodka that his mate had made. I knew from his deep frown and concentrated look that he was up to something the minute he walked through the door. We lived in a rented ground-floor flat in the city centre at the time. Every single time we heard a police siren, which was a lot, he was out the back where he had hidden his booze stash, transferring them to the bin. Then bringing them back when the sirens faded. He hardly slept until they were gone, donated to the house party of a distant friend.

And then there's his temper. He has a tipping point, something that, over the years, we have negotiated and I protect him from. I know he would never hurt me, I am absolutely sure. But I have seen him on the edges of pub fights in the early days and, later, neighbourhood arguments, and it is there.

But Frank. He has terrorised Sheila, controlled her, and now he's trying to control this situation. He's trying to menace me, too. Is it him? I'd checked out his pockets; no telltale second phone, but there is only evidence of the latest iPhone, sleek and slim. I don't want to accept the Xboxes and I can't help but question where they came from, but Janice has already started to unpack them.

Her ethos is that every little helps and if we don't actually know they are stolen, then we can accept them. Donations are so few and far between, especially for the children here, because they truly are forgotten. This is a family service, but the focus is on the women, even though their children have suffered the same.

Frank's visit has shaken me, but I did fine. I didn't cave, and I got him on record just in case this goes further, which I have a strong gut feeling it will. Danny is fine, my stalker still hasn't been in touch and all is as well as it can be. I can hear the women come back and as I walk through Sally's children chant, 'Ria, Ria, diarrhoea; Ria, Ria, diarrhoea.' For the first time in ages, I smile.

Janice hands an Xbox to each of the children and it is like Christmas Day, except completely silent. It is only when people have been to the depths of sadness and hurt that you see their true gratitude. These little people cannot believe that they are being given something. They look at Sally for approval. Then back at Janice, who is organising the rough couches at the back of the room around the game monitors also supplied, overlooked by the twinkly branches. The children hold the boxes as if they are pots of gold. Janice laughs loudly.

'Come on! Shape yourselves! Mario's not going to find them pizzas himself, is he?'

It's a golden moment as they and the other four children we have with us at the moment settle down and Janice sets everything up. Soon, they are mesmerised in quiet concentration. Sally stares at them and then I see it. I see her, like so many of the women before her, break.

She has spent every minute since she arrived completely focused on her children. The guilt of what has happened, that they have been ripped from their homes, even though it is not her fault, is building steadily. The children's well-being is the dam and guilt and shame are the flood, just waiting for a gap in the responsibility and here it is. She buckles. Physically. I see her and catch her and guide her to a side room. I shut the door just in time, because she lets out a wail, deep and visceral. I hold her as she grieves the marriage she thought that she could save. The man she loved once and the innocence of her children that has been lost somewhere in the shouting and fighting they have witnessed.

I hold her and rub her back, my cheek against her hair and I think that this is exactly it. This is what the funders, with their spreadsheets and their calculators and their tick sheets, would be denying. This physical witnessing of the consequences of prolonged pain and torture endured. The open channels for tears and welcoming of uncertain explanations because we are not in court, we are just here for each other.

She cries for a long time and then she wipes her reddened eyes and her nose.

'He's back. He's out there again.'

I nod. 'The thing is, they will build a case against him. It's good he was arrested. Couple more times and you can get an injunction.'

My words sound empty and her face crumples.

'What does he have to do to me? To us? He's already … and I thought that was it. I thought once I was here and he started, the police would sort it?'

She begins to cry again and I hug her and look out of the window. Jim is sitting there in the front window of the pub, back in his usual position, staring menacingly at the door of SafeMe, where Malc stands guard. Jim has a black eye, no doubt from his struggle not to be arrested and to 'just see his wife and kids'. Sally sobs into my shoulder and my gaze moves along the street to a red Skoda parked just outside the gates. I peer at the shape in it, then, still holding Sally to me, flick my screen on to the CCTV image on the gates.

There's someone in the car. Parked outside the gates. Just watching the gates, he and Jim both focused on this building. I feel Sally's grief-racked body and my own fear rise slightly. But there is no law against sitting in a pub or parking on the street. I make us both a coffee and add this to my diary. I check myself. It could be completely innocent. Or it could be someone waiting for me. Sally sees me staring and follows my gaze.

'Is that the social worker? Nice he was. He was in here yesterday.'

I swallow hard.

'Here? Where?' I say it evenly. I don't want to scare her.

'In here.'

'In my office?'

She nods. I rush outside to Malc.

'That guy yesterday. Sally said it was a social worker ...'

He sighs. 'Duty. Yeah. He was here about an hour.'

I can feel sweat dripping down my back, soaking into my T-shirt. He was here. He was here.

'What did he look like, Malc?'

He makes a face. 'Fortyish. Might be a bit older, I suppose.' Then he stands up straight. 'He had the right paperwork. I checked.'

I breathe out.

'Right. Is that his car?'

We both look up the road at the Skoda. Malc frowns at me.

'I don't think so. Look. Is everything OK? I mean, I did check ...'

I shake my head. Is everything OK? I don't know. It probably was the duty social worker. He had the right paperwork. I am losing it.

'Yeah. Sorry. Sorry. I'll just check the CCTV. Can't be too careful.'

Malc's hurt and his face shows it. I'll make it up to him, I promise myself. I rush back to my office and rewind the CCTV. This guy isn't hiding. He's sitting in my office, back to the camera, chatting to

Sally. Then he's walking through SafeMe. Black jeans. Black hoodie top. Brown bag slung over his shoulder. But I never see his face. He could be anyone. Or he could just be the duty social worker.

I phone Social Services to check. They have no record of it, but then again they have no record of Sally on their files either, at first glance. I rub my eyes. This is how it gets you. Suspicious. Paranoid.

I try to ignore it and Sally tries to ignore Jim. By the time I leave to go home, making a show of talking to Malc to make things right, the car is gone but I am still shaking.

Tanya

Diary Entry: Monday

It's late Monday night and I'm sitting near the base of the shower again. The water is running. Today has been excruciating. On the outside everything continued normally, but on the inside I was seething. My new-found knowledge about Al's life has pushed me closer to cracking point, the point where I annoy him so much he lashes out.

He says it's my fault and it probably is. I know I am heading there now. It feels like I am in a car with no brakes but I don't care because anywhere is better than where I was before. The morning routine went as usual, except I couldn't help but think of Tina and how I missed her even now. Words like 'bastard' and 'monster' rose into my mind, but I pushed them down in case they slipped out. I knew that outwardly he could never know what I was thinking. I am well practised.

I got into the car and shut the door gently. No slamming. No signals that I was upset. Instead, as I waited for him patiently as he preened in the hallway mirror, I looked at the mileage. 56,782. I repeated it over and over again in my mind during the journey and, once in my office, I wrote it down. I watched as he drove off, just to make sure there was no pause, no slight hesitation that happens when he suspects something is going on.

I don't have a mobile phone, which caused much hilarity when Karla and Jade found out.

'How do you text people, then?'

Jade was genuinely curious. I shrugged.

'I don't have anyone. My dad's dead. Just Al.'

She pouted. 'But what about your friends?'

I didn't answer her. I got on with my work. But yes, what about friends? I didn't have any friends, obviously. But it wasn't always like that. I had plenty of friends at school. I was quite popular, mainly because I look exactly like Sissy Spacek in *Carrie*. Everyone has a best friend. I had her. We grew up together. We slept in a tent at the end of my garden, lay underneath the bright stars on that hilltop holding hands. We swore we would never be apart.

I don't really like to think about her. Not after what she did with Al. We had been so close, gone everywhere together. But he told me. He said he had to tell me the truth. We had to have honesty if we were going to be together for ever.

She went after him. I saw it that first night, in the disco. Her eyes were on him as much as mine were, and when he chose me she was livid. In the back of his car on the way home I saw her trying to catch his eye in the rear-view mirror. He would smile at her, then at me. But he chose me.

It didn't stop her. She tried to cause trouble, telling my dad he was dangerous. Ha. I have to give her that one, but she could never have known what would happen. She was trying to split us up, to come between us. So she could get her claws into him. Which, of course, she did.

So even if I wasn't in this mess, I would actively choose not to have friends, because I don't trust anyone. That's what I was thinking as I sat at my desk: that I didn't trust anyone. Not him. Not her. Not Mrs Simister. Not Jade. I felt a big tear run down my cheek. It took me completely by surprise, and I sniffed heavily. Was he with her now?

Five o'clock ticked by and he pulled up outside. I got my coat and said goodnight to everyone. 56,782. I am good at maths. With nothing else to do – I am rarely allowed books or newspapers and only selected films when it suits him – I have taken advantage of the Microsoft Office help files on my computer at work. I had to teach myself as I am not allowed a computer. We can't access the internet at work, but I have heard everyone in the office discuss it. So I have done what I can without it.

56,782. It is twenty-two miles from our house to my work. So he would have done sixty-six miles today so far. That's if he had gone home and stayed there. I have no idea where this haulage company where he works is. I expect it is in Oldham, so add ten miles for the journey to and from work. I glanced at the mileage. 56,899. 117 miles. So today he's driven 51 miles.

It just meant that he hadn't been at home all day. Maybe he'd decided to go into work. My pulse was banging in my head. I regulated my breathing, so the seething did not escape. But it was even worse than I thought. When we stopped outside the house he reached on to the back seat and pulled over a Tesco bag. I saw the outline of Jacob's Cream Crackers. Miniature cheeses and tubes of Primula. The crunch of crisps. This only meant one thing. I didn't know if I could carry on. If I could have got out of the car and run away at that moment I would have. But I was frozen to the spot.

Chapter Fifteen

Day 15

I go through my morning routine of cornflakes and teeth brushing and combing out and waxing hair and skin. I push on wellingtons as it is raining and we will get wet. He is not giving up. He is not giving up.

The thought stops me in my tracks, little hands pulling at mine until I look at my children. A red car approaches. It isn't him, and I am relieved when I pass the school gates and step into relative safety. I scold myself for being paranoid. But someone saying they are watching you is different from seeing them do it. I see Simon's teacher.

'Hi, Lucy. Hi. Look, can you remind the office that neither of them is to go with anyone else?'

She frowns.

'Is anything wrong, Ria? You look exhausted.'

'No, no. Just, well, reports of a strange man in our area. So just checking.'

I walk away and turn back to see Jennifer filing into her class and waving at me. She is holding hands with her friend Janet and I can't help but think about school and Alice. All this always comes back to me when I am stressed. I want to warn Jennifer not to rely on Janet, that she could hurt her like Alice hurt me, but I also remember the love. The friendship. The sharing and the laughing. I also recognise Jennifer's longing for Janet's life. The way she stares longingly at Janet's mother and the cockapoo in the back of the status car. I was like that with Alice. Her dad Dougie, laid-back and academic, in contrast to my racist, sexist father. Her messy home, no one tidying up after her. She could draw on her bedroom wallpaper and not get into trouble. Maybe that was why she was always smiling. That's why I leave Jennifer be. I wave back. Simon is with his friends and, for a second, my heart feels warm that he has settled.

I walk to work, think all the way about making a police report. I make a note to at least write it down in my diary, just in case, so if anything did happen to me someone would know – what? By the time I get there the day is in full swing. There are two new residents: a young woman who has no recourse to funding and has had her children taken into care – she is crying loudly in the main room – and a family of three, a woman and two sons, the older son who came with her had to move into a hostel because he was over sixteen.

It is completely heartbreaking but I must do my job and do my best for them. Janice punches me in the arm.

'Another day, another dollar. Anything else from dick pic?'

I smile. 'No. Nothing,' I lie, because I know if I tell her my now paranoid mind thought he was parked up outside she will immediately call the police. Maybe she should. 'Hopefully he's given up.'

She nods. Her look tells me she is there for me every minute of the day, but she just says: 'Yeah. Right.'

We glance out of the window and Jim is in the pub nursing a pint. It is ten-fifteen and we know that he will sit there all day drinking until he is either asleep or banging on the door with a blunt instrument demanding to see Sally. She comes over.

'Still there.' She seems brighter today. I hug her.

'You're doing brill. Honest. We'll get something sorted out for you soon, you know.'

She looks at me. 'I worked in an office at the hospital, you know. I had a really good job. The kids were settled in school. Good reports. We weren't one of them families. You know.' Her voice is pleading, her expression desperate. Janice laughs.

'Yeah, I know. *Shameless*. No, I know, Sally. I know you are an intelligent woman. And this is just a blip. You'll get support out there.'

We all look outside and Jim takes a gulp of his pint. Is it only words? No. She will get support. She will get outreach and a panic alarm and everything we can arrange to keep her safe. Will it be enough? It all depends on what Jim does. Yet there he is, free as a bird, and here she is, trapped in a cage.

We are in a glass bubble of safety here, and right now I am thankful for it. My children are safe at school and I am safe here. Danny texts at lunchtime, triumphant.

> Day 15. We're halfway there, babe! The next two weeks will be tough but after that I'm all yours. I love you x always x

I go to text him back, but decide to ring instead. He answers in one ring.

'Everything OK?'

I suddenly realise that he would think this was trouble, but I turn it around quickly.

'Yeah. Sorry. I just wanted to speak to you. Hear your voice. You know.'

I suddenly realise that I have been lonely. Donelle and Janice are the best friends anyone could wish for, but Danny is different. He is laughing now.

'You soppy bugger. Mardy arse.'

I laugh too. 'Well. Absence makes the heart grow fonder and all that.' I sound sarcastic because after twelve years and two children and the day-to-day slog I am severely out of practice. But he is game.

'When all this is over I'll never let you out of my sight. Or my bed.'

I feel a thrill like when we first met and this is it. This is what I want out of life. This feeling. I giggle and he giggles and then he asks the question that I know is on his mind.

'Soon be back to normal. Donelle OK?'

'Yeah. She's fine, been dropping the kids off and rushing off so I've not spoken to her about this guy yet, not even stopped for a brew, but she seems OK. Your mum is on top form as well.'

He sighs. 'Right. Back to it.'

I hear the drilling and hammering in the background.

'Yeah. Me too. See you soon, love.'

He is gone and I do miss him already. I wish things were back to normal, with us in our little flat with the rumble of trains comforting us, the birds singing outside our bedroom windows and the kids running in and jumping on our bed. And no constant buzz of fear that something terrible is going to happen. It won't. It won't. I tell myself over and over again that this is just some arsehole who is fucking with me. As the day goes inevitably on in its march towards evening, I almost believe it until another message arrives.

I see it bounce down on the cheap phone on my desk right in front of me as I am checking the invoices for the catering services. The ping is jolly, lulling me into a false sense of security until my eyes scan the words. I almost don't want to open it. I feel like leaving it sitting there, walking away into the distance and never coming back. But the anger rises, 'the how dare you' fuckery that always proceeds fear. I open it.

I KNOW WHERE YOU ARE. I'M ALWAYS WATCHING YOU.

I am fucking fuming. I am beside myself with anger and frustration and I hit 'reply' and begin to type.

LEAVE ME ALONE OR I WILL GO TO THE POLICE

I press 'send' and my rational mind, the one under my raging angry-bitch face, knows this is the right thing to do. The start of resistance. A reply I can send on to the police and to legals if it comes to it. But at the same time, on planet psycho, I know that it could also be perceived as the beginning of 'the game'. Where the hunted kicks back and attacks instead of running for their life. I have no way of knowing which way this will go, but I do know that I feel physically sick.

I toy with the idea of forwarding the message and my reply to Carole, just to alert her, but I know deep down that she will repeat that I have no ID. I go through every scenario in my mind and arrive at the semi-comforting position that I have told whoever this is to back off.

But the phone pings again and a photo appears. It's me leaving the police station after my chat with Carole. A message follows.

LOOKS LIKE YOU ALREADY HAVE. ANY LUCK? DIDN'T THINK SO. STILL WATCHING.

I am unable to eat, and when I get home in the evening and Donelle has cooked egg, chips and beans, a perennial favourite, I pick at it, pushing the food around my plate. She touches my arm gently.

'Are you OK, Ria? It's not that guy, is it?'

I sigh. I am half relieved and half sad that I can't confide in her further. I can't risk her telling Dan. I'm keeping silent about this now.

'Just some stuff at work.'

She nods. 'God, I don't know how you do it. All that, day in, day out. When Dan's done with this job, you need a holiday. I can get you cheap flights. Anywhere.'

I smile. Donelle is so kind, just like her brother. She dotes on Jennifer and Simon and I pray that she will meet someone – the right someone – and have kids herself one day.

'Maybe. But we'll be busy house-hunting.' I see Simon wince and duck his head. She sees it too. 'We're looking in this area. So the kids can stay in school.'

She laughs. 'Wow. It's really happening, Ria. I'm so happy for you both. You all.'

Over a glass of wine that I sip slowly, she tells me about all the difficult passengers this week. A heavily pregnant woman flying Manchester to Edinburgh who needed the loo every two minutes. A businessman with a huge sense of entitlement who insisted they put a pillow behind his head for him and adjust it every time it slipped. I snort.

'Sounds like you've got your hands full as well. See, I couldn't cope with that.'

She waves the comment away. 'Ah, you get used to it. We don't care. Just A to B with a coffee service. Anyway, I've got a lot outside work at the moment. The kids and ... Oh, by the way, I'll get them from school all next week, but if anything changes?'

But it's too late. She has hinted at something and I see a glow about her.

'Ah. How's it going with lover boy?'

She fakes embarrassment. But I need some good news.

'Early days. We'll see.'

'So the worries ...?'

She waves her hand to dismiss the thought. 'Just silly stuff. Only because he cares. I did the right thing and asked him about it. We talked. I guess he has a point. I just wish we could be together all the time but his work and my work ...'

She has a wistful look. It lifts me. Seeing someone so happy is a complete contrast from the broken relationships I face at work. My heart lifts and I cling to the good things: Danny's 'halfway there', Donelle's happiness, both my kids safe in bed. Suddenly life is not so bad and I drink my wine. Eventually Donelle goes to leave.

'See you tomorrow, Sis. Get some sleep. I know you miss Dan, but it's all for the good, yeah?'

When she has gone I text Danny. He'll be on his way home from work but I need him to know.

I love you x always x. Just sayin'

He texts back almost immediately.

Me too, babe, always. Goodnight, beautiful x

It almost makes the day right. Almost. But not quite.

Tanya

I am not at work. I am in the house with the shutters down and Al has gone somewhere. I don't know why I am writing this diary now because I have lost all hope again. This is never going to stop. All the diary has done is make me think I can do something, anything. But I can't.

I knew as soon as I saw the carrier bag. Al never carries Tesco bags by the handles, he grabs the neck of the bag. It both annoys me and frightens me because I know what happens next. There is no pattern to it and this is not the same as when I have annoyed him. In a lot of ways it is worse.

I tried to act as normal as possible as we went inside, even though I was shaking. I started to get out the pans to cook dinner but he was already arranging the cheese and crackers on a tray. Emptying the crisps into the little bowls we usually use for cornflakes. Then he handed me a black and gold plastic bag. I knew what was inside without looking.

I am not allowed in Al's study at all. I am not usually allowed in Al's bedroom, which used to be ours, either. But I know the drill. I found myself sitting on the king-sized bed in a transparent black baby-doll nightdress, the horrible nylon stiff and new. The bedroom is spacious but seems dwarfed by the huge screen on the wall facing the bed. I was mesmerised, watching the bright colours and people speaking and laughing on some kind of game show.

The cheese and crackers were on a table at the end of the bed and Al appeared with a bottle of fizzy wine. I could feel the panic grow. He took the glasses and filled them to the top and handed one to me, smiling. I automatically smiled back. Any falter would have only made it worse.

He fumbled with the remote control, his excitement palpable. Visible. The screen dimmed, then flickered to light and for a second I saw myself reflected, my eyes wide with fear. The title screen flashed on: Jane Mourino. *Hotel Getaway*. Running time 126 minutes. Al licked his lips.

It started innocently enough, like it always does, with a young woman in some kind of normal-life situation. Al handed me the fizzy wine and I sipped it slowly. He patted the bed and I moved nearer to him. I have heard Jade and Karla talk about their boyfriends 'watching a porno' and they think it is fun. But I am fairly sure that what comes next is not the same as what they are doing with their men.

My eyes fixed on the screen as Jane Mourino submitted to two men in her hotel room. They started to have sex and Al tipped up the bottom of my glass and I forced the liquid down. He left the room for a moment to fetch a condom or use the toilet and this is where I usually try to vomit, but it never works. So this time I looked around. He is untidy and there were clothes strewn on the bench under the window. I pulled open a drawer and saw a wallet and some keys.

Then I saw some receipts – bank and credit card statements. I used to go through them all for him, balance his bank account, but over the past year this has stopped. I grabbed them and folded them up as small as I could. The window was open – the only window in the house that actually opens – and I quickly pushed the folded paper through the gap. I knew it would land on top of my clematis. Al does not go into the garden.

I jumped back on to the bed and lay there feeling the fuzziness of the drug Al always puts in the drink to stop me screaming wash over me. I wondered vaguely why I cared about her when I would do anything to be rid of him. But I concluded that I am damaged. Damaged. He came back into the room and pulled at me, manoeuvring my floppy body into a position where he could do the most damage.

I can never go to work the day after. And sometimes the day after that. I suspect that sometimes I should have gone to hospital, but he never takes me. I sometimes wonder if that is why I have never got pregnant. Because I am too damaged. Today I am groggy, too. I hate myself and I hate him.

I managed to go outside when the shutters were up, telling him I was emptying the bin. I grabbed the screwed-up, damp papers I had thrown out of the window and almost put them in the bin too because who am I kidding? All I am doing is torturing myself by thinking anything can change. I'll go to work tomorrow and everyone will ask me how my cold is and I will nod and smile.

Now, though, I am looking at his bank statements. The income column shows his salary, but halved, and my meagre weekly wage. The outgoings are the usual bills and credit card payments. I move on to the credit cards. He has bought a lot of new clothes over the past three months. Hotel bookings … I mentally calculate the dates and they tally with when he said he was away at work. But then I remember he isn't working.

I stop and think. He is obviously with her. Not that I can do anything about it. Or is he? He could be working on and off. There are payments to Ann Summers and a few restaurants. Tesco.

I rip up the documents and flush them down the toilet. I shower again for the fifth time and lie on my bed. I am playing with fire. I can feel the burn deeper inside me now and I know that this is not going to end well. But I am not going mad and I am going to have to do something.

Chapter Sixteen

Day 14

By the time we are all up and having breakfast it's nearly time to leave for school. I drew a heart shape from shaving foam on the mirror to remind me of Danny when I feel bad and Jennifer and Simon giggle when they see it. I take it as a good beginning to this Wednesday halfway through the week and make a flying start by cooking pancakes and dusting them with icing sugar and lemon. We eat them on the sofa. I let them watch children's TV for a while, savouring the warmth and comfort because each day seems to be getting harder and harder.

When I have dropped them off I head to work, more confident now I have confronted this bully. He is still on my mind, but I've stated my case. I have nothing to be sorry for. I repeat it over and over again, telling myself that it will all be OK.

When I approach SafeMe I see that there are more immediate matters to deal with: Jim is standing beside the front door staring at Malc. Malc is guarding the doorway and staring at Jim.

'Come on, Jim,' I say as I get nearer. 'This isn't going to achieve anything.'

He turns to face me. I can smell the stale beer and tobacco, the sweat from unchanged clothes.

'Fuck off. It's your fault I can't see my kids.'

I face him. 'Do you want them to see you like this?'

He staggers backward and raises his arms. 'Like what? Like fucking what, you stuck-up bitch.'

He's pointing at me and then suddenly he does the comedy 'watching' signal. Two fingers on his eyes then towards me. I face him. I move closer.

'It's you, isn't it?'

He steps back. A wide grin emerges, speed teeth and whisky-chaser breath. I can feel Malc behind me. Jimmy opens his arms in an exaggerated shrug and stares at me?

'What?'

I lunge forwards but Malc catches me and guides me through the front door, my pulse racing. Janice is waiting. She looks worried even though the scene behind her is children playing computer games and the women chatting with coffee.

'He's been there an hour. Shouting. This is escalating and Malc can't be there all the time.'

I think. I wanted to field Sally away, get her settled without a scene. But it looks like that isn't going to happen.

'I'll call the cops.'

But as I say it I hear a crash and a rock hits the mesh outside the window. Unable to make any headway on the door, Jim's throwing stones and, as I watch, he finds a thick piece of wood and starts to batter the window. Malc doesn't know whether to leave the door unguarded and stop him or not. Janice is dialling. I look around. Sally has herded the kids into the children's room and levered a chair against the door, effectively locking them in. The other women stand around the main room, unsure what is happening, but I know. I know exactly what she is about to do.

Before I can reach her she has unlocked the bolt on the front door and she is outside. She is standing in from of Jim, screaming at him.

'Come on then. Come on. This is what you want. Finish it, big man.'

He stands in front of her, holding the piece of wood like a bat, aimed at her head. Malc cannot get to him in time to stop him if he swings. He shouts at us.

'See. See what I have to put up with. Crazy fucking bitch.'

Sally is crying.

'You said you were going to kill me. You said that. Even if I am crazy, which I'm not, I don't deserve that. But I don't have a choice, do I, cos you won't leave me alone. So go on then. Do it.'

I see the police car pull up and two officers get out and come up behind Jim. He sees them and raises the wood.

'You took my kids away.'

She nods. 'Yeah, I did. Because they're scared of you. You took all my money. You never saw them, always in the pub. So now you want to see them? And this is the right way to go about it, is it? For once, Jimmy, you can't have it all your own way. You can't bully me and frighten me. So do your worst.'

I see a flicker of regret cross his face.

'What happened, Sal? How's it got to this?'

She looks like she is going to cry, but faces him off.

'You. You did this, Jimmy. You bullied me and made me scared to leave my own house. You made me lose my job and we might both lose the kids. All because you wanted to go to the pub. Cos you wanted to shag other women. You've ruined all our lives.' She finally breaks down, but still stands there. 'So come on, big man. Do it.'

I see him raise the wood further and Malc reacts a fraction and then the policeman behind Jim grabs Jim's arm. There's a scuffle but Sally stands frozen to the spot, her hands covering her mouth. The police lead Jimmy away and she shouts after him. 'I want to make a complaint. I want him charged. I'll go to court.' They bundle him into a police car and I can see she still wants to help him, she is still trying to care for this man who has taken everything from her. As they drive him away and another police car arrives to deal with the aftermath, she turns to us, shaking. 'I'm not scared of him now.'

I hug her and Janice goes inside to make sure the children, who will have been oblivious to this but, unsupervised, are all right. This time Sally is not sobbing. She hugs me back and I can feel from her stance that now this is on her terms. She draws away and wipes her eyes.

'I don't know what took me so long.'

I take her inside. She hugs her children and I know what I have to do now. I go over to Janice.

'Taking an early lunch. Now that's out of the way.'

She smiles.

'Bloody hell. I wasn't sure which way it would go.'

'Me neither. He'll be bailed but I don't think he'll be back. Unless he comes to Perps.'

I need to face this. I need to go and tell Carole that my situation has escalated. Just like Sally's situation, this has dragged on and on and I need to hand it over. I don't care if I have no ID. I'm going to insist. I wait at the bus stop and watch as the policewoman who will take Sally's statement arrives. I go over the details of what I will say in my head. Danny texts me, a short interlude in my worry.

Morning, love. Two weeks to go. Every day is a day closer. I love you xxx always xxx

I deliberate about telling him what I am about to do, telling him what has happened. But I know that it will be better if I can keep this to myself, just report it. Hand it over to someone who can deal with it.

I don't text him back. I just get on the bus and watch the backstreets of Manchester turn into the modern new builds of Central Park and the police station. I've been here many times before with women who are finally making statements or answering bail themselves because sometimes they are implicated in crimes that are associated with their partners. Even if they have been forced to cover up for someone, in the eyes of the law they are still complicit, which makes their torment twice as bad: a criminal record for something that they were forced to take part in.

I swing through the double doors and sit in the foyer waiting my turn at the front desk. My phone pings. Of course it does. In the back of my mind I already know it will be him. I know he is watching. I go up to the desk and stand at the end, with my back to the window, so he will think I am talking to the desk sergeant. Instead, I am breathing deeply to stop my insides shaking, the fear building inside again.

I have to open the message. I have to know what it says before I reach Carole. A man and a woman are arguing with the desk sergeant over access to their friend who is in a cell. With shaking hands, I tap the phone buttons.

I'M WATCHING YOU. YOU WILL PAY FOR WHAT YOU DID.

I flick up the screen to the accompanying picture. It's a video. It's me and my children leaving my home this morning. I mentally check my actions. I am sure that I checked for any unusual cars or people. Is this someone I know? I spin around but there is no red car. I leave the police station and I hurry along the road back to the bus stop. My children. He's watching my children.

I'm so preoccupied that I don't sense someone behind me, someone following me, until it is too late. I don't hear the footsteps, quicker in a split second, until I am walking in the space between the terraced houses, the scrubland where a mill used to be, where buddleia is growing wild between the self-seeded saplings make an enclosed space.

I hurry up, telling myself now that this is nothing, that it's just someone late for work hurrying behind me. I half run but he is behind me, his hand over my mouth. Leather gloves. His grip is tight. I struggle, pulling away, my scream muffled by his hand firmly over my face. He's tall. All I can think is that this isn't Jim. It can't be. Jim wouldn't wear leather gloves. And his shoes: black, shiny shoes. It all happens in a split second, and then my instinct kicks in. I'm looking at his shoes because I need to locate his foot. As he drags me towards the trees I resist and I stamp on his foot. His grip softens and this is my chance. I elbow him and suddenly he lets go.

I do not turn around to see where he has gone, because I know he ran into the trees. I heard the snap of the branches, loud in my danger-sensitive ears. Instead, I run and run. I can still smell the leather and taste my fear. Eventually I stop. This is it. He is watching me. He is taking photographs of me. And now he is trying to hurt me. That uncertainty has gone. I shudder. My lungs hurt. I slow down and walk the rest of the way – all I can think of is SafeMe and safety. I bend over to recover and try to calm myself. What was he going to do? Where was he taking me? And what for? My God.

I head for a bus stop and sit down in the shelter, so I can think about what to do next. I can feel my body tense, the anxiety shifting gear.

Pay for what I did. Who would go to these lengths? It seems risky for someone who already has form in violence against women to do this. My mind slips over the edge of the current vista of angry men and scans wider possibilities.

There is suddenly a sinking feeling in the pit of my stomach. *Pay for what I did*. I didn't tell anyone. I never told anyone what happened to Alice. What he did. The leather gloves. And Alice getting into his car. Then she was gone. The questions.

I panic. I feel my breath quick and fast. It was all so long ago. And I kept my word. I never told anyone what he did. I text him. Even this feels strange. Personal, now. Yet it can't be. Can it? He is buried deep in my memory. But it suddenly strikes me that he is capable of this. My hands are shaking as I text.

WHY ARE YOU DOING THIS?

I stare hard at the vista and think of Sally. She faced Jim, risking everything. But he's got me. My children are in that picture. My children are everything to me and he obviously knows it. My phone pings again.

WHY NOT?

I'm cornered. I can't risk telling Carole now because whoever this is knows where I live. He knows where my children live. He's got me. And if it is who I think it could be, I already know how dangerous he is. I'm more fucked than I thought I was. I need to think.

I go back to work and do as much as I can in this state of mind, telling Janice that I am doing admin as I watch the clock creep towards five. Then I go home and chat to Donelle, who tells me she is thinking of getting her own place. That she's asking her guy to move in but he's saying it's too early. Why doesn't she stay with him, at his place? I smile on the surface but inside an invisible hand is twisting my gut and I am shaking.

There is never really a time when I ask myself why he is doing this. Because I know what people are capable of and sometimes there is no reason. Sometimes it is pure badness; most times it is complete self-interest. Going to such lengths to have other people live life the way they think it should be lived. To curtail someone else's freedom and to manipulate them into a position where they have no choice but to comply. This is what he is doing to me.

I can't decide if my new suspicions about this – that it is someone from long, long ago – are real or just a figment of my fear-induced paranoia. I thought it was over. I thought those horrible events would never crop up again. Maybe I am wrong, but I have a niggling feeling. *Pay for what you did.* But I didn't do anything. And I never told anyone. I never told anyone it was him who took my best friend. And more.

Tanya

Diary Entry: Wednesday

I am off work again. But Al has gone to work at the normal time. Last night he came home at the usual time too. Despite the fact that I could hardly move, he expected me to make dinner and we ate it in silence.

I could feel his eyes on me. At one time I would have thought he was concerned, even sorry. He used to cry and apologise and beg for forgiveness. He would claim that he was drunk and didn't know what he was doing. I was caught up in it and I still am most of the time.

But I have this clarity. I don't know if it's the diary or another episode of my madness. Am I really going crazy? I know what will happen. Once, years ago, we had what I thought then was an argument and I just walked out of the house. He'd told me I couldn't watch TV any more. That it was making me into a slut. I was young and stupid and I was striding down the road.

When I heard him behind me I even smiled a little. He didn't want me to go. He loved me. He wanted me back. He caught my arm and he looked at me. His face was gentle and he held me tight. I held him back.

'Come back,' he murmured in to my ear. *Everyone argues*, I reasoned with myself in that moment. *He does love me.* He held out his hand and we walked back to the house. Once inside, he kissed me and hugged me and I thought that we were going upstairs to make love. But he guided me to the spare room – my room now. We went in and he shut the door behind him.

That was the first time. He pinned me against the wall by my throat and hissed in my ear, 'Think you're clever? Eh?'

I struggled, of course, but he's strong. I managed to kick his shin and he was hopping in the spot, still holding me.

'You fucking bitch. You'll pay for that.'

He kicked me back. I felt the contact then a sharp pain. I screamed.

'You've broken my leg.'

He laughed.

'Try that again and I'll break both your legs. You're going nowhere.'

I screamed more. I was screaming, 'Help me.' But he had his hand over my mouth and was unbuckling his belt. No one came to help me. No one could hear me.

My leg wasn't broken, but there was a huge black bruise that took weeks to fade. Before it did there were more incidents, more arguing. The more I annoyed him, the more he kicked me and punched me. Then he would plead for forgiveness. He would cry and hug me and tell me that we would have a child, a son. That we would be married.

So now I am risking everything. It's that or live like this for ever. I sent that letter. I have no way of knowing if anything will happen over that, but I don't regret it. Someone should know what he is like. I have no idea how this will play out. I know full well that he could snap at any moment and the best thing would be to keep quiet until I see a way out.

But I can't endure one more night like the other one. I've tried to see it as 'role play', as Al described it to me the first time. 'Harmless fun'. The girls in the videos look like they are enjoying themselves. Sometimes. But I'm hurt. And it gets worse every time.

I have to do something. I know I keep saying it, but it's finding the right moment when the blinds are up and he is in the shower. When he has become complacent. But I must not become complacent myself.

I can hear him downstairs now. The shutters are rolling up and light floods into my bedroom. I listen, frozen to the spot. He is in the kitchen, running the tap. Filling the kettle. He is early. He will have seen that I haven't even washed the breakfast dishes yet and that the washing machine is full of dirty clothes. He is at the bottom of the stairs.

I have to stop writing now and hide the diary. I am so scared.

Chapter Seventeen

Day 13

> Day 13, babe. Less than two weeks then we can lie in bed
> eating toast and drinking tea ☺ I love you x always x

Danny's text comes mid-morning. The morning routine went without a hitch, despite my mind being entirely elsewhere. I had lain awake most of the night, wishing Danny was getting into bed and spooning me, his breath gentle as he fell into a deep sleep. We are one day closer to our goal and I should be deliriously happy that he's doing this for us. Instead, I am seething.

I fume. Scared as am, I cannot just leave this alone. If Sally can stand up to Jim, I can do this.

I write it down in my diary and mentally run through the police response if I report it now. There is no law against sitting in your car on the street. He grabbed me, but I have no witnesses and I have no idea who 'he' is. Just like Carole said, the most they would do is go and have a word with him. He would show them the texts and say I'd been texting him, it was a misunderstanding. Just a bit of fun. Sure, he would leave me alone now.

Fuck. I flick back through the diary where I have written detailed notes and think about my mother's *she's got a good imagination* line which she constantly chided me with as a child and wonder what he can really do? All he is good for is standing in the shadows and creeping around at the back of pubs. Sending texts and pictures. But the kids. He's taken photographs of my children.

I have to go round to the accommodation to collect some worksheets from the warden and I pull on my coat, hands shaking. I slam the office door and set off, head held high, just in case he is somewhere watching, taking time to stop and talk to Malc.

'Jim not been back, then?'

I know he hasn't but I need to make myself visible. Show I'm not fazed by him. Watching.

'Nah. He's been bailed. Reckon he's gone home. Close call, though.'

I shake my head. 'We knew it was coming. Good for Sally.'

I am smiley and animated when all I feel like inside is, *Fuck you*. I know he is watching. I can feel him on the edge of my consciousness. Malc nods but he doesn't smile.

'Yeah, good for her. As long as he doesn't turn really nasty.'

In the normal turn of life what happened yesterday would have been nasty enough. But we both know if Jim had wanted to hurt Sally, right there and then, he would have done. Next time it could be much worse. We know Jim was bailed and told to go back to Gloucester. To the family home. He was told that Sally was being rehoused in Manchester. That she was seeking an injunction. But we have no way of knowing if he was listening.

Just like I have no way of knowing if my stalker will turn into a violent psychopath instead of just keeping it mostly psychological. Just. As if that wasn't enough, there's the constant pressure. I laugh at the thought and keep my chin up as I walk up the road, past the pub and Jim's empty seat in the window. I cross over like I've not got a care in the world and walk around the bend towards the warden's flat. I ring the bell and wait, looking up the road. Looking for him. Finally, the shift warden, Carla Groves, opens up and I go in. I stand by the window and wait for her to fetch the paperwork, all the time looking for him looking at me.

'Here it is.' She breezes in and I turn to smile at her, but then I see it. A huge wide-screen TV in the adjoining room. She follows my stunned gaze. These flats are sparsely furnished from second-hand donations and the TV looks entirely out of place, almost filling the whole length of a wall. 'Oh, that. Yeah. All the flats got one. Arrived this morning. Early on.'

I fume. It's obvious what this is.

'So who let them in? You?'

She shakes her head. 'No, Sheila. She was waiting with the key. She told me you knew about it.'

Frank. I remember his parting comment: *I could completely refurb this place.* The Xboxes. Huge TVs for everyone. He just doesn't fucking get it, does he?

'Well, you should have checked. Did you sign for them?'

She looks sheepish.

'There was no signature. Just these blokes who brought them in from a van. Four of them. All the ladies seemed very pleased. With the TVs. And they all had a cup of tea with the blokes who brought them.'

I roll back the CCTV and watch as the women come out and stand watching as four burly guys wheel the TVs in. Frank isn't there, which is a relief, but I see Sheila in a slightly different light as she directs the proceedings, the guys deferring to her. She is in charge, and, just for a second, I wonder if she has ordered the TVs. She must have money because she pays her own rent. Unlike the other women here she is self-funded and not on benefits. And for another second, as she slips the guys tips in the form of ten-pound notes with the same movement as him, the line between her and Frank is blurred.

They all go inside. I fast forward to see the guys emerge with Sheila, chatting to her and pointing at the van. The van pulls away and she lights a cigarette, watching it as it goes down the road. But my attention is drawn to the space where the van had been. I backtrack the footage to just before the van arrived at 7.35 and it wasn't there then. I go back to eight-fifteen, when the van leaves, and there is the red Skoda. Empty. I watch, panicky, thinking now that I have completely got the wrong end of the stick and that this isn't his car at all. That I have imagined it and I am going mad. Then I remember the car outside the gate at SafeMe. The registration is the same. My blood runs cold. This isn't an opportunist at work. This is more than some messages. If his car is parked outside my work, where is he? This is more than a disgruntled ex. An angry perp. He is planning something. He is calculated. But he is also taking chances, grabbing at me in broad daylight.

This is someone unhinged. Something shifts deep inside me, a memory of a time when I felt this way before. When I knew what was happening really, and I failed to act. Look what happened then. Look what happened to Alice. And to me. I always put that bit to one side, because compared to Alice and all the newspaper reports and scandal, it was nothing. But it's a kind of deep instinct, a knowledge that something is bad.

I feel sick to my stomach. Like so many times time before, usually in that mellow space between sleep and awake, I'm back on that narrow path. The moorland where we would run, arms outstretched. The path up to the pond where Alice and I used to splash around as kids, where we sunbathed as teenagers. I am hormonal angry and pathetically naive. In a car with my best friend's boyfriend. He came between us. I would show him. I would save her. But I didn't. I couldn't. Not after what he did to me.

I usually wake up screaming. But now I simply add him to the long list of terror. It sinks slowly into the thick soup of my fear and dread across the years. It couldn't be him, could it? After all this time.

Tanya

I'd gone downstairs to pre-empt the problem.

'I'm still ill.'

He had stared at me.

'Right.'

I moved towards the sink to start the dishes but he stood in my way.

'What have you been doing all day?'

I stared at the floor.

'Sleeping. I don't feel right, Alan. I think I need to go to the doctor's.'

He was nodding. I thought for a minute he was going to get his car keys and take me. Instead he just stood aside. I ran the hot tap, squirted the washing-up liquid. Went through my usual routine of fantasising over finding something heavy enough to hit him over the head with. Planning my escape.

He went upstairs. I stood very still and listened. If he went into my bedroom and searched it and found this diary … No. He went into his room. The TV was on loud and I could hear a voice but not the words. I washed the dishes and reluctantly started the washing machine – that meant I could not listen for footsteps behind me. I prefer it very quiet.

Half an hour later he came down with an arm full of clothes on coat hangers. He laid them on the table and went back upstairs. More clothes. Then a suitcase. I could feel him behind me.

'I'm going on a conference. I've told Jeff Simister you'll not be in this week.'

I relaxed a little. A conference! This is both good and bad. Good because I will be alone and not afraid. Bad because I can't go to work. Or outside. There is no point asking. It will just mean trouble.

He packed the bag and left it by the door. I had expected him to go there and then. But he was in his study all night. I could hear his TV and his chair creaking as he shifted around. He didn't go to bed. He left this morning without the suitcase.

When he had been gone about an hour, I opened it and looked inside. I counted the shirts. There were enough clothes for about three days. He'd packed a bag of toiletries and I opened it and sniffed the musky shower gel. I went to the sink and squirted it down, leaving a tiny bit in the bottom. It is little things like this that make me feel more in control. Then I saw the condoms. A pack of ten, squashed down in the bottom of the bag.

I took the pack and, with shaking hands, opened it. I counted them and there were eight. I carefully placed them back in the bag and zipped up the case. Then I went upstairs and checked the bathroom cabinet. The condoms he used with me were still there. A pack of ten. With two left, like before.

So he was definitely sleeping with someone. This was no business trip. He was going away with her. I burst into tears. I should be pleased. I should be celebrating that he is going off with someone else because then I will be free. But I still have a sliver of self-respect. I still get upset when he is lying to me. I still get upset when he stays out all night.

I have tried my hardest to control it, God knows I have had enough time on my own to analyse it. I know, deep down, even through periods when I try to defend him in my own mind, that I don't deserve this. And I am suddenly pleased. All the manipulation, control and violence has not worked. He hasn't broken my spirit.

Chapter Eighteen

Day 12

I have no choice. Even though the footage of the car outside the accommodation block has completely shaken me, I have to carry on as normal. It set me on yet another trajectory of wondering if I should report it, but after almost an hour of weighing it up when I should have been working, I wrote it in my diary. He's playing a game of cat-and-mouse with me. It's almost as if he wants me to call the police so he can laugh at me.

Even so, yesterday I made sure that Malc knew to keep the gates shut and locked at all times and not to let anyone in without asking me or Janice. But I carried on, making the kids tea. I did not want to leave them but I am damned if I am keeping them off school. Damned if I am sitting trapped in our flat all day. They are edge-to-edge safe. I laughed and chatted with Donelle when she came home later with a takeaway. She asked me if anything else had happened with the stalker and inside I was screaming, *Yes, Donelle, yes; he won't leave me alone.* But I shook my head and hugged her. What would I say? *I saw him outside my work? He was in the pub the other night? He tried to abduct me?*

It sounds mad, even when I practise telling Donelle and Janice everything in my head, as if I'm making something of nothing. I know this is exactly what happened back then, when I sat in the newly refreshed lounge with my mum and dad and they quizzed me about Alice. Why had we fallen out? Was he my boyfriend? Had I had 'relations' with him? They actually said 'relations'. I knew that she had gone with him. That she was obsessed with him. I knew everything about her because we were like sisters. But they wouldn't listen. I even tried to tell them what had happened to me, but all they wanted to know about was her.

I know deep down that this is why I am working at SafeMe. I became what I am that day: someone who stands in the background, behind all the drama, managing it for other people. And, when it happens to me, I push it deep down with my memories of beautiful Alice and our friendship. Now, as I sit on the wall outside Sheila's, Danny texts me.

> Hey, babe. Fri-yay! Day 12. We're doing it. Not long left now x I love you x always x

I type a reply. I don't trust my words to not convey how scared I am inside, so I just type:

'XXX'.

I'm staring at my phone, willing him to send something back, a heart or a smile, when Sheila appears beside me. She's already defiant and feisty; she knows that I know about the TVs.

'All right, Ria. Coming in or just lookin' like it?'

She's already walking back to the flats and I watch her, stomping up the pathway. She's wearing gold open-toe sandals, black leggings and a gold shiny top. Her eyes are lined with black kohl, making the whites of her eyes look even more yellow. I follow her.

The usual aroma of her flat, tobacco mixed with Estée Lauder Youth Dew, has a faint tinge of brandy. I glance towards her bedroom and see a sequined dress flung over the back of a chair. Sheila is smoking still, the corners of her mouth sticky with spit, her breathing heavy. She throws a newspaper at me. It's the early edition of the *Chronicle*.

'Thought I'd show you this before you see it anyway.'

The paper is folded at an article headed 'Manchester win for bantam-weight belt'. Underneath are several photos of celebs going into the arena. One of them features Frank and Sheila with the caption 'Ex-mayor Frank James and his wife show up for pre-match gala'. Shelia is watching me carefully. Sheila in the picture looks glamorous and is smiling widely. Her arm is linked inside Frank's and he has his hand over hers. I look at her.

'Was it good, then?'

She snorts. 'Yeah. Course it was. People hitting each other in the face is always a bloody treat.'

I'm annoyed and she knows it. Not just about this, but also about the TVs and her not telling me.

'So why go?'

She blows smoke at me as she speaks.

'No law against it, is there? I mean, not in prison, are we?'

I see a wall go up. Not that it's ever really come down with Sheila. But she is right. There is no law against any of the women going out. Socially. In fact, they go out most Friday nights, taking turns to babysit the children. When we explain that they are free to come and go as they please, people are shocked. It's as if they think SafeMe is a kind of institution, where these women who have been abused should be grateful and stay inside, looking after their children and doing crafts.

But this is pure bollocks and the opposite of what it really is. The women here have done nothing wrong and are not having their freedom curtailed. They have already been in a kind of prison, physical, psychologically or both.

'Nope. You're not in prison, Sheila.'

She flicks her ash.

'Frank's lads came and said he wanted me to go. The other day. He said that it wouldn't do any harm. Sent me some of my clothes over.' She points to the bedroom where I see a black suitcase leaning against the wall, one that I haven't seen here before. 'All the nice stuff. Said he wanted to take me out.' She stares at me, her eyes dark now. 'Court me.'

I nod. Of course he does. *Start again. Like it was. When we first met. Dating. Courting.*

'And how do you feel about that?'

She sighs. 'He sent a car for me. Just like that first night when he changed it from paying me to taking me out. Just like that. Black limo, Frank's style. Little present on the back seat.' She flashes her non-smoking hand and I see a diamond ring on her little finger. A new one. 'Real, that is.'

I nod. She's holding out her hand and it shakes slightly.

'Look, Sheila. It's up to you what you do. I just want you to be safe.'

'When we got there, he was waiting in the car in front round the corner. I saw him get out and then get in with me. The windows in them cars, they're blacked out, you know.' She drops her diamond-studded hand into her lap and stubs out her cigarette. I see a tear drop.

'Oh, Shelia, love. What did he do to you?' I scan her for injuries, but apart from the cast on her arm, which is partially covered by a gold lamé scarf, I can see none. But that doesn't mean that there aren't any. 'Has he hurt you?' I go to hug her but she leans backwards, more agitated now.

'I saw her. She was in the car. In the back.' She picks up the newspaper and points to a young blonde woman walking two people behind her and Frank, head slightly turned. She looks confident, taller than Sheila and perfectly coiffed. I can see, even from the black-and-white newspaper picture that she is wearing Christian Louboutin high heels, and her short skirt is expensive designer-wear. Her right hand is raised to brush her bleached-blonde hair out of her face and she is wearing a simple tennis bracelet that has caught the camera flash. She appears to be about twenty-five. I touch Shelia's arm, but she is up, rooting in boxes and pulling out folders of photographs. Eventually she finds what she is looking for and sits down. She pulls out a photograph which is sepia with age, corners folded.

'See. Look at me there.' It is almost a replica of the newspaper photograph, Frank and his entourage entering an event. He clearly has a set piece, where he leads, his woman beside him, his right-hand man just behind, then his ranks filtering behind him. Sheila points at herself.

'Look. What you have to understand is that he will have told everyone exactly how he wants this to look. Everyone in these pictures will have received strict instructions, and sometimes the clothes to make the right impression. It's very important to Frank that everything looks right.' I picture him last week in the perps meeting, his golf swing and the cufflinks. Sheila's jaw is set. 'Yeah. He bought me that dress and shoes. I had to wear them, exactly those. And that bracelet.' I study the picture. A tennis bracelet.

'But I don't understand. Why would he ...?'

She is crying now. Her face crumbles and her eyeliner makes rivulets down her over-tanned skin.

'I knew. He thought he could keep it from me, but I always

bloody knew. I even asked him, plenty of times, but he just said, "Don't be bloody stupid, woman."'

She throws the newspaper at me and its pages flutter through the air, landing all over the sofa.

'That's the bloody problem. What he didn't say. Me and Frank have never had a proper relationship. It's always been what he wants. If I couldn't give it to him, he'd go and get it elsewhere. And that's what's happened here. He's gone and fucking got it somewhere else. And of all the things he could have got me to go to, he wanted me at this one. I knew when the car drew up and I saw her in his car.' She wipes underneath her eyes, a practised motion that removes most of the mascara and eyeliner, and wipes it on her leggings. 'He kissed her on the cheek and got out.'

She takes another photo. Frank kissing the cheek she offered to him.

'I'm so sorry, Sheila. It must be awful for you. Is this the first time he's done this?'

She suddenly stops sobbing.

'Done what?'

I'm confused. She's just shown me Frank's mistress, his twenty-odd-year-old mistress who he brought on this supposed date with his estranged wife.

'Well, this woman ...'

She starts to laugh, a snotty bellow, right from her lungs, mixed with her black tears.

'No. No, no, no. Well, granted, that would be fucking bad enough. But this is worse, love. Much worse. That's no high-class hooker, or even his girlfriend, love. Nah. There's been loads of 'em, but I've had to turn a blind eye. No.'

She laughs long and hard.

'No, this time he's took it further. He's proper rubbed my stupid little nose in it. Not that I had a bloody choice, and he knows it. But he picked his moment. Gives me a diamond. Sends a car. Has me believing that all this can be fucking bearable because how much worse could it get. Eh? How much worse?'

She's pulling photographs out of the folder, her face scarlet, and she's ripping them up. The fragments cover the floor around her, fingers working quickly. She grabs another handful of photographs and begins to tear, but the bundle is too thick and it will not shred in her hands. She throws them to the floor.

'See? I can't even do this. I can't even rip up a few photos.' She lights a cigarette with shaking hands and the smoke drifts into her back-combed hair. 'I can't keep a baby inside me.'

I start to pick up the tiny shreds of photos and pile them into a carrier bag.

'Come on, Sheila, love. The fact that we're sat here talking, in this flat, shows that you can do something. You got away. This is just a blip. You knew there would be bad days.'

She nods and wipes mascara tears across her face.

'Not this bad. Not this fucking bad. But I'm not surprised. Not really.'

I put my hand over hers.

'So now you know what to expect. You know if he asks you again. You don't have to go, you know.'

She smiles a little. 'Yeah. But he has his ways and means. I did it for this lot. And you, lovely.'

'Oh. For who, Shelia?'

'Well, he said he'd promised to do a refurb, like, you know, to help.' She says 'help' in the most sarcastic way possible and I know then that she knows it is all just a game to Frank. 'So he said if I went to the boxing with him he'd get a wide-screen TV for every flat. It's all some of 'em have got here, TV, Netflix and that, so ...'

Unbelievable. He's blackmailed her.

'But he didn't promise anything. I never agreed. He turned up with some Xboxes for the kids and Janice took them, but no plans were made. I wouldn't let him, anyway.'

She laughs and mimics me. '*Wouldn't let him*. Funny. You don't let Frank, love. Oh no. He'll just do it and bugger the consequences. If he wants to send everyone a gift of a TV, then he will. But he said if I didn't go with him, you know, take up his little "first date" offer, then he wouldn't. And he'd make things difficult for you. I told you, love. He'll stop at nothing.'

I straighten now. It's hard to see how he could make things more difficult than they are right now, but Janice and I always say, *Just when you think you've seen everything*, so I pay attention. Maybe he was going the extra mile already.

'But you did. And the TVs arrived. I didn't agree. And you should have asked, Sheila. I don't want stolen goods here.'

She laughs. 'Oh, lovely. They're not stolen! Frankie would have bought them fair and square for something like this. Loves to pay cash, he does. A good way to get rid of it, this sort of thing.'

She picks a few sepia strands from down her armchair. 'No. He knew what he was doing all right. He can't get to me here. No arm twisting or pinching or scaring here. So he thought he'd do it another way.'

She's looking at the newspaper now, staring at the woman in the picture. I look upside down, Frank his usual collected self, no sign of cufflink jangling here, where he is king of all he surveys. She turns the paper round again and shows me the picture.'

'You see, he's kept her hidden. Not been to owt like this before.

But I've been told. A few meals out, been seen at the Trafford Centre. But in the same car. That's my place, that is. But not any more.'

She's tearing up again. I try to reason with her.

'The thing is, Sheila love, you and Frank are split up. I know you were there last night and, yes, that is a dirty trick. But you might meet someone else as well.'

She laughs again, guttural and deep. She leans forwards, a sneer on her lips.

'Bloody hell, love. You are dense, aren't you? That's not his bloody girlfriend. It's his daughter.' She shoves the paper at me. 'And her, in the background. That's her mother.' I squint at a small woman, younger than Sheila, dressed in a long black gown, two people behind her daughter. 'All Frank's women. All together. Bloody hell.'

I hug Sheila now as she cries hard. I know how hurt she was over Bobby and how she, and, I thought, Frank believed that it was at the bottom of their marriage problems. But this. Frank has punished her for all that he feels she has done. For leaving. For not returning. For telling me about Bobby. He has dealt a blow that will last for ever, striking over and over again at Sheila's soul.

I look around at the flat, in even more disarray than when I arrived. Sheila is at rock bottom, and I know that this is the time when many women just give up and return to their old lives. I rub her shoulders as she sobs into my chest, desperately trying to think of a remedy to this solution. But Frank has it sewn up. It's all out in the open now, his daughter and his mistress out with his wife. It's laid out in the newspaper for all to see. The ultimate betrayal. Sheila stops sobbing a little.

'All for a couple of tellys.'

She is deliberately missing the point. The TVs were a small

enticement, a signal that Frank had control. Even here. She would have gone anyway, desperate to recapture whatever fucked-up origins their relationship had. But now she is desolate and there is no comforting her. I look around the flat.

'Yeah. But where's yours, Sheila? Where's your TV?'

She snorts. 'What do I need one for now?'

Tanya

I am writing this now in case something happens to me. I have this feeling a lot, mainly on Friday as I leave my desk and wonder if I will ever see it again.

I did the unthinkable. He didn't come home on Thursday night. He came back for the suitcase today, at teatime. I hadn't made tea but it didn't matter because it didn't look like he was staying. He came in with another, larger suitcase and opened it on the table. Then he went upstairs and brought down more clothes. A suit, some casual clothes. Three pairs of shoes. Socks.

Then he went into his study and brought out some papers. He placed them and a laptop in the suitcase. I sat at the kitchen table and watched him.

'How long will you be away, then?'

He stopped and stared ahead.

'Why?'

I could feel it bubbling up inside me, a cauldron of hate. I tried to keep it inside but I couldn't. It slipped out like treacle, thick and soft but more than I intended.

'It's her, isn't it? You're going with her?'

He turned to face me.

'For fuck's sakes. Have you learned nothing?' He stepped towards me. I got up and pressed against the sink. 'Shut. Your. Fucking. Stupid. Mouth.'

I was shaking. But there was no way I could stop the tirade.

'You never stopped sleeping with her, did you? That's why—'

But he grabbed me. He grabbed me by the throat and he bent me backwards over the sink.

'You think you're so clever, don't you? You think you know everything. But you don't even know what happened back then.'

He let me go, but I was glued to the spot, my legs like jelly. He went on, pacing around the kitchen.

'She never chased me. She was never interested in me. She was fucking snooping; trying to find something she could use to get you back.'

I interrupted. Not something I would normally do but this was new.

'But you said you slept with her…'

'Fucked her. Yeah.' He moved closer to me again. I turned my head but I could feel his breath on my cheek. 'I did fuck her.' He grabbed my chin and pulled my face towards him. 'I raped her.'

I felt my face flush and bile rise in my throat. He was smiling. Smiling widely.

'Up at the rocks. I needed to make sure that she would never say anything about us going away. And she didn't.' He pressed himself against me. 'And now …'

He let me go and I sank to the floor, my knees too weak to support me. He walked over to the large suitcase and slammed it shut.

'So are you going to her now?'

I heard the words come out but it didn't sound like me. Not the strong voice in my head that was driving this madness. He snorted.

'Have you not been fucking listening, Alice? She's was nothing. But you. You're already gone. Invisible. They've been looking for your body since the day we went. So no one is going to come looking for you.'

He picked up his car keys up and I ran at him. Full force.

'You can't do this. You can't hurt her…'

He punched me and knocked me on to the floor, then crouched over me, holding my arms.

'That's where you're wrong. I can do anything I want to. Anything. I'll say one thing for her, she's a trier, not a fucked-up mess like you.'

I stared at him. If this was going to be my last breath, I would make it good.

'You did this to me. You. You're a violent rapist. I hate you.'

He stared down at me for a long few seconds then he jumped up, took the suitcases and was gone. I lay there, the sun on my face through the window. She hadn't gone after him. She hadn't tried to steal him from me. I'd hated her all this time for nothing. He hadn't been with her. But he would have been with someone …

I touched my face. It was swollen and sore where he had punched me with his full force. I could feel my ear swelling. My mind raced over the pointless, childish, petty scenarios as it avoided the real issue. The room was becoming darker and darker as the shutters closed.

Chapter Nineteen

Day 11

After Sheila's revelation yesterday, and the aftermath of her deep sadness, I felt reluctant to leave her. But I had to rush home. I finished the day tucking my children safely in their beds and kissing them hard on their foreheads. Donelle had picked them up from school, feeding them fast food and sugary drinks then chasing them up and down the road, until I caught her checking her phone.

'OK?'

Her sad eyes are enough.

'He didn't call.' I hug her. She looks bereft. Like me, she's putting on a brave face, doing everything she should. But inside she is tortured. 'What's wrong with me, Ri?'

I held her closer.

'Nothing. It's his problem, not yours. I'm here, Don, anytime. I mean it.'

But she doesn't take me up on it. She stares at her phone, waiting for the ringtone, the name. His name. It doesn't come and she leaves looking completely dejected.

When I wake at 9 a.m., Jennifer is standing beside me, looking very intense, with a bowl of cornflakes in one hand and a bottle of Diet Coke in the other.

'Mummy, are we going to see Grandma today?'

I nod and relieve her of her load. I see the time and quickly check my messages. I'd asked Janice to make sure Sheila was checked more often, I'm deep-down worried about her. But there are no alerts. I consider phoning her, but it's Saturday and I need to be with my children.

'Yes, yes we are. Unless ...'

'So has Grandma got a husband?'

She's trying a different way around. My two are obsessed with family, with relationships. It's fairly easy at Danny's end, with Danny and Donelle being obvious siblings, just like Simon and Jennifer. Vi and Danny Snr rubbing long side by side, just like me and Danny. But Mum ... I can understand the mystery. In their life suddenly, just for a couple of hours, then gone. No context for her, not even me. But I'm not going to lie to my children. Not because of my dad's small-minded prejudice.

'Yeah. My dad.'

She makes an O with her mouth.

'Your daddy? Like Daddy?'

I laugh. No. Not like Danny at all. Unless, when they went into that little Dorma bungalow at night, they suddenly collapsed into a giggling heap of familiarity. Their relationship was more like an agreement, sharing ideas heaped up against the world. No. Not like Danny at all.

'Yes, Jen, he is my daddy. But not so much like your daddy. Quite different.'

She picks at her nails.

'So where is he then?'

My smile fades. She wants a definitive answer. But this is all part of the innocence of children. That they don't have to understand people who take against them for nothing; they are protected against it.

'He lives with Grandma at their house.'

'But why don't you see him, if he is your daddy?'

I see the horror dawn on her, the terrible realisation that is inevitable in this conversation. That, one day, she might not see Danny. I hug her.

'Oh, sweetheart. It's not that I don't see him. It's just that he's busy. He's...'

'An astronaut? Or a giraffe keeper? Because they would be busy.'

I nod vigorously, pulling her into me. The warmth of my bed is pure tranquilliser, and we lie there for a few minutes.

'Don't worry, kiddo. Your daddy will always love you. No matter what.'

We get up and go into town. As we approach Boots I see Mum, all dolled up again. Even more this week. As I get closer, I see a streak of lipstick across her mouth. Expensive, stay-on lipstick, understated but pearly bright. She looks ten years younger. She turns to see us and Jennifer and Simon run towards her. Her worried glance at me alerts me to something not quite right.

'Hello, you two.'

Hugs are had, and I loiter around, not really knowing if there will be a repeat of last week. She would need to suggest it as I cannot afford the damage rejection from her would do right now. But she points in the general direction of the games centre.

'Coffee again?' She seems more confident this week. I nod. 'Been taking a leaf out of your book this week. I've been volunteering. Cancer Research charity shop. But I might have to do the odd Saturday so ...'

I smile. 'Great. That's OK. You know you can see them anytime. So how's Dad?'

It just slips out, like a giant wriggly snake that wound itself around us, strangling out any conversation we might have had. She is silent and we watch the kids run ahead. We reach the shop and sit, and she goes to the counter and orders exactly the same as last time, without asking. She doesn't turn to smile at me and she doesn't even smile at Jennifer when she shouts at her. Something is wrong. When she sits down with our coffee, I open my mouth to speak but she pre-empts me.

'I'm glad you asked about your father. He's been ... well, over-interested in recent goings-on.'

I almost know before she says it. Her flushed cheeks and her demure manner tell me that she is going to talk about when I was still living at home. She has a certain stance, where she becomes more upright and formal. I take the bait.

'Goings-on?'

She nods.

'Yes. All that stuff with Dougie Peters never really went away, you know. I mean, after a decent period he should have accepted what had happened and got on with his life. '

She is looking into her coffee. My anger rises.

'Well, I would certainly want to know what happened to my only child.'

She nods. 'Oh yes, of course. But some questions don't have answers, do they? I mean, you never find out why some things happened.'

I cannot tell if she is telling me or asking me. Or why. I panic.

'Mum. You know what I think—'

She interrupts in a high-pitched, louder than necessary voice. 'Which was why I was surprised when your dad said that there had been police up by that pond. You know, up that little path way over the hill.' She swallows. 'I got in yesterday and your dad wasn't there. I panicked a bit as he's always in his chair. So I walked up the road to see if he'd gone up to Tom Lovell's looking at his Triumph – he does now and again – and there he was. Him and Dougie, standing halfway up the hill, watching the police milling about up near the rocks.'

I feel like I am going to faint. My head spins and the pond comes into sharp focus. This was all part of why I left and why we are so distant. It's something I do not think about.

'There were about seven of them, a car and a van. I stood there for a bit, but they just seemed to be looking. It's not cordoned off or anything. I heard Dougie telling Martin Jackson that they were reopening the investigation. That they had a new potential lead. Looks tired, Dougie does. All thin and sunken.'

I can hardly think. The terror inside me threatens to take over but I focus on Jennifer and Simon.

'Yeah. Well. Like I said. You'd be upset too, after what he's been through. Well, some of us would. Others wouldn't be so bothered, would they?'

She looks away.

'He had his reasons.'

I nod and scrape my chair out.

'Yes. He did. But look at those two. And Danny. Fucking stupid reasons.'

I get up but she grabs my arm. Her fingers dig in and I see the fear in her eyes.

'Don't go. I wanted to ask you ...'

I sit back down. I am so tense that I feel brittle and my children's laughter as they play cuts through me.

'Oh. Right. Finally?'

She nods. 'Did you have anything to do with it? Because this is serious now.'

She says it like I am a child, like I didn't think it was serious before. I laugh too loud.

'And it wasn't then?'

She looks unsure. She looks around, at the door, at the children. She could run now, not face what she must know in her heart is true.

'But Dougie said that you were his girlfriend. That if she had gone, it was because she found out about you and him.'

I seethe. Surely she can work it out. She has all the evidence.

'I wasn't his fucking girlfriend. He ... he ...'

She looks affronted. But I am on the edge. I try to regroup. 'So why did you stay with Dad, then? He's a bigot. A racist. He's quietly bloody bullied you all your life.'

'That's different. We're married. Back then you did what your husband wanted.'

I snort. 'It wasn't the 1930s, you know. Anyway, I should thank you both. You gave me a perfect fucking example of what not to do. He was Alice's ... boyfriend. I told the truth back then. Not that anyone was fucking listening.'

I fold my arms and she looks offended. I know she hates bad language, but I can't help myself.

'Well, I hope it keeps fine for you, Ria. Because marriage isn't easy. Anyway. Did you?'

I can't believe it. I look at her now and wonder whether I should tell her about what happened that day. I want to. I want to tell her about the horror of it all. But I don't because I would just be punishing her. But I tell myself. Again. This is why I have avoided her. This is exactly it.

It was all so quick. I was reaching the pinnacle of my bravery. I marched around to Dougie's to tell him what was happening, what Alice was planning. But Dougie wasn't there and Alice was. She told me she hated me and she never wanted to see me again. She was hysterical, shouting that after everything we had gone through, best friends for ever, I had slept with her boyfriend. I was dumbstruck.

'I haven't. Alice. You have to believe me. I haven't.'

She'd screwed up her face, eyes shut, and screamed at me. 'He told me. How you'd come on to him. How you'd tempted him. How you ...'

She was crying, sobbing, and I went to hug her but she pushed me backwards. We stared at each other for a while. Then I ran. Out of her house, away from her, tears streaming.

Suddenly his Ford Fiesta was cruising beside me. He hopped out and stood in front of me. He grabbed my arm and pulled me, my strength no match for his, and before I knew it I was in his car.

He acted perfectly normally, just like he had when he used to pick me and Alice up from the disco. He drove along, telling me about his day at his job in a tyre-fitting bay and how one of his customers had kicked off. I panicked a bit when he turned to go up the lane toward the rocks, but I told myself not to be silly. *Ria's got a good imagination.* That's what dad was always saying too, agreeing with Mum. I wondered if Alice was right and he did like me?

He parked up and leaned across to me. He began to kiss me, not gently like the boys at the disco. Hard. Hissing in my ear, 'You like it rough, don't you, little girl? Don't you?'

I pushed him away.

'Don't. Don't.'

He backed off and held up his hands.

'OK. OK. Let's just walk.'

I got out of the car and he pushed me forwards. I stumbled over the heather, looking for an escape on the open ground, but he was behind me all the way. I could hear him unbuckle his belt and when I turned around he had his hand down his pants. I didn't want it to be like this. I wanted the romance and the kisses. I was scared now. Scared of what he would do. But I'd got in the car. I'd gone there willingly. I never said I didn't want to. Not until now.

We stopped at the rock and I looked into the pond. He came up behind me and cupped my breasts, squeezing. It didn't feel right at all. He had gloves on, the black leather driving gloves from his car. Then he spun me round and I could feel him against me. His hands were in my hair and I panicked and whispered in his ear. 'I know what's going on. I know what you are planning. With her.'

He stopped dead. I stepped backwards but he pulled me towards him.

'What do you mean?'

'She told me. You're running away.'

He nodded. He was just standing there, disgusting and obviously aroused.

'Are we now?'

I was crying. Sobbing lightly.

'Yeah. She tells me everything. She told me just now that you said you'd slept with me. Why would you say that?'

I started to cry harder. It was fear rather than upset. And my immature, fifteen-year-old self let it all pour out. I could have shut up. Then he would never have known and what happened next would not have scarred me for life.

He stared at me, his cold eyes all over my body. Then, quick as a flash he grabbed my hair and dragged me over to the pond.

I screamed but he pushed my head under the water. My scream went silent and turned to bubbles and I tried to breathe in. He lifted my head out. His lips were close to my ear.

'If you mention this to anyone you will pay. I will hunt you down and kill you. Understand?'

I didn't have time to answer or even nod. My head was plunged into the icy water again and all I could think about was keeping my mouth shut so the water could not get in. He lifted me out again. He lifted up my dress and pulled my pants down and he was inside me. It hurt and I screamed at him to stop but he didn't.

He pushed me on to the ground and he was on top of me, holding my shoulders as he forced my legs open. I stopped screaming and he carried on, on and on until finally it was over. His body went limp and heavy on me and he raised himself up on his arms.

'Now it's not a lie, is it? Now you have slept with me. Is that what you wanted?'

He pulled me to my feet. Again, he plunged me under. Longer this time, and I felt the world blacken, but the tug at my hair brought me back. I felt my knees buckle. And he let me sit. I gasped and he spoke into my face.

'You will not mention this to one living person. Not the police. Not Dougie. Not anyone. I mean it. Not ever. Understand?'

I sobbed and nodded.

'You will never speak to me again. Or Alice. And if you ever tell anyone what she told you, I will come after you.'

And he was gone. His car sped down the hill. I watched as he reversed at the end of the road and disappeared. It was a hot day and the stone around me was drying fast. I could not move. The shock penetrated every part of me and I shook in the blazing sunshine. I didn't know anything could hurt so much as my bruised lungs and my scalp where he had pulled out my hair.

I just went home. That was why my hair was wet and why they sent me upstairs, shouting at me for dripping on their pristine carpets. That was why my lips were sealed, from then until now. This is the first time since then I have been able to piece this together because I had to pretend it didn't happen just to carry on. Hands over ears, lalalaing my way through life with this weighing me down like a huge boulder. And even now I am terrified just thinking about it. But I do. It's here, right in front of me. But I never told anyone and Dougie thought Alice was dead.

I didn't tell. And if he did anything else he will be found out for raping me and grooming Alice. She was fifteen when they left. Fifteen. I never wanted to think about this again. I should never have got closer to Mum. But I did and life must go on.

I can feel the weight of the threat, the pain of hair bursting from my scalp. The cold, cold water as my head is pushed under. My lips pressing together to keep the icy water out and being too scared to utter a single word about this. I shake my head. I shake out any thought of ever letting go of my secret, because if any time would have been right, it would have been now. But I can't. I am Sheila, too horrified to admit what her husband has done. I am Sally, running as fast as she can and chancing her life before she reports Jim's violence. I am every woman who has passed through SafeMe. I only told a tiny fraction of the story back then, keeping the bigger part inside because it's too much for another person to bear. So, even now, I don't tell her any of it.

'I went with him because I believed in love. That kind of love where someone cares about you, has your best interests at heart. Understands what you want and helps you to get it. You know?'

She looks puzzled. Of course she doesn't know. She's been

tiptoeing around Dad, making him pies in her flowery apron as she looked out at the possibility of the Manchester horizon. The city laid bare before her, a city she could never explore or even know because Dad might want a cup of tea. We sip our coffee and suddenly it's as if the preceding conversation hasn't happened. But I need to seal it.

'So if anyone asks, that's what happened. Right? It was nothing to do with me. She left with him. He made her. Like I said back then. No one believed me and in the end I didn't believe it myself. I was fifteen, Mum. Remember? And he was fucking twenty-five. I was very different then. Soft. Quiet. But now I know the score and while I was happy enough to try to forget about everything that happened to me, if it comes up again I'll be telling the truth. About everything.' I can already see her considering how this will affect Dad, and consequently her, and not me. My temper rises again. 'I don't blame you. Or Dad. I blame the person who was responsible for this. Bloody hell. I thought this was gone.'

She nods.

'Yes. I expect you did.'

I lean forward.

'It had nothing to do with me. We were kids.'

She looks directly at me and I see her fear. I see it in her eyes. Does she know what happened? I tried to tell her at the time but in the end I just left.

'I know. But I can only speak for myself. Let's hope your dad and Dougie Peters see it that way, though.'

Dougie Peters. I shudder with the sudden memory. He always blamed me for what happened. That day I went round, after she had left, he was weird. He called the police when there was no need. She left. I tried to tell them all what happened, but they wouldn't listen. So I left too. That's when I met Danny.

I knew where she had gone because she told me. I tried to tell them. And when I tried to tell them something had happened to me it was worse. But this was so long ago, and although it all had a huge effect on me, I erased it with Danny then the kids. Now, though, I picture Dougie and his dogged determination that Alice was dead. His eyes fixed on me. Watching me as I walked up and down the road to school.

I summon Jennifer and Simon and we all settle down to a sandwich. Normality reigns on the outside, but on the inside I am in turmoil. Why are the police up there? I am sweating and trembling and Jennifer is telling Mum about how Danny is buying us a house and how Mummy is Superwoman. Simon is watching and laughing in his quiet way and, out of everyone, he would suffer most. He is sensitive and intelligent and so like Danny that it hurts.

The afternoon is nearly over and the kids run off again to play. Mum picks at a jam and cream scone and leans in, towards me.

'I know you resent me. And I wish some things had turned out differently, but I've done my best. I've always kept up contact with the children and tried with you.'

I think about Sheila and how she would have loved a daughter, not simply endured one, and I wonder if, deep down, my mum has ever allowed herself to feel love. We're all doing our best and the struggle is real.

'Yeah, well, I have done the right thing. I might not be smart and pretty like you wanted, or have a good job or a husband you approve of, but at least I have integrity.'

We leave her at the door of the cafe. Jennifer and Simon hug her and kiss her and there are lots of 'see you next weeks', which throws more doubt into my mind as she stands stiffly in the doorway, hardly responding to my hug.

I sense her watching us as we skip away, me instinctively bending to kiss Jennifer, Simon holding my hand even though he is almost grown. But when I look around she is gone. I told her part of the truth. The part of the truth that I told her back then in my awkward, petulant teenage stroppy tones, which she dismissed as hormonal or inventive or daydreaming.

I don't blame her. I don't blame Dad. Not for that, anyway. Yes, they should have stopped it. They should have objected to an older boy (read: man) taking out a child in a car to who knows where. But they didn't and what happened happened and I moved on.

Incredibly, I find myself sitting on a bus with my children going over the ground I played on as a child in my head. Where the police would be, what they might find. It was nothing to do with me. Not directly. I imagine the police reopening the case and knocking on my door, questioning me again about Alice. I can't even remember what I told them back then. But I know I can never tell them about him raping me. I just can't. I am almost at breaking point. Pressure piled on pressure. It swirls around in my head until Simon nudges me.

'Mum, it's our stop.'

I ring the bell quickly and we hurry off the bus and down the road towards our flat. Once inside, I text Danny.

I love you, Dan x

He responds almost immediately.

Everything OK? x

I stand in the messy hallway with my phone in my hands, staring at it. This all looks so normal. A tangle of coats and trainers, a scooter and two footballs. A pile of books behind the door that I had dropped there months ago and never moved, along with winter wellies that would live there all summer, just in case of a rainy day. Danny's love of hats evident on the coat hooks, my love of scarves wrapped around the wrought-iron hooks. Kids' school bags, gym pumps and football boots. A huge wired heart of white fake roses, hung about the door but slightly offset with the constant slamming in and out. The detritus of family life. Yet nothing is normal. Not any more. It's all skewed, the colours distorted by the terrible anxiety I feel as this situation deepens. Eventually I type.

Absolutely fine x

He sends a smiley back and I stand there, hands in pockets, chilled to the bone, and realise that my stalker doesn't even need to email me or text me now.

Tanya

He has been gone for one day. My face has swollen badly and I think something might be broken. Add this to my other injuries and I am in a pretty bad way. But my body will heal. I am not sure that my mind will after what he has done.

I can't stop thinking about what he said about Ria. He made me think my best friend had betrayed me. She tried to tell me. She warned me about him. I can hear her voice now. *He's too old for you, Alice.* Lovely, kind Ria. All those years we were together, from junior school to secondary school. Sleepovers at weekends. Plaiting each other's hair. Borrowing each other's clothes. Running through the heather on the moor, arms outstretched.

I was sure she liked him. I saw her looking at him. Or did I just conjure it up in my stupid teenage imagination? Was I jealous and territorial? He raped my friend. And it was my fault.

I'd abandoned her to be with him. I was obsessed, mesmerised. In love, I thought. He pushed me into sex, telling me that everyone was doing it. I liked it. Then. I liked everything about our relationship. He was attentive, always around, all over me. His arm around me as he picked me up and dropped me off. Ria watched and waited. She came round to my house when he wasn't there but I was too busy getting ready or doing my hair. She eventually gave up and I wanted her to. I wanted rid of her. I just wanted to be with him.

But then she was back. I don't know what happened – at the time

I assumed it was to poach my man – but she was around me, warning me, her eyes flashing. Ria was brave. I knew it really and I loved her for it. But I loved Alan more. Or what I thought was love. I can see now that it was a childish infatuation coupled with him making me into a princess. His princess.

I suppose I was a bit jealous of her. Jealous of her normal life. Her mum and dad. She was pretty and smart and level-headed. Attractive. I did not want anyone attractive around Alan. I wanted him all to myself. And that is what I got.

I spent today sleeping. It's all been a shock. My life has collapsed in on itself. Nothing I thought was real is true. I agreed to leave because getting Alan away from Ria was my ultimate goal. He made me think that he had chosen me. That I was special. That he wanted to spend the rest of his life with me. It was all a lie.

He is completely evil. I thought it was me. I thought that I was lacking in some way. That I was annoying and irritating. I stupidly thought that he had made a bad choice, picked the loser, and, in my weakest moments, that he was noble for putting up with me. But I was the fool. I put a teenage crush before a lifelong friendship.

I am writing this in the lounge, lying on the sofa. The house is perpetually dark now and I am relying on the clock on the lounge wall to tell me if it is day or night. During the day I have to put on the stark white light until bedtime. There is no in between. I cannot turn on the heating as he has the code for boiler timer. There is enough food in the cupboards to last until he gets back from the conference. On Monday. I have time to make a plan.

Earlier I poured myself a huge bowl of cornflakes and milk – with sugar – and ate it on the sofa. This is banned. But I don't care. I don't care if he walks back in right now because I have had it. I'm done with it all now. I am going to do what I want to and take the consequences. He might kill me. He might hurt me. But I am going to take my chances.

And when I get back to work I am going to walk away at lunchtime and never come back.

Chapter Twenty

Day 10

I wake up thinking about how working at SafeMe has brought me into contact with a wide range of women. I am learning all the time. But one thing I see every day is what I saw in Sally: the well-practised ability to hold it down in the most difficult and dangerous situations. For their kids, for their jobs, for their parents, friends, always, always, always for someone else.

It was almost as if they rose out of their bodies and monitored every expression, every tick and movement for fear it would give away what was really happening to them. Sheila, brassing it out, cigarette in hand, a hard look on her face. Karen Green, a capable mum of three, who wore leggings and long sleeves all summer long to hide the cigarette burn scars from her children and, at the start, from us. Paula Bell, who sat silently, staring ahead, because every time she had looked away her husband had accused her of looking at other men and had beaten her for it.

I already know the truth: that it was easier for them to get through if they showed no sign of there being the slightest thing wrong. They become Oscar-standard actors, playing the role of normal people, when really they were deeply traumatised and, in some cases, badly injured. But, like Sally, they would crumble, usually when their kids were elsewhere, and we would find out the extent of what had happened to them. Paula once put it in a nutshell: it's the only way I can stay alive. To play dead. If I start to cry, I will never stop.

I thought I understood this. I thought my teenage experiences had positioned me perfectly to understand these women. Yet I had never fully experienced it myself: a whole other life of fear going on inside me whilst, on the surface, I maintained an oasis of calm. Sure, I'd kept stuff to myself. Buried it deep, sealed it in. I thought that was enough experience to know what it is like to live, day in, day out, under disproportionate pressure. But I had escaped. I had got out.

Now I am back in and, this Sunday morning, as I get dressed, Danny texts me about how this is day ten, yes, just ten days left until we can have a full bank account and start house-hunting. I push it to the back of my mind like I have so many things, until my eyes are focused on Donelle. She tells me that this guy did ring after all and it was all a big mistake. That he's only pissed off because she is away so much. She's going to take part-time hours and that, yes, he is right. And I am constantly smiling. I am somehow externally monitoring myself for any tiny sign I might give away.

We sit down for breakfast and I smile as I set the table. Donelle pours coffee and the kids play on their tablets on the sofa.

'So how did it go yesterday with your mum?'

I pour and smile.

'Yep. She was the same. Had coffee with her. Bit more uptight but—'

Jennifer interrupts without taking her eyes from the screen.

'Mummy shouted at Grandma.'

She says it in a baby voice and I glare at her. Donelle sees it and I revert to my fixed smile.

'Oh, did she? What's that about, Ria?'

I laugh. 'Oh, you know what she's like!'

It's all a bit too bright and breezy and she frowns.

'Come on. Shouting in a cafe? Bloody hell. This isn't like you, Ri. Are you OK? What did she do?'

Jennifer parrots her, again without looking up.

'Bloody hell.'

I see Simon redden and hold it down. Donelle looks to me for guidance and when I carry on sipping, she tuts and steps up.

'Jenni. What've I told you? No swearing.'

She sulks.

'Mummy said a bad word. Mummy said "fucking" to Grandma.'

Donelle stares at me, eyebrows raised. I am calm. On the outside. Controlled.

'Jennifer. What's got into you? What would Grandma Vi say? Go to your room until you can behave. I've explained before that Mummy and Grandma sometimes have a little argument. We're adults. Adults sometimes say naughty words. I'm sorry for shouting and swearing. Grandma was just a little bit annoyed.'

It comes out like I am reading a shopping list and Donelle intervenes.

'Right, kids, go and wash your hands before big breakfast. Go on.'

They hurry into the bathroom and she listens for the tap to run. When it does, she puts her arms around me.

'Ri, Ri, Ri. What's up? And don't say nothing. Is it the guy that's pestering you? Have work dealt with it?'

I don't say anything but she has already made the assumption that someone else will deal with this. I pull my hair back and tie it up, and she pulls me close. I want to tell her but how can I explain it now?

'It's all got on top of me. Work and you know ...'

She kisses my forehead.

'Danny being away? It's only for another week and a bit. I can put Ian off, go to me mam's with you and the kids. Oh yeah. And that flat I went for. I knew there'd be a fucking catch.'

I smile at her.

'Aunty Donelle said a naughty word.'

She laughs and we listen for the kids.

'Massive service charge. But ...' She looks down at her shoes. 'Ian says move in with him.'

I look at her. She's searching my face for ... what? Approval? Agreement? Permission? When Danny and I knew the time was right, wild horses wouldn't have stopped us shacking up together.

'Is that what you want, Donelle?'

I'm glad she's gone off the subject of me, though. It releases a bit of the tension.

'Yeah. I think so. It's just that he seems a bit ... possessive? I don't know. Wanting to know where I am and all that. I'm not used to it. But it might just be me.'

Alarm bells. Blaming herself.

'Don't move in unless you are sure, love; if he's worth it he'll wait.'

She hugs me tight.

'Aw, Ria, just talking to you helps. Thanks.'

Two hours and one big breakfast later, we are sitting in Vi's kitchen. Danny Snr is getting his backgammon set out in the lounge and Simon is waiting eagerly. Jennifer is colouring in and Vi is peeling potatoes. Danny Snr shouts through to the kitchen.

'No Donelle? Where is she?'

I laugh. Vi wipes her hands on her apron.

'Working. She wants to move out. Got a new man.'

I smile widely.

'What's he like? Have you met him? Dad approve, does he?'

Danny Snr repeatedly proclaims loudly that no one is good enough for Donelle. Vi laughs.

'Only glimpsed him. Outside, picking her up. Took her to a fancy restaurant. All dressed up, she was. Seems nice. Works at the council. Good job. Own house.'

She pulls a satisfied face and I laugh.

'Own house, eh? That'll be us soon.'

I see her stir the gravy faster, her annoyance showing on her face.

'You could have it now. If you took the money. Danny wouldn't need to stay away all hours. Leaving you alone.'

I interrupt. I dare not even hint at the debt we have racked up. Vi and Danny Snr don't even have a credit card.

'It's OK, Vi. I'm fine. It's only for ten more days, then he's done. I did ask him. He won't take it. Keep it for the kids. And Donelle's kids.'

Vi makes a harrumph sound.

'She won't have kids ...' And suddenly something else gets my attention as she talks about Donelle and children and how she and Danny Snr got their money. I see, out of the corner of my eye, a picture of some moorland on the TV on the kitchen counter. I sidestep to get a little closer so I can hear it. Danny Snr is engaged in a heated argument with Simon about backgammon so I listen harder, watching the screen flick to Dougie talking.

'... and then there were the accusations against me, which, I can say with full confidence, were completely false ...'

A reporter fills the screen now, and behind her I see the familiar winding footpath over the grassland up to the pond. I feel sick. I can see police cars up there and I scan the background.

'Police say that they have no further details of the new witness, just a detailed report of someone seen running away from the alleged crime scene the same evening. Investigations continue.'

They go back to the studio and my heart is thumping in my chest. I see the children playing with Danny Snr as he's arguing with Vi all through a kaleidoscope of confusion. She ran away. Why is Dougie doing this? Why can't he accept it?

My head is spinning as the reporters in the studio go over the timeline, Dougie's various campaigns and denials. There is a map of our street, with the dirt path highlighted.

'So was this area not searched in the original inquiry?' asks a female reporter.

The man with the map explains. 'Yes, Jane, it was, briefly, as Alice Peters was a registered missing person. But with no clues to go on, it was difficult to know where to begin the search. The police formerly had no evidence of anyone in the area at the time. But with the new evidence that has been submitted, evidence that clarifies previous evidence, they feel that the case can be re-opened and the area investigated. But at this stage it remains an informal investigation only. As stated earlier, someone must know something about this case and now is the time to come forward.'

There is more footage of police cordoning off the area around the pond. Dougie Peters standing behind the police cordon, staring into the distance, holding the photograph of Alice and her mother that I have seen in their house so often.

I feel physically sick. From grief and from guilt and from shock. I know every inch of the area around the rocks and I would have known if the ground up there had been disturbed. But that was back then, without hindsight. That was without the knowledge of what happened next, the claustrophobic atmosphere that contained us all on that small avenue.

I know the panic is growing inside me, and I almost sense my mother pulling herself up inside herself, all her relaxed attitude ebbing into uncertainty and then fear as she rapidly realises what is happening. When they don't find Alice up there, she will work it out. She will know that I was telling the truth. But she didn't help me then and she won't help me now.

I turn back into the room, towards my children and towards Danny Snr, who is now hugging Vi tightly. I jolt, reminding myself that this really has nothing to do with me, and no one can prove otherwise. And even then, I can defend myself, tell the truth. Yes. Nothing to worry about. I was the one who was hurt. I just don't understand why this has come up now.

Donelle arrives and talks about Ian, who works in the legal department at the council. She sings his praises, tells us he is newly single and is well up for a relationship. Loves Chinese food, not worried about her being away with her job. Which sounds better than before.

'Taking it to the next level ...'

She high-fives Danny Snr and we all laugh. Then it's time to go and we sing all the way home in the car. Then the kids are getting ready for bed. I am sad. Every day used to be far too short, a disappointment at the end because there was never more time to spend with those people. But now I am counting down until the next time I can be alone to obsess over who is messaging me.

When Jennifer and Simon are tucked up in bed, I put on Sky news and wait. And wait. And wait. For what seems like a lifetime for the report to appear again. The same report repeats and I watch it closer than close for any 'further details' but all I see are police cars and blue lights bouncing off my childhood playground. I am mesmerised by my avenue on TV, like an extra insight into my life from different angles now. The camera pans onto Dougie's house and I see the books through the window, the shelving and the layered photographs that sparked my jealousy as a teenager.

Why couldn't my parents be like him? Instead of super tidy and minimalist. Why couldn't they be laid back and lounge in the back garden in hats drinking gin and tonic? Rather than Dad's constant window vigil and Mum's flowery apron kitchen uniform, which she tried to overlay on me one Christmas as she attempted to teach me to cook? I remember asking her what happened to Dougie's wife and she just stood there, shaking her head and glancing at Dad under her lashes. I stayed for ages, expecting her to tell me when he wasn't listening. Like she'd told me about periods when she was drunk the preceding Boxing Day even though I had started mine years before.

But she didn't. She never mentioned it again. Every time I brought it up she walked out of the room, making herself busy. She kept quiet back then, just like she did when I asked her about pregnancy and sex and how I could get a job. And anything about school.

I check my phone now. The more I think about this, the more I think it could be anyone. But the past is awake. I knew that this would happen if I connected with my mother.

I finally go to bed. It's perp counselling tomorrow and the final funding meeting on Thursday. No matter what happens to me, I still need to step up for SafeMe. I have to find a way to separate this from my life and my work. I get up and look in on my kids. Jennifer is rosy-cheeked and sleeping outside the covers as usual. Her room is messy like my childhood room and she truly is mini me. Simon is tidy and, Vi tells me, a mini Danny. Or Danny Jnr Jnr, as they like to joke. His room is spotless and his clothes hung up. His many certificates are pinned in lines on the wall by his bed. Long-limbed and curly-haired, he even lies straight like Danny does.

My heart bursts with love for the pair of them. I push down the fear I felt earlier in case it seeps out of me and into them – Jennifer is already playing up and I wonder if it is my erratic mood that is getting to her. I hardly remember a time when I didn't have these two to care for. The time between leaving home and giving birth is a faded memory punctuated with meeting Danny and the times we became closer.

I can't imagine life without them. Any of them. I have to find a way to straighten this out. I go through all the options again but I am helpless as it goes on and on. My mind races into anxiety, towards another sleepless night worrying about Danny and the kids. Worrying about Dougie Peters, wondering what happened after I left. After she left. But what's the use? No one believed me then and no one will believe me now.

Tanya

Diary Entry: Sunday

I spent all day searching for something I could use as a weapon. I'm almost laughing as I write this. It seems so unbelievable. I haven't showered and I haven't brushed my hair. My face is still swollen. It's turned blue now and I know that in three days it will turn a light green, then yellow, then disappear. Except I will still feel it every time he comes near me.

The house seems huge without him here and I roamed around the rooms, opening drawers and looking in cupboards. I need something heavy. It would need to be a complete surprise – I would wait behind the door for when he comes in then hit him over the head. I almost pass out at the thought of it.

A knife would be useless, I might not kill him and he would have time to get me. This way the door would be open and he would be unconscious. I wavered all day between deciding that this wouldn't work to standing behind the door on the footstool from the lounge. I held a sponge in place of the heavy object I was yet to find.

About six o'clock I began to panic. My whole plan rested on doing this right. I didn't really want to kill him or even hurt him; I just want to get away. I thought if I didn't do this now, I would never do it. I knew he would not be happy about what I said just before he left. And from previous experience he would be even more furious after having had time away to think about it.

But didn't this make me as bad as him? I don't want to hurt anyone.

Even as a young teenager I liked kittens and I made sure spiders and stray bees trapped in the house made their way back outside. I've often wondered what would have happened if I hadn't left with him. The searing pain of my father and what he must have gone through when he found me gone pierces me. And how he must have died alone, in pain. It is this that stops me thinking back, thinking how stupid I was and how many people I must have hurt.

But I have to now. I have to face what really happened if I am to get out of here. I told myself, and still do sometimes, when things are really bad, that he loves me. That he did then and he does now. That I chose to leave and cut off everything that I knew.

I was fifteen. Nearly sixteen. It was all drama. All boys and clothes and falling out with friends. But I had Alan. I met him at the local teen disco, which, now I know how much older than me he actually is, seems strange. We all fancied him. He had a car and cigarettes. He was very cool. He made a beeline for us and I prayed that it was me and not her he liked, even then. Even right at the beginning.

She was protective of me. She would screen potential boyfriends and write down the pros and cons in two columns in blue Biro. The night she stood in front of me, slightly to one side, and watched as he asked me to dance. I made a 'squee' face and flicked my ponytail. Although we had played together as children and, even though we had gone to different junior schools, hung out in the holidays and after school, we were very different.

Ria kept up with fashion. She dyed her hair at fourteen and bought the latest jeans. She loved Manchester music. I had kept my blonde hair long and wore it in a tight ponytail. The only thing I looked good in was jeans and a T-shirt. I was too skinny for fashion. All the boys loved Ria. Her thick mascara and her short skirts. Me, not so much. But Alan did.

As he took over my life she dropped back, going out with Kim and

Linda. But I would feel her eyes on me as I got in Alan's car. We lived four doors apart and she was always watching. She was always staring at us. I thought she was staring at him but I'm starting to realise that it was me she was watching. She was scared for me.

Around teatime I opened the freezer and reached right to the back. I kept a tub of Häagen-Dazs ice cream for special occasions when I would be allowed a desert. Alan does not eat desert. He doesn't like sweet things. So, by default, neither do I. I ate the full tub. I felt a little bit sick, but I held the ice-cold container against my face and it made me feel better about it. I pulled out a big bag of frozen peas and held them between my legs.

This time tomorrow I would have carried out my plan. This will be my last diary entry because I will be either dead or free.

Chapter Twenty-one

Day 9

I'm caught. Every thought is preceded by a 'what if?' and I am stifled in my own life. I sit in our tiny flat with my beautiful children and all I can think about is the fucked-up game that someone is playing that makes no sense.

I am used to it. I speak at conferences all over the country about domestic violence, gaslighting and abuse. I know what the enduring questions are. Close behind 'why didn't she leave?', which is entirely explainable in practical and psychological terms, is 'why did he do it', which inevitably leads to 'and how can we stop it?'.

So the angry buzzing in my soul is asking the very same things. Why would one human being do this to another human being? And why is he doing this now? These questions, I realise only too well, form the basis of any complaint I could make. The police and legal services work on logic – cause and effect. To them, he is an unknown. Unpleasant, but unknown.

But to me, like anyone who has had long-term contact with a bully or abuser, he has steadily built up a regime of fear and blocked any means of complaint. Probably reasonable and approachable on the outside, they do their worst in secret and promise more of the same if you tell. I know for sure that to most people it is difficult to believe, especially if the person is plausible.

I chose well with Danny – beautiful, kind Danny, who I know would never hurt me or anyone else. Yet here I am, embroiled in a situation where all this hurt is happening to me. I am trying to think it through, to see where I can push through and get someone to believe me, to find a way to trip up whoever is taunting me and make people see what he is doing. Because I know that, like all abusers, when he is cornered he will deny everything. He will tell them it is my fault, that I led him on, that I am a psychotic liar.

Jim stood there, about to batter Sally with a blunt instrument, and he was still blaming her. Look what you made me do. Frank, blaming Sheila for Bobby, while he did the worst thing he could do second to hitting her – he had a child with someone else. Dougie, insisting for years that someone was responsible for Alice's death, accusing anyone on the basis of some thin theory, when in reality she had left.

Why? Why did they do it? Why is he doing this? The answer is this: because they can. The very fact that it is not logical, not what you would expect, disproportionate, is how they are able to get away with it. Because when I come to pull the story together, to explain it, even to myself, it sounds like some hugely exaggerated made-up story with little evidence. It did happen. It did.

I drop off my children, waving and smiling, but immediately scanning the landscape for a red car. He is not there. I haven't heard from him all weekend. Why is he doing this? I ask myself for the millionth time. But I know the answer. Because men like him do what they want, regardless of the consequences.

Yes, this is the inside of my mind on my way to work. Wondering how someone else's mind works, which is always a losing battle. As I approach SafeMe and see the men who are here for perpetrator counselling standing outside the gates, not looking at each other,

I wonder if I am in the right state of mind for this. But it's too late: Malc has seen me and he throws open the gate. The guys walk towards the yard, carefully avoiding me and each other, as if they were here by accident.

Once inside, I help Janice set up. She's on good form, packing the women off to the accommodation block while the meeting is in progress. She's sweeping the floor and dragging the tiny chairs into a circle while I sort through the register and notes.

'See Sheila in the paper? What do you think?'

I nod. She knows I'm attached to Sheila.

'Not good. But there's more to it. Bloody Frank. He's clever.'

She shakes her head and does her best Don Corleone. 'Frankie, Frankie, Frankie.' We both laugh and it feels good. I feel like I haven't laughed for a long time.

'So do you think he'll turn up today?'

'Yeah. He'll be here, sticking his beak in till he gets his own way. Gave all the flats widescreen TVs.'

She snorts. 'Yeah, I heard. Not good while funding's looking at us. Not without donation forms.'

I produce some donation forms on cue.

'Well, if he does turn up today, I'll get him to fill them in. And for the Xboxes.'

She sweeps and I sort. Finally she brings up the subject we're both nervous about.

'So funding meeting. Thursday. We need a Plan B. What if we don't get it?'

We both look around at the main room. We've seen so many things, so many people, so many lives turned around. So many lives lost. I can't imagine my life without SafeMe. Worse, there will be no provision for the women. Or for the perps. I feel tears prick my eyes.

'I don't know, Jan. Let's cross that fucking massive bridge when we come to it.'

We're ready. I signal to Malc to open the doors and the men flow in, rushing to the seats furthest away from the front. There are a few new faces and I recognise Amanda Perry's husband, Tony, back again. I'd heard she was back in hospital and her children in foster care. She went back because they couldn't rehouse her with her four children. Six months ago, in this very room, Tony swore on his children's lives that he would never hit Amanda again. Turns out his children's lives don't mean that much to him.

I glance out of the window and see the black limo. The rising anger inside me takes me by surprise. Frank, fresh from his outing with his mistress and his daughter to teach Sheila a lesson, has shown up. He emerges and two guys, different from last time, follow him with boxes. Malc opens the door and Frank is standing in front of me. He motions at the boxes.

'Electric blankets.' His eyes meet mine and he is mocking me. He leans forwards slightly. 'For the children.'

I don't flinch. Not even a raised eyebrow. I won't give him the satisfaction. Janice hurries over.

'Ooo. More donations. That's very kind of you, Frank.' Her tone says 'uncharacteristically kind'. She hands him the donation forms. 'If you could just fill these in. So our funders know where these have come from. And the TVs and the Xboxes.'

He passes the forms and pen to his accomplice, who moves to a table and begins to fill them in.

'So, ladies, what's on the agenda today?'

Janice touches his arm and his other minder steps forwards. He smiles.

'OK, boys, you can wait in the car. Frankie's safe here.'

He sits at the back, looking at his phone, as Janice goes through the motions with the perpetrators. One of the guys is truly sorry and in floods of tears and Frank looks up, disgusted. There is a long debate about dealing with jealousy and flashpoints, and Janice hands out some sheets which detail alternatives to violence. The session ends and the men rush to the front to get their attendance cards stamped. This is so that either their probation officer or their social worker will approve. Then they leave. Except for Frank. He waits, scrolling his phone, until the last perpetrator has left, and then he looks up.

'Ria, may I have a word?'

Polite as anything, yet my hackles rise. I don't have a choice, really. It's part of the perpetrator service.

'Of course, Frank. What is it?'

He looks around. His lazy gaze rests on the CCTV camera that points both towards the exit and into the room.

'In private? It's about Sheila.'

I look at Janice, who is moving the chairs back.

'OK. In my office. Is that all right?'

He follows me into the small room, where he can intimidate me better, and we assume last week's position. I watch as he checks for CCTV cameras. He's wasting his time, because the cameras in here are webcams, activated by the switch under the desk. He seems satisfied and sits, one leg pulled up over the other, opposite me.

'Right, Ria. How's Sheila?'

I nod. 'She seems OK. I saw her on Friday.'

The conversation is loaded with Thursday night's events, but I will not be the one to mention them. He nods slowly. Then he touches his cufflinks – gold with a tiny diamond in each. He's nervy and the atmosphere changes. I flick the switch under the desk to record.

'Right. Right. The thing is. I think we are making progress here. Sheila agreed to accompany me on a social event the other night. It went well. Did she mention it?'

I smile. 'You know I can't disclose the conversations I have with Sheila, Frank.'

He nods. He is calculated, slow in his movements.

'No, no. Of course. The thing is, Ria ... this is private, isn't it?' I nod. He knows it works both ways. Unless anything criminal is disclosed, of course. 'So this place. I wanted to do something to make sure it carries on. With the funding coming up. And I looked into donating privately but how can I be sure that my money would be used correctly?'

I stare at him.

'We have audited accounts. And we are accountable to the funding body.'

He nods and holds up his hands. 'Yes, yes, oh, I wasn't suggesting anything ... inappropriate. But in the course of wondering what the money was used for I met up with someone from the funding body ... Trevor ... I forget. But he was very helpful. Very helpful indeed.'

I can feel myself flush. My face is burning.

'And what did Trevor say?'

Frank shrugs casually. 'He told me that this could be a private concern, set apart from the other services, because of the specialist care. He agreed that Sheila didn't really belong here. Her place could go to someone who really needs it.'

'But she really needs it, Frank. That's her decision. Not yours or Trevor's.'

He smiles. 'Oh yes, of course. Of course Sheila has a choice.

While this place is open, anyway.'

I check, from the corner of my eye, that the red recording light under the desk is lit. It is. This conversation is being recorded. I nod.

'Yeah. True. Who knows what will happen next week, with all the cuts?'

He leans forwards, and I instinctively lean away.

'Well, one thing's for sure, even if you lose your funding, Frankie can help. For people who need a place. Not like Sheila, who have their own homes to go to.'

I regulate my breathing. I hold in my rising anger.

'So are you offering funding, Frank? Conditional funding? Just so we understand what you are offering?'

He presses his fingers together as if in deep contemplation.

'Let's just say, if the council funding doesn't come through, which I have to say from my conversation with Trevor is looking unlikely, I can offer whatever you need to keep this place running. I am sure, under those circumstances, that Sheila will see that this has been a huge misunderstanding and will decide to come home. After all, no charges have been made. Or indeed, no complaints. So ...'

I stand up.

'Let's see what the funding decision is, Frank.'

He stands too, very close to me, close enough that I can smell his expensive aftershave and his blossom-fresh clothes. His minty breath is on my face. He speaks very quietly.

'The thing is, love, unless something drastic happens, you won't have any choice. If you get my meaning.'

I know I should shut up now, but I can't. This means too much.

'I'm afraid I don't know what you mean, Frank. You'll need to explain it to me.'

Frank doesn't like me. I see his face flush slightly and sense a change in his stance. More tense.

'Right, love. What I mean is I want my wife back home. And I want to support this place and its good work. I know Shelia takes notice of you, she's mentioned you numerous times, and you can talk some sense into her. I'd really appreciate that.'

I have a comeback.

'But we should get the council funding, Frank. It's very kind of you but I don't think we will need your help. It's a big commitment.'

He pauses and looks around again, weighing up the odds of him getting caught.

'You won't get that funding. I have a lot of sway in this town and I can assure you that I am easily able to convince Trevor that the funding would be better going to, I don't know, the lads' boxing or the WI thing about World War One. Wasn't there another organisation who could take this over or something?'

Trevor Jones. He's definitely been talking to Trevor about a potential merger. I play dumb.

'OK. Well, I guess the council will make their decision and if it's a no, then we'll be in touch about your kind offer of a donation.'

He shakes his head. 'I want her home, and, believe me, love, I'll do anything to get her. She's had her bit of fun now.'

I stare at him.

'A broken arm is hardly a bit of fun, is it?'

He turns quickly.

'Like I said last time, nothing to do with me. None of it. Understand?'

I hold up my hands.

'Yes. Of course, Frank.'

He opens the door.

'Mr James, to you. From now on. You won't get that funding,

and I'll be your boss. Have a think about that.'

I sink into my chair and, when I see his limo pull away and Malc has deposited the usual bribe into the charity box, I turn off the recording and check the file. I watch it back, Frank's manner looks much more threatening than I experienced. I save it to the hard disk and to a flash drive, just to be sure, and then I call Janice. She slumps into the chair opposite.

'He's bribing Trev.' I show her the conversation. 'In return for Sheila coming home.'

Janice sighs. 'Bloody hell. What can we do? And he's offering to replace the funding money. God, Ria, we can't.'

I shake my head. 'Oh no. That is not happening. A bloody perpetrator running the show. Jesus.'

We watch the recording run in a loop.

'All those years of hard work and in the end it comes down to a twat like Frank James. Is there any hope, Ria? Really?'

She wipes away a tear and I think about how this is yet another kind of control. Getting their kicks from being king of their castle. Knocking down strong women, who are trying to make a difference, women who support other women to be strong; that's their speciality. I smile.

'Yeah. There's always hope.'

She sniffs and wipes her eyes. I pass her a loo roll and she rips a big piece off and blows her nose hard.

'Is this the bit where you rip your shirt open and you're Superwoman underneath?'

I laugh. Superwoman. Ha. Right now that is the biggest joke ever, but somewhere deep inside I still have a spark.

'I never said I was Superwoman. But the fuckers haven't got us yet, Jan. Not yet.'

Tanya

Diary Entry: Monday

It's almost midnight. I eventually found something very heavy; it was staring me in the face all the time. Our cast-iron skillet. It takes me two hands to lift it up and all my strength to pull it down from the hook on the wall.

I expected him to come home this morning. He would need to change before he went to work. Then I remembered that he hasn't got a job. And he's probably not at a conference. Nevertheless, I stood behind the door on the footstool holding the skillet from seven o'clock until a quarter to ten. My nerves jangled, but I had to admit that I have no idea what time her would be back.

I poured the last of the cornflakes and the milk into a dish and sat at the table eating them. When I had finished, I opened the freezer and looked for something I could make for dinner. That was when I realised that I was not going to carry out my plan. My head ached and my legs were like jelly and now my arms were heavy from holding the skillet.

I'd eaten most of the frozen food over the weekend. The peas were still there and there was a pack of haddock that was too frostbitten to eat. I opened the fridge. Two eggs and some butter. There was a crust of a Warbuton's loaf in the bread bin and nothing else.

Alan doesn't like frozen food. He likes everything made freshly. He has never once cooked a meal yet he has criticised every single dish I have made, even if it was only with a silent lip curl. I had recipe books and my signature dishes were lasagne and salad. Mainly out of boredom, I had made my way through the only real reading material I was allowed. I made detailed shopping lists, the contents of which would magically appear in the kitchen on my return from work.

I opened the top cupboards. Flour, cooking oil, tomato sauce. Tins of beans and kidney beans and chopped tomatoes – no good to me as Alan would not let me have a tin opener without him being there. Same with knives. A biscuit tin with no biscuits. A Jacob's Cream Cracker box with two crackers in the bottom.

No doubt he would come waltzing in with bags from the butcher's he loves so much and Tesco's. He always puts the food away and brings me knives and tin openers when it's time to cook. He stands there, watching, as if I was going to slit my wrists at any moment. Don't get me wrong, I have considered it. But this is just another failure on the long list of things I am too weak and scared to do. When I have finished cooking, he stands there while I taste it.

This is how I know that there is something wrong with him. After our first big argument and the shutters, but before Tina, he got it into his head that I was trying to poison him. He picked me up from work and he looked as white as a sheet. We'd hardly got home before he was rushing to the toilet. I heard him vomiting and I wondered what was wrong. He was in bed for three days, so I was off work, tending to him. All the time he made me taste the chicken broth and the dry toast.

As soon as he was better, he confronted me. I was in the kitchen and he swung me around, soap bubbles spraying across my apron.

'What did you put in that sandwich?'

I often don't know exactly what he means and my answers are so nerve-laden that I say the wrong thing.

'Today? Ham. You said ham.'

I felt the sting across my cheek. Red, burning hot.

'Don't get smart with me. You know exactly which sandwich I mean.'

This happened a lot. He would tell me that I knew exactly what he meant when I didn't have a clue. I had to flounder around, trying to second-guess him and hoping that I was right. I racked my brains and eventually he filled in for me.

'You tried to poison me, you fucking bitch.'

I shook my head. 'No, Alan. I would never do that.'

I wouldn't. Because I am not brave enough. But that was beside the point. From that day I had to cook what he wanted and he would buy everything. No more supermarket for me. Not that I went much anyway. My world narrowed until the only place I went was work and a walk at the weekend, often to a remote moorland where I was sure he was going to murder me and bury my body.

But he didn't, he preferred to keep me like a little pet, a dog to kick when he felt like it. And here I am. He hasn't come home. He must have meant Tuesday.

Chapter Twenty-two

Day 8

I fell asleep on the sofa last night. Danny must have texted late.

> Day 8 – three weeks down, one week to go. We're nearly
> there! I love you, Ri, always x

I switch on the TV. I'd scanned the news last night, but the media eye had turned away from Springhead and towards more pressing matters. I search the internet for any updates, but there are none. For an insane moment I consider skipping work and going up there, just to see what's going on. But every time I think about it I flashback to panic, icy water setting my teeth on edge and the blackness of almost drowning.

I never thought of it as rape. Not until I was older. I don't know what I thought, except it was very wrong. Every time I thought about it I felt sick. Ashamed. I wanted to tell someone, scream it out. To a teacher. My mum. Anyone. But I couldn't. So I just didn't mention it to anyone. Alice was gone; that was all anyone cared about. By the time I had escaped and realised what had happened to me it was all a distant memory. Distant, as long as I kept away from home and my parents. So life went on.

I exhale. Yesterday's conversation with Frank has made me even more determined to rise above. I need this job to make mine and Danny's plans work. It's no use having a deposit for a house if there is no job to get a mortgage. And we can't get a mortgage with a bad credit record. The funding meeting is on Thursday and we have submitted the bid now, so all we can do is wait and see. Frank could easily be lying about meeting Trevor, but how would he know about the merger? Janice is as worried as I am. I can see it in every movement, every glance around the room. Even the twinkle of the fairy lights somehow seemed brighter, as if the whole place is making an effort.

I check the cheap phone. Nothing. It's like a brief interlude in a hectic schedule that barely stops, where I am lying very still and enjoying the gap in the proceedings. I stare at the ceiling of the tiny flat. I will miss this place. Everyone thinks I am mad, but I love living like this. I am not someone who needs their space to be tidy. I need it to be lived in.

I will miss it. I don't think for one moment that Danny is suddenly going to change into Mr Tidy. No. He just wants something of his own to mess up. He needs a show home even less than I do and is as fond of bright colours as I am. None of the houses we have seen so far have fitted his wish list fully, but we will know when we see it, when we glimpse our dream home. I feel a pang of apprehension as I think about my job and the funding meeting, about Simon's reluctance to leave his school that limits our choices. But most of all, I am anxious at the prospect of a day ahead of me with someone watching my every move.

It all disappears as Jennifer runs in asking for her PE kit and Simon appears to be singing an X-rated version of a rap song. He looks at me, all innocent.

'Daddy sings it.'

I turn around and smile. So it begins. We gather up all our belongings that the day demands and start the trek to school. I wave them goodbye in the playground.

'Aunty Don will pick you up. OK?'

They nod and wave and hurry towards their other life with their friends. Simon is high-fiving and bumping fists and I see him growing into a teenager almost before my eyes. I am smiling and walking away from the school, through the streets and towards SafeMe, when I see it. A red Skoda parked a street away from my workplace. I hurry away from the car, looking back and wondering why it is parked here. Where is he? The gates to SafeMe are locked and Malc is standing guard. He smiles as I approach.

'Mornin.'

I stop. He wouldn't have let him in, would he?

'Mornin', Malc. Any visitors?'

He shakes his head. 'Nope. One of the ladies' partners was here overnight but the police collected him. Going to court this morning, by all accounts. Your mate's already here. And they've changed shifts round the corner. Couple of cars there early on, seeing Sheila, I think.'

I momentarily forget about my own problems.

'Sheila? What time?'

'About nine. Pulled up. Went into hers. Weren't there long. She came out and waved 'em off.'

I look at SafeMe. It's not Sheila's day and the other women and the funding bid need my attention as well. Maybe that's what Frank is relying on.

'Right. Ta, I'll go and see her.'

He nods.

'Nasty piece of work, that; you need to watch yourself there.'

I stop in my tracks.

'Frank? Was he there?'

'Both of them. Don't underestimate anyone around Frank James. He'll have them doing his dirty work. Just sayin'.'

As I walk around to Sheila's flat I wonder if I've missed something. She seems like a woman on a mission to save herself, but can Malc see something I can't because of my attachment? Her front-room light is on and I see her shadow cross the room. I buzz her and she lets me in.

'All right, love?' The room is thick with cigarette smoke and she is flushing the remnants of the ashtray down the toilet. 'I've had company,' she explains as her hand wafts the air. I leave the door ajar.

'So I heard. Just checking all is OK?'

She nods. 'Yeah. Fine.'

I glance around. Some of the boxes are gone. She watches my eyes, waiting to jump in, her mouth twitching. Her bright red lipstick, the one she always wears if men are around, has bled into the lines around her mouth, suggesting she applied it quickly, without much care. 'Had a bit of a sort-out. The lads came and took the stuff I was throwing to the tip.'

I nod. 'The tip being back to Frank?'

She shakes her head. Her eyes harden. 'No, lovey. To. The. Tip.' She explains like I am a child. Then she stares at me, unsmiling. We are at loggerheads for a full minute before she breaks.

'Why are you here?'

She is still hostile.

'I just wanted to make sure you're all right, Sheila. It's up to you what you do, you know.'

She nods. 'Yeah. I know. And I'll do what I want in the end.

When I know what's what.' She lights another cigarette and I note her chain-smoking is much, much worse. 'That's if these don't finish me off first.'

I know this is a strategy for many of the women. Slow suicide. Drink, drugs, cigarettes, anything that might end this existence of torture from which there is no escape sooner. Some of them even admit it, but for most it is subconscious and part of the work we must do to help them recover. It is a long, hard road, for them. Sheila's narrowed eyes as she regards me tell me that something has happened to make her take a step backwards. We were getting somewhere, she was opening up. Now she is not so sure about me. She sits down carefully on the armchair in front of me.

'Frank came to see you, didn't he?'

I nod. 'Yep. You know he was at Perps. You saw him go in.'

It hadn't escaped my attention that Sheila was standing on the corner when Frank's limo pulled up. She always is.

'He stayed longer, though. What was that about?'

I shake my head and put down my cup. 'What do you think it was about? You know I'm not able to tell you …'

She's up and ranting, red face and hands flying around.

'Oh, don't give me that bullshit. He'd have got it out of you. I know what he's like.'

I stay calm. 'What out of me, Sheila?'

'Her. About her. If I knew. If I said owt. What I thought.'

I stand up. Enough is enough.

'That's where you're wrong. Frank would not get anything out of me because I am a professional. I'm not invested in the nuances of your relationship with Frank or his with you. That is your business. I'm concerned with your safety. And I would never break your confidence.'

She flies at me. 'You're no different to anyone else. He could make you say anything. Anything. He could.'

She collapses into the chair, crying. I go to her, but she shrugs me off.

'But I didn't. I didn't say anything about you, or her. It was never mentioned, by either of us.'

She is sobbing, inconsolable.

'Yeah. Well. Praps not. But he'll get you another way. If it wasn't that, it'll be something else, and you won't escape. Nobody does.' I touch her shoulder but she jumps away. 'Go on. Get out. Sling yer bloody hook. Bleedin' do-gooder, you.'

I leave, reluctantly, and close the door quietly behind me. I text the warden and ask her to keep an eye on Sheila and walk back past the parked car. It's gone. It's only as I open my office door that I hear that phone ping. I am so used to Danny's texts that I think it is him, reminding me that it is day 8, but it's not.

CLOSER AND CLOSER. I'M RIGHT BEHIND YOU.

The argument with Sheila has upset me and I kneejerk reply.

FUCK YOU.

I press 'send' and my heart beats faster and faster. I spin around and there is an electrician looking at the fuse box. I scan him but how could he possibly message me from up a ladder? I see red. This could not have come at a worse time and I am losing the plot. I can't do it. I can't play his game. I type fast.

> JUST TELL ME WHAT YOU WANT. WHY YOU ARE DOING
> THIS? WHAT I CAN DO TO MAKE IT STOP.

I have sent it before I realise that this is exactly what he wants. That I'm engaging. Before I have a chance to think more, to dread, my phone pings again.

> NEWTON'S THIRD LAW. EVERY ACTION HAS AN EQUAL
> AND OPPOSITE REACTION.

My temper flares. I have a lot to lose, but I'm going to lose it anyway, so I might as well go out with a fight.

> YES YOU'RE RIGHT. I'M BLOCKING YOU. STOP STALKING ME.

I block his number and block his messages. It feels good for about fifteen seconds until I realise that I have just raised the stakes and given him a free hand. What the fuck does that mean? Every action has an equal and opposite reaction? What sort of fuckery is this?

Fuck him. Let him do his worst. What can he possibly do now? Him and Frank and Jimmy and Dougie and everyone else in the business of scaring the shit out of everyone around them. Well, they've picked on the wrong person because I'm not going to give up without a fight.

I sit at my desk and fill in my diary. If something happens to me, at least people will know. They will know exactly what he has done. But here I am, at the safest place in the world. He can't get me here, and he can't get my children: they are safe too. Now I have stood up to him it can go one of two ways: he will back off or he will escalate.

I will be ready. I am done with being scared and worrying because, in reality, he will do what he is going to do whether I am or not. And in a week Danny will be back and we will be looking for a new place, away from here. Yes. I can hold it down for a week.

Especially a week with the funding meeting in it. It feels like a defining time when I will know exactly what my future holds and I will finally be free. Let him terrorise me. Let the funders make their decision. At least everything will be out in the open. I even consider going to Carole again, but the only thing that holds me back is the tiny piece of me that still thinks he is a normal person who will only take this so far. Who will finally realise that he can no longer manipulate me.

I know that some perpetrators will give up when they realise they could end up in prison. It's as if they have believed their own hype for so long that when shit gets real they are surprised and back off. This little game they have been playing is private torture, not public humiliation. It is for their eyes only, watching another human being squirm and struggle under the weight of their violence and abuse.

I also know that when it threatens to go public, in court, or even into the street, well, where's the fun in that? And there is the problem of looking like a fucking coward. Only cowards hit women, persecute children. Not the big man when everyone knows what they really are. But others do not stop there. The real psychopaths do not care what anyone else thinks because they are convinced that they are right. That their women belong to them, that their power extends to the control of another human being. They will argue with police and hire lawyers to defend themselves, even when the evidence is clear. Their victim is never safe because, even after years in prison, they will return to get what they believe is vengeance, because they are offended just by them being alive.

I finish my diary and tap, tap, tap my pencil on the desk. Which one is he? I don't know. He may be the coward, eager to play a clever game but knowing when to stop. Or not. But now I have stepped up, I am about to find out.

Tanya

I've waited all day and he hasn't come back. This morning I waited behind the door, certain I had got it wrong as usual and it was today he was coming back. About half nine I suddenly realised that he was testing me. He was probably watching me doing all this. He told me once he had cameras installed in the house and he does seem to know everything I do.

Then I remembered the space underneath the unit where I keep my diary and the tiny cards and Tina's collar, which I found in the dustbin. He can't have cameras because he would have seen all that. Even so, I moved the footstool back into the lounge and brushed the cornflake crumbs off the settee. I got the hoover out and pushed it around the house. I felt weak and dizzy but I managed it.

The kitchen was spotless. The carpets were pristine. I walked around the house, listening to the silence, my footsteps making no sound. It was as if I was not here. And in a way I am not.

When Alan and I left we came straight here. We came straight to bed and we stayed there, feeding each other chocolate and eating takeaways. I never questioned why Alan would have a house like this, I only found out later that his parents were both dead. He kept telling me that we could never go back. That no one could ever find out where I was because he would get in trouble.

The police came round. We saw them pull up and he told me to stay in the little bedroom. He pushed my bag in behind me and we were giggling. Actually laughing. Somehow I was so stupid that I thought it was funny that my dad had called the police. Because no one understood Alan and me. Not Dad. Not Ria. Certainly not the police.

I could hear them downstairs, talking in low voices. All very reasonable. I held my breath, wishing them gone. Then I could hear them in the hallway. Alan's voice different. Older.

'Yes. If I hear anything I will.'

A woman's voice.

'You can understand our concern, though. But it's all checked out so thank you.'

'No problem at all. Glad to help. Let me know what happens and give my regards to Mr Peters.'

My dad. I should have run downstairs right then and just gone with them. Gone home. I should have told them it was all a mistake and I wanted to go back to school. Instead, stupid teenage me thought it was all a game. Me and Alan against everyone else.

I don't think he ever meant to keep me prisoner because at first we went out to a lot of different places. We went to Blackpool. We stayed two nights and ate ice cream. When we got back he told me he was worried that we would be found out. I laughed and said we should move away. I saw a shadow cross his face then.

'No. This is my parents' home. I'll never move away.'

And that was that. He told me I couldn't be Alice any more. To pick a name. I chose Tanya. Tanya Cartwright. I loved it. I just knew it was only a matter of time until we married, and then I would really be Cartwright, because naïve little me did not realise that I would need ID to be married. To get a passport. To open a bank account. And Alan told me that if I did any of those things he would be arrested and sent to prison. *Did I want that? Did I?*

So Alice was gone and I was Tanya. I liked it at first. Alice was for little girls with hairbands. Tanya was sophisticated for a grown woman having sex with her boyfriend. He called me Tanya and I didn't mind. But now I realise that what he was doing was shaping me into what he wanted. We went out less and less and he became more careful about where we went. Then he told me about the job. In Huddersfield.

I was excited. I felt free. A year was a long time to be sat indoors, only sneaking out for short walks or weekends far away. I wanted to earn my own money. I wanted to go into town and buy clothes. When that did not happen I became angry. And that's when he started to hurt me. To make sure I was invisible. Making me pull myself up inside myself, so careful not to slip up and annoy. I was no longer Alice. I was a shell of her. A scared, empty shell.

Now, sitting writing this diary, I am wondering what Mr Simister thinks. Have they missed me? Has Mrs Simister, who clearly suspects something is wrong, tried to find out what is the matter? But Alan will have told them I have flu or some other ailment that takes as long to fade as bruises do.

The truth is no one is looking for me. There is no one.

Chapter Twenty-three

Day 7

I wake up and Lily Allen's 'Fuck You' is my earworm. Seven days to go. I can hardly believe that we have got through it. That it's been only three weeks since the awards ceremony and that the funding decision is due on Monday.

There are no signs that he has regrouped – he can't text me now as I have blocked him. The kids appear and I make boiled eggs and soldiers and we all tuck in. I broach the subject with them.

'OK. So what do we do if anyone we don't know approaches us?'

Simon thinks hard and answers through chewed toast.

'Tell an adult.'

I nod. 'Good. And do we go with them?'

Jennifer shakes her head. 'No. Stranger danger.'

I high-five them both.

'And strangers are anyone we don't know. Even if they say they know Mummy and Daddy. The only people you leave school with are family.'

Simon chews and thinks.

'What about Terri? And Simone?'

The babysitters. Fair point.

'You know them. You know that Mummy and Daddy know them. But if someone you don't know tries to get you to go with them, you scream. Loud.'

They both look at me incredulously. This is the opposite of what I have told them to do on every occasion so far. I am usually telling them to be quiet. I laugh.

'Come on. Let's practise.'

I scream really loudly and they stare at me.

'Your turn.'

I scream again and they join in, quietly at first, then very loudly. We all collapse on the lounge floor, laughing helplessly.

'Good. Good. So that's what you do when a stranger tries to take you. Or even tries to talk to you. But no need to worry today: Aunty Don is going to collect you.'

Jennifer is screaming and shouting 'stranger danger' and it is time to go. It continues until we are nearly at the school gate and I don't stop her. She needs to get it into her head just in case ... no. I'm not thinking about it. This is the new, positive me. The new 'Fuck You' me who is going to take no shit. I drop them off and wait until they are safely in school.

There are no incidents on the way to work and when I get there Janice is supervising the knitting group. Sheila is there and she looks at me sheepishly. Sally is in the corner and her kids are in the family room on the Xboxes. Janice hurries over.

'Bloody good news for a change: Sally's housing has come through.'

I smile. Finally. Sally's request was an unusual one. After a lot of consideration she had presented us with a list of her requirements for accommodation. Usually, faced with a new start, we are given a wish list that is way above what the local council can provide. But Sally's appeared to be the opposite.

'I need a three-bedroomed flat – the lads can share. I can even bloody share. Lounge and kitchen. Bathroom and toilet. A shower would be nice.' She had looked at the ground. Anything that concerned her safety was difficult to talk about. 'One way in, one way out. As high as possible in a tower block. Fully alarmed with a panic button and a reinforced steel door.' A slight smile. 'Balcony for a few plants.'

We know that the council would have provided a three-bedroomed semi in a rough area with a garden side, back and front, but Sally didn't want that.

'I want to be high up. So he's not climbing in the windows at night. Or sneaking in the back door if one of them leaves it unlocked. One way in. One way out.'

One of the more inexperienced workers told her that 'it would be fine now, there's an injunction in place'. But men like Jim don't observe an injunction. Sally is clever. She made her own plan for her own safety. She will be taking no chances this time. I look over at her, focused on her knitting. She sees me and comes over.

'What's up?' Her expression changes. 'Is it Jimmy? Is he back?' She looks over her shoulder in the direction of the pub.

I smile. 'No. No he isn't. The thing is, the council have given you somewhere. Treehouses. In the tower block. Three bedrooms. It's yours if you want it.'

For the first time since I met her she smiles widely.

'Honest?'

I nod. 'Yeah. You can move in as soon as you want.'

She looks past me into the distance and I know she is suddenly seeing her future stretch out in front of her. She has a second chance. And that is what SafeMe is all about. Sally is on to the next thing.

'Course I'll take it. Wait till I tell the kids.'

We all look over. Her children, who have gone through so much, will have school places and a stable home. I turn to Janice.

'That's brilliant, Jan. Can we get her some furniture sorted?'

Janice beams. 'On it. Already phoned Mustard Tree. Taking her round today.'

They've been here ages, away from their home. Away from everything they know. But hardly a tantrum or a tear. Same with Sally, stoicism built in. She's slept in a single room with all her children to avoid having to go back to Gloucester, where Jim could take up where he left off.

Janice follows me into the office.

'Right then. Funding meeting tomorrow.' She drags up a chair. 'We still need a Plan B. In case it all goes tits up.'

We look at the sign on the office wall.

Each time a woman stands up for herself, without knowing it possibly, without claiming it, she stands up for all women – Maya Angelou

I look back at Janice.

'There is no Plan B. This is it. We can't take Frank's money, if that's what you were thinking. He'd want something back.'

She smiles. 'He just wants Sheila.'

'No. He doesn't. He wants to win. It's part of his game, part of his control. Just like the TVs and the Xboxes.' I know that she knows this but I also know she is desperate. 'And Sheila. Jesus, Jan, she's vulnerable. She's on the edge. He's just looking for a reason to whip her back there and it'll start all over again. When she's been doing so well.'

Janice sighs. 'What else is there? There must be other funding? Other charities?'

We both know I've done the legwork. I've appealed to every single celebrity who might want to support us. Started crowdfunders, done social networking, rattled tins on the street. There is nothing.

'Nope. No lottery funding any more. If we don't get this council funding, we're fucked.'

She sighs. I think about the first time I met her. I had been working for SafeMe as a development worker for a year when the manager left. I was thrown in at the deep end, with six months' worth of admin backlog and a cash loss. I rolled up my sleeves and within four weeks I was up to date and interviewing for two new workers. I secured funding, back then when the council still cared about what happened to people and not just about their jobs. Janice applied.

She was the only one who was properly qualified and the only one who had answered the question on the application form 'why do you want to work at SafeMe?' with the correct answer: because I care.

We hit it off from the very start, the good cop, bad cop double-act. The Friday-afternoon party in the spare flat that doubled as an office before we extended outwards into the mill next door. Jelly, ice cream and full-fat cola. Virgin cocktails in proper cocktail glasses and trays of tiny sandwiches balanced on cake stands from the local charity shop. We would herd in the women and children. Sad-eyed, shell-shocked residents who had sat for days in a white-walled cell of a room, suddenly confronted by a room full of happiness. It was a start, and we knew it. A start to a new life where there were treats on a Friday afternoon and where opulence was allowed, nay, encouraged.

The trees and fairy lights were Janice's idea. I contributed the china teacups and teapots and we had some donated chesterfields reupholstered by a local furniture class. Very soon the SafeMe main hall was like home: a mixture of my messiness and Janice's boho style. No need for housework or continual tidying. No pressure to 'keep house'. We were all in recovery here. All supporting each other, feet up, having a brew, in our safe, secure, grotto.

'They'd try to take the settlement workers to the merger. And us …?'

I laugh.

'I doubt it. Troublemakers, us. Renegades.' They would never take us. Not after the arguments and protests to get the ever dwindling-funding over the past years of government austerity. I lean over and touch her arm. 'But if we do lose this place, worst-case scenario, we can still carry on. Kind of freelance. Outreach. Helping them stand up for themselves. It won't end here.'

But we both know how difficult that would be. We both know the consequences for the women and their children. They will be out of our reach, out of public view. Hidden away behind a set of statistics as someone in a research department ventures out once a year to interview a token victim for the *Guardian* opinion column. They will become another column on a spreadsheet, a paragraph in a government report that someone will read out, assuring us all that this problem is being dealt with, while these women step on and off the ever-spinning merry-go-round of abuse, until they fall off for good.

So Janice and I know that it will end here. In practice, anyway. The embers of the service will survive in our hearts, and we will never stop fighting for what is right, but if the funding bid is rejected SafeMe will close.

Janice stands. I smile at her.

'It's not over till it's over.'

Mid-afternoon my phone beeps and I grab it. It's Vi.

'Hello, Ria. It's me, Violet. Look, Donelle's cancelled for the kids. Meeting her man Ian. I'm really sorry but Danny's got a hospital appointment or I would ...'

I'm suddenly alert.

'It's OK, Vi. Don't worry. I can ask Terri. I'm sure she'll do it. If not I'll go.'

But alarm bells are ringing. It isn't like Donelle to drop everything and run after a man. I think about what she said, how she mentioned that he was demanding. Had I listened enough? I make a mental note to try to talk to her. I dial Terri's number.

'Hi, Terri love. Can you get the kids from school? Please? Sorry it's short notice but ...'

She laughs. 'Course. But I have to leave at four-thirty for my shift.'

'Thanks. I'll make sure I'm back.'

I see two missed calls from Donelle, both at lunchtime when I was in the archive room. It would normally be OK but I am suddenly filled with fear. Terri is great with the kids, but I haven't warned her not to let anyone near them. No matter what.

I pull on my coat and dial a taxi. I am dancing foot to foot, waiting in the yard. Janice comes out.

'What ...?'

'Kids. Donelle's cancelled.' I hold her by the shoulders. 'Do not worry. I will be here, fresh and early, for the meeting tomorrow. Everything is ready to go.'

I meet her eyes and she nods. The taxi arrives and the driver tuts when I tell him the address, only a short distance, but I need to get there quickly.

We pull up outside the flat and I throw a fiver at him. I turn the key in the door and I see Jennifer's coat in the hallway and breathe a sigh of relief. I panicked for nothing. I can hear her, giggling and singing, and Terri is laughing. I relax. It's all OK, Ria. It's all OK.

But as I turn the corner into the tiny lounge, I see a huge bunch of flowers on the kitchen table, my lovely bright yellow painted table. Terri beams when she sees me, looking at the flowers.

'Surprise. Aren't they beautiful?'

They are exactly the same flowers as the ones delivered to SafeMe. Fucking roses. I freeze.

'Where did they come from?'

Terri's smile fades and Jennifer stops jumping up and down.

'This guy brought them. Said they're for you.'

'Was he here? In here?'

I move closer to her and she backs away.

'Yes. He brought them in and set them up on the table. He knew the kids. Called them by their names. I thought ...'

I look at my children. He was here, with them. In my home. I gather them to me. Terri is mortified. I move very close to her.

'Who was it? What did he look like?'

She stares at me, suddenly tense.

'I don't know, Ria. I've never seen him before. Average height. Average build. Darkish hair.'

'How old?'

I see the tears spring up.

'Forties, I think. Look, Ria, what's this about?'

'What exactly did he say? Exactly?' I realise I am shouting at her. Right in her face. 'Sorry. Sorry. It's just ...'

'God, Ria, I'm sorry. I thought ...'

I regroup.

'It's not your fault, Terri. He tricked you. Did he say anything else?'

She shakes her head. I spot a card on the flowers, in a sealed envelope. I grab it and rip it open.

WANT TO PLAY THE GAME, RIA? LET'S SEE HOW GOOD YOU ARE.

Tanya

I don't know what is going on. Another day has passed and he's not back. Maybe he's had an accident. But the police would have been here. I've eaten everything. There is no more food, but plenty of tea and coffee so I'm drinking black tea.

I woke up late this morning and I didn't feel too good. Apart from being hungry, my face seemed more swollen and red. I sat on the coffee table in the front room cross-legged and tried to clear my mind and think what could have happened. He hadn't left because most of his things were still here. He would never leave this house.

Not an accident. No. Illness? He would be in hospital and they would try to contact next of kin. Arrested? I was suddenly alert. The letter. I posted the letter. I started to laugh and I could not stop. I was hysterical. I knew the police were looking for me. Well, Alice. I knew. I pretended I didn't care. That I was blasé about the whole thing. But at night I would cry silently for my dad. I knew him. He put full effort into everything and he would put all he had into trying to find me.

But I also knew that if I went home Alan would be in trouble. He told me he was nineteen. He told everyone he was nineteen. But I saw his driver's licence and he was twenty-five. He would be in deep trouble. So time just went on and I let my imagination change the story. I imagined that I really was Tanya and Alice was buried up near the rocks, near where Ria and I used to swim and where Alan and I first made love.

So when my addled brain told me that he was seeing Ria still, that when he was away he was with her, that she was waiting for him in swanky hotel rooms, I wrote the letter. I told them that Alice's friend knew where she was. That I was a friend of hers and she told me that she was jealous and had harmed Alice. That she had told her about that night when Alice went missing from her bedroom. The bedroom with the wooden rocking horse and the pink bedspread with butterflies on it.

Oh yes, I had told them down to the last detail that Alice's friend had described the room and Alice's demise. That I was a close confidante but couldn't bear to keep this secret; I wished to remain anonymous. I didn't mention Ria by name - even when I hated her I just couldn't. I just described her.

I had laid it on thick and made sure that the police knew this was real. And that Alice was up by the pool where I had imagined her. Me. I don't know what is real any more. But I also mentioned that her boyfriend helped her. So if they have arrested Alan and Ria I have sentenced myself.

My laughter turned to tears when I suddenly realised that he might never come back. That he might have just left me here. I know there is no way out because if there was I would have found it years ago. I have water but no food. I don't know how long someone can last without food.

I traced my fingers around the walls, around the windows, trying to find any way that I could get out. I know the attic door has a padlock on it. I knocked on the outer walls to test for weakness but this house is solid.

I spent the rest of the day just waiting. I went through everyone we know and ranked them in order of if they would miss me. Finally, just as I felt like I was going to pass out, I realised that no one is coming for me. Somewhere, outside my body, I heard someone begin to scream. Then I realised that it was me.

Chapter Twenty-four

Day 6

I did consider phoning the police. Terri could not have been more apologetic, but I told her that it wasn't her fault. He told her he was a friend; he knew my name and Danny's name, the names of our children; said he had just come to drop off some lovely flowers? All very plausible. The kids needed their tea and I needed time to calm down.

Then Danny phoned and said he would be back early. There was a dust storm brewing, apparently, and he would be flying back as the job was nearly finished anyway. He sounded worried.

'I don't know if they will pay us the full whack. There's work locally when we get back, but ...'

I exhaled. Danny would be back soon and I hadn't sorted this.

'It's OK, Dan, just get back safe. We can save. Don't worry.'

I panicked. I needed to deal with it before Danny did. I dialled 101 and then ended the call. What am I reporting? An old friend calling round? I know it is more, that he is threatening me, but I cannot prove anything. Except that I have texted him and asked him to leave me alone, but then they will ask me why I didn't do that in the first place.

So, instead, I lay awake all night, waiting for Danny to text me with his travelling times. Worrying. I walked the kids to school and did the 'stranger danger' drill, impressing upon them that they must not go off with anyone. Vi is collecting them today, the day of the funding meeting, as it is likely I will be home a little later, and Donelle's shift starts at six o'clock.

'Grandma Vi will pick you up. You must only go with her.'

Simon grips my hand.

'Are you OK, Mum? You look tired.'

I nod and smile. 'I miss Daddy. Just like you do. But only a few more days. Then we will be back to normal.' *Normal*, I tell myself, even though my addled brain has almost forgotten what normal is.

I watch them go inside and wait until the doors are shut and locked. I scan the area. No red car. I can't get the flowers out of my mind. He was in my home. I promise myself that, the next time he pulls something like this, I will call the police straight away. When I get to work and there is no sign of him, I write up last night's debacle in my diary and lock it in my desk drawer.

Janice and I keep our business suits in the lockers at the end of the office. I open my locker and pull out a black Next trouser suit and a white blouse. The meeting will start in fifteen minutes and I watch through the window as the agency representatives file in.

It's taking place in the family room, and Janice has moved all the Xboxes and screens and set up a projector and laptop for presentations. I carry her suit through. She has made the room look businesslike, even down to jugs of water and glasses, and a duo of hot drinks dispensers on the side with eggshell-blue cups. I feel out of place in here, in my red jeans and white T-shirt, my hair unwashed and approaching deadlocks. Janice looks down at her smock, black with a splash of breakfast.

'Better get changed. God, I feel nervous.'

She is a shade of ashen white and I know this place means everything to her.

'Que sera sera. Nothing we can do now.'

She nods. We hurry through to the toilets and get changed. I pull my hair back in a tight plait and rub on the obligatory foundation, followed by a lick of mascara and some pale pink lipstick. The result looks semi acceptable, and at least I have made an effort. Janice squeezes into a black dress and black tights. Her over-bleached hair is reluctant to be tamed, but I manage to brush it through and capture it in an elastic band, the pony tail spiralling down her back.

We are both uncomfortable and it makes the atmosphere thick and awkward. Janice pulls at the dress and I breathe in to fasten the button on my trousers. I give up with the jacket.

'Fucking hell, Jan. Fucking hell.'

She sighs, deep and long.

'They are a bunch of bastards, but some of them must have a heart. Until I know, I'm not giving up.'

We watch as the council officials file in now behind the police representative and the CAFCASS woman that we usually deal with. Marjorie Bates is herding them in, all bonhomie. My lips curl as I see Trevor Jones step into the yard and look upwards at the building looming before him. Then, behind him, a slim figure, all dressed in black. Adele Baker. Janice whistles.

'Well, fuck me. She came.'

Adele Baker is the head of the council. She is an almost mythical figure who spearheads all the positive change in the town, but is mysteriously absent from anything that goes wrong. When I heard the funding was in question this year, I wrote to her and asked her if she wanted to be the head of a town that has no domestic violence provision, one that can't prosecute offenders because there is no one to defend the women. I used the 'someone think of the children' tack that I am so loath to roll out, because abused women should be enough, but they never are.

I asked for money not only to continue SafeMe as it is but also to extend it into a children's unit. I realise now, at this late stage, that I hadn't mentioned this part to Janice. But it won't matter. Because she was observing and I was doing the talking. I had prepared my death by PowerPoint presentation and, even in my highly stressed state with my personal life teetering on the precipice of disaster, I will myself to stick to the plan.

The council do not like emotional interludes where people throw away the meeting agenda and stand on chairs crying. I know this from long experience of funding meetings, mostly other people's in other parts of the country where I have been drafted in as an independent observer. The Rias and Janices usually start well. But, greeted by stony-faced number-crunchers, they grow determined to get their messages across.

So I must not do that. And Janice must not do that. We will sit and nod and smile and listen and make notes until it is my turn to give my presentation, which I will do calmly and eloquently, even though I already feel like screaming the place down. Then we will listen again and shake hands and show them out, awaiting the result in a couple of days. All as if it is in a day's work. Maybe one of our last here.

I look at Janice.

'Ready?'

She nods and we go in, our double-act vibe never stronger. She has made name cards, and everyone is sitting in their designated place. I cannot help but stare at Trevor, who is messing with a clipboard. He doesn't meet my eyes and no fucking wonder.

Everyone is fussing around Adele Baker. Does she want a coffee, a biscuit? Is that chair OK, Adele? Is it warm enough in here for you, Adele? Close up she looks quite normal, in a very thin, over-groomed kind of way. Younger than I thought. Silent.

We begin. There is an introduction from the head of the team that has been considering the funding bid, Emma Lewis. She goes through the budgets and the proposals for an hour and a half and I am almost losing the will to live. I made the mistake of sitting opposite the window and I watch as Sheila goes to the shop for ciggies and comes back. Malc walks up and down outside and there is a delivery of potatoes. Eventually, Emma finishes, and there are a set of reports from the agencies. This lasts another hour and it is lunchtime. I watch as the buffet delivery company fetches in some hot and cold platters and everyone grabs a plate.

I nibble at a sandwich, seething, but smiling. This is not going well for me. Nothing unexpected has been introduced, and Janice is being the friendliest person ever, even twirling the end of her ponytail as she chats to George Allinson from the police liaison unit. Emma is talking at me, explaining how she single-handedly saved the budget of the local library open days. How this has benefited the children of the area, which, I admit, is admirable, but it does not answer my question.

I drift away, fantasising about a time when I can walk into the local police station and tell all. I consider running a hypothetical scenario past George, just to see what he says. But I already know. Proof. Evidence. Catching someone is the act. Proving harm. Yada yada yada.

'So in the end we had to settle for puppet shows.'

Emma is obviously expecting an answer, and I oblige by nodding and smiling a 'Really?' in a very interested voice. The platters are bare and Janice is pouring elderflower cordial into a jug and topping it up with expensive sparking water. I push down the derision and smile, smile, smile. Janice sees my fake bonhomie and raises me.

'Right, lovely people. Shall we reconvene?'

We smile at each other. Next on the agenda: Trevor Jones. I sit and clasp my hands in front of me. He clicks his PowerPoint controller and tests the laser pointer on the screen.

'Right then. Ladies. Gentlemen. Madam Chairman.' He gives a little deferential bow to Adele Baker. 'Shall we begin?'

He clicks through the facts and figures, which are really only a rehash of my proposals and budgets and what has been presented today. He is merely regurgitating it, without passing any opinion, but I know it is coming. I can feel it as the slides click on. I am fine, calm, collected until he stretches to point at the screen and I see the cufflinks. A set of gold squares with a tiny diamond in them. It riles me beyond what I can bear and I feel my face set solid. Janice frowns but no one else notices as I glare around the room. He finally reaches his conclusion.

'So based on this, I have reached my decision. My final decision.' He says it like he is Simon Cowell on *Britain's Got Talent* and I roll my eyes as Janice visibly wills me to stop it. 'I hear all of you. I hear all the good things about SafeMe. About the boys and girls here and about the good work. But facts are facts. And there is a perfectly good space in a duplicated service only a couple of miles down the road that can provide adequate services.'

People are making notes. Janice is bright red and I am past anger. George asks a question.

'So is this based solely on budget decisions?'

Trevor nods enthusiastically. 'Budget savings, George. We simply can't afford to keep this facility. But no services will be lost and most of the staff will be re-contracted. Those who fit the services, anyway.'

I watch Adele, taking it all in. Quiet and solemn. Trevor looks around.

'Any further questions? No? Then it's over to you, Ria.'

I walk over and take the clicker. It's like I am walking on air. As if I am hardly in the room. But I keep it together, I have to. I shine the laser pointer on the screen, testing it, then I look at Janice and shine the red dot onto Trevor's forehead. She looks alarmed.

'Oh, it's working.' I give a little laugh. 'Right. Can you dim the lights, Jan? Thanks.'

I click my PowerPoint presentation into action and go through the slides, one by boring one. They are facts and figures and just another rehash of the same figures dressed up differently. Unfortunately I am not allowed to show them pictures of the women's injuries or the footage of Jim beating down the door with a claw hammer.

But I do finish with a slide about two women per week on average being killed by their partners. Trevor sighs and looks at his watch.

Adele speaks. The room is silent.

'Please could you give us an example, Ria? Of someone you have helped?'

I look at Janice. She mouths 'Sally'. Adele nods as I speak, taking in Sally's story, how we successfully invoked an injunction and how she will be rehoused. I have not completely finished speaking when Trevor interrupts.

'Yes, yes, yes. But all this would be possible with the new plan.'

I hold it in. I hold in all the anger and the sadness and the feeling that SafeMe is slipping through my fingers.

'But there would be no mentoring. No groups. It would just be accommodation. With no security. There would be no emotional support.'

Adele raises her eyebrows and writes. Trevor sees her and interrupts again.

'But that could still be provided. With external funders. I understand that a local businessman is prepared to fund those elements of the service. External to council funding.'

Janice clenches her whole body. I see her fists bunch into white knuckles and her knees go tight as if she has just been attacked. All eyes are on me. I can feel myself still smiling, my laser pointer making a red streak on the table. I switch the clicker off.

'Thank you for your attention. That is the end of my presentation. I think you have almost everything you need to make your decision. Except for one thing.'

I go over to the laptop and unplug the media plug. The huge wall-sized screen goes dark and the room is suddenly lit only by the light from the window, making it feel cold and empty. I swirl my finger on the touch pad, selecting the SafeMe Network and finding my user area. I select the correct file and plug the screen back in.

Frank's face fills the wall, mid-word. I glance at Janice who is staring at me, shocked to the core. I look at Trevor, who is struggling to make sense of the picture in front of him, until he hears Frank's voice boom out over the speakers.

The whole conversation about Trevor and the decision and the funding and what he will do plays to a room of wide eyes and open mouths. The footage stops, but I wind it back to the part where Frank is assuring us that Trevor will make the right decision, the part where he is messing with his cufflinks. I focus the screen in on the cufflinks. Then I turn the clicker back on. Trevor is pulling down his sleeves, anticipating my next action. But it is too late. The red dot is on his wrist, the tiny diamond twinkling red and the gold glinting.

I turn off the footage.

'Any questions? No?' They stare at me in complete silence. I nod. 'That concludes my presentation, ladies and gentlemen.'

I walk past them, flicking on the lights so that they blink into the harsh fluorescent glow. I throw the clicker on to the table, leave and slam the door behind me. I rush to my office and Janice is behind me. I watch through the open door as they file out, Adele Baker storming through the double doors and to her car, Marjorie, George and Emma running behind her. Trevor stalks through, shooting me a dirty look and I respond with my middle finger and a mouthed 'Fuck You.'

Janice sits down in the chair opposite.

'Fucking hell, Ria. Fucking hell. Tell it like it is, girl.'

I shake my head. There are no words. The truth is out there. Some of it, anyway. The caterers arrive to take away what is left, and Malc opens up the accommodation doors and in no time everything is back to how it should be. Except Janice's face, which shows a reverence I have never seen before.

She gets up and goes to the safe. She clicks it one way and then another and extracts one of the tacky golden Superwoman stars left over from the awards night. She passes it to me silently.

Tanya

Diary Entry: Thursday

I slept all Wednesday night and most of Thursday. When I woke my face didn't feel so hot and sore. I looked in the mirror and my eye, which had been almost closed and puffy yesterday, was open again. My headache was gone and somehow I felt positive.

It's fairly clear now that he isn't coming back. Somewhere in between sleep and awake, in my delirium, I took this thinking a bit further, pushed it to the limit. He isn't coming back yet. He will come back eventually, of course, but I will be dead then. It gave me a kind of peace. An understanding.

But when I woke up I felt more determined than ever to get out of here. I wondered if I could use the skillet to hammer something and break the lock on the door. I tried to do it with a spoon which bent on contact. Instead, I swung the skillet at the door. It bounced off, leaving a small dent. I'd heard him say it many, many times.

'We've got composite doors. And roller shutters. No one's going to rob us.'

I swung again, and the rebound spun me round. I sat on the kitchen floor in the corner. I was very hungry. Very. I looked up at the cupboards. Two tins of tomatoes, two tins of beans and one tin of kidney beans. I rushed over and placed one on the tiled floor. I lifted the skillet above my head and brought it down on the can of beans. It buckled and popped, the contents spraying across the tiles. I stared at the mess. But beggars can't be choosers. I scuttled around picking up every individual bean and dipping up the tomato sauce with my fingers.

When I had finished, I ran the shower and filled up the washing-up bowl with warm water. I got out the squeegee mop and cleaned the floor. If I was going to eat off it I need to keep it spotless. For what, though? I'm just prolonging the agony.

Chapter Twenty-five

Day 5

I rushed over to Vi's after the meeting was finished, phoning on the way and checking everything was OK, that there had been no surprise visitors. The kids ran to hug me and the bitter victory of showing Frank's video at the meeting began to feel a little bit reckless. What if I lose my job? If I had been a 'good girl' and toed the council line at least I would have references. This way, I'm fucked. No one will touch me after this.

But the overwhelming feeling is relief. It's not often that this kind of underlying behaviour is outed. The lying, bribing, influencing that goes on. It's usually an internal whistleblower followed by an inquiry that buries the wrongdoing and wrongdoers in detail, them long gone after a three-tier investigation that takes years. But this is different, and we all know it. Especially Adele Baker, who clearly had no idea this was happening. Her face was pure anger and my stomach turns over at the thought of what will happen next.

The good feeling that I have made a difference is overshadowed when, first thing in the morning, I feel Danny's side of the bed, realise he will be back soon and think about my stalker immediately. He has contaminated my home, and I get up and clean every surface he could have been near, wiping the door handle with bleach spray.

I get a text from Danny, which stops me in my tracks and makes me sip my tea as I read it.

> Morning, babe. Five days then we can have a lie-in. I'm on my
> way! There's a short contract at home, shit money but if I work
> it, I will get the bonus. Have a good Fri-yay. See you later –
> can't wait x I love you x always x

I feel the relief flood through me that Danny is coming home. I just have to figure out a way to keep my fear inside and hope my stalker doesn't pull another stunt before then. Jennifer appears and rubs her eyes.

'Mummy.'

I hug her.

'Daddy's coming back. He'll be back soon.'

She sighs. 'Can we have a puppy?'

Simon is behind her. 'No. we can't have a dog. We can't leave a dog on its own all day.'

Jennifer's bottom lip trembles and I feel my stress levels shoot up. She lets out a wail.

'I want a dog. Janet's got a dog. They take it on walks. It's not fair.'

I put their cereal on the table and pour them orange juice.

'Life isn't fair, Jen. And Simon's right. Mummy and Daddy have to work and we can't leave a dog all day.'

She pouts. 'Janet's mummy doesn't go to work.'

I nod and smile tightly. 'Good for her.'

Jennifer stares at me. 'Where's Grandma's granddad?'

I go to the kitchen and rest my hands on the sink, staring through the window into the shared garden. I know Jennifer is still tired. We were at Vi's until late and she was cranky when she went to bed. I know that these inquisitive questions are perfectly normal for a seven-year-old. But I am worn out. My nerves are frayed and now I am on the verge of snapping at my overtired daughter. .

I take a deep breath and carry on. I have no choice, but something needs to change, and quickly. Outside the school gates I watch as they walk in, Jennifer hand in hand with Janet. I glance at Janet's mum, who flashes me a cosmetic-dentistry smile. She is blonde and pretty and she has parked her shiny Audi in the no-parking zone – again – but she is the type of person who will get away with it every time. The rules don't apply. They live in a detached house on the new estate, the one Danny calls 'plastic paradise'. Her husband owns a builders' merchant. Jennifer has been to birthday parties at their home and I have sat outside as she runs in. I'm not jealous, but I sometimes wonder what it would be like.

It is this mood that takes me along the backstreets of terraced houses to SafeMe. These are the streets of my kind of people, the kind of folk who were not born with a silver spoon and who somehow have to overcome problems just to get through. Most of the time I like it. I like the challenge and I know that an 'easy life', one like Janet's mum, directed and paid for by someone else, would not fulfil me. But when I am uneasy, unsettled, it is what I yearn for. Someone to make it right for me. Danny in regular work so I would have a chance to breathe.

Right now I am almost suffocating. I'm watching all the time for the red car and some sign of who is watching me, now etched into my day, and I'm ever vigilant. He is nowhere to be seen and I feel doom. If he isn't here, is he somewhere else planning something worse? The doom deepens as I see Malc waving at me down the street.

I hurry up to the gates and he points around the corner. My mobile rings and I see the warden's name. Shit. Sheila. I hadn't thought about what impact yesterday's performance would have on her. I divert and rush past the gates and around the corner. Her living-room light is on and the warden isn't outside. My phone rings again and I see Karen at the window of the warden flat. She rings off but points to Sheila's flat.

I'm out of breath, my flat glittery pumps pounding the pavement, but when I buzz, she answers normally.

'Hello?'

I catch my breath.

'Sheila. It's me.'

She buzzes me in instead of coming to the door. The flat door is open and cigarette smoke has filled the hallway as well as her living space. I go in. she's sitting in her usual chair, but half of her furniture is gone: the glass cabinet and all her little dolls; the glass coffee table with the octopus base. I look into the bedroom. All her clothes are shoved into black bags. I stand in front of her. She is clutching a holdall that is slightly open. I can see her jewellery box, the charm bracelet on top, and several sleeves of her favourite brand of cigarettes.

'Bloody hell, Sheila. I wondered what had happened. The warden—'

She snorts. 'Yeah well. Thought I'd be gone before you got here.' She smiles a little. 'Part-timer, you, lady.'

The kitchen is still intact so I make a brew. Our usual tea in her brown earthenware pot, poured into china teacups and then milk added, with Sheila's customary two spoons of sugar. I put hers down in front of her. Neither of us speaks for a while and she does not meet my eye. But I can't leave it like this.

'Why, Sheila, love?'

She nods. 'I'm tired. It's never going to stop.'

I shake my head. 'Is this about yesterday?'

She looks confused.

'I don't know. Why? What happened yesterday?'

I debate whether I should tell her or not, but maybe she needs to know. And maybe I need to say it. I speak gently to her.

'Well, we had our funding meeting. I found out that Frank had been ... influencing one of the council people and I told them.'

She laughs harshly. Her throat rasps and she sips her tea through the bright red confidence lipstick.

'What's fucking new?' She laughs some more. 'Of course he has. You might as well face it, love: Frank'll get what he wants.'

I nod. 'Yes. So I see.'

She puts her cup gently down beside the saucer. Sheila's not a saucer person.

'That's where you're wrong, lovey. I've decided to go back. Me. I've decided.'

Her frown is deep and I can see that this is important to her.

'But why? He hasn't changed. You know what will happen, Sheila.' I take her hand, arthritic before its time, deeply tanned with fake tan and yellow and brown speckled with nicotine. I've grown fond of these hands. Their warmth. 'Please. Don't go.'

She pulls in her lips.

'I have to. Because you know what will happen if I don't.'

I shake my head. 'No. I don't know. But I know you will be in danger. Please, Sheila. Think about it. We can get you new stuff.'

She pulls her hand away and lights yet another cigarette.

'He won't stop till he gets his own way. He'll start on this place – you and her, if he hasn't already. I'm back home. And all them girls who come here, what'll happen to them?'

Her logic is flawed and she clearly doesn't realise that SafeMe is in danger in any case – or perhaps she thinks Frank is behind it all. I have a sudden insight, a sudden questioning. What if he is?

I don't have an answer to tell her. I don't lie and tell her everything will be OK if she leaves. Or that everything will be OK if she doesn't. Instead, I sit quietly, fighting back tears and swallowing tea. I pour again.

'What about you, lovey? I've watched you, you know, losing weight, dark circles under them pretty eyes. Somat's up with you. So come on, tell your Aunty Sheila before it's time for me to go.'

My eyes brim and I pull at my T-shirt, pulling it down over my knees like I used to do as a teenager. Eventually I manage to speak.

'This guy … he's, he's … harassing me. I'm a bit scared of him.'

She pats my knee.

'You know them photos I showed you? When me and Frank were courting. At the boxing? We were a real item and we were on the same wavelength. I always knew what he was, you know.'

I stare at her. 'Did you? But …'

'Yeah. But I could overlook it. We laughed and talked and then all that over Bobby, secrets, not speaking, punishing each other. But the worst thing was keeping it inside. I never once told him the truth. How hurt I was. How upset. For us both. I still haven't. It's lingered there between us, and he could have helped me. It's not always been like this, you know. But I just became another thing to him. Another asset. I'd pull away now and again and he'd push me back into line.' She sees me wince. 'I know it's wrong, yeah, and I know who Frank is. What he does to people. I just never thought he'd do it to me.'

She rubs the plaster cast.

'I'm worried for you, Sheila. What if he …?'

She grabs my hand, hard.

'Never mind me, love. Save yourself. Tell the truth. Tell your fella. Tell the police. Tell everyone. That bloke, whatever he has on you, face it and start again, while you still have time.'

She is crying now.

'This place. Solid bloody gold. You and Janice, you're good women, like I've never known before. Standing up to them cruel bastards and talking sense. Take your own advice, for once, love. Or mark my words, you'll end up like me. Trapped inside here.'

She taps her temple. I wait a while.

'But what about the other day? His ...'

'Daughter? Yeah. I always knew, really. And look at the bright side. She'll be there to look after me when I'm old and decrepit. I might get to know her. That'll piss him off.'

She smiles wickedly, her face crinkling sadly. We both look at the window as the light is blocked by a big white furniture van. Two men appear and Sheila nods slightly. They start to move black bin bags out of the bedroom. She's still gripping my hand tightly and I see a trace of panic.

'It's not too late, Sheila. You can stay with me. I can move Jenni—'

'What, and bring Frank to your door? Bloody hell. Sounds like you've got enough problems as it is, lovey. No. It is too late. It's the only way.'

The men finish with the bin bags and start to pack up the kitchen, bringing in removal boxes and silently packing things just as they are – a tea caddy full of teabags, the brown teapot, the cups and saucers. Toaster, microwave, leaving only the items Sheila has stuck red dots on, the SafeMe fixtures and fittings. Her eyes follow them, yellow and super-watery now, and she still grips my hand tightly.

We step aside as they take the leopard-skin rug and the animal-print throws. Sheila twists her diamonds and fusses over some crumbs on the floor, fetching a dustpan and brush. Keeping busy. Finally, all her belongings are gone. The only trace of Sheila is Sheila, and I hug her tight. She reaches her lips to my ear.

'Thanks for everything, love. I've thought of you as a kind of daughter, you know. If I'd had a daughter, I would have wanted her to be just like you.' She holds my cheeks in her chubby fingers. 'You're a lovely girl. Lovely.'

I take her hands. My heart is breaking.

'We could meet up. Have a brew somewhere? I just want to make sure you are OK.'

She shakes her head. 'No, lovey. You know that's not what's going to happen here. I told you to tell the truth, and I will now.' She squeezes my hands tighter until it almost hurts. 'You won't see me again. It's for the best. For everyone.' I feel the tears, hot on my cheeks, but she brushes them away with her thumbs. 'Superwoman. That's how I'll always think of you, love. Bloody Superwoman, you are.'

She lets go suddenly, grabs the holdall and leaves. A small crowd has gathered outside and I watch through the window as she stands at the top of the path and Janice talks to her. Janice has the tenancy folder and I see her pointing to the signature line, and Sheila taking the pen and signing. She looks back at the doorway and I wonder if she has changed her mind. The van drives away and for a moment I think she will come back in, sit down in the chair and light a cigarette.

Instead, she kisses Janice on the cheek and moves towards the other women; they are holding her hand and laughing, the easy camaraderie of a soldier going into battle. I see the 'good lucks' and the pats on the back, the arms-folded solidarity of women who know full well what this battle entails because they have all been there.

I compose myself and go outside, past Janice, who catches my eye and nods, through the small crowd and to Sheila.

'Good luck, Sheila. I know what you said, and I'll never chase you, but you know where we are if you want us.' I hug her. 'Where *I* am. Anything, yeah? Anything at all.'

She nods and looks into my eyes.

'It's over for me now. You do what I told you, you hear me, lady?'

I nod. We all watch as a black limo pulls up and almost silently draws to a halt, the back door aligning exactly with the gravel pathway. Sheila hardly misses a beat as she holds her head up high and, as the door opens and I catch a glimpse of a pair of golf shoes, she turns and waves like the queen. Everybody laughs except me, and she is gone. The door shut, the limo pulls away and disappears around the corner.

The crowd disperses and Janice is beside me.

'Another one bites the dust.'

We stare at the space where the limo was, arms folded and sombre. Malc paces up and down, I can see Sally's kids through the family-room window playing. A bird sings and the sound of the M60 rumbles in the distance. All as usual. Except Sheila is gone. Janice shakes her head.

'Come on. We'll sort that lot out later. We'll need a couple of pneumatic drills to get the nicotine off them walls.'

I have to smile because what else can I do?

'I'll just be a minute.'

She hands me the keys and I go back inside. She really is gone. *Tell the truth*, she said. And I will. I root around in my bag for a tissue to blow my nose and feel something soft and furry. I already know what it is before I pull it out. The blue fuzzy ears emerge and I hold it there in front of me, conclusive proof that Sheila has given up: Bobby's rabbit.

Tanya

Diary Entry: Friday

I am weaker than ever but I have made a breakthrough. I am trying to drink lots of water as well as tea and coffee, but I have to make the tins last as long as possible. Last night I bust them all open and scooped them up into freezer bags, tiny portions in each. I put them in the fridge and it looked like a decent amount.

Mid-morning I made a big decision. I knew that Alan kept biscuits in his study because I have seen the empty packets in the bin. Boxes, sometimes. And chocolate. I have never been allowed in there, even at the beginning. He jokingly called it the 'man-cave' but there was more truth to that than I imagined. Today, though, I would break in.

The bedroom, too. He had told me to never go in there, so I never had. Sitting at the table, thinking about the letter and every combination of what could happen until I felt sick, I suddenly realised that his bedroom didn't have a lock on the door. I had just never dared to go in alone.

I rushed upstairs and tried the door. Sure enough, it opened. I crept inside and opened his wardrobe. Quite a lot of his clothes were gone, leaving big gaps. I searched through the drawers. No food. No sweets. Not even mints.

Then I turned around. The TV. I can watch TV. I switched it on and turned it up. Loud. It was a game show. Lots of people stood behind illuminated boxes. Just the sound of human voices made me less panicky.

I made my way downstairs to the study. I'd seen Alan lock it so I knew this wouldn't be as easy as the bedroom. I tried the handle but immediately felt sick to my stomach. What if he comes home now? I ran back upstairs and switched off the TV. At least I would hear him.

The study door is just dark pine, the same as all the other internal doors in the house. I tried to smash the handle and lock first, but a fortunate near-miss hit one of the panels and splintered it. I hit it again, harder this time, and it smashed out. I tore away the splintered wood and climbed into Alan's man cave.

It wasn't what I expected. Unlike the rest of the house, the furniture was dark oak. He had an old desk with green leather inlay and a computer screen on the top. There was a TV in the corner and an ox-blood chesterfield against the wall. I opened the drawers one by one and bingo! A biscuit tin. I prised it open and there were just four Nice biscuits. I gobbled them down. Better than nothing.

There was a brown leather bag. I opened it and inside was a badge with Alan's picture on it. He must have got a job at Social Services. Maybe Jenny got it for him. Then I saw a drawer with a key. I turned the key carefully, wondering what he would lock up in an already locked room. There were some more photographs of me as a teenager and some strips of tablets. I suddenly wondered if he was ill and if that was why he was doing all this. But they were Cerazette. I vaguely recognised the name, but I read the leaflet all the same. The mini pill. My hand went to my stomach. He'd taken away the one thing that could have saved me. Not that I wanted his baby. No. But I would have liked the choice.

Then I turned around. On the wall behind the door was a cork board. There were a few pictures of a woman and two children. There was a picture of me all those years ago as a teenager, all teeth and hairband. I looked closer. There was a newspaper cutting pinned to the top of the photographs. It was photocopied and highlighted.

There was a woman holding a small trophy, smiling.

'Ria Taylor – Local Superwoman.'

My blood ran cold and the familiar icicles of jealousy began to form. Then I remembered what he had done to her. Done to us. I read the rest of the report.

> Local mother of two Ria Taylor ran an evening to highlight the plight of women experiencing violence. Ria, who runs the SafeMe Centre, said, 'Two women per week are killed by their partners. I am making it my life's work to stop this happening, whatever it takes.'
>
> The Centre provides accommodation and recovery for women who have undergone abuse. Ria explained how she got involved in this work.
>
> 'An incident in my teens made me realise that I wanted to help other people who had been harmed by violence or coercive control.'

I chilled even more. He had highlighted 'An incident in my teens'.

Pinned next to the picture of Ria were various photographs of an older woman and another woman with lots of children. A picture of a building. A picture of a terraced house. A picture of a school with a different woman with the children Ria was with in the first picture. Ria going into the police station.

What the hell was this about? Has she reported him after all this time? Is this why this has come up now?

I ran my finger over her face on the newspaper cutting. She looks happy. I'm glad. I know what the 'incident in her teens' means. She would run to my house, her face still red, vivid hand marks. She told me her dad hit her. Slapped her. I never understood it really. Not until now.

But Alan would obviously think it was about him. The self-obsessed bastard. I shocked myself. I had long ago regulated myself not to get angry and not to swear, even in my head, as it might inevitably slip out and was punishable.

I wonder where he is now, what he is doing to her. If he has her trapped too. But Ria is brave. I bet she would fight, unlike me. As usual, I am helpless to do anything except fade away.

Chapter Twenty-six

Day 4

Nine o'clock on Saturday morning and I'm in the foyer of the police station waiting for Carole Barnes. Simon is entranced by the desk and the sergeant and the man who has just been brought in wearing handcuffs. Jennifer is playing hopscotch on the multicoloured tiles.

I cried myself to sleep over Sheila and I was exhausted from the past couple of days. I knew as soon as Frank's car pulled away that I would be sitting here this morning. I am not responsible for Sheila's safety, but I am bound by my own integrity to report any criminal activity. It isn't the first time I have given the police a heads-up on a potentially dangerous situation.

Bound by my own integrity. Yes. For other people, but not for me. Here I am, sitting in the police station and I don't even have the guts to tell the truth. I will. I definitely will. Carole appears.

'Ria. Hi. Come through.'

Simon is delighted that we are seeing the inside of the police station. Carole waves to a woman on the desk.

'Paula, can you give our VIPs the guided tour?'

Paula smiles widely and herds Jennifer and Simon towards the staff canteen and the play area. I follow Carole to her office.

'So. What can I do for you?'

I take a deep breath.

'Sheila James. She's returned to the family home.'

Her face clouds. 'Frank James's wife? Did she go of her own free will?'

I nod. 'She'll say she did, but ...'

We sit in silence for a moment. Carole stares at me.

'You know I can't log it. I'll put a note on the file but she has never made a complaint.'

I roll my eyes. Of course she hasn't. She's never really admitted that Frank has hurt her. Not officially.

'Yeah. My problem is that he's tried to get over-involved with SafeMe. Tried to interfere in the funding process.'

Carole makes a face. 'What, Frank? Bribery? Fraud? Never.' She is sarcastic and scathing. But then she realises what I have said. 'God, Ria, is it that time? Funding apps? What'll happen?'

I shrug. 'Hard to tell. The council guy recommended against it. So I showed them Frank's arse.' I remember she is the police. 'Oh. Sorry.'

She smiles.

'But the service provision?'

'They claim it will go to Redeem. But they don't have a specialist service, do they?'

She pales. 'You're kidding. The women ...'

'I know. They would just be placed anywhere and then they'd be sitting targets.'

Neither of us speaks. I know that she is imagining the same scenario that has haunted me for weeks: someone in danger with nowhere to go. Someone in need of protection, turned away.

'Was there representation from us?'

I nod. 'Yeah. George came along. Adele Baker was there too. But I can't call it. It doesn't look good.'

She puts her pen down and leans forwards.

'What about you? That guy you told me about?'

I swallow and I feel my face redden.

'He turned up at my flat. He grabbed me. Hurt me. In the street. Been texting. And even though he's scaring the shit out of me there's nothing I can put my finger on or prove that it's actually him doing all these things. Except ...'

She stares at me.

'Is there history?'

I think. I do not fucking know. It could be anyone. Terri described a generic white male delivering flowers.

'I don't know. I have no idea who this is. It could be ... anyone.'

I feel the words come but they stick inside me. I struggle and she sees me falter.

'So has he approached you directly?'

'Someone grabbed me. Someone cut my hair on the bus. But like you said when I first told you, there's no proof it's connected. I live in a high crime area. And unless sending flowers is illegal ...? And last time I checked it wasn't. The problem is, he hasn't done anything illegal. Not that I can prove. Not yet. Except keep texting.'

She seethes. 'Did you go to the hospital? When he grabbed you? Did you...?'

'No. I didn't.' No I didn't do exactly what I tell the women to do. Report everything.'

'You can still report it. Or just talk to someone? Look, Ria, I know you work with violent people, but is there anyone at all who would want to harm you? Would want to hurt you? Even in the past?'

The moment is here, the moment I have imagined for twenty years. I am sitting in the police station with a friendly police officer asking me what happened that night. But I will never tell. If I haven't told it can't be him.

'Not really. Whoever this is has scared me. I expect he will give up or Danny will stop him.'

She sighs. 'Have you told Danny, then?'

'No. He's working away, but when he comes back I will.'

'As long as you're sure, Ria? You know where I am. And I'll try to look out for Sheila James. But I can't promise anything. Frank's got it sewn up.'

She stands and it's time to leave. At least she is aware, I lie to myself as my children run towards me. At least she will keep an eye out for Sheila, let me know if anything happens. And if anything happens to me, she will have a starter for ten.

As we walk away from the police station, both kids talking at once about what they had seen and what they had done, I spot the empty red car. I look away and almost turn back, but Jennifer is pulling me towards the tram and I let her. He can't know that I've seen him, that he is winning, so I plaster on a smile and fix it.

But my phone beeps. Not the cheap phone with the blocked messages. I stop dead and read the message.

I'VE GOT SOMETHING OF YOURS.

I check the number and it is the same. It's him. What has he got of mine?

Off the tram and walking towards home, Jennifer is demanding to know if we are meeting Grandma.

'Can we have ice cream? Janet has ice cream with her nana and grandpa. Can we, Mummy? Where is our grandpa?'

Even Simon looks at me and raises his hands.

'We don't have another one, Jenn. Just Granddad Danny.'

She folds her arms and sets her face.

'But Janet has two: her daddy's daddy and her mummy's daddy.'

I feel my temper rise. Bloody Janet. '

Simon shakes his head and runs towards the front door as I do my usual checks. No red car. I know he's planning something. I know he is. But I need to stay calm.

'Well, we get what we are given, don't we?'

Her eyes fill with tears. 'Is your daddy in heaven? Is that why we can't see him?'

I gather her up in my arms. Bless her. She must be wondering all kinds of things. I have been distracted and Danny hasn't been here. I make a mental note, as I close the door, to speak to Danny about explaining everything. Everything about my dad. Everything about difference and everything about how we will always support her and Simon. Simon is finding out the hard way. Shunned by friends, I have caught him staring at himself in the mirror and trying to straighten out his beautiful curls. He is only too aware of how cruel people can be; now he has found friends he is militant about not letting them go. I hug them both, counting the hours in my head until Danny is back and we can be a proper family again.

Almost as soon as we settle down there is a knock on the door, firm and hard. I stiffen. Is it him? He would know I was on my own with the kids. I stand behind the door as the knock comes again. I can't live like this, not wanting to answer my own front door. In fear of what will happen next. My anger rises and I pull at the latch, ready to turn him away. My phone ready in my hand.

But it isn't him. It's equally surprising: it's Mum. She is standing there, glancing around, a look of doubt on her face. She fixes her gaze on me as she cancels out my shocked face.

'Oh. So this is the right address.'

I don't say anything immediately. All I can think is that something terrible has happened. We both know she is banned from visiting me. But when she doesn't announce a disaster, I shake myself into life.

'Yes. Hello, Mum. Come in.'

The kids see her and make a run for her, nearly knocking her wiry frame into the door post. I shut the door behind her. We stand in the tiny living room, the crowding eyes of the tiny faces of the ornaments all looking at me now, questioning me and my obvious contrast to her neat and tidy beige abode. The Lurex scatter cushions and purple velour throws, grubby with stickiness, all jump out at me. She scans the room and fixes on the back window.

'Oh. You have a garden. I wasn't sure ...'

She walks over, towards the light, around the unmatched chairs and the crumb-covered table. I stand beside her – anywhere in here would be beside her as it is so small – feeling teenage huge and ungainly at the side of her slender grace and elegance. She looks outside. I can see her reflection, thin lipped and uncertain.

'I'm sorry, Ria.' She murmurs it almost incomprehensibly. 'I'm sorry. I should have come here before. We've missed so much.'

I fold my arms.

'But it was difficult for you ...'

She shakes her head and her hair, lacquered to a sheen, does not move.

'Not really. I could have just come. But there would have been questions. Consequences.'

I put the kettle on. It suddenly reminds me of Sheila, how we would sit and endlessly drink tea. I feel the lump in my throat. Mum perches on a chair at the table, looking around. What must she think? But this is me, without her influence. Pure Ria. No pallid colours in sight, no laundry-fresh room deodorant. A pile of unironed clothes in the open, shoe stragglers under the table. Every surface covered in tiny monuments to my women. Unframed photos of me and Danny and us and the kids pinned to the kitchen cupboards with dressmaker's pins. A bare, concrete kitchen floor because we always wear socks, not slippers. This is us. Take it or leave it.

She takes it. She sips tea and watches Jennifer as she brings out her favourite toys. I find some ginger biscuits under two packets of hair dye and as I pour them on to a plate, she takes off her coat and hangs it neatly on the back of the chair. Eventually the kids lose interest and go to their rooms to stare at their tablets. We are left alone with no Jennifer conversation filler. Mum looks around again.

'This is very you. Very you.' I am on guard, but this is no insult. She says it softly and kindly. I reach for a biscuit and she touches my hand then withdraws. 'I'm not doing very well here. But something's been bothering me. The police were up by the rocks again this week. Dougie was out, talking to anyone who would listen. Your … father. He was standing outside and I heard them talking about it. I went out.'

I shake my head. 'Look. You don't need to do this …'

'No. Hear me out. I knew it was wrong. I knew all along. But your father, he … he's a difficult man. Not really a bully. Not really … anything. I feel terrible telling you this because he's your father but he'd shut me down long before you were born. With his "shoulds" and his silence. He would listen to me and then say, "No. That's how it is, Dawn. That's just how it is." And if I disagreed or went against him, he wouldn't speak to me for weeks. Months, sometimes. And yes, as you have guessed, he did occasionally hit me. And I'm sorry he did it to you. And that I didn't intervene. I'm so sorry. And he took all the money, saying we could have an allowance each, but if I … well, he just wouldn't give it me.'

I stare at her. I knew it was bad, but suddenly, this man who had been wrapped up in 'Dad' to me was suddenly another insecure man who controlled his little kingdom. I nod at her.

'So does he know you are here today?'

She looks into her tea.

'Yes. He does.'

'And what will he do?'

'I don't know. But I don't care now. I need you to know that I was never any part of this. I remembered what you said about Dougie and I went out and asked Dougie, right there and then on the garage path, if that bloke had been questioned. That he was a lot older and it could have been our daughter.' Her breathing is fast and I can see a pulse in her temple quicken. 'He just stared through the gap in the fencing, out over Manchester. He told me that he had a cast-iron alibi. That he hadn't been round for weeks because he was bothering with our Ria. The police had interviewed him. So it's not your fault. Even though you didn't tell them everything, it's not your fault. Even if you would have said, he would have had an alibi.' She sighs. 'I just wanted you to know. It wasn't your fault.'

I don't say anything. My breathing is even and calm and I think about that day when she didn't believe me. I wonder whether I should tell her now that because of that he raped me and persuaded a fifteen-year-old girl to go off with him.

'Why didn't you stop it?'

She makes a little noise, a groan.

'I spoke to your father about him. Told him he was too old. That I didn't trust him. He told me that I didn't know men. That it was normal. That you were practically sixteen and out there with boys anyway. That he had money and a car and didn't I want the best for you? That he was nine years older than me, so what was the problem?'

I gasp. 'Nine years older than you?' Yes. He must have been. But somehow it didn't seem a big age gap, and I suddenly see the trap people fall into. 'So how old were you …?'

'It was different then. I was sixteen. We went out for four years then got married. Then I had you later on. It was different times.' She leans closer. 'So you see, it was my fault if it was anybody's. I should have put a stop to it.'

I remember the days at his house with Alice, Dougie and his books seeming so interesting and normal. Then his eyes following me down the road. I shudder. I raise my eyebrows and she responds.

'His wife. She left. Had an affair and left. He lost the will to live. Alice was out day and night, or stood staring through the window. I used to see her running over the fields at eleven o'clock at night, up to the rocks, arms out like a little bird. I had a word with Dougie but he just laughed and said it was her mother's fault. But I could have done something. I could have.'

I pull my chair closer.

'But it wasn't your job.'

'But it was to look after you, and I failed. I know he hurt you.' Her eyes fill with tears. 'I knew and I couldn't ask you. I couldn't do anything. I did care, though. It's eaten away at me.'

I sit back in my chair. All these years and I never knew. I thought they were well rid of me. But all these years she has been torturing herself. It would be so easy now to deepen her guilt. To tell her exactly what he did to me. But I don't. I decide that instead I will seek help. Counselling. Anything but this. Dumping it on her is not fair.

'It's OK. We can start again. From scratch.'

'But Danny?'

'Danny will be fine. He's a good person.'

She sobs and I hug her.

'I'll always support you from now on. Never mind your dad. I've learned a big lesson from you, love. You could have turned your back, and you would have had good reason, but you didn't.' She stiffens. 'But about your dad. He's … he's … been to anger management. We went to couples' counselling. Because I was going to leave, Ria.' I almost laugh. Dad. Anger management. 'Just so you know, he isn't like that any more. So let me know what I have to do and I will do it.'

I hold her tight. She doesn't get it. She doesn't know what she has done by taking a stand. By standing up for me after all this time.

'That's just it, Mum. You don't have to do anything. You never did. You're free now.'

Tanya

Diary Entry: Saturday

I was so overwhelmed by my breakthrough yesterday that it made me think everything was going to be fine. But how can it be? Even if he came back now? He would know I had been in his study. I smashed his door. He would know I had tried to escape by the dents in the back door.

During the night I had woken up with terrible stomach cramps. I was weak and hungry but, most of all, I was angry. I had caused all this: selfish little teenage me, who ran away to be with her boyfriend. I wish I could say I had changed but I haven't. I sent that letter. If, God forbid, the police had acted on it, it would only fan Alan's flames. He would think Ria had told them.

Something inside me snapped and I went around the whole house with the skillet, swinging it and smashing the windows. A shard of glass bounced and cut my leg, but why not? I was a mass of injuries. My cheek was dark blue and there was movement in my cheek bone when I touched it. I still could not sit down without pain and now I was bleeding. I reached through the lounge window to the tough steel. I hoped that there would be some give, some way that I could force it. But it was thick and solid, the steel reinforced and tightly knitted.

When I turned around I saw the devastation: glass, blood, wood splinters. Alan's cream wool carpet smeared with my bright red blood. If he walked in right now I cannot imagine what would happen.

I sat down and ate the last of the beans. I drank a pint of water –

the coffee was nearly gone and there were ten teabags left. This was it. I lay down on the chesterfield in the study holding the picture of Ria. I am so weak. So tired. Whoever finds me will know that I did care about her and that none of this was my doing. It's too late to tell my father now. But at least Ria will know.

Chapter Twenty-seven

Day 3

'So she just turned up, no warning?'

Danny is lying next to me, looking at his phone as he twirls a strand of my hair between his fingers. It's like he has never been gone. I hook my legs over his and reach over for the hot tea he brought me.

'She knocked on the door. I'd just got back from the cop shop ...'

He drops his phone on the bed and looks at me, his full attention on me.

'Oh? What for?'

I don't want to say it. I don't want it to be real. But I know I have to get used to it.

'Sheila's gone back to Frank.'

He throws up his arms.

'What? Oh God, Ria. Why would she do that?'

I've told Danny about Frank. No details, I would never break their confidence, but he knows of Frank James and his dealings. Everyone does. Frank makes it his business to be notorious. All gracious and giving up front, with the bribes and the bullying round the back.

'I don't know. I guess she's given up.'

He hugs me. 'Bloody hell. After all the work you've put in.'

'Yeah, well, they don't all work out. It's the funding result tomorrow as well. Look, Dan, what if it doesn't go my way?'

He holds me away from him.

'We'll just wait. You'll get something else.' He picks up his guitar and plays the first bars of Tracy Chapman's 'Fast Car'. *We'll just wait.* He wants this so much, but he is so reasonable. We'll just wait. He's worked twenty-seven days straight and he's happy to just wait. He puts down the guitar.

'As long as I finish the thirty days the money's in the bank. Three more days after today. It's not going anywhere. So we can bide our time. Don't stress, babe.'

I relax a little. I know I need to talk to him, tell him all about what happened while he was away. If I'm going to even consider going to the police, or even if I'm not, he deserves to know. But I just can't. Mum coming round is an excuse to bring it up, but I feel guilty. He's so tired. I can see it in his beautiful face, his droopy eyelids and the way he pulls his lips in to stifle a yawn. Maybe, like the house move, it can wait until after he's finished the contract. It's only a few more days. *Maybe, maybe, maybe.*

'What time do you have to leave?'

He glances at the phone. It's only six-thirty on a Sunday morning, but I'm glad we woke and had this time. The kids are still asleep. It's just me and him.

'In about an hour.' He puts his arms around me and kisses my neck. 'Just enough time to get familiar. It's been a while.' He nuzzles me and I feel the heat from him. He fills my mind with the possibility of what is about to happen and for the first time in weeks I feel happy. This is what my life is about and I will do anything to keep it.

Then he's gone. I half hear him shower then say hello and goodbye to the kids, who are playing in their rooms. I snooze in my happy haze, all the problems I had smothered under a sunny glow left by Danny and me and thoughts of this for ever. But it doesn't last long. My phone buzzes and I see a text from Donelle.

> Come round early. Haven't seen you properly for a while. Let's have a catch-up.

I would usually wait until lunchtime to impose on Vi and Danny Snr, but today I feel like being out and about. Doing something and not thinking about Sheila or my stalker or the past. So we walk over mid-morning and Vi is in the kitchen as we come in the back way.

'Oh. No Daniel? I heard he was back.'

I shake my head.

'Nah. But only another couple of days until the contract's finished. Then you'll be seeing a lot more of him.'

She's peeling vegetables and I sit at the table. Donelle is talking to Jennifer and Simon; Danny Snr is watching a gardening programme.

'Yeah. So did you ask him again about the money?'

I tense. She's not going to like this.

'I did, Vi. But he said no. Again. He said save it for the kids' uni fees. He wants to do it himself.'

She drops the knife in the sink and I see her grip the edges, white knuckled. The kids are silent, staring at her. She turns round and her face is like thunder.

'You know, I just don't understand it. We save for all this time and then you turn your noses up. Danny and now her.' She waves towards Donelle, who looks at her hands. 'We're just trying to help.'

Danny Snr intervenes. 'Let them be, Violet. They're your kids, they're thinking about their kids. You'd be the same. It's how we brought them up.'

She pulls on her coat and shouts to the kids. 'Come on, you two, let's go to the shops. Spend some of that money. Seeing as your daddy doesn't want it.'

They bound after her, pulling their coats back on, and Donelle joins me.

'Cos of me, this. She's in a tizz cos I'm moving out.'

I can't help but smile, and she grins widely.

'You're kidding me? When?'

She laughs. 'Soon. That's what I wanted to tell you. I won't be able to get the kids no more. Well, once in a while, but not all the time like I used to. I'm making a go of it with Ian.'

She looks so happy. She is positively glowing and I can't help but smile with her. Donelle has waited so long to meet the right person. Her job, with the long hours and two-day stopovers, means she hasn't been able to hold down a relationship. They never last long and she has a myriad stories. One guy dated her for months then took a loan out in her name. First thing she knew of it was when the bailiffs turned up to repossess a car – he had been staying over when the statements were due, then dumping her, only to hook up again the next month. Another one had been married. He told her he wanted to wait. That he didn't want to disrespect her and sleep with her until he knew her properly. But she followed him and he was still living with his wife.

Donelle and I had laughed about the bastardometer and she had a range of scores for 20 per cent right up to 80 per cent Some of them had tried to manipulate her, but she is wise. Donelle knows the score and I know that all she has been waiting for is someone decent who will love her. She is self-sufficient and doesn't need anyone – she would have to want them. I laugh.

'Ooo, Donelle and Ian ... I want every detail.'

She thinks, rolling her eyes.

'Well, he's tall, handsome, treats me like a princess.'

'And have you stayed at his much?'

'Yeah. Course. You have to try before you buy. No, seriously, he's got a nice gaff. And if it doesn't work out, I can always get somewhere of my own.' She looks around. 'Much as I love them, it's time to go.' She pauses. Then she's serious. 'I don't think Mum's keen on him. I mean, she's a bit funny with him. He's been here a couple of times and she goes all weird. Eyes all big and suspicious. But he's never been anything but nice to her.'

This is one of the reasons why I love Donelle. Not just because she is the sister I never had, but because she doesn't realise her own value.

'You're her baby, Don, she's not going to let go that easy. Bloody hell, she's still trying to give Danny pocket money. So what chance have you got? She'll come round. Anyway, tell all. Will there be a housewarming?'

She smiles with her eyes. 'We'll get round to it. But he's quite a private person. A bit quiet and, dunno, a bit shy. Not many friends. But he works hard and he's cool with my job. Now.'

We stare at each other, both our excitement palpable. I get a strange feeling, like even when things are on the brink of going wrong, there is still a chink of light. My early-morning Danny encounter and Donelle's happiness lift me just enough to be optimistic. Just enough to believe that the funding bid might be ours. That Sheila will hold her own and will whip Frank into shape this time. That my problems will back off and fade into nothing. Danny Snr lets out a big snore and we both laugh.

Vi arrives back with the kids. They are clutching comics with plastic bags full of tiny toys and novelties stuck to the front. Jennifer is holding a diary with a key and Simon has a box of dinosaur pieces that I know he will take hours painstakingly building. I sense a quiet afternoon and, although Vi is clearly pissed off, she makes a beautiful Sunday lunch and Donelle and I tuck in and talk Netflix box sets and shoes.

At three o'clock it's time to leave. I hug Donelle and Vi tears up. We know that this is the last time we will do this, that next time Donelle will be attached to Ian and he will be here with Danny, making man talk. That this is the last Sunday lunch in this era, and everything will change.

'So when will I meet him?'

She is coy.

'Soon. Like I said, he's private. Just likes it with us two. But we're … I'm making an announcement and you'll be the first to know.'

I touch her arm.

'I'm pleased for you. Let's all go out to eat.' I turn to Vi. 'You and Danny, too. All of us.'

Donelle doesn't look sure and I am just about to query this, but Vi laughs and she hugs us to her.

'My girls.'

I'm reluctant to leave. I know that sitting alone on a Sunday night, the kids bathed and in bed early, is not going to be productive. But what choice do I have? We walk home through the empty streets and the further away from Donelle's joy I go, the more dejected I feel. The kids skip along in front of me, still clutching their comics and toys. Simon has half built the T-Rex and Vi has glued it and popped it in a see-through bag, which he is careful not to swing against his leg. Jennifer is holding her diary against her like it contains state secrets, and I tease her about what she has written. Is it about a boy? Someone from school. She is bashful, and she in turn teases Simon about a girl in his class called Carly. They bicker and swing around the two-year-old saplings that have been planted near our home to screen the rubbish that is regularly fly-tipped.

We are home, and I habitually check the road to make sure the red car is nowhere in sight. It isn't and in no time I am embroiled in the bathing and oiling of skin and waxing of hair ready for the new week. I think about dying my hair, but it's eight o'clock before we are done and they are tucked up in bed, giggling and reading books. I read to them for half an hour from *Lord of the Rings*, then it is lights-out time.

As soon as I am alone a sense of dread falls over me. SafeMe means so much to me, and losing the funding would be a catastrophe. We have no Plan B. Janice and I would get through, but it isn't me I'm worried about. I know that, even after the Frank incident at the meeting, the decision is already made. One way or another, we will know tomorrow and no amount of worrying can change it now.

I make coffee and grab some biscuits, even though I am full after Vi's dinner. I flick on the TV and half watch *The Antiques Roadshow*, but my mind drifts to everything that can go wrong this week: to Sheila, to the funding, to SafeMe closing and us ending the week with no jobs. It's an uneasy feeling with an edge of sadness, tainted by a sense of injustice that I can do nothing about.

I assess my situation. Am I in danger? Any more danger than someone on the Tube who has been sent a dick pic and some horrible messages? Been videoed and had it sent to them? This flat is like Fort Knox, it has to be round here. But I am in danger of going completely mad. I think yet again about telling Carole everything. But I also think about the children, the police turning up and having to explain it to two distressed, tired kids, who would tell Daddy and then he wouldn't want to leave me on my own. With only three days to go until the end of his contract.

I am fifteen again, in my bedroom, hugging myself as I worry about what will happen next. How this will play out. I am sitting amongst my dolls and posters and my school books, thinking adult thoughts and worrying adult worries that I was not supposed to know about. I was worrying and my head was filled with half-cocked scenarios that I could not fully envisage because I didn't know the world.

But now I do know the world. I know the ultimate bad things that happen to others. But they are happening, they really are. Yet when I tell people they sound trivial. Petty. A man sending my picture of his cock. Even the police had normalised it. He parked outside my work; called on me with flowers. I haven't even told anyone except Carole he grabbed me or cut my hair because it sounds too crazy – that he could do that and not be arrested? Put it all together and you have a sinister, cruel, psychopath who is out for kicks. I shudder.

I get the baby gate out from a cupboard and carry it to the lounge doorway. It is loud and tinny and, if anyone got in I would hear it immediately. I check the locks on the front and back doors and peep behind the curtains, my heart beating fast; I check the window locks. There is no way in. I will not come downstairs until it is light and I can see out and see he isn't there. He is closer now. But I am closer too. Closer to him doing something drastic that I can report. I cling on to this; it gives me a sliver of comfort as I climb under the quilt where Danny and I made love only this morning. I am shaking as I wait for tomorrow to come.

Tanya

Diary Entry: Sunday

I am writing this last entry now as a confession. I don't think I am going to make it. My leg won't stop bleeding and I am so weak.

So here goes. I fully knew what I was doing when I ran away with Alan Cartwright. It was no one else's fault except mine and his. Ria is completely innocent in all this. She was never anything except the best friend in the whole world to me. She was the kind of kid who would give you their last sweet, and I let her. She looked after me, kept me safe when my mum left. No matter what he says, she has done nothing wrong.

It's all so clear now. I could have just walked away from him. People tried to help me. I didn't. Because he would always be there, out there somewhere waiting for me. He would get me. He told me he would find me. And Tina. What he did to her. So I couldn't. I had no proof. We just looked like any other couple.

There was one time I did mention it to someone, a lady who asked me if I wanted any help when he sent me into a newsagent's for a paper once. When I still had hope. I knew she meant help with the papers, or the mints I was clutching, but this was my only chance. I could feel his eyes on me so I spoke quickly.

'Yes. Yes. My husband, he …'

She's looked at me in a strange way, her face changing to a blank expression. She had pushed the change into my hand and looked away.

'He hits me.'

She looked up, scanning me for injuries.

'Go and see your doctor, love. They'll help.'

I'd taken a deep breath. This was my only chance.

'He said he was going to kill me.'

I'd expected horror, but instead her face relaxed into a kindly smile.

'It's a figure of speech, love. He's not really going to kill you.' She looked past me, into the car. 'Look. He's looking for you. Doesn't look like he's going to murder you, does it?'

And she was right. It didn't look like that to anyone. It just looked like he was the doting husband. I'd told someone and nothing had happened. That was when I finally lost hope.

But it isn't a figure of speech and I always knew it wasn't. I always knew it would come to this. And here I am. But Ria. She has suffered because of me. She has had to keep secret what he did to her for all this time. I know him. He would have threatened her too. Made her do it. Now I have forced it into the open. Whoever finds me, please tell Ria I love her and I never meant to hurt her.

Chapter Twenty-eight

Day 2

Monday morning and Danny has been and gone. I must have dozed off and the next thing I knew he was climbing out of bed. I watched him through barely open eyes, wanting desperately to beg him to lock the doors behind him, to check them twice, three times.

Instead, I crept down when I heard the door close gently and made sure the catch was on. I'd had to unbolt the front door and move the baby gate before I went to sleep otherwise Danny wouldn't have been able to get back in, and now I stand behind the door, too scared even to look outside. It is light and I check my phone. Five o'clock. I go back upstairs and lie there until the kids erupt from their rooms.

The walk to school is fraught with red cars passing me. I drop them off and tell them again about stranger danger. It's wearing thin now and they roll their eyes and run to their friends. I stand there until the door close and watch Janet's mum breeze away to her car. Today is going to be super difficult. I know in my heart that the funding bid is not going to be straightforward. Not after the meeting the other day.

I arrive at SafeMe and I am right. Janice is waiting for me on the front steps. She's wearing a business suit and I look down at my Day-Glo blue dungarees.

'Today's the day. Adele Baker herself is coming over to deliver the decision. At one. Straight after Perps.'

We both automatically look at the gate. There are several men gathered there and a few standing by the pub. All ignoring each other. Malc is watching them, arms folded.

'Bloody hell.'

We look at each other in a 'this can mean anything' kind of way, and it can. Adele might be coming to make a show of good news. Or she might want to explain why it's bad news. Either way it's going to be today. At one. Then we will know for sure what the future of SafeMe is. And our own futures. Janice nods towards the men.

'So d'you thing Frankie will show? You know? Just to make a point? He must know what we did.'

I snort. 'What I did. It's not like I ran it by you, is it? And I'm sorry about that. But there was no alternative I could see. I wasn't letting that slimy little bastard get away with it.'

She smiles and pats my arm.

'I wish I'd thought of it. Quick off the mark, you, Ria. That's why I love you, mate.'

We go inside and prepare the room. All the while I am watching for Frank's car to pull up and for him to walk nonchalantly into the main room, his boys bearing gifts behind him. The men file in and sit down and Janice plugs in the tea urn. The weather outside is grey and pallid, a little bit dark, which only serves to make the twinkly fairy lights on the branches above the perpetrators brighter and more cheerful. They, by contrast, look miserable, like they would rather be anywhere else.

We wait a while but Frank does not show. I'm not sure how I feel about it, slightly panicky perhaps, because he is my only lifeline to Sheila now. Not that he would divulge anything to me, but if I saw Frank I would think of her. Funny. I thought he would be here to prove a point, to gloat over us. To deliver another bribe. But, now he has what he wants, why would he? I try to imagine them having a cup of tea in their home, sitting together all made up and happy, Sheila chain-smoking and Frank knocking golf balls into a cup across the lounge.

In my heart I know this is not the case. Just as my life, blessed as I am with Danny and my beautiful children, should be fabulous and carefree, but it isn't, Sheila's financial-worry-free existence is haunted by other pressing matters. It rarely is that simple. For all I know, Janet's mum could be the loneliest person in the world, sitting in her show-home alone all day.

Time ticks on and the perpetrators are unusually quiet today. I finally admit to myself that Frank will not come to any more meetings. It really was all lies, all front, and why would I be surprised? I glance at the clock and I look outside. It starts to rain and I go to the window and check that the red car isn't parked in its usual place, three cars up in the road by the gate. It isn't. I wonder if I imagined it. If I am losing the plot. Going mad. Getting it all out of proportion. *You always had a good imagination, Ria.*

One of the perps is crying, having a breakthrough as Janice explains that everyone can have a fresh start and that their partners are just as entitled as they are. Explaining about what fear does to a person, how it shuts them down, silences them. He is sobbing, and I go and sit by him. I know what he has done; I know what he was charged with. I don't hate him. I don't feel sorry for him either. I'm just glad that he's reached a stage on his journey where he understands, where he isn't in denial, and where he wants to make amends.

I pass him a tissue and smile at him, while the other men sit, arms folded and legs crossed, their faces contorted into expressions ranging from disgust to envy. The meeting comes to a slightly premature end and they filter to the back of the hall and get tea or coffee while we tell Lee how to access counselling and ongoing anger management. It's a small triumph in a sea of tragedy and desperation, but it is worth it, and as I turn around I see that Adele Baker thinks so too.

She is standing in the sheltered entrance, hands deep in her black trench coat pockets, watching us. She smiles gently and I am suddenly aware of my clothes, my hair and my make-up. No time now to rush to my locker and change into my business suit. I hurry over and hold out my hand.

'Hi. Hi. Sorry. We just had the perpetrator counselling. I ...'

She takes my hand. She has a strong grip.

'Yes. I've been here about fifteen minutes.' She looks around the room. 'This place. Extraordinary.' She stares at me now, her dark eyes piercing. 'Look, Ria, I wanted to meet with you and Janice prior to the official decision meeting. Is there somewhere ...?'

I bet she does. I feel my temper rise. Of course she wants to meet us. The business between Frank and Trevor has been contained so far, and I knew she would want reassurance that it would go no further. Adele's reputation on the council precedes her. Social Services refer to her as the smiling assassin as she doles out cuts to services without a hint of regret. She has done wonders for some areas but others have been left to rot. And SafeMe is right in the centre of the crap catchment as we refer to the rubbish-filled alleyways and rat sightings. I signal to Janice and she speaks to Malc, who supervises everyone out of the building. Janice waves her into our office.

'Right. Here we are.'

Adele looks around, upwards. I nod.

'No. We're not recording you, Adele. The only reason I recorded Frank was because I felt in danger. You could see his attitude: threatening.'

She nods and brings some papers out of her bag.

'Yes. I've watched the footage several times. I can only apologise for my colleague's behaviour. I can assure you that he has been dealt with appropriately.'

Janice's eyebrows shoot upwards. 'Oh. And how might that be? Slap on the wrist. Cufflinks temporarily confiscated? He took a bribe.'

Adele shifts in her chair uncomfortably.

'He did. And that is what I am here about.' She hands us the recommendation report. We read it as she continues. 'As you can see, the recommendation is that SafeMe does not receive full funding.'

I throw my copy on the desk. The pages skid across the surface and teeter on the edge. She goes to save them but I just stare at her.

'OK. So the recommendation is to leave this area without a specialist service?'

She shakes her head. 'No. It would go to Redeem—'

Janice intervenes. 'Which is not a specialist service. Come on. You know this. You just don't give a fuck.'

I stifle a laugh. Oh yes. Let the games begin. Adele's eyes widen, but she stays calm.

'It isn't a case of not … caring. It is budget considerations. As you know, too. Obviously if we could keep all the services we would, but …'

Janice smirks. 'So what would you rather have: a newly built meeting room for the council scrapped or dead women? Because that is the reality, isn't it?'

Adele looks at me, then Janice. She is lost for words. I step up.

'Let me help you. If you don't fund this place, people will suffer. Really suffer. Not just have nowhere to go on a night out or some rubbish in the street. It really is life or death for some of them, Adele.'

She rummages in her bag.

'And that's why I am here.' I look at Janice, who gives me a *that is definitely not why she is fucking here* glance. 'What I wanted to ask you is ...'

I shake my head. It's fucking obvious why she is here. She knows that no matter which way this goes, the council has been bribed by Frank James, ex-mayor and councillor. No one knows yet, and she is here to make sure that they never do.

'... are we going to tell anyone about Frank James bribing Trevor? Opening that particular can of worms where, and I am seriously wondering this now, with you sitting here, there might be more despicable shit such as this.' I look at Janice, who nods imperceptibly. My 'Ria stare' hits Adele and she sits upright. 'All I am going to do is tell the truth. Whether you give us the funding or not, I will tell the truth. It's not whistleblowing anonymously or telling tales, it is just not lying. So ...'

Adele is thinking. Her face is a study in concentration.

'So even if I endorse the funding you will go to the press?'

I laugh.

'I never said I would go to the press, although that is an option. To be honest, Adele, I'm quite busy with stopping very angry men assaulting their partners, so writing an email to journalists isn't on the top of my list. But if I had more time and more reason I might. But I would be just telling the truth. So, no, before you think or say it, I am not bribing you. I am just telling you that I will not keep quiet about what has happened. Even if you give SafeMe the funding, I will tell the truth.'

I hear Sheila's voice in my ear, her yellow-stained fingers twisting her diamonds. *Tell the truth, lovey.* I feel tears rise as I think I hear her say it's too late for me now and me telling her it's never too late. I believe it with all my heart. It is never too late. Adele has to take a chance. She has to go with what she believes. I help her along.

'The thing is, Adele, you have to go with your conscience on this one. It's not all about spreadsheets, is it? And budgets? It's about people. Not us. Them.'

I look towards the open door and Sally is bringing her kids back through from the accommodation. Six-year-old Annie spots me and starts the 'Ria, Ria, diarrhoea' chant and, in seconds, they are all doubled over laughing. I turn back to Adele.

'Only six weeks ago they were so scared they couldn't speak. Including their mother. Look at them now. Off to a new home next week. They're from Gloucester. It was their last chance. Otherwise they would still be enduring … it.'

She looks at the paperwork, then she puts it in her bag.

'We'll find it from somewhere. One year.'

I come back quickly at her.

'Five years.'

She's as quick-fire as me.

'Three years with an option to review and extend at two.'

I look at Janice. She covers her face with her hands and her relief floods the room like sunshine. She nods.

'Done. But you are not buying our silence. I expect you to make a statement about what happened. And that Trevor will never work on the SafeMe decisions in the future.'

She smiles. 'He won't be working for us in the future. We've started proceedings against him. I shouldn't tell you this but what the hell. He's admitted everything but said Frank James threatened him so he had no choice. So if, by some strange twist of fate, he is reinstated, I'll make sure he is in a completely different department. But that still leaves the Frank James problem.'

I shake my head. 'His wife returned to the marital home.'

Adele shows real emotion for the first time in the whole time she has sat there.

'My God. Could you not stop her?'

I shake my head. 'No. She hadn't reported him to the police and there was no injunction. We were just getting her to open up when she went back. In the meantime, he's been delivering TVs and Xboxes and swanking around like he owns the place. I was a bit worried he would turn up today.'

She sighs deeply. 'I'm sure I don't need to tell you this, but he told Trevor that he would finance the funding if it failed. If he does offer ...'

Janice laughs. 'You've got to be kidding. He's got what he wants now. He's got his punchbag back, his pride is back intact. I'm guessing that was a time-limited offer, just until we returned Sheila.'

We see Sally usher her children into a side room and Aisha carry her baby through as the other council workers arrive. Adele smiles at us, then she dons her stony-faced mask as she stands and walks through the main hall, past all her open-mouthed staff and into the family room. I follow her, suddenly realising that we hadn't prepared it for a formal meeting. But she waves her hand and laughs as I try to move the Xboxes and screens.

'No need! We're too used to it, the special performance for us. It'll do some of them good.'

She's back to serious Adele again as the others troop in, confused at the boxes of crayons and the scraps of paper left by Sally's children and baby Ameen. Adele addresses them once they are sitting down.

'OK. So could everyone move the screen in front of them to the space behind their chairs? And the games machines can be moved on to the table.'

Some of them look at me and Janice as if we are going to spring into action. But eventually the table is clear. Adele continues.

'Good. OK. We're here today to give the decision on funding for SafeMe based on the application made. Due to extenuating circumstances where an employee of the council has taken a bribe ...' She pauses and her eyes rest on me. I smile. She is telling the truth. 'I have taken personal responsibility for this decision.'

She takes the paperwork out of her bag again and everyone shuffles theirs. Some of them get out laptops and load complicated spreadsheets on the screen. Adele stands up. She takes the papers one by one and rips them in half. There is complete silence. When she has finished, she sits again. All eyes are on her.

'So. I have decided on emergency measures. SafeMe will receive full funding for three years with an interim review. This will include all service provisions at the current level with staffing review meetings quarterly.'

One of the men in suits speaks quietly. 'This was not the original decision. To complete the records, can you confirm where the funding will come from within the council budget?'

Adele nods and looks around the room.

'No. Not right at this moment. But the funding would have gone to Redeem to provide the same services, would it not? Or that's what it said in the report.'

The suited man reddens.

'There would have been a forty-five per cent saving.'

She fumes now. I can sense her anger and I am starting to see why she is in this job as a leader.

'So a forty-five per cent saving on the same services. How does that work?'

He stutters. 'Well, the services would have been more general ...'

'So not specialist services? So how would these women have been helped in the same way?' There is silence. Everyone is looking at the papers in front of them. She continues. 'So what has actually happened here is that Ria and Janice were right all along. In the previous meeting and in the application, where they stated that the provision would be lost.'

I stand up very straight at the mention of my name. Adele is scary. She bangs her remaining paperwork on the table and picks up her bag while pulling on her coat. She pushes back her chair. The meeting is clearly over.

'My office. Tomorrow morning. All of you. Julie, you will prepare the funding documents. The rest of you, you'd better have a good explanation for this.'

She hurries out, pausing at the door to beckon us. Once outside she smiles.

'Ladies, this has been a learning curve for me. And all of us. But my eye is on SafeMe now, and I will make sure you are fully supported. I'm so sorry about it all.'

She stands awkwardly for a moment, and then she moves towards me and hugs me stiffly. I put my arms around her and pat her back. I can smell her expensive perfume and her desperation for validation. I give it to her in a whisper.

'You did good, Adele. This is how it should be.'

She is nodding and I swear I hear a sniffle but, when she emerges to hug Janice, she is composed and calm again.

Chapter Twenty-nine

Day 1

Naturally I text Danny straight away. I couldn't believe it. My job was safe for three years. I stood outside with Malc, texting and waiting for Danny to text back. It was almost instant.

> OMG, babe. We're on the up! One more day for me then it's
> D-Day. This is our time, Ria. Nearly done. I love you x always x

My heart flew. Not for myself, well, hardly. More for the women that would come through SafeMe in the future and their children. It's funny really; I thought I would be more emotional. I suppose I was, in a way, because I forgot about all the bad things. All about whoever was sending me messages, and Frank and Trevor. Instead, I was calm and collected. A little bit excited.

As the news filtered out we were inundated with phone calls and emails of congratulations and the evening, once I had collected the kids and brought them over to Nando's in town, was a further round of chicken, chips and celebrations. We booked half the restaurant and brought everyone: all the kids, all the women and even Malc and his lovely wife, Malc proclaiming himself our 'token man'. It was wonderful. Ecstatic. A ray of sunshine through the shit storm that has been my life for the last month or so.

Which is why, when my phone rings as I walk away from the school, registering a number unknown, my heart is in my mouth again. Every scenario goes through my mind. Danny? No. He just texted me to say he was picking up the kids later. The kids? No. They are in school. My mum? My dad? The stalker from another phone? Vi? Danny Snr? No. No.

But it isn't any of those things. When I do answer, it's Carole. I recognise her voice.

'Hi. Is that Ria?'

I know before she says it.

'Yeah. Yeah. This is Ria speaking.'

I hear myself, calm and clear as a bell, not the turmoil that is suddenly spinning inside me. Carole pauses.

'Ria, it's Sheila. I said I would update you. I'm so sorry.'

I stop in the street. The sky is crashing down on me and I hear myself let out a cry.

'What happened?'

Carole pauses again.

'I can't go into detail, I just needed to let you know because I know you cared so much about her. I'm so sorry.'

I can feel my mouth moving and hear the sounds coming out.

'Thank you, thank you for letting me know. Bye. Bye.'

I disconnect the call and hurry towards work. My feet drag along the pavement and all I can hear is Sheila's laugh and all I can smell is the thick, toxic, smoky odour that followed her everywhere. My God. Sheila is dead. Every possible cause runs through my head and then I am frustrated because chances are I will never find out what really happened. Then, just as I reach SafeMe and Malc and the gates, Janice runs out and hugs me in the street. She is crying and now I am crying. They are the tears that have wanted to come out since I received the very first message.

We never cry, Janice and me. We hear about our clients and their situations but we are as hard as nails. But Sheila was different. She was tough. She was brash and hard peroxide-blonde. She was yellow-stained and scarlet-lipped but she was kind and lovely and had the most devilish laugh I have ever heard. She was our Sheila. And she was still laughing, still smoking, still having the last say. Even after everything she had endured, which was a lot. I had seen her hospital records.

I never told her I had. But I knew what that woman had been through. Janice sobs and makes us a cup of hot sweet tea and everyone is very quiet. The funding documents have been emailed and printed but suddenly I don't feel like looking at them. Or celebrating. I stare out of the window and, one by one, Sheila's neighbours bring flowers and place them at the gates. I see Malc wipe away a tear and, when the flowers threaten to spill over into the road, he bends down and gently arranges them along the barbed wire on the top of the gates.

Janice finally speaks.

'Go home, Ria. I'll sort this lot out.'

I check the time on my phone. It isn't even lunchtime.

'No. I'll stay. No point going home moping.'

I push through with the help of Diet Coke and Janice changing the subject. No one mentions Sheila again and I know that this is how it will be for the time being. Her memory is held in the silence of the day. I want to walk round to her flat and breathe it in one final time, but I know she is gone. There is no point.

Around two I look up from the funding notes. I am tired and my eyes are sore and red-rimmed. I check my phone for texts, but there are none. I check my Facebook page and scroll up and down, uninterested and preoccupied with hating Frank. Up and down, school friends on holiday, ex-colleagues having babies and getting married. Donelle moving in with her new man. I shake my head as she stands there with a key in her hand.

'New man. New pad. New start.'

I look closer at the montage of photographs she posted yesterday. She is in a car and she is smiling. I can see the reflection of Ian in the window behind her except it's someone I know and I can't place. I open a browser on my computer and load the picture on there and magnify them. The shape of his head and his haircut is familiar. In another picture he is caught in profile and it is him. The guy who took Alice. The man who raped me. Or am I going mad? I look closer and closer. It is him. Older, fuller-faced. But it is him. I scroll down her feed, panicky, and finally find a picture from last week. Donelle with her finger at her lips captioned, '*Sneaky pic. X no publicity.*'

He is paying for petrol. It is him. Behind her in a sneakily taken selfie. I read all the posts carefully, reprimanding myself for only half listening to her story on Sunday. Pictures of new dresses. Glasses of champagne. A huge bunch of red and pink hand-tied roses, complete with a beautiful pink ribbon. *Every action has an equal and opposite reaction.* She is moving in with him. She has a key. It is today. *I've got something of yours.* He didn't have Sheila or Sally or one of my childhood toys that I had left in Alice's room. He had Donelle. I fumble for my phone and dial her number. It goes straight to answerphone. I send her a text.

Donelle. Ring me immediately. Stop what you're doing and ring me.

I can't tell her. I can't make her panic. He will become suspicious and God only knows what will happen. She texts me back.

Can't call now. In transit. I'll call you later x

I try to phone her again but her phone is switched off. I think fast. Danny. I need Danny. I call him and he answers in one.

'Hello, gorgeous. How's it going? I just got in and—'

I shout down the phone. 'Dan, ring your mum and get her to pick the kids up. Then come and get me straight away at work.'

He laughs. He thinks I'm joking. We mess about and have a laugh like this and he thinks I'm joking.

'Why? What's up?'

I think. *The word*. I need to say it then he will realise how serious this is.

'Superwoman.'

The phone goes dead and I know he will be here as soon as he can. It takes him seven minutes. He screeches to a halt outside and runs through the yard. He grabs me and holds me to him.

'Are you all right? Are you OK?'

I nod into his shoulder.

'It's not me, Dan. It's Donelle. He's got Donelle.'

He lets me go.

'What do you mean?'

I show him the Facebook pictures and point him out.

'Alan Cartwright. Look, Dan, there's something I need to tell you.'

I use the computer at work, logged into the social security system, to find him. It's illegal but this is an emergency. What if he's changed his name? I knew his date of birth because I'd seen his driving licence when Alice and I were in his car. And there he was. I press print and throw the sheet at Danny. 'Just drive me here. She said she's moving in with him. This is his address.'

We drive, up the Manchester Road and out to Saddleworth. I tell Danny everything. All about when I was fifteen and what happened up at the pond. That Alice and I had grown up together but he had turned her against me. How scared I was. How my mum and dad acted as if nothing had happened. How I hated myself every time I saw Dougie. How Alan Cartwright has been following me. Filming me. Watching me.

When we are very near Alan Cartwright's house he pulls over. He is crying. He takes my hand.

'Ri, it's OK. Honestly. It's OK. This man is not a real man. Real men don't do this. You've kept this inside …?'

I sob.

'I blocked it out, Dan. I never thought … I thought … He was at our flat. With Terri. I didn't know what to do. How to tell you. He … he …'

'Did he touch you?'

'He grabbed me. Near the mill ground. That's all. He didn't—'

He hits the steering wheel hard.

'I'll fucking kill him.'

He starts the engine and we drive up the lane. Just as we draw to a halt my phone rings and it is Donelle. I fumble with it and answer.

'Don, don't say anything. Is he there with you? Are you inside?'

I stare at the house. There is a long garden, immaculately manicured, full of rose bushes in bloom. I swallow bile as I smell them. There are white shutters at every window.

'Yeah. I'm inside. Why? Look. What the fuck is this about, Ria? Have you gone fucking mad?'

Danny shouts at me. 'Is she inside?'

I scream down the phone. 'Donelle. This is very important. Is he there with you? Is he?'

'No. he's gone out for a bottle of wine. He's been a long time, actually. What the actual fuck?'

Danny is out of the car. He has the boot open and he is rummaging around. He produces a crowbar and rushes towards the door. I run after him.

'Stand back, Don. Get away from the doors and windows. Danny's coming in to get you.'

He levers up the shutter on the front door. It is a white UPVC and it doesn't budge. He goes back to the car and gets a lump hammer and hits the crow bar. The door moves and after a few more swings at it, it flings open. He runs in, shouting.

'Donelle? Donelle?' He runs into the house and then he appears again. 'She's not there, Ri.'

Donelle is shouting down the phone at me. I scream back.

'Where are you? Which room are you in? Are you upstairs?'

'I'm in the fucking lounge. What is this about?'

'Get out of there. Ian is really called Alan. He's been stalking me. He's dangerous. We're outside. Just come out.'

I hear traffic in the background.

'I am outside. You're not here.'

I look at the house. No. It can't be. He took her somewhere else. Danny grabs the phone and puts it on speaker phone.

'Look, Don, Ria's telling the truth. Where are you?'

'I'm in town. He's got a flat in town. On Princess Street.'

'Right. Get a taxi back to Mum's. Now. Just trust me, Donelle.'

There is silence. Eventually she speaks.

'This had better not be a fucking wind-up. Seriously.'

She ends the call. I lean against the wall, head in hands.

'This is his place, Dan.' He puts his arms around me and the tears start. 'Sheila's dead. Carole rang me this morning. She's dead.'

Deep sobs rack my body and he strokes my hair. He whispers shhh in my ear and I know he feels my pain. I am devastated, but suddenly I realise that I have told someone. I have told Danny. I don't have to hide it away any more.

'I wanted to tell someone, Dan, I swear. But I was so scared. I still am. He's hounded me. Parking outside work. I didn't know it was him. He pushed me to the fucking edge.'

He nods and kisses my head.

'I should have been here for you. Instead of chasing the cash. Look at us. We're both shattered and I wasn't there for you.'

I am horrified. It isn't his fault. I won't let him think that.

'No. I should have said something twenty years ago. He's been following me, messaging me. I thought it was Frank at first. Or Jim. Or anyone it could have been. Watching me. I'm sorry, Dan. I should have told you.'

He sighs. 'Let's go and get Donelle. Then we can figure out what to do from there.'

He goes to retrieve his hammer and crowbar, swinging them hard. I watch as he looks into the house, his face changing from the kind, gentle Danny I know to the streetwise teenager who had to defend himself in his younger days. I wipe my eyes and blow my nose on a scrap of tissue from my bag. Danny is trying to close the door when I see a movement. In a split second a woman runs out of the house and launches herself at Danny, holding on to him. I know before I see her face it is Alice. She is still willowy and her movements graceful. Her natural blonde hair is waist length and she is wearing a white slip dress covered in blood. Her legs are bare except for a white strip soaked in blood.

She turns her head, still hanging on to Danny, and her eyes squint against the bright sunlight. Danny pushes her away but she holds on tighter. I move towards them and reach out to her.

'Alice. Alice. It's OK. It's Ria.' She cowers away from me, and then looks a little closer. She is very thin and her skin is almost translucent, apart from a deep bruise on her face. 'It's OK. We're going to get the police. It's OK.'

She says my name like it is a strange word.

'Ria? Oh my God. Ria. I'm sorry. The letter. I sent the letter. I'm sorry ...'

She holds me. I never thought I'd see her again. I nod.

'You're safe, Alice. We'll get the police.'

She hangs on to Danny even tighter. She is agitated, panicky. Yet her voice is very, very quiet.

'No police. He'll ...'

I nod and smile at her.

'He won't. You are safe now.'

I prise her away from Danny and lead her to the car. She is clammy and shaking. I sit in the back with her, holding her tight. She looks at me.

'He ... he ... and he just told me that if I ran he'd ...'

I nod. Invisible walls. Yes. He'd trained her like a dog. If she went outside, told anyone, called the police, he'd kill her.

'It's OK. We'll sort it out.'

She grips my hand tightly.

'He ... he ...'

I nod and hold her to me.

'I know, I know. But you are safe now. Safe.'

She is stiff with fear and brittle with the possibility that he might suddenly appear from nowhere. I hold her close and stroke her hair. Danny halts at the end of the lane.

'Which way?'

I catch his eye in the rear-view mirror.

'Four doors down from my mum and dad.'

He pulls away and in minutes he pulls up outside Dougie's house. She looks out at a wall-sized poster of her fifteen-year-old self.

'He never stopped looking for you.'

I see movement in the house and the door opens and Dougie stands there, white with shock. Danny gets out and opens Alice's passenger door. She is unsteady and I rush around and help her. She sees Dougie and her face crumples. She is still beautiful, still ethereal. She is still Alice and I still love her. Her feet are bare but she runs across the gravel path and towards her father. They hold each other like they will never let go and we go and stand in the doorway. She is sobbing.

'He told me you died. He told me you were dead.'

I hear Danny's phone ring.

'Don, where are you?'

I watch his face. It is relief, love and anger rolled into one.

'Yeah, well, stay there. We'll be over to explain as soon as we can. Are the kids OK?'

I look up the road, toward what used to be home. He is there, standing in the window, watching everything that is going on. The door opens and Mum appears. She walks up the road and her hands go to her mouth when she sees Alice. She walks towards me, arms outstretched, and I think she is going to hug me, but she doesn't. She goes to Danny and puts her arms around him.

'Danny, I'm sorry for how I behaved. Can you forgive me?'

He smiles a little.

'I'll have to see. It all depends on whether you make a brew. One sugar. Please.'

We get Alice inside. Dougie is already calling the police, telling them that Alice is found. We drink our tea and wait for the liaison officer, who arrives and takes our details. She tells us that she will take Alice's statement first as she will need to go to the hospital to get checked over, then ours. But Alice does what I knew she would.

'I don't want to press charges. I don't want to see him again. I can't.'

The police liaison sighs.

'We need to find him. It's wrong what has happened. He shouldn't have done this to you.'

I speak up.

'I'll press charges.' Mum comes and stands beside me. She squeezes my hand. 'I'll press charges. He assaulted me years ago, around the time this happened. And he's been stalking me for weeks. I wrote it all down in here. In my diary.' I hand the diary to her. 'I told Carole Barnes. She will fill you in.'

She flicks through the diary.

'Are you willing to give a statement?'

I nod. 'Yes. But not today. None of us are up to it. You just need to find him. Let him know it's over.'

Danny rings Donelle and she gives him the address of the city centre flat. We pass all the details to the liaison officer and we are free to go.

'We'll send someone to take a statement.'

I say goodbye to Mum and Dougie. Alice is sitting on the sofa, still tense. As I pass her, she catches hold of me.

'I'm sorry.'

I shake my head. 'What for? You didn't do anything, Alice. No need.'

She stares into the distance. Into another time, twenty years ago, a time that neither of us will ever forget.

'He told me what he did to you. I could have told you. I knew what he was like. I never warned you. I thought you and he were ...'

I sit down beside her.

'And I could have told someone I was worried about you. And him. But I didn't. But you know what? We were both children. How could we have known?'

She smiles. She is still childlike, innocent-looking. Except her eyes. Her eyes show the depth of her pain. She touches my hand.

'Are we ...?'

Just like when we were children, no words are needed. I nod. There is a future for us.

I follow Danny out to the car. He looks down the road, towards our house. Dad isn't in the window. He's walking down the road towards us. When he reaches us, Mum stands beside me, arms folded, unsmiling. He holds out his hand to Danny.

Danny hesitates, but I know him. He's a good guy. He will do anything for me. He takes Dad's hand but he doesn't smile. He pulls Dad towards him and half hugs him, pats him on the back.

'Easy, mate. Takes a big man to do that.'

Dad nods and looks away.

'Aye. Took me all that time to admit I was wrong.'

He stands with Mum as we get into the car. And all the time Alice watches us from the window. Twenty years has made hardly any difference at all, it turns out.

Chapter Thirty

Three weeks later

On D-Day Danny and I stayed in bed. After we left Alice, we went to collect the kids and explain to Donelle what had happened. She was devastated but safe. We took our children home and locked our doors and waited for any news.

Danny didn't go to work on the last day of the contract. Instead, we took the children to school then, exhausted and emotional, we went to bed. I called Janice and she agreed it was the best thing. Danny was philosophical.

'Yeah, I'll miss the bonus but what the hell?' We look around our cosy bedroom, arms and legs entwined. 'That fucking creep is busted now and you are safe. We are all safe. But what I don't get is why? Why now?'

I think about the response I received to that question. *Why not?*

'He think I told. He thinks it's my fault. He won't even admit he's done anything wrong.'

I know that Danny is bothered about the bonus, really; I know that he is annoyed that he put his heart and soul into the thirty days and now it's for almost nothing – he will get paid an hourly rate and no bonus. But Danny can see the bigger picture. He can see that we need time to recover, to talk about what has happened. He asked me why I didn't tell him and I explained, this time in detail, about the pond and the threats. I showed him the texts. I showed him the picture he sent to me.

He wants to hurt Alan Cartwright, but when the police arrived to interview me he saw that this was a better way. He came with me to see Carole. He witnessed her sadness at everything that had happened.

'Ria, I'm so sorry. About Sheila. About this guy.'

I nodded and held Danny's hand. I don't want to talk about Sheila, but I do want to talk about Alice.

'Alice has refused to give a statement or press charges. I know that it's not the usual route as I'm personally involved, but I wondered if you would consider allowing me to work with her. At SafeMe. One day she might be able to open up.'

Carole spins her pencil, thinking hard.

'Are you sure you are up to it? With all this with Sheila? And all that has happened to you?'

I fix her with my 'Ria stare'.

'I'll never give up, Carole. Never. Sheila's death has made me even more determined.'

I feel Danny squeeze my hand and see a slight smile out of the corner of my eye. He is not comfortable around the police. As a teenager living in Manchester he was stopped and searched more times than he needed to be. But he's here and he's supporting me. I don't think I am lucky, this is normal behaviour, what good people do. Support each other. I squeeze his hand back. Carole shakes her head.

'I don't know, Ria. She sent a letter to us incriminating you. Obviously we know what she said isn't true now, but still. Leave it with me. Maybe Janice can work with her?'

I nod.

'I don't care who works with her. It's not a personal thing. Just as long as she gets the help she needs.'

I can see she is waiting to say something else. She blinks at me, weighing up if this is the time. The tension in the room is palpable.

'Look, there's something you should know. We looked at Alice's case and why Alan was never picked up. He had an alibi.' I hold my breath. I know this. Doesn't she think I know it? But she has more. 'The thing is, the girl who gave him his alibi. She was reported missing later on.'

I exhale.

'How old was she, Carole?'

I feel Danny tense next to me. Carole shakes her head.

'Fourteen at the time of the incident. Daughter of one of his work mates. He was bringing her home from a night out. A favour, she said.' We are silent for a moment as it sinks in. Then Carole continues. 'Naturally, we'll look at this more closely.'

I shiver like someone has walked over my grave.

'I hope you will, Carole. I hope you will. This time.'

Carole catches my eye and I see her understanding. I stand and offer my hand. 'Thanks for everything.' She takes it.

'Thank you, Ria. And again, I'm so sorry about Sheila.'

I think about this as I stand in Hollinwood Cemetery next to Sheila's coffin. Frank James stands opposite, staring at me, and I stare back. I am flanked by Janice and Sally, who we have employed as our admin person now she is settled in her flat and we have our funding. Malc joins us, all dressed up like our minder complete with black shades.

The service was a full Catholic funeral at St Thomas's where Frank and Sheila were married. He is dressed in an expensive black suit and his daughter and her mother stand behind him, black

veiled and Armani-clad in identical outfits. The people associated
with Frank fall back into rank behind him in order of importance,
faces I have seen on election broadcasts and in the local press.

Carole and three plainclothes police officers stand behind us,
and some of Sheila's neighbours behind them. It is a good turn-
out. It's what Sheila would have wanted. There is a huge framed
photograph of her at the side of the grave. She is smiling, her
blonde hair piled on top of her head. She is wearing a diamond
necklace and holding a glass of champagne. Her charm bracelet,
with a charm for every year she knew Frank, is hung over the
corner of the frame. I look closely at the photograph as I pass it
to pay my final respects and see the yellow nicotine stains on her
fingers and the bright red lipstick. I miss her so much. I can hear
her saying 'Tell the truth, lovey' and it will never ever leave me. I
did tell the truth. I did, Sheila.

Frank's eyes are ever on me. He did not tell the truth. He told
the police that he found her dead in bed when he took her a cup
of tea. There was no autopsy. Sheila had a heart condition and
Frank insisted that she had chest pains the night before. Frank's
private doctor signed the death certificate. I considered protesting,
insisting, making trouble, but it would not bring Sheila back.
Instead, I stayed quiet and now, here I am, returning Frank's stare
in the absolute knowledge that we both know what he is. What
he has done. To Sheila.

We file past the headstone that bears Bobby's name. I glance
at it and at Frank and raise my eyebrows. His daughter and her
mother also stare at me from under their lacy veils, willing this to
be over and Sheila to be forgotten so that they can step into her
shoes. But I do not care. I'm not even wearing black, I am wearing
a red jacket over some smart black trousers, with a neon yellow

T-shirt. Oversized sunglasses. And obviously, bright red lipstick. It's what Sheila would have wanted.

I am spoiling Frank's little performance piece entitled *I Love My Wife*, pissing on his parade. Everyone will wonder who I am. But I don't care. We pass the headstone and pass the coffin. The mourners who preceded us have placed red roses on top of the coffin and it is piled high. I reach into my bag and pull out the blue rabbit. Bobby's rabbit. Frank's eyes follow my fingers and he turns a bright, angry scarlet as I place Bobby's rabbit on the top of the roses, nestling it in. I kiss my hand and touch Sheila's forehead on the picture, then I walk away. I don't need to see anything else.

We are silent as Janice drives us back to SafeMe. She has given me my own space lately, time to consider all that has happened. Everything about Alan Cartwright's arrest and bail. It's the same old same old – just like all the women here – arrest, charge, appear in court, get bailed, live to abuse another day. Donelle and I have an injunction in place. When police went to the flat, they found the phone he had used to text and photograph me and handcuffs and a gag, which he claimed Donelle like to use during sex.

But Alice has refused to make any charges so far and will not leave her father's house. This means that the only accusations are my own, backed by my mother and Donelle.

He has denied everything. Told them that it was just a huge misunderstanding. That he never touched me. That Alice was never a prisoner and could have left at any time. She has also stated that the door was not always locked and she could have left, but we both know that she was too scared to. Terrified. Conditioned.

And this is the key. This is the behaviour that people who have never had their life threatened can't believe: that someone could be so scared that they cannot leave. Alan Cartwright – quiet, smart-suited, well groomed, nicely spoken, Alan Cartwright. *What a nice man*. Even Donelle fell for it. But the truth is this: Alice was conditioned like an animal not to step outside without permission. I was conditioned not to tell. Donelle was on her way to the same. God only knows who else he has manipulated. Or worse.

But there was one thing. The police searched Alan Cartwright's house and found the one thing that would link us all. Pinned to the wall of his study was a copy of the newspaper article that declared me Superwoman; he had highlighted the words, 'An incident in my teens made me realise that I wanted to help other people who had been harmed by violence or coercive control.' I never said that. Never. I was hitting out at my childhood, at my parents, but doesn't every sociopath think this it is about them? I was misquoted but that is what he believed. That I had told.

He even tried to have Danny charged with breaking and entering his home. This means that I will have to appear in court to give evidence when he goes to trial – if he does. Because it is my word against his; Alice is in no fit state to say what happened.

But one day she will. I truly believe that with all my heart. With the right help and support, she will, one day, be able to. There is no time limit on this, no sell-by date. And when she does, I will be standing beside her, her best friend, making sure that Alan Cartwright pays for what he has done. Over the past few weeks I have come to a realisation. He is no murderer. He is no different from any of the other perps. The cowards who keep other people as their prisoners, either by physical violence or by psychological abuse, or both. He even faked social worker credentials, and I thought I was going mad. He'll get done for that, if nothing else.

I should have listened better to Donelle. Everything she told me about him. All the alarm bells pointed to the fact that this man was another violent Jim, a cruel and manipulative Frank. Not a man like my Danny or Malc, who have the same drive and anger but manage to hold it in a place where it can be dealt with safely, channelled into protection or passion for the good. It all fits now. Where is the love? I should have talked to her more.

Now, though, all the power he held over me drained away with the truth, to leave a weak, insecure and frankly deluded man who will lie until the last second. Instead, I have my power back now.

We are back at SafeMe. Janice stops the car and we look out at the small crowd that has gathered outside. Malc gets out of the front seat and joins Danny and the kids, who walk around to the front gates. Sally hurries into the building to set the tea urns going and to switch on the fairy lights. I look at Janice.

'This is it, then.'

She nods and smiles but I can see she is crying.

'We did it, Ria. Against all the odds and without taking a penny off Frank James. We fucking did it.'

I watch as Sally's kids march by with the other children who are currently living here. They see me and, even through the thick windows of the new people carrier, I can hear them chanting, 'Ria, Ria, diarrhoea.' They are laughing and I watch as they file by and up to Danny and Malc and Simon and Jennifer. All smiles. All messing about and all happy. This is how it should be.

We are a bunch of misfits, a crowd of the parts of society that life has not been kind to. We don't fit in. We may be different, affected by drama and trauma and currently unable to walk back into the world outside, but we are doing the best we can. The very best. The women file out now, those who don't mind being in press photographs and on the local news; the others stay inside, watching through the windows, hiding away just yet. Janice backs the people carrier into the parking space that Alan Cartwright's red Skoda used to occupy, next to Adele Baker's BMW.

We get out and stand at the side of the road. I turn to her.

'Thanks, Jan. I must have been a fucking nightmare.'

She sucks in her lips. 'Well, I won't lie, you were hard work. But we took the scenic route, mate. Nothing about this was ever going to be straightforward.' She punches me gently on the arm. 'Anyway, you're Ria Taylor, services Superwoman.'

I snort. Neither of us can laugh and joke because too much has happened, but we are both proud. Some of the most effective paybacks are done quietly, steadily, without drama. No need for shouting or violence. No fireworks or grand gestures. We walk towards SafeMe, through the gates, and over to the newly furbished extension of the old mill building that houses us.

Adele Baker joins us, and the cameras roll. Flashes blind us as a bank of photographers capture every moment of this, and I smile inside because I want maximum exposure for what is about to happen. I see Danny at the front of the crowd with his mum and dad and Donelle. He's wearing a shirt and tie for the first time since our wedding and smiling his best 'I love you x always x' smile. As soon as this is over we are going on a road trip. Danny says the house can wait until later because as long as we are all together it doesn't matter where we live. Jennifer shouts 'That's my mummy!' and my eyes fill with tears as I wave at her and Simon, who has brought his two best friends. Mum and Dad— yes, Dad – stand behind them, Jennifer holding Granddad's hand tightly.

Finally, we reach the doorway to the new section of the building. Everyone is cheering and Adele pushes me forwards gently as someone hands me a pair of scissors. I stand back and look at the now-huge crowd gathered outside. At the women in the windows, waiting for their freedom. I think about Alice and what she has endured, and about every woman and man who has used SafeMe over the years.

At the back of the crowd I see a black limo, the back window slightly lowered. I turn and snip the cord in front of me and the plastic sheet falls away from the newly erected sign that fills the side of the building.

The Sheila James Family Centre

The logo is a blue bunny rabbit, and Janice and Sally are handing out blue rabbits, just like Bobby's, and blue rabbit pin badges, as a huge blue rabbit balloon suddenly appears above the building. Adele laughs.

'Well done, Ria. This will make a real difference.'

I look through the crowd and the black limo pulls away. I nod. No one will ever forget Sheila now.

'Yes. It will. It already has.'

Acknowledgements

I would like to thank everyone at Corvus Atlantic Books, particularly my editor Sara O'Keeffe for her insight, and Susannah Hamilton and Poppy Mostyn-Owen for their guidance. Also, Kirsty Doole and Jamie Forrest for their publicity and marketing superpowers, and the whole team for their help.

I cannot thank my friend and agent Judith Murray enough for her guidance, advice and patience. None of this would be possible without her and I am eternally grateful. Thank you to everyone at Greene & Heaton for your dedication and help.

I want to thank my fellow writers for the opportunity to try out stories and learn from their experiences. Special thanks to Anstey Harris who has listened endlessly to me over the years. I cannot list you all here, but you know who you are.

In writing this book, much of the research came from talking to survivors of domestic abuse and their families. I want to thank every survivor, and every member of a family who has survived, for their bravery at speaking out. This story is not about you, but hopefully contains an understanding of what you have been through.

Thank you to Refuge and Women's Aid and to those people who work in refuges, in outreach and in independent living, making the journey back from domestic abuse more bearable. Again, this story is not about any one of you but hopefully I have captured your spirit.

Funding for domestic abuse services has fallen sharply in the past five years. Funding cuts have hit at the heart of women's and men's safety and austerity has made it almost impossible to provide enough specialist services for people suffering domestic abuse. Police funding has also been cut making it even more difficult to prosecute perpetrators. I want to thank everyone who is still fighting to reinstate this funding and services and shame on those who took it away in the first place knowing that it will cost lives. My hope is that this story highlights the complexities of domestic abuse and helps in some small way to keep people safe and form support networks.

Thank you to my friends who listened to me as I talked the story through. To my children and my grandchildren who I love very much. To my brothers who never doubted that writing was a life for me.

As always, biggest thanks to my partner Eric for his love, support, patience and for making me laugh endlessly. I couldn't have done this without you, love.

Book Club Questions

What emotions did the ending evoke? Was anyone brought to justice? (Please feel free to let me know via Twitter, Facebook or Instagram #HowToPlayDead)

The story of *How to Play Dead* revolves around Ria and her strength. Did you feel that Ria had any weaknesses?

Did you think Ria and Danny had a strong relationship? Why could she not tell him what was happening?

After reading the story, what does the title 'How to Play Dead' mean to you?

The story is set in a women's refuge. Is this how you visualised a safe place for women? Has your view of women's refuges changed?

The female characters in the story are all very different people but have a lot in common. Do you think that their suffering unites them, or divides them?

The women in the story have all been affected in some way by abusive behaviour, either personally or vicariously. Do you think they are survivors? How have their lives changed?

Ria's parents made mistakes. How much did that influence her life and her decisions? How does it affect her relationships? How does it influence her own parenting?

The early incidents in Ria and Alice's life with Alan take place in the 1980s. They were fifteen and he was twenty-five when they met. Do you think this kind of behaviour was more acceptable then? Why did Dougie and Dawn allow it?

Did you believe that Ria did not initially associate Alan with the messages? Would you associate something that happens today with events long ago?

When Ria was attacked, why did she not report it to the police? Why did Tanya, Sheila and Sally not report all their abuse? What does this say about domestic abuse in general?

Tanya was able to leave work at lunchtime. The door to their home was not locked. Why did Tanya not leave Al?

When did the turning point come for Tanya when she realised that she was trapped?

Some of the men in the story are perpetrators, but not all. Did you think that the balance reflected real life? If not, did you believe that the extra insight gained by the reader from looking inside a women's refuge gave a more realistic picture of perpetrators that is usually hidden from view?

Sheila was an older woman who had been married to Frank for a long time. Did this make his treatment of her more – or less – acceptable? Did his social status affect your view?

Did Sheila's fate shock you? Two women per week in England are killed by a partner or ex-partner. After reading *How to Play Dead* did you believe these statistics more?

Donelle complained to Ria that her boyfriend was both attentive and difficult. Why do you think she continued with the relationship?

'Dickpics' or cyber-flashing has been normalised by the media reporting that it is a common occurrence. Is it really sexual harassment? Or is it something people can just ignore? Is it stalking?

The violent and abusive men are all referred to as perpetrators throughout the book. The police repeatedly state that they can't investigate without knowing who Ria's stalker is. Alan is both a stalker and a domestic abuse perpetrator. Are they really the same thing, or does society separate them out according to whether the victim is known to them or not?

How has this story made you feel about domestic abuse and its criminality?

Helplines and advice

If you or someone you know is experiencing domestic abuse, domestic violence or gaslighting, or anything in this book has affected you, please call one of the helplines below. Domestic abuse is a crime. **If you are in immediate danger always call the police, and always dial 999 if it is an emergency. They have a duty to protect and help you.**

24hr Domestic Violence Helpline – run in partnership between Refuge and Women's Aid. Freephone: 0808 2000 247 (24 hours)

Refuge – refuge.org.uk

Women's Aid Federation of England – womensaid.org.uk

The Hideout – website for children and young people witnessing domestic violence. thehideout.org.uk

CRUSH – CRUSH is a structured programme of group support and empowerment for young people in the age range of 13 to 19. 0800 014 9084

Love Don't Feel Bad – aimed at 16 to 25-year olds, Love Don't Feel Bad explores what is and isn't a healthy relationship. lovedontfeelbad.co.uk

Scottish Women's Aid – 0800 027 1234 scottishwomensaid.org.uk

Northern Ireland Women's Aid Federation – 24hr Domestic and Sexual Violence Helpline: 0808 802 1414 niwaf.org

Broken Rainbow – National Lesbian, Gay, Bisexual and Trans (LGBT) Domestic Violence Helpline. Freephone: 0800 999 5428 brokenrainbow.org.uk

FCO Forced Marriage Unit – Helpline: 020 7008 0151 (or 0044 20 7008 0151 if you are overseas) fco.gov.uk

Honour Network – Karma Nirvana – Helpline: 0800 599 9247 karmanirvana.org.uk

ManKind – Helpline: 01823 334244 mankind.org.uk

Men's Aid – Helpline: 0871 223 9986 (8am to 8pm daily) mensaid.co.uk

Abused Men in Scotland (Mon-Fri 9-4) – Helpline: 0800 800 0024 abusedmeninscotland.org

The Dyn Project – Helpline: 0808 801 0321 dynwales.org